Desmond Lov

film technician

career, first a

novelist with *The Boondocks*,

Bellman and True, *Boudapesti 3*, and *Sunspot*.

He lives in Sussex with his wife and children and is able to indulge his love of good food and wine by helping to run a pub-cum-restaurant.

Also by Desmond Lowden
in Pan Books

Bandersnatch
Bellman and True
Boudapesti 3
Sunspot

Desmond Lowden

Cry Havoc

Pan Books
in association with
Macmillan London

First published 1984 by Macmillan London Ltd
This edition published 1985 by Pan Books Ltd,
Cavaye Place, London SW10 9PG
in association with Macmillan London Ltd
9 8 7 6 5 4 3 2 1

ISBN 0 330 28608 0
Reproduced, printed and bound in Great Britain by
Hazell Watson & Viney Limited,
Member of the BPCC Group,
Aylesbury, Bucks

for Jane and Chris
and an early summer evening
in the Folly

1

There was nothing about that Friday morning to say it was going to change the course of Dan Wyatt's life.

It began like any other day, with Wyatt waking up and wondering where the hell he was. Until he recognised the apartment in the rue Meynardier in Cannes, the bashed kind of apartment quite a few of the pilots used who had a stopover at Nice. From his watch Wyatt saw it was just after seven. He got up, made coffee, showered and shaved. He put on the tan-coloured shirt, slacks and windcheater that made up the uniform of Custom Air (sole proprietor and pilot Dan Wyatt). He left a hundred francs in the tea-caddy, picked up his flight bag, and left.

At the end of the rue Meynardier the market stalls still had the deep blue shadows of early morning. But out on the avenue de la Liberté it was bright day. Wyatt threaded his way through the traffic and stood in the sunlight at the corner of the harbour.

Cannes, he thought, was just as it should be in early June, just as he liked it. An ice truck was crawling along the warm flagstones of the quai St Pierre, delivering from yacht to yacht. Beyond, a tall two-stick schooner was manoeuvring out of her berth. There was the sound that was unlike all others – a big marine diesel spatting down onto sunlit water. And the morning haze of a Mediterranean harbour that was unlike all others – a haze part yacht-smoke, part hangover, and part last night's lies.

Wyatt walked under the café awnings across the road from the quay. He went into the Yacht Agency just short of the Nautique Bar, and up the stairs to the first floor office that handled charter flights. There he left the keys of the rue Meynardier apartment, and asked for the day's lists.

There were two of them. The Commercial List – the

companies who wanted to fly their executives across Europe. And the Yacht List – the bronzey-bronzey boys who wanted to fly from yacht to office, or office to yacht. The first list Wyatt wasn't interested in; he crumpled it up and threw it in a waste paper basket. The second he took back outside with him to the sunlight. He sat at a café table and studied it. As usual it was going to take some time.

Because there was an art to flying the rich. It wasn't just a question of cleaning out the plane's ashtrays, making with the wall-to-wall grin, and flying the pretty way. It wasn't just the bronzey-bronzey women who spent every waking hour changing their minds. Nor the godawful English nannies. Nor the picnic-cases that suddenly started barking like Pekineses the moment you were lining up for Heathrow.

It was something else, something recent. In the past couple of years the rich had looked up from the Stock Market prices in the newspaper and started reading the front page. In the past couple of years they'd got frightened of kidnap, of other people knowing about their movements . . . And nowadays the Yacht List was printed out in a certain way. No names, no pack drill, just numbers. A date/time code that changed every day.

For example:

YL06032300 . . . Antibes–Liège. 4 persons. Pickup Antibes 1100 hrs, June 4 . . . Confirm.

And:

YL06040130 . . . Calvi–Lyon. 3 persons. Pickup Calvi 1400 hrs, June 4 . . . Confirm.

The first job was the obvious one. It meant no more than a taxi-ride along the coast for the pickup at Antibes. Then an easy flight up the Rhône valley and on. . . . But it was the other end, the Liège end, that worried Wyatt. He sat back in his café chair and looked out at the harbour.

Then he got up. Jimmy would know.

Towards the end of the quai St Pierre was an English sloop, a Moody 29. And sitting in the yacht's cockpit drinking coffee was an Englishman, Jimmy Shardlow. And Jimmy, Wyatt reckoned, was one of the more successful people he knew. He'd sold up his business in Croydon at the age of forty-six. He'd kept his money in exactly the right sock under the bed. Seven months of the year he sailed the Mediterranean, which brought him a deep ochre-coloured tan. And more than this, there was a calm to Jimmy – smooth circles of round face, round stomach, and fat round thighs. To Wyatt he always seemed like ginger in a jar.

'Dan Wyatt.' The man looked up now from the cockpit. 'For heaven's sake, how are you? Come on board.'

Wyatt took off his shoes and crossed the gangplank.

'You want a coffee?' Jimmy asked.

'No, thanks. Just had one.'

'What then? What can I do for you?'

Wyatt got out the Yacht List. 'There's this job,' he said, 'Antibes to Liège. And I wondered if you'd know anything about it.'

'What kind of thing?'

'Liège,' Wyatt said. 'Nobody goes to Liège unless they live there. Unless they're a Belgian.'

'And?'

'Well, it was a Belgian I had these problems with last week,' Wyatt explained. 'Belgian with a big flashy yacht called *Leontine* . . . I wanted to know if the boat was at Antibes right now.'

'*Leontine.*' Jimmy frowned. 'Bloody great gin-palace of a thing? Streamlined stack? Two speedboats?'

'That's the one.'

'Yes, it's berthed at Antibes.'

'Right,' Wyatt said. 'Then that's the job I don't take.'

'Why's that?'

Wyatt put down his coffee cup. 'You got five minutes?'

'I've got all day.'

'All right, I'll tell you.' He leaned back, remembering. 'About a week ago I did this Yacht List job, Ostend to Toulon. And I got to Ostend, what, round about midday? . . . Anyway there was this long wheelbase Merc parked there, and out of it stepped this Belgian. And he was followed by his valet, his kids from his marriage, his sixteen-year-old girlfriend in a fluffy coat, and a St Bernard dog.'

'Jesus,' Jimmy said.

'No, I can handle that, no problem at all in this new plane I'm flying,' Wyatt said. 'But then there were the two CQR anchors he wanted me to bring along. Big anchors, for that great gin-palace of his.'

'*Anchors?*'

'That's right. He said he'd got them cheap, cheaper than he

could down here. They had to come.'

'And you told him no?'

'I told him no, and he told me yes. In the end I said I'd try it, but the kids weren't coming. They were staying behind in the car.'

'Too damn right,' Jimmy said.

Wyatt nodded. 'Okay, so we tried it. We went off down the strip . . . Grass it was, a Belgian flying club, and halfway down I knew we weren't going to get up in the air. So I slammed on the brakes and buried the nosewheel. We dug it out and went back to the car.'

'And took out the anchors?'

'No, he still wouldn't have that. So I called the chauffeur of the Merc over. I got him as witness and I got the Belgian to sign a blank laundry-slip. I told him a plane was quite simple, it could do one of two things. It could go up in the air or it could come down and hit a tree. And I said, as I was flying the thing, I was going to be the one who came out of it alive.'

'But it made no difference,' Jimmy said.

'None. We went back to the strip, using all the grass there was, and tried it once again. And once again I hit the bleeding brakes. So then I told the Belgian somebody had to stay behind. And we sat round playing "who do we throw off the raft?"'

'And who did you throw off?'

'You tell me,' Wyatt said. 'There were the anchors, the valet, the girlfriend and the dog, remember.'

'And the anchors stayed?'

'The anchors stayed.'

'All right, he threw off the valet and the dog, and he kept the girlfriend.'

'No,' Wyatt said, 'he was a Belgian. He kept the bleeding dog.'

'I don't believe it.'

'You haven't heard half,' Wyatt told him. 'We got up in the air. The nose was up, the anchors started sliding back, and we hit a stall situation. So the bleeding St Bernard slid down to the back too, and the Belgian went after it . . . Jesus, I was cutting barley-stalks out of this field with my tail.'

'You're joking.'

'No, and there's more . . . Because we got out of that. We had the Belgian hauling in on the anchors, yo-ho-ho, like some bleeding pirate. We had him pulling the dog up the cabin by its ears. And then we were flying, everything was dandy . . . until maybe half an hour later when we were caught by this tail-gust. And what happens? The anchors come up and wrap themselves around my feet. The plane goes into a nosedive. And the St Bernard is shot forwards into the co-pilot's seat, flying the bleeding thing.'

Jimmy put his head back and laughed.

'Not funny,' Wyatt told him. 'Not at the time.'

'No, I don't suppose it was,' Jimmy said. 'So what are you going to do? Forget the job with the Belgian today?'

'Too damn right.'

'And is there any other job?'

Wyatt nodded. 'Calvi–Lyon. Pickup in Calvi at 1400.'

'Well, what's wrong with that?' Jimmy asked. 'I mean, I don't have to tell you, do I? . . . Calvi means Calvi Week. Which is the Ocean-Racing Series going on in Corsica right now. Which is the big sailing yachts, the *real* bronzey-bronzey boys . . . And a fat tip coming your way at the end.'

'I know that,' Wyatt said. 'I flew a job there earlier in the week.'

'Well, then?'

'It's just that today, on paper, the Antibes job looked quicker.'

'On paper it's the other way round,' Jimmy corrected him. 'You fly from here to Calvi, all right? You leave Calvi at two, and get to Lyon easily by five. You do your cringing act for the tip. You turn the plane around, and you're back here in time for a late dinner.'

'Back here? Cannes, you mean?'

'That's right,' Jimmy said. 'Because tomorrow's Saturday. And tomorrow you're coming sailing with me.'

Wyatt looked round at the yacht's cockpit. 'It's an idea.'

'More than an idea. Listen, we fill the boat up with booze. We pick up a couple of slinky ladies who're waiting around for the Film Festival. And we point out to sea.'

'Could be.'

But Jimmy leaned towards him, irritated. 'Dan Wyatt, I want a firm promise out of you. I mean, where the hell've you been recently? Last season we were sailing together, what, one weekend in two? This season I've hardly seen you.'

'Yes, well,' Wyatt said. 'I've been flying the mountains a bit . . . Switzerland . . . Switzerland mostly.'

'Why Switzerland?'

'Company jobs. I seem to have been flying the Commercial

List a lot.'

'The Commercial List is contract work, regular hours,' Jimmy said. 'That's not you.'

'I don't know.'

'There's a woman in Switzerland, isn't there?' Jimmy said.

Wyatt shrugged. 'Yes and no.'

'Serious, is it?'

'Not really,' Wyatt said. 'She's a divorced lady with two kids. And she has a certain style. She's got this flat overlooking the lake. It's at a place called Horw, near Luzern. And you know how the Swiss arrange these things . . . There's this dish-shaped balcony that goes with the flat, and it's got grass and rose-trees growing on it.'

'Jesus. Grass and rose-trees on a balcony,' Jimmy said. 'That's serious.'

'No, she's the one who's serious,' Wyatt told him. 'I mean a serious kind of person. She's got all these books on the shelves, and records. She listens to a lot of music . . . Mahler it is, and Schu-somebody . . . bert or mann, I forget which.'

'Mahler?'

'That's it.'

'Mahler is bad for the golf-swing,' Jimmy said.

'You're right.'

'And Schu-somebody is bad too.'

'Yes. Like I told you, it's not serious. We haven't seen each other for a couple of weeks.'

Jimmy stood up suddenly. 'Listen,' he said. 'I'm going to do you a favour, and you're going to thank me for it afterwards . . . Tonight I buy the booze, and make a date with the slinky ladies here in the town. Tomorrow you come sailing with me . . . Is that a date?'

Wyatt thought a moment, then he nodded. 'A date.'

He stood up, touched Jimmy on the shoulder, and went back up the gangplank to the quay. His weekend, as he thought, mapped out.

As he *thought* mapped out.

Because later, in the Agency office, he got the girl to send a Confirm on the Calvi job. And, although he didn't know at the time, that was the start of it. The tapping of those telex keys was like a time bomb ticking underneath him.

2

The plane, a Piper Saratoga, was almost brand new, with no more than a hundred and eighty hours on the clock. There was the smell of the eight leather cabin seats behind Wyatt, and the softest of hisses from the air-conditioning.

Waiting to roll out across Nice airport to the turning-circle, he called up the tower. 'Custom Air Golf-Alpha-Charlie,' he said. 'Flight-plan to Calvi. Request taxi instructions and take-off.'

But there was no answer, and he came back on the throttles to save the engines. The sun-visor ahead of him cast a blue-grey shadow over the instruments. And there was a blue-grey too to Wyatt's face. He'd shaved no more than three hours ago, but a dark metal was there in the line of his jaw, just as it was in the tight black curls on the backs of his hands.

They were large hands. Wyatt was a big man who'd boxed light-heavy in the RAF about a million years ago. The flattening of his nose came from that time. The lines around his mouth came from trying to stay in shape at the age of forty-four. And he'd managed it. Or thought he'd managed it. Because there was beginning to be that touch of the ageing pro about him, the tennis pro maybe who hung on too long in the singles courts.

'Custom Air Golf-Alpha-Charlie,' he tried again. But the control-tower came on then, curtly, cutting him short. And Wyatt saw why. With a building roar, a Pan-Am 747 lumbered over from the commercial apron ahead of him. Scheduled flights had preference, and the voice from the tower took on a respectful tone. 'N453PA to New York, good morning,' it said.

Wyatt waited for the chat to finish. Then a shrieking gale got the jumbo rolling down the airstrip. Slowly, incredibly slowly it rumbled away. In the distance it suddenly sat back and was airborne, leaving four snail-like trails over the bay of Nice.

The gale subsided. The voice from the tower came back. 'Custom Air Alpha-Charlie. Line up and home.'

Wyatt released his brakes and edged forward to the circle. He turned, and the lights of the runway were ahead of him, meeting far away by the sea.

'Custom Air Alpha-Charlie. Stand by for take-off . . . Go.'

He had a slip sideways out over the water. He had two left-handed circles to gain height over the bay. Then all was haze below him, sea, the sprawl of Nice, and its beaches. Only the Alpes-Maritimes were hard-edged, an old blue willow-pattern above darker hills, with wisps of white cloud clinging to their faces.

Wyatt did the things he had to do, got the undercarriage up, trimmed the plane, and throttled back. He found the list of frequencies he'd need to update his weather-map. He located the chopper flying far below him at Cap d'Ail that Nice tower had warned him about. Then he flew the coast at 5,000, keeping well clear of the commercial lanes.

Monaco came up quickly, its streets an old copper colour in the haze. Then Italy, the white ribbon of the autostrada threading the hills, with the flare of greenhouses above it, and the pink roofs of yacht-harbours below. Wyatt went as far as San Remo before he turned out over the sea.

There was a sudden change to blue, a huge saucer shape of blue, where haze reached up from the horizon at every point. As he flew on into it, the peace of what he was doing rose up in Wyatt. There was just the occasional updraught to stop the plane flying itself. But apart from that, nothing. Time passed slowly in the creamy note of the engines and the unbroken sky ahead.

It was a time for sitting back and thinking. Thinking how he hadn't told Jimmy the whole truth back in Cannes this morning, how it hadn't been the right time or place.

And thinking more particularly about a woman who lived in a lakeside apartment at Horw, near Luzern. A dark-haired woman, gentle, frighteningly honest, with two frighteningly honest kids. They'd made no secret of their liking for Wyatt, their need for him even . . . And they still didn't know he'd left, wasn't coming back.

The plane gave a lurch. He corrected it and came back on course. Other pilots, he knew, blamed everything on the life they led, the waking up in different cities, the days and nights away. But for Wyatt it wasn't that. It was the peace he felt inside him at this very moment. The almost total control he had over an almost perfect way of life. It spoiled you. You never got lonely up here. Ever.

Except that . . . Hanging over the back of his seat was his tan-coloured jacket. And in its left-hand pocket, moving as the plane moved, was a heavy object. A knife. One of those trick Swiss

Army penknives with the trick pair of scissors, and the trick saw-blade sharp enough to cut off the leg of a chair . . . The kids who lived in that lakeside apartment had given it to him. They'd seen him looking at it just once in a shop window, and they'd had pocket money saved.

For Christ's sake, Wyatt thought, forget the jokes with Jimmy this morning. Forget the Mahler and the rest of it. Given time, he thought, Mahler and he could have come to some kind of arrangement.

It was that it *had* got serious.

He flew on through the haze, a speck of bright shiny metal crossing a wide saucer of blue.

Corsica appeared on the horizon, and grew larger. Wyatt swung round on the compass, left Cap Corse to the east, and crossed the wide sweep of the Gulf of St Florent. After a while land came up again, a line of brown haze under cloud.

And then he saw it, the thing he'd been waiting for, the white sail. Followed by the second, the third . . . until the whole fleet opened up in front of him, big yachts, ocean-racers, thirty or more of them scattered over the shining sea.

They were a fine sight. A sight that got him swinging the plane up on one wing, swinging the blood through his veins, as he went in towards them. An excitement – what was the best way of describing it? . . . All right, that arrow they stuck onto street-plans in big cities . . . You Are Here.

Here, as opposed to keeping a bed and a ready-made family warm in Switzerland. Here, as opposed to flying the mountains as he'd done recently. The Commercial List, contract work, regular hours . . . And somebody, however nice and dark-haired and gentle, making sure those hours stayed regular.

Wyatt lost height. He throttled back as he approached the yachts so as not to disturb their wind. Sails came towards him, small, like sharkteeth at first. Until suddenly they were great soaring arcs of canvas, taut and jittery, beating a path out to the sun. He shielded his eyes. There was the white of sea, the white of long curving decks, and a champagne white as spray burst up from their bows.

He circled and came round with the sun behind him. Came low, and singled out just the leading yacht. There was colour then, and something else too to the boat – he couldn't say what it was exactly – maybe a race-car feel. It was the hull, a bright race-car red, and polished to a race-car shine. It was the low flat deck, without so much as a cabin-top to give shelter. And the precision of what was going on – even sitting up in his pilot's seat Wyatt could feel it – the thing that was highly-tuned. It was there in the stillness of the crew. Ten of them he counted, wearing bright red oilskins and sitting out in the spray. An eleventh man was crouched over a genoa-winch, letting out the huge triangular sail no more than an inch at a time. And finally the helmsman, taut, concentrating, flicking the long steel spokes of his wheel.

Wyatt climbed again, and from his new height could see the whole pattern of the fleet . . . To your average cruising yachtsman, he thought, it would have been surprising. Yachts were pointing in half a dozen different directions, scattered from the gold of deep water to the darker shadows inshore. And it wasn't tide they were fighting – there was no tide in the Mediterranean – he knew that. But the answer was there in the day's weather-map beside him. There was very little wind, he saw, forecast for the sea around Corsica. What there was was local, a thermal action as the land-mass of the island warmed up and brought an onshore breeze. A breeze impossible to predict, varying as the day wore on.

At the moment he could see it was strongest offshore. The yachts out there were heeling over, were pointing high, seemingly doing well. Except that, with a long tack out and back, they had the greatest distance to cover. While the yachts inshore had less wind. Their sails were slack, then filling as they crabbed towards the dark flurries on the water that were gusts. It was all a gamble, Wyatt saw, a throw of dice on the blue chequerboard below.

Then the game came to a head. Fighting, crossing each other's bows, the yachts narrowed on an orange buoy. All seemed chaos until on each individual deck he saw precision. Ant-like crewmen ran forward, worked quickly, and on the outside of each genoa sail rose a twisting snake of coloured cloth. It burst out to become a spinnaker, shivering, almost collapsing on itself until the big genoa was dropped. Then it filled, and in a swirl of sun-dancing water each yacht went round.

Still Wyatt circled above. The race was now a corner in the

sea, a narrow angle where sharkteeth sails became round spinnakers. And they were like nothing else he'd seen, those spinnakers. They were huge bell shapes, thin, almost transparent. After a while only the jagged colours of their sail-patterns could be seen, a ghostly procession of triangles, arrows and stars going away into the haze.

The sight of those sails stayed with Wyatt as he turned back on course. Because, apart from anything else, they were rare. A fleet this size came to the Mediterranean only once a year, for Calvi Week on the odd-numbered years, and for the Sardinia Cup on the evens. This year was Calvi. It fitted in between the SORC races in Florida, and the Admiral's Cup series at the home of yachting in Cowes. And the whole shebang was known as the Ocean Racing circuit, the playground of a group of millionaire yachtsmen who travelled the world . . . The *real* bronzey-bronzey boys, as Jimmy had said.

Wyatt flew on into empty blue sky. And that sense of calm returned to him. What had he called it just now? An almost perfect way of life? . . . That it was, no question about it. And, no question too, he was a bastard to walk out on that dark-haired woman in Switzerland. Let's face it, there wasn't a lot to be said in his defence – except that life hadn't always been perfect. It had been a hell of a fight just to get here.

The years of flying freight for a two-man outfit held together with promises and bad cheques. The years of sweating in the Far East while the oil-rig money grew. And then the break, the first look at what could happen – owning his own plane.

A man called Jackman. An Englishman with a quiet voice, tailored suits, and that English kind of straw-coloured hair.

The parcels of money he'd flown for Jackman on the back seat. Or, in the case of bigger consignments, the metal boxes hidden in the fuselage behind the luggage compartment.

And the kind of airstrips Jackman had fixed him up with. Even-Stevens flying it was known as. The strip where it was car-headlights and an arrow out on the grass, showing the direction of the wind. Or the strip where it was just a couple of huts and some goats.

No, it hadn't all been cleaning out the plane's ashtrays and flying the pretty way.

3

CALVI WEEK, 8 JOURS CALVI, SETTIMANA CALVI . . . The posters flapped past Wyatt's taxi window as he went into town. Just short of the old harbour with its red-tiled roofs was the marina. It was new, its flat white concrete seeming to crumble at the edges in the haze. And it was empty too, the yachts not yet back in.

Wyatt paid off the taxi. The Calvi Week office was labelled in three languages too, and he went inside. Over in the corner he could hear English spoken, and he found an Australian kid there behind the counter, wearing a guess-what tee shirt.

Taking a copy of the Telex Confirm out of his pocket, Wyatt handed it over. 'You're going to tell me I'm early,' he said.

'Yeah, early. Like half a day,' the kid said. 'Or even a day.'

'What d'you mean?' Wyatt pointed. 'Read what it says there. Pickup fourteen hundred hours.'

'That's right, sport. Only your client's out there in this ocean race. And it's no flaming race at the moment. Wind's dropped. Not a puff.'

'Dropped? But I flew over the fleet, what, an hour ago? There was wind then.'

'That's right. But the forecast wasn't good, was it?'

'No.' Wyatt remembered.

'And that's how it goes with yacht-racing.' The kid shrugged. 'One minute your guy's expecting to be here with his toothbrush packed. The next he's out at sea picking his feet, same as the rest of them.'

'And there's no way of telling when he'll be back?'

The kid looked at the telex again. 'Custom Air. Wait a minute, we had a message for you, sport. They want you to hang on, call back at midnight tonight . . . But it could just as well be flaming tomorrow, the way things are going.'

'Jesus,' Wyatt said.

'He'll help, yeah.'

'I mean, I turned down another job this morning. And there's this brand new plane I'm flying. The bank's kind of interested in me keeping up the payments.'

'That right, sport?'

Wyatt turned away. A good day's wages gone, he thought.

Not to mention a day's sailing with Jimmy tomorrow.

But the kid called him back. 'Maybe I got good news for you,' he said. 'There's this thing going the rounds. Don't know if you're interested, but it's a short-haul job, San Guielmo and back. You could do it, *allay-reetoor*, and be back here talking to me by midnight. Easy.'

'Where was that?' Wyatt asked. 'San Guielmo?'

'I never heard of it either,' the kid said. He reached round for a map. 'Here we are. Small place. Reckon it has to be one of those new holiday-developments going up on the west coast of Italy. You know, where for years the tourists've been whining on about run-down hotels and the trots. And now they've got sterilised toothmugs, paper covers on the loos . . .'

'. . . And the trots,' Wyatt said.

'You've got it, sport. But, listen, if you want the job, it's yours. These three guys, they had a plane booked, but there was trouble with the elastic, wouldn't go up in the sky.'

'What are they?' Wyatt asked. 'Yacht-people?'

'Bound to be,' the kid said, 'this week.'

But they weren't yacht-people. They were locals, Corsicans, and if you were being charitable about it, business-people. The kind of business that got your flesh sagging away from your bones at the age of twenty-five, and got you sitting in the back seat of a taxi as limp as your silk shirt.

At least, two of them were like that. And Wyatt wasn't wild about them. All the way out to the airport there was this hair-combing routine going on behind him. While the other man played a good amateur game of golf on his left nostril, before switching courses to his right.

And the third man, he was a real lulu. Older, much older, around sixty, he had skin tanned the colour of parchment, and a thin mouth that kept arguing. He argued through Customs, he argued as they went out to the plane. And when Wyatt went through the no-smoking-during-take-off speech, he lit up. Wyatt let it go. He decided to skip the clown act with the life-jackets, and went forward to the pilot's seat.

It was just after two, and there was quiet over the field. Wyatt got up into the air quickly. He set course over the mountains, and once past them, reached the wide blue sweep of the sea. And it was just as it had been this morning, cloudless, a huge saucer of blue curving up from the horizon.

Time to sit back and think again. But not about the woman who lived at Horw, near Luzern. There was a limit to how long you could go on caning yourself on a sunny Mediterranean day . . . Instead Wyatt found himself going way back, eight years back in fact, to the time when he'd flown for the Englishman with the straw-coloured hair . . . Jackman . . . And those parcels of money that had been on the back seat . . .

Then he looked up. And in the cabin-mirror he saw something that hadn't been there before. A parcel. On one of the empty seats.

The old Corsican must have been watching him. Because he spoke. 'It's a parcel of shirt-material,' he said in his rough French. 'I go to do business in Italy, but I go also to have shirts made up. Because I refuse to pay the prices they ask back in Calvi.'

'Yes,' Wyatt said.

But he knew what Jackman would have made of it.

And, half an hour later when they reached the Italian coast, he knew what Jackman would have made of San Guielmo airstrip.

Because it wasn't a new strip for some holiday-development, as Wyatt had been led to believe. It was old rough concrete, potholed, with grass growing up through the cracks. There were some falling-down buildings. And on either side of them were these light-coloured circles where animals were tethered.

Jackman-style flying, in fact.

A strip with just a couple of huts and some goats.

Wyatt had been involved with airplanes since the age of seventeen. He knew they went sideways, upwards and downwards, but they didn't go back. He went on in. And there was only one way in, he saw, low over the sea, with a bump maybe from the warm watermelon fields beyond.

There was a bump. He sorted it out and made a perfect three-point landing, followed by a second perfect three-point landing as the nose kicked high. There was a string of Hail Marys from the passengers behind him, but then they were down, the props screaming in reverse pitch. They reached the end of the potholed strip, and Wyatt turned off towards the buildings and parked in their shade. He opened the cabin door, got the steps out, and helped the Corsicans down onto the ground.

But then he hung back. If there was one thing he wasn't going to do, it was walk through Customs and Passport Control with those three. Because the parcel was hidden from sight again. And it had to be under the folds of the raincoat one of the younger Corsicans was carrying. Otherwise, for God's sake, why carry a raincoat in this heat?

Wyatt did a couple of unnecessary jobs on the plane. And while he was doing them he listened, but heard no sound from inside the buildings. Then, maybe five minutes later, he locked up the Saratoga, put the keys in his pocket, and went slowly in through the door marked Passaporto.

To find nothing had happened. Passports and Customs were one and the same man, a guy with a hole in his shirt where his vest showed through. And maybe the Corsicans had known that all along, just as they'd known about the potholed airstrip and the goats. Anyway they were now through a door at the end of the building, standing out in the sun with the parcel still hidden under the raincoat. Wyatt kept his face expressionless. He showed his passport and was nodded through.

There were two taxis parked outside on a gravelled area. The Corsicans took one of them. They told Wyatt they were going to a business meeting in town, and then on to the shirtmaker's. They wanted him back here for the return flight at six. Wyatt nodded. He watched them drive away in a cloud of dust. Then he took the second taxi and breathed out a long slow sigh of relief.

All the way into town he called himself names. If anyone in this world knew about parcels on the back seats of planes, it had to be him. If anyone knew about derelict airfields run by men with holes in their shirts, it had to be him. What had he been using for a brain?

The taxi was moving past crumbling cement-fronted houses now, and Wyatt realised it wasn't just the airfield that was derelict. Because the centre of San Guielmo, when he reached it, was a throbbing hub of civilisation, a riot. It was a small main square with buildings that were sandy-coloured in the sun and a drab grey in the shade. It was two blocks of tarmac road before the dirt and the potholes began. And it was siesta time. There was the kind of silence where the nearest sound was a radio two streets away, and everyone else had gone to a war.

All in all, a great chance of a big-deal business meeting being held here. Not to mention a big-deal shirtmaker's, worth a round-trip of two hundred miles.

Wyatt gave it up. He crossed the square and found a trattoria that had half a shutter open. He sat inside it with a plate of good fish and a glass of bad wine. Then he sat outside with a coffee and watched the biggest show in town. Which was the kiosk-owner over by the corner, a man who moved his chair every twenty minutes or so, following a strip of shade. Wyatt watched for an hour. Then he got himself another coffee and sat through the second show.

By then it was twenty minutes to six, and he got up. It was over, he told himself. All he had to do now was get back to the airfield, fly the Corsicans back to Calvi, and then sit around waiting for the bronzey-bronzey boys to come back from their yacht race. After that, normal service would be resumed.

But when he reached the airfield he found a lot of people in the Customs hall. There were men in big city suits. And there were the Corsicans in a line over by the wall. They had handcuffs on their wrists, and they were fastened every five metres or so to a chain.

Life got serious. Wyatt was grabbed. He found himself joining the chain-gang. And he found his Italian stretched only so far. The word, it seemed, was *Douana*, Italian Customs. Any other words that came his way were all No . . . No telexes, no telegrams, no phone-calls out.

Handcuffed by his right wrist, like the others, Wyatt knew he had three choices. He could shout in English. He could shout in English louder, in the classic style. Or he could make the smart move and wait. He made the smart move, and it seemed to be the right one. Because gradually he came to understand that they were going to be taken away to the big city. And then would be the time for the telexes out. To the Calvi Week office first of all, and then sure-as-hell to the lawyer who handled Wyatt's business.

The Customs men began shouting, and the chain-gang was led outside, Wyatt bringing up the rear. And he was surprised. He'd expected to see some sort of paddy-wagon out there, with bars over the windows. But there were only the two taxis he'd seen earlier. And they didn't seem to come into the picture either, because Wyatt found himself hauled straight past them, and on down a gravel track to the shore.

It was then he saw the small jetty, built out on the end of the rocks. There was a motor-cruiser bobbing alongside, and this, it seemed, was going to take them to the city. The Customs men got them aboard. They lined them up along one side of the deck and fastened both ends of the chain to the rail. Then they started the engines and cast off.

Wyatt looked around. Ordinarily, he told himself, it would have been a hell of a fine evening to go batting out in a fast motor boat. The sun was low to the west, a heavy swell was running, and there were these dark lines coming in on a golden sea. For about five minutes the cruiser headed into them, and spray rose up from the bows like fire. But then they altered course. The cruiser started across the mouth of the bay and set to thudding and rolling. Which made the line of chained men swing out into the centre of the deck and then smack back against the rail. It was insane.

Most insane of all was what was happening to the old Corsican on Wyatt's left. He looked all of his sixty years now. And while he could manage the normal run of the sea, the big vicious waves jerked him suddenly against the ship's side, and his face showed the yellow putty colour of pain.

And nobody did anything. The helmsman steered, and the head Customs man stood next to him, lighting a fag with this big Zippo lighter.

Wyatt had had enough. He called the head Customs man over. He held up his handcuffs and made the sign of the key. And then he started shouting. He had a British passport, he shouted, and he was a member of the Commercial Pilots' Association. He was related to the English Lord Chancellor, he shouted, and a personal friend of Prince Charles . . . He went through everything he could think of, right down to his boy scout's firelighting badge, and his season to Regent's Park zoo.

But the strange thing was it seemed to work. The Customs man watched him a moment, clicking the cap of the Zippo lighter. Then he looked round. The cruiser was well out past the arm of the bay, the motion of the sea was bad, and he told the helmsman to slow down. Then he gave other orders. The front and rear end of the chain were unfastened from the deck-rail. And Wyatt thought he'd won.

But the Customs man took over the ship's wheel. He whispered something to the helmsman and sent him away. The man went to a locker, opened it, and pulled out a heavy anchor.

And Wyatt didn't understand. He thought for some reason they were going to anchor out at sea. But then he turned and looked at the old Corsican. And suddenly he got the message about that putty-coloured face of his. Not pain, but fear.

The man with the anchor dragged it over to the front end of the chain. He shackled it to one of the links. There was screaming from the men around.

Wyatt darted a quick look at the old Corsican. He was clinging onto the rail, shouting out, 'No. *No!*'

Up ahead the man swung his arm back, paused, then threw the heavy anchor over the side. The first Corsican was jerked up, out, over.

The speed of the boat hissed water past, hauled the chain back, bunched them all up. The second Corsican went.

Wyatt felt but didn't see the old Corsican smack back into him. His brain was out of lock. All he saw was the Customs man by the ship's wheel. He was lighting another fag with that big Zippo lighter of his. It was steel, and it had this enamel design on it – one three-pointed star set on top of another.

Then even that was gone. A dark shape passed. The old Corsican flew up into the air.

Wyatt felt a huge jerk on his right wrist. His left hand tried to scrabble at the rail. But he was flying. Out. And there was a dark hole in the curl of a wave. For him.

He went down. To nightmare, growing pressure, death. Below him the chain was straight. Faces were upturned, white, screaming in great goldfish bowls of air that passed him. Down. Dragged on by that huge machine on his wrist. And, Jesus God, the pressure. It lined him inside out, cracked his head like a walnut. Down and on down. To black.

Then the machine stopped. He was hanging upside-down, the anchor bottomed down there in the black. But a hissing in his head. His head no longer hard but soft, like wax. And the black rushing up inside him, a black fur crowding his brain. The end . . . coming . . . now.

But the banging. On his arm. From his pocket, his jacket pocket hanging down. Something heavy there . . . A knife . . . Swiss Army knife with the trick . . . trick Swiss blades . . . He reached with his left hand, got it out . . . He didn't know why. Just an action. His last.

The black fur was finishing him. There was just a line down the centre of his brain that saw . . . Then in front of him another line, a blade, a trick saw-blade . . . Then a third line . . . Where to cut.

He sawed. Pain hit him like a wall, and he sawed on, twisting through bone. His right thumb flapped away from his hand. He wrenched the hand through the metal cuff. And rushed upwards like a cork.

His head screamed and hissed. There was light which hurt, and air which hurt. Jesus God it hurt. He hung onto one last grain of sense and saw in the distance a motor boat blasting away on the waves. Then he let his head hiss and flap, hiss and flap, in the motion of the sea. Until he realised it wasn't the motion of the sea. It was inside him. That narrow line of vision was still there. It was still crowded in by black fur, and what's more it was flapping now. Pressure. The pressure underwater, and coming up too fast . . .

Sense was denied him after that. He knew he was in water. He knew he had to keep his face out of it or die. And he knew, as time passed, he couldn't keep his face out. He was swallowing water, more of it, choking.

Then, unbelievably, hands. Hands reaching out for him, pulling him up.

4

Days passed. Quite a number of days, Wyatt didn't know how many. There were times when he was unconscious, careering along on some mad merry-go-round. And there were other times when he came to. But these didn't help. Everything seemed just as mad then.

He was in a bed, he knew that, an old bed made of black iron. He couldn't see much because of that godawful pumping and hissing in his head. But what he could see were blankets, rough grey blankets covered in stains. Then he saw the stains came from his right hand. There was a pool of blood there, around the pulpy wound where his thumb had been. He tried to move to see more. But he found both his wrists were tied.

Fear made him see beyond the bed. There was a man, an old man, across a room. His face was like a skull round old gums, his skin was dark and leathery, and he had the shine of sweat on him as he bent over a stove. There was a pot on the stove, with dark liquid bubbling inside it, like tar. The old man picked up a cloth. He used it to hold the pot-handle. Then he came close to Wyatt and poured hot tar over his hand.

Wyatt screamed and passed out.

The next time he came to, it was daylight. He moved again and realised his wrists were no longer tied. And on his right hand, over the wound, was a black spider-shape of tar. The pain seemed less there, a great deal less. But what worried Wyatt now was his head. That pumping and hissing were still there, and the black fur that crowded his sight.

He touched himself and realised he was naked. Then at the foot of the bed he saw his clothes. They'd been dried and folded. And on top of them was his money-belt, with its canvas pockets of deutschmarks, francs and lire.

He saw the old man too. He was staring down at the money-belt, and he seemed worried. Maybe it was a large amount of money to him. Anyway he came towards Wyatt and made signs as though he was phoning. '*Polizia?*' he asked. '*Polizia?*'

'No,' Wyatt said. 'No *polizia*.'

And passed out again.

When he came to for the third time there was a different light. It was faint, the thin blue light of dawn. The old man was there, crouching by the bedside. When he saw Wyatt was awake, he brought him soup, a thin clearish soup made of fish. Wyatt didn't want any but the man made him eat, patiently, as if feeding a child. Then in Italian he told Wyatt to sleep again.

And he did sleep, as against passing out and riding on that mad merry-go-round once again. He slept, he woke, and he ate the food the man brought him. And gradually beyond the man he began to make out the rest of the room. It was small and poor, made out of whitewashed breeze blocks. There was space in it only for the bed, the stove, a wooden chest, and the chair the man sat on. Sometimes he just sat there watching Wyatt, and sometimes he knotted small hooks onto gut. His hands were white and soft, Wyatt noticed, while the rest of his body was dark brown. He was a fisherman, and from beyond the room-door came the sound of the sea.

Wyatt listened to it, the sea. He connected it with the hissing and the black fur in his head. And it was beginning to scare him now, what was happening in his head, because it never seemed to grow less. He watched the old man as he worked on the hooks.

He would know about the sea. He would know about going down too deep and coming up too quickly. There was a word for it that made Wyatt shiver – the bends.

He made signs that he wanted to get out of bed. The old man said no, but Wyatt made him help. Together they staggered to the doorpost, and Wyatt nodded out at the sea, the flat water beyond the rocky point. He tried to get one simple question across. How deep was it out there?

In the end he managed. And in the end, counting on his fingers, the man showed him it was forty metres, a steady forty metres, a flat shelf.

Wyatt fought his lurching head and worked it out. The chain he'd been handcuffed to – Jesus, he could hardly think about it – had been maybe twenty metres long. And he'd been up at the top of it. So he'd been round about twenty metres deep.

He managed to get that across to the old man too, about being down there for maybe a minute, and coming up too fast.

Twenty metres? The man swivelled the words doubtfully with his hands. Maybe okay, but . . .

It was on the borderline.

But by then the old man's face had changed. He seemed to be putting certain things together because he looked once again at the handcuff-mark on Wyatt's wrist, and the wound where his thumb had been.

'*Polizia?*' he asked again. '*Telefono polizia?*'

'No,' Wyatt told him. 'No *telefono polizia*.'

Two more days passed. Wyatt was clearer about that now, where daylight ended and darkness began. His head was clearer too. It could have been the old man telling him that twenty metres' depth was 'maybe okay'. It could have been food and rest. Anyway the hissing sound and the black fur were beginning to relax their hold. He could see more of what was around him, and knew more.

The old man's name, for example, was Gennaio – January. He had a small red-painted boat he kept down among the rocks. And he fished using a long line with hooks knotted to it every metre or so. This line he kept in a big coil-basket, with the hooks sunk into the straw of the rim.

The house was his too, the house with the bed where Wyatt slept. It stood alone on the beach, with white windtorn sand in either direction. And it was more of a shack than a house, just the one room, made out of the broken ends of breeze blocks. There was a rough courtyard in front of it, marked out by dented oildrums. Two of these had poles set in them. They held up a roof of straw wattles that buzzed in the wind like wasps. Wyatt sat in their shade and looked out at the bright line of the sea where Gennaio fished.

Then on the second afternoon the red boat disappeared. Wyatt was alone in that deserted landscape for an hour or more. Until the *tonk-tonk* of the boat brought Gennaio back along the shore. He was waving something.

It was a newspaper. Wyatt saw his own photo on the front page. There were the photos of three other men too, three faces it took Wyatt some time to recognise as the three Corsicans.

And you didn't have to be a genius to work out what the headline said . . .

CRASH AT SEA. HOPE ABANDONED FOR MISSING PLANE.

Crash? Missing plane?

Wyatt didn't understand. Nothing made any sense at all. All he felt was a slow burning anger at the loss of that new Piper Saratoga.

Then, as he stared on at the newspaper, he remembered Gennaio asking him again and again about going to the police. And he saying, no police. At least he'd got something right. Because there wasn't a policeman, nor a Customs man, nor any damn man in uniform he was going to go to. Not in this part of the world.

His head began to ache again as he sat in the shade. Afternoon became evening, and he watched Gennaio fishing in his boat. The man was under the path of the sun, hauling his long line from the water, hook after hook.

. . . And under that golden reflection on the water, Wyatt thought, there was another line, with other hooks. Only it was a chain and they were handcuffs. And three dead men were hanging there, upside-down.

He had to get the hell out of here.

In the blue twilight Gennaio came up from the beach. Wyatt stopped him. He had two words of Italian ready. '*Dovè?*' he asked. '*Dovè telefono?*'

'*Telefono?*' the man asked. '*Telefono polizia?*'

'No. No *telefono polizia*. Just *telefono . . . Dovè telefono?*'

'*Café*.' The man pointed, along the shore to the right where he'd been in the boat this afternoon. Beyond the higher rocks on the skyline.

'Okay,' Wyatt said, 'that's good.'

And at last he was thinking, putting one foot in front of the other. Because this evening he was going to get Gennaio to take him in his boat along to the café. And from there he was going to phone England. Phone the one man he'd met in his life who could handle this, get him out of the country, no questions asked.

Jackman.

5

Jackman came the next evening in a big shiny hire-car. He was alone, but the world he lived in came with him. It was there in the smell of his cologne, the smoke of his cigar, and the way he smoothed back his carefully-cut fair hair. To Wyatt it was like going back eight years.

And what was like going back eight years too was the passport Jackman held out. It was one of the old ones, British, registered under the name of Douglas, but with Wyatt's photo inside. And there was the British Airways ticket with it, first class, Rome to Heathrow.

Wyatt held Gennaio's hand and said goodbye. He sat in the hire-car, heard the hum as the window went up, felt the softness of the seat and head-rest surrounding him. But then the whole thing fell apart. As they drove off, an old man was left behind them on the beach, staring down at a handful of money. And Wyatt found himself stopping the car, running back, and putting his arms round Gennaio, crying.

For a moment Jackman was confused. But only for a moment. He got Wyatt into the car again. On the long drive to Rome he asked him questions, careful questions, about the scars on his hand and wrist. At Rome airport he put in a call to London. And at Heathrow he led Wyatt quickly to his Rolls Royce in the carpark. He said it was time for a short stay in a place he knew. Just a short stay.

It turned out to be a clinic off Albemarle Street. It had small private rooms and corridors with highly polished floors. And there Jackman's smooth operation clicked into place like a well-oiled lock. Just as it always had done.

A fortnight went by. A fortnight when they taped wires and electrodes to Wyatt, patched up his hand, and gave him red capsules, yellow capsules, every damn colour capsules. But at the end of that time his head was clear, the hissing and blurred vision gone. The wound on his hand no longer had that spider-shape of tar covering it, but a new white dressing. And – something he felt bad about – the days he'd spent with Gennaio on that beach seemed part of another world. Even the man's brown leathery face had become dim.

But against that England was all around him. The calm stone streets of Mayfair outside with their purring limousines and well-dressed passers-by. And inside the room the voice of the BBC TV newsreader, again calm as he told about the latest in the string of IRA bomb-attacks in London, told it in some disbelief, as if he were reading from a foreign menu. Nothing had changed, Wyatt thought. England was still the same country he'd lived in all those years ago, when he'd worked for Jackman's organisation.

On cue, at the end of the fortnight, Jackman's Rolls Royce appeared. He came into Wyatt's room with a suitcase full of new clothes, everything from a tan leather jacket down to socks. And he had the clinic's medical report with him too. It was a hundred per cent, he said. No problems at all.

But there was one. To Jackman and the rest of the world Wyatt was fit. Even to the doctors with their wires and electrodes. But there was something none of the machines had been able to reach. A dream. A nightmare.

It had begun two nights ago when the effects of those capsules they'd given him had begun to wear off. It came often, and it was always the same . . .

First there was the handcuff on his right wrist. Then the long chain with that motion it had, like some unstoppable machine. The black hole in the curl of the wave . . . Down . . . Until, for some mad reason, everything became steel, a big steel Zippo lighter, with an enamel design on its side . . . One three-pointed star set on top of another.

Jackman drove him through the traffic and out of London. They took the M3 and headed on towards Southampton and the New Forest. But once off the motorway the roads seemed narrow and winding to Wyatt. And he remembered thinking the same thing before. As an air-taxi pilot he'd returned to England often in the past few years. And each time the roads seemed to get smaller, and Jackman's houses larger.

This one, just outside Lymington, was no exception. It was a mansion at the end of a long curving drive. There was that luminous glow of wet lawns that could only be England. Beyond were the long thin shadows of cedar trees. And the house itself had that old soft brickwork that seemed to have been dipped in honey.

Inside, as usual with Jackman, there was the right kind of pale carpet. There were big rooms through double doors, a tall gilt drawing-room, a billiards room and then a library with one of those old stepladder affairs on wheels. And then there were smaller rooms, some with just a single piece of spotlit furniture.

Wyatt had the tour. He met Jackman's wife, standing small in a huge Swedish kitchen. She was the same as ever, until you looked under her bright make-up and saw she'd got even smaller. But Jackman? Wyatt couldn't make out if he'd changed. Maybe he'd slowed up, maybe that white moon-face of his was heavier. But as for the rest of him it was difficult to tell – the suits he wore were too good.

One thing about him hadn't changed though. Back in the gilded drawing-room he up-ended a Courvoisier bottle into a glass the size of a bucket, and started pouring the stuff down.

Wyatt helped himself to a beer, then put his right hand quickly back into his pocket.

And Jackman noticed. 'You're lookin' a bit down, Ace,' he said. 'A bit pissed off, int that right?'

'Could be.'

The man came up and pressed a fist fondly against his stomach. 'What's up then? Int you had it in lately?'

'No,' Wyatt said.

'Bleedin' fall off, I tell you.' Jackman finished his brandy, and went out, as he said, to mow the tennis lawn.

Wyatt watched him through the french windows. He saw him sit in his shirtsleeves on a big Ransome's mower. Saw him drive up and down, dark strip against white, a heavy barrel-like figure with that straw-coloured hair. And that force about him, the violence that people often mistook. Jackman looked as if he bought shirts from a cut-price store. But they were silk. And with him violence was silk too, the real thing.

Again Wyatt thought back to the days when he'd flown for the man. The trips to the Continent with parcels on the back seat, bulky parcels, banknotes. The golden days, as Jackman had called them. Because banks had been built differently then. 'Jesus Christ,' he'd said. 'There's only this staff-door up one end of the counter, int there? And it's only locked by a single bleedin' Yale. And it only opens inwards so as not to inconvenience the customers. *Inconvenience* the customers?'

Towards the end Jackman and his firm had got it down to ninety seconds, a tap with a hammer, pick up, and away . . . To where Wyatt was waiting across the county with a plane. He remembered those times, the van appearing, bumping over the grass. And the time in particular when Jackman was swearing, clutching at his gut. Wyatt thought he was hurt.

'Hurt? Listen,' Jackman shouted. 'Bleedin' Hawkins come out first with the hammer. Maurice come out next with one of the shooters. So I had to come out with the Securicor sacks . . . Jesus, I come out with a double-hernia. You ever carry those things?'

Wyatt never went in with them, he always kept apart. As far as Jackman was concerned he was just Ace, who flew planes. But he travelled a lot with Jackman, sitting in pubs and looking over the banks beforehand. And why? Because he liked Jackman, liked him a lot. It wasn't just that the man was different from him in every way. There was something else, a crudeness, an unfinished feel about his stumpy hands and blank round face. A sawn-off feel, like the shotguns.

For example there was the pub where this big man was sitting. This big man who was angry, hauling off about a white girl he'd just seen on the arm of a blackie.

And, listening to him, that innocent look came over Jackman's face. And that soft breathy voice of his came out. 'Never,' he said. 'White girl with a blackie?'

'That's it,' the big man said.

'Well, I heard about it happenin',' Jackman said. 'I mean, I heard about it but I never seen it.'

'Diabolical,' the man said.

'Yeh,' Jackman agreed, still innocent. 'But, you know what, my son? You got it easy.'

'Easy?'

'Yeh, I mean, you can see who it is you hate. You can walk in a place and see blackies straight off. Only with me it's different. Me, I hate people who come from Derbyshire. And when I walk in a place I got to go up to each bugger in turn and ask if they come from Derbyshire. Then it's . . .' He reached out and smashed a bottle on the bar. '. . . Wallop, the light ale bomb.'

It was just a thing Jackman had, Wyatt thought, a thing people like him had, about needing to raise the temperature when they went into a room . . . And there was the other thing too, the need there was in Jackman. It came regular as clockwork, twice a day. And was satisfied . . . Wyatt knew all about that.

For example, the time when they were working out in the sticks, well out in the sticks, the land that Jackman referred to as 'roadhouses and Jeremys'. And that particular night there were Jeremys – estate agents and solicitors – a whole mob of them in the bar where they were drinking.

Jackman had his ration of Courvoisiers. He looked round. And he picked out this thirty-fiveish faded-looking woman, standing in a group.

'Never,' Wyatt said.

'Oh, yes, my son.' Jackman picked up the car-keys. 'You're walkin' home.'

He went over there to the group. And he changed not a word of his act. They gave him Jeremy-talk, he gave them South London. But half an hour later the thirty-fiveish woman went out to powder her nose. Jackman went out to his car . . . And Wyatt walked home.

'You just got to like doin' it enough,' Jackman explained later. 'If you like doin' it enough, it shows . . . And it's always goin' to show on somebody else too. There's always your oppo, one in every room.'

And that was Jackman . . . Or *was*, Wyatt thought, as he finished his beer in the tall gilded drawing-room. Because there were things around him that were news. There was the collection of silver that looked serious. And then the big oil-portrait of Jackman and his wife and two boys. The kind of portrait where all the hard lines had been softened by guineas.

Wyatt looked up at it. He wondered if he wasn't counting on too much. If it hadn't all been too long ago.

6

After lunch they sat out in the garden. They finished a bottle of what Jackman called 'good pudden' wine, and they started another.

Then the man leaned across. 'All right, Ace, you tell me what it's all about,' he said. 'All I know so far is you got stuck somehow down under the sea. And you used this knife to get clear.'

'Yes,' Wyatt said. And he told him. Everything.

Jackman's face began to take on that blank look, that dangerous look. And when he spoke, it was with that soft breathy voice.

'Let's get this straight,' he said. 'Right at the beginnin' you're flyin' over to Corsica. You got this job, to pick up a guy on this thing called the Yacht List. Which is a list where it's just a number on a telex and no names . . . On account of the rich go about things that way.'

'Yes,' Wyatt said. 'But that was before. Before any of the trouble started.'

'I need to see it all, Ace. That's the way I am,' Jackman said. 'Now as it happens, the guy on the Yacht List doesn't turn up, on account of he's still out at sea. So you take this other job with three Corsican heavies. And it turns out they're carryin' a parcel on the back seat. And they got you to land at a Mickey Mouse airfield, just like the old days.'

'That's right.'

'Which is where, later on in the afternoon, the Customs lay hands on you. Only it turns out they int Customs. It turns out they're hard men. Very hard men indeed.'

Wyatt nodded. He kept his right hand in his pocket.

'You got any thoughts about that, Ace? Have you?'

'Well, as I see it, they have to be some kind of a mob,' Wyatt said. 'Corsicans maybe, I don't know.'

'Yeh, but both lots,' Jackman said. 'I mean, two mobs. One takin' on the other over this parcel that was on the plane. What we got here is mob violence, right?'

Again Wyatt nodded.

'But the point I'm makin' is it int small stuff. My Christ, no,' Jackman went on. 'Listen, these guys that slung you into the sea on that anchor-chain, they decided to do away with a whole plane-load of people that afternoon. Not to mention the plane itself. Not to mention squarin' it with *everyone* who could've seen you out at the airfield.' He paused. 'Ace, I'd say you was up against a whole barrel of money here.'

'Yes,' Wyatt said.

But Jackman was watching him closely. 'I mean, you do see what I'm on about, don't you?'

'What?'

Jackman sighed. He got up and walked away over the grass. Then he turned and looked back. 'If I was to ask you, Ace, what it was you wanted to see out of all this at the end . . . what would that be?'

Wyatt took his time. 'There's a man somewhere,' he said. 'And I don't think I've even met him yet. But I'm going to find him. And when I do, I'm going to take him out in a small boat. I'm going to take him out deep, and show him on the chart just how deep it is. Then I'm going to show him the anchor, the chain, and the handcuffs. I'm going to let him look at them a long while. And it's all going to happen very slowly . . . right up until the time I throw the anchor over the side.'

Jackman's face didn't change. 'That's what I was afraid of,' he said.

Suddenly Wyatt took his right hand from his pocket, held it out. 'You try going down there,' he said. 'You try. Just once.'

'Yeh.' Jackman nodded. 'But you still don't get what I'm on about, do you?'

'No.'

'I mean, Ace, where's all the gags? All the laughs we used to have? Eight years ago, remember, when we was sittin' round in the pubs?'

Wyatt didn't answer.

'Gone, right? Gone down there in the bottom of the sea with half your mind.' Jackman's eyes never left him. 'Ace, listen to me careful. You and I worked together, what, a matter of months? And it was good, and there was laughs, and you stayed on the outside, away from the hard men on the street . . . Because, Ace, you int hard. Not like Maurice was, or Hawkins, guys who would go right in the middle of it with a razor or chain, because that's what the street was all about.'

Still Wyatt didn't answer.

'But now, eight years later, suddenly you're in that kind of trouble,' Jackman went on. 'You want help. There's no way you can go to the Law. So you come to me for the kind of help there is on the street.'

Wyatt sat there a moment. 'Yes,' he said.

And Jackman walked further away. He went down the bank to the tennis court below where they were sitting. He looked at the straight lines he'd mown on the grass. He looked at the net-posts and the coiled-up net. 'Ace, the street's a long way away,' he said. 'I mean, you can see for yourself, you come to me at the wrong time. I got two kids at Cheam, which is the school where the Royals go. I got sports day comin' up, and after that it's Goodwood.'

'Yes,' Wyatt said.

'For Christ's sake, you must've noticed, each time you come back to England, how I been movin' further and further away from the Smoke. And why? Because there's a better class of C.I.D. out here. They don't come knockin' on my door. The past is the past.' He pointed back at the house. 'Ace, she keeps Siamese cats now, and she goes to flower-arrangin' classes. I promised her I'd retire. And that's just what I done. Retired.'

'Yes,' Wyatt said again.

Jackman shook his head. He looked round at the tennis court as if it bothered him. Then he came back up the bank and sat down suddenly, scarring the turf with his heel. 'But that int goin' to stop me helpin' you,' he said softly, close to Wyatt's ear. 'And I'll tell you why . . . I'm forty-four years old, and what do I do all day? I sit, that's what I do. I sit in my Rolls Royce, I sit in my Range Rover, I sit in my bleedin' motor-cruiser. Just sit in them, one after the other.'

7

They were both sitting in the Rolls Royce, driving through the back lanes of the New Forest. And of course it was raining.

Wyatt was on edge. Maybe it was the rain that had fallen for two days now, the summer that had been washed away. Or maybe it was that Jackman had been away on business, as he called it, for the same two days. And when he returned he'd been washed too – washed and scrubbed clean of the women he'd been seeing. Wyatt knew it. Jackman's wife knew it as she sat at one end of the dinner table. But that bright smile stayed on her face. Maybe she'd retired too.

Which was fine for Jackman, if that was the way he went about his marriage, but it wasn't exactly getting Wyatt any further. And nor was this morning. Jackman had brought the Rolls round to the front door at midday. He'd put his golf clubs in the boot, put Wyatt in the front seat, and driven for half an hour without saying a word. Now, still in silence, he turned off the country lane, crossed a cattle grid, and went in through a large stone entrance with wrought iron gates. A notice said: Ferndene Golf Club, Members Only.

They drove on through parkland with white metal fences and grey trees on either side. Then ahead of them appeared an ornamental lake and a house – one of those vast country houses with the long portico of stone pillars and the wide stone steps. Jackman pointed to it. 'They tell me, Ace,' he said, 'it's the only club to join.'

They went round the lake and parked in a line of other cars on the gravel. Jackman opened his door but then waited a moment before running through the rain. 'Don't look so bothered. The golf-sticks are only for show,' he said. 'Why we're here is we're meetin' this guy.'

'Is that right?' Wyatt asked.

'Yeh, but I'm not promisin' it'll do any good, mind. The thing is, he's retired, same as what I am. But I did hear he still had some dealins in foreign trade.'

The man who dealt in foreign trade was waiting for them inside. His name was McGilray. He was about fifty but his head was like a skull, and it was tanned a deep rich brown that went through to the bone.

McGilray took them through to the dining-room. It was huge and echoing, with dark oil paintings that rose up to the dimness above. There were marble columns too, and as Wyatt followed the others over to a table his shoes clicked on a marble floor. He sat down and listened to the talk around. It was all of shortfalls and downturns and currency flows.

There was little talk on McGilray's table. The man said nothing through the *asperges vinaigrette*, he spoke hardly at all through the venison. But then he said, yes, all right, he did still have some dealins he kept open in Europe. But only through a front man, they had to understand. He himself kept well back.

The strawberries arrived, and the subject of Corsica came up for the first time. No, McGilray said, there was no way he was ever goin' to get himself involved in Corsica. Corsica was trouble.

With the coffee, Jackman pressed him about this trouble. And McGilray seemed ready to talk . . . Corsican mobs were okay as long as they kept to their own back yard, he said. It was when they started crossin' the water. And a week or two back this had happened. A Corsican mob had got big, too big for its boots, and gone in with a European partner. It had bought its way into this partnership with half a million dollars . . . And the story was, he said, that this sum of money had left Corsica in a light plane. The wrong hands had got hold of it. There'd been bother.

Jackman glanced just once at Wyatt. He ordered liqueurs and waited for them to come before he pressed it further . . . This plane trip, he asked, how had it ended?

McGilray sipped at his drink. Nobody knew, he said, except it was bad.

How bad was bad? Jackman asked.

In Corsica? McGilray looked back at him. Then he put his liqueur glass down and talked about a couple of scores which he said were just small scores, just starters. And as he spoke, for some reason there was a lull in the business talk all around.

'They got this habit of takin' chunks out of people with pairs of pliers,' he said in the sudden silence. 'Or shavin' people's heads.'

Two days later Wyatt and Jackman were in the Range Rover, bumping over the long grass of a racing gallop. The wheels were sliding too on patches of mud, the rain had only just stopped. All around there was a very white overcast look to the day, a hot-house feeling that Wyatt remembered from English summers of long ago. Steam rose from the slope of the gallop ahead, it rose from the wheat-field to the left. And on the right was this long avenue of beech-trees, tall and grey and dripping.

Then, in a gap between the trees, there was colour. Another Range Rover, light blue, was parked there, and two men stood by it. One was a racing-trainer, the other a man in a red turtle-neck sweater and check trousers. And the sweater was too new and bright. It looked as if it belonged in a colour-page about the country rather than in the country itself.

Jackman drew over into the gap and parked. He got out.

'Arthur,' he said to the man in the sweater. 'Arthur Windlesham.'

'Hi, Jacko. How you doin'?'

The two of them talked, until the racing-trainer raised his binoculars and turned away. There was just a drumming sound at first. But then a string of racehorses appeared round the wheat at the corner of the field. They leaned steeply inwards to make the turn, and Wyatt was surprised at how far their hooves slid – maybe a foot and a half – carving long strips of mud up from the turf.

The man called Arthur was angry behind his binoculars. 'Don't he know it's been rainin' these four days?' he shouted. 'Don't he knew he's got my forty grand between his knees?'

'Easy! Easy!' the trainer called out.

The horses grew larger, trailing steam that was thinner than the mist. Then they passed, their jockeys small and hunched on their backs. Wyatt watched them go away, down to the end of the gallop where the white rails of the stables began.

'Seems to be goin' all right, don't it?' Arthur said.

'Yes,' the trainer told him. 'You picked yourself a good little mover there.'

Jackman walked between them. 'Don't kid me he knows anythin' about horses,' he said.

'I know the end that eats,' Arthur said. 'I know the end that's costin' me a hundred and fifty a week.'

The trainer edged away at that. Moving the way a lot of racecourse people did, Wyatt thought, as if walking on thin ice.

Jackman waited till he was out of earshot. 'Wanted a quiet word with you, Arthur,' he said then.

'What about?'

'Dockland.'

'Dockland? I int been there in ten years. And for the same reason you int been in certain places in ten years.'

'Southampton docks in particular,' Jackman insisted.

'What d'you want me to tell you?' Arthur said. 'Southampton docks is history. There's the new container port up the river. There's nearly no liners calling in there any more. And if the Southampton Law sees someone out on the municipal course weekdays, working up his handicap, then they know he's signed on at the docks.'

'Maybe,' Jackman said. 'Except, as I heard it, there was this story you was tellin' a mate of mine the other evenin'.'

'Where was that?'

'Round the Conservative Club.'

'That?' Arthur nodded his head, just slightly, towards Wyatt.

'He's all right,' Jackman said. 'He's with me.'

Arthur hesitated. 'Well,' he said, 'well, it's like this. There's this guy.'

'What guy?'

'Just a guy. You wouldn't've heard of him. One of the ulcer-men from a few years back.'

'What d'you mean, ulcer-men?'

'Where he's never far from a phone. Where he's always on the phone in a bar or pub, doin' the talkin'.'

'A grass, you mean?'

'No, not that. Not to the Law. This guy just knew dockland first to last. He heard the whispers. And if any new racket come up, then he knew where to place the information. So there'd be sweeteners, money changin' hands, and a bit for himself. Everythin' nice and tidy.'

'And?'

'Well, for years he int had a livin' wage,' Arthur said. 'Like I told you, the docks is history. There int been the trade because there int been the boats in in a long while.'

Jackman nodded.

'So he's in trouble, int he, this guy? Trouble with his rent, trouble with his missus, walkin' round and smokin' other people's fags . . . Until recently, that is. Because suddenly he's smilin'. Suddenly he knows where information's goin' to be to hand. Real information, he says. Shipments, regular shipments. The old days of foreign trade comin' back.'

'Foreign trade?' Jackman asked. 'Here? In Southampton Water?'

'Who knows?' Arthur asked. 'But that's what he said.'

'And you mean, that's the end of the story?'

'No, not the end . . . Listen, I told you he was one of the ulcer-men, dint I? And why they got that name is it's a very chancey business, information. There's people get very sudden and start hittin' back.' He frowned. 'Foreigners especially. And foreigners is what I got to tell you about now. Though nobody saw them come in. Nobody saw them when they was here. And nobody saw them go away.'

Jackman waited. Arthur stood by his side, looking out at the gallop and the wheat-field in the mist. 'It was one of those hot days we had last week,' he said. 'You know, when we *had* a summer. And it was down in St Mary's Park in Southampton. There was people sittin' around on benches, and there was this cricket game goin' on out on the grass. And then this guy I'm talkin' about turns up, walkin' out on the cricket pitch. Nobody notices him at first on account of the white shirt he's wearin', they reckon he's part of the game. But then they see he's moanin'. And they see these two red spots on his shirt.'

'What?'

'He had his two nipples and a pair of pliers in his trousers pocket,' Arthur said. 'Foreign way of doin' things, all right? Though I int heard of nothin' like it before.'

The two of them went down to Jackman's motor-cruiser in Lymington. It was getting towards the end of June now but the summer still hadn't returned. White hazy days had given way to white windy days, and as they left the narrow streets of the town they met dust kicking up from the boatsheds along the river. Jackman drove past them and parked on the hard behind the yacht club. Then he led the way round to the front of the building, and they looked out at the marina.

The wind was stronger here. It was booming in from the Solent, rattling the masts and slapping the water underneath the mooring-pontoons. But there were other sounds as well. It was a Friday afternoon and there was the whir of the coming weekend. The flap of oilskins as crewmen marched out to the yachts. The scrape of sailbags on deck. And then the sharp crackling sound as sails were hoisted.

Wyatt followed Jackman along to his cruiser. It was much as he'd expected, a great eggbox of a boat riding uncomfortably high on the water. It had a square white stern, a lot of flashy chrome, and these two long fishing-rod aerials. They whipped from side to side, the whole damn boat rolled from side to side, as gusts caught it coming up-river.

'Not the greatest sea-boat in the world,' Jackman said. 'But that wasn't down there on the colour brochure. What *was* on the brochure was forty-four feet of high class knockin'-shop, eight feet of which bein' double-bed, and eight feet of which bein' bar.'

And he was right. They crossed the white afterdeck and went down a companionway to the saloon. There was a grey twilight down there from the tinted windows. And only a ship's wheel and a navigation-console up for'ard to say it was a boat. The rest of the saloon, as Jackman had said, was bar.

They sat down one on each side of it. The companion door rattled behind them, the rows of bottles rattled in their racks. Jackman poured, drank, and unusually for him drank silently. He'd been away from home again for the past three days. But this time he hadn't come back scrubbed and clean. He'd seen no women. He just looked tired.

'What's up?' Wyatt asked.

'I don't know.' Jackman shrugged. 'I mean, I been askin' a lot of questions on your behalf. Only I int been comin' up with answers, just more questions.'

'Like what?'

'Okay, let's take it from the beginnin',' Jackman said. 'A story we heard, right? A simple story . . . This Corsican mob gettin' big and expandin' into Europe. Takin' on European partners and puttin' half a million dollars in the kitty. The money leavin' Corsica on a light plane.'

Wyatt nodded.

'Which is where you come into it, Ace. By chance you happened to be the pilot of that plane. And it was chance, because the way you told it to me you went to Calvi on another job altogether.'

Again Wyatt nodded.

'All right, now I want you to think back to that day. I mean, as I understand it, it all happened very sudden-like . . . You were let down on the first job. You heard of the second job. You went straight round to the hotel where these three Corsican comedians were, and you clinched the deal in a matter of minutes.'

'Yes,' Wyatt said, not understanding.

'What I'm talkin' about is time, Ace,' Jackman said. 'I mean there wouldn't've been time for anyone . . . anyone workin' for those Corsicans, say . . . to fit up your plane?'

'What d'you mean? Fit it up?'

'The way we used to do it in the old days when we carried certain shipments,' Jackman said. 'The important shipments, where we used to unscrew a fuselage panel in the plane, and slip a couple of cases in behind the luggage compartment.'

'No,' Wyatt said. 'Christ, there wouldn't have been time to do that. It's a tricky job. You have to make racks for the cases to keep them secure, and to keep them clear of the plane's control-lines.'

'So that's out,' Jackman said. 'All right, tell me one other thing . . . Those Corsican comedians, were they carryin' anythin' else? I mean, apart from that parcel they had?'

Wyatt frowned, remembering. 'Just a raincoat. The raincoat they covered the parcel with, going through Customs . . . But, if we're talking about half a million dollars in large notes, what's wrong with the parcel?'

'The parcel they said had shirt-material inside?'

'Yes. What did it have inside?'

'Shirt-material,' Jackman said.

'*What?*'

'There int no doubt about that, Ace. These three got shirts made up in the town of San Guielmo.'

'But . . .' Wyatt stared at him. 'I don't get it.'

'Me neither,' Jackman said. 'A parcel of shirt-material gets three people drowned on an anchor-chain. It gets fellers doin' each other over with pliers in Corsica. Not to mention a feller gettin' done with pliers over here . . . *Here*, in Southampton.'

'Yes,' Wyatt said.

'I mean, Ace, we int got a story, we got lots of little bits of a story, none of them tyin' up. For Christ's sake, what's the connection between what went on in Corsica and here? There *has* to be a connection.'

Wyatt didn't say anything. He wasn't feeling like saying anything. The rolling of the deck-saloon, the motion of the egg-box of a boat, was beginning to get to him. He put down his drink, went up the companionway and out on deck.

The wind came at him across the marina. He walked over to the taffrail and stood there leaning against it. And as he looked out, it was there staring him in the face. The connection.

He didn't see it at first. He saw only the yacht in the next bay, the tall-masted sloop. It was big, and it had a curving red hull, as shiny as a race-car. And on it crewmen were working in shiny red oilskins.

And where, Wyatt wondered, had he seen that particular yacht before?

Then he remembered. In the Gulf of St Florent off Corsica. The red boat had been part of the fleet of ocean-racers. But why here? Now? Fifteen hundred miles away?

And he remembered that too. The Ocean Racing circuit. The Florida races in February. Calvi Week in June. And Cowes in late

July and August.
Here, on the Solent.
But he still didn't make the connection. Not until he saw the other big yachts in the further bay. The huge curves of sail they were hoisting, spinnakers, flapping loosely in the wind to dry. And, glowing against grey clouds, were their brilliantly-coloured patterns . . . Triangles, arrows, stars.
Stars.
Because beyond them was another sail. A sail that was new to Wyatt, with a much simpler design.
One three-pointed star set on top of another.

8

The wind was stronger. Wyatt was back in the deck-saloon, hanging on in the bigger gusts. Jackman faced him, his body wedged between the bar and the racks of clanking bottles.
'Right, Ace,' he said quietly. 'Connections . . . And we int talkin' about nothin' that's hearsay, either in Corsica or here. We're talking about what you saw with your own eyes . . . Racing yachts, Ace. And a certain Zippo lighter with a certain design.'
Wyatt nodded.
'Because it alters things, int that right? It alters one hell of a lot. Because what we been doin' is lookin' at it the wrong way round. We been lookin' at those three Corsicans you flew that day. But what we should've been lookin' at was what came *before*.'
Again Wyatt nodded.
'I mean, the Yacht List, Ace. Startin' way back there. That famous list where it's just a number and not a name. That should've bothered the hell out of me a long time ago.'
'And me,' Wyatt said.
Jackman leaned towards him. 'Now I can see some of it,' he said, 'but by no means all. So what you do is talk me through, tellin' it the way it seems to you now.'
Wyatt thought a moment. 'All right,' he said. 'That particular day I took the Yacht List job with the pickup at Calvi, fourteen hundred hours. But I got there early and took a taxi into town. I would've been away from the plane for, what, a couple of hours. Which meant there would've been plenty of time for somebody

out at the airport . . . a mechanic maybe . . . to get into the fuselage, and fit a suitcase in behind the luggage compartment.'

'Right,' Jackman said. 'But why? Who for?'

'For the Yacht List client, the guy who'd booked the flight in the first place,' Wyatt said. 'Because *he* has to be the guy who's going partners with the Corsican mob. He has to be the one taking the payment.'

'Right,' Jackman said again.

'But then it all started to go wrong for this guy,' Wyatt went on. 'Because when I tried to meet him, I was told he wasn't there. He was still out at sea in a yacht-race. I was told to wait, wasn't I? Come back at midnight? In ten hours' time? . . . And. Let's face it, in that ten hours I wouldn't be expected to fly out of the island and back in again.'

'But you did,' Jackman said. 'You picked up those three Corsican comedians.'

'Who seemed kind of heavy,' Wyatt said. 'And, all right, who were maybe kind of heavy . . . Except that they were travelling clean that day. Doing business in Italy and getting shirts made. Just like they said they were.'

'Right.'

'But what they didn't know was that they were flying with somebody else's half million dollars.'

'Right.'

'And what they didn't know was that this somebody else would send people chasing after them. Later on in the afternoon, I mean, when the yachts finished the race . . . Somebody on the Yacht List. Somebody with a fag-lighter that ties in with the sail we've just seen.'

'Right, Ace,' Jackman said. '*Right.*'

They were out in the Solent.

The wind had risen higher. It was now a steady Force Five, gusting Six, or so Jackman said from the radio-reports. And it was wind against tide, as he said too. Which brought short seas, ugly seas, with the lights of copper blue and green in their troughs. They came at the cruiser. They buried its engine-note in the belly of the waves and raised it to a scream at the crests . . . And all this, Wyatt thought, not half a mile from Yarmouth harbour on the Isle of Wight . . . Jesus, he wished he were back in the Mediterranean.

Next to him on the cruiser's bridge, Jackman fought the wheel, trying to keep the damn eggbox of a boat headed to wind. 'How many?' he shouted. 'How many now?'

Wyatt looked through the binoculars. 'Five,' he shouted back. 'No, six . . . Six.'

And they were there, coming in from the Needles, the six spinnakers with the double-starred design. Six among a much bigger fleet of balloon sails, tall, majestic . . . and racing, while every other sail Wyatt could see was a small tight-reefed triangle, scurrying for home.

'Six?' Jackman shouted. 'Where the hell do they come from? That many?'

'I don't know.'

'I mean, we only saw one before, didn't we? One back at the marina?'

'Yes.'

'And what the hell's it mean anyway? That double star? Some sort of badge, is it? They all come from the same country or somethin'?'

'I don't know,' Wyatt shouted again.

He raised the binoculars. The fleet with the tall balloon-spinnakers was bearing down on them . . . And those yachts came fast, unbelievably fast, with great bow-waves lifting on either side, and white water piling under their sterns. But even so Wyatt wasn't prepared for the risks they were taking. He could see how twitchy they were as the waves coming behind lifted them, see how fast the helmsman spun the wheel to keep those huge sails off the wind, a balancing act where if a gust came on the beam, the boat would be dragged over.

And something else he could see too, how the crews in bright oilskins were bunched aft to keep the weight back, and how some of them were standing, as calm as if they were on a pavement.

The leading yachts passed. Kicking, screeching through the short seas. Then swinging round as a gust almost keeled them over. Then swinging back.

But it was the sounds he hadn't expected. The violence of the sounds. The smack of sails like thunder, the scream of sheet-winches as slack was clawed in, the crashes of surf and metal.

Then the sound like a gunshot . . . The yacht that swung off, slewed round in the big gust, heeled. A bellow of metal as an alloy spinnaker pole dug into a wave. The hiss as the vast sail touched water, threw its shape and filled from the top, dragging the yacht over. More metal, a thunder of metal as the main boom swung in a gybe, as white water pounded the stern and fifty feet of yacht went over, floundering, shrieking in the surf.

There were the screams of men. Men clutching each other in a tangle of limbs as water poured over them. Only the helmsman was upright. He hurled his rage at the sky, fought, and in a mad white arc behind him the wake curved round. The yacht came head to wind, roaring like an animal, trying to shake itself free. Then sixty feet of metal mast rose up, stalled, rose up again. A huge spinnaker, backed, tried to flog itself to pieces against the rigging. A white mainsail rose, pouring water down its length.

And the boats around? The boats around gave two fingers as they skeetered past on the following sea. As in a hiss of surf, men ran for'ard over pitching decks to swing out on the spinnaker guys and put their weight against the main boom.

They took avoiding action. And, as quickly as it had come, the fleet was gone.

To be followed, maybe five minutes later, by the yacht that had broached, had gone over. With a new spinnaker hoisted, and the old one cut away.

'Kind of hard men,' was all Jackman said.

9

The summer had come back.

From the Lymington Yacht Club the river seemed wider in the sunlight. The wooden pontoons lay in straight lines, calm and unmoving, and the yachts moored there seemed to be set in a sheet of silver. Half a dozen of them had masts taller than the others. Half a dozen were shapes that only a child would draw – low lean hulls with just a triangle of rigging above. The ocean-racers were back from their wild ride. Their decks seemed bare without last evening's twelve-strong crews. Cordage no longer littered them, and their spinnaker poles lay lengthwise near their bows. Poles which Wyatt had last seen trying to dig into a screeching sea.

He looked down now from the bar of the yacht club. It was ten minutes to eleven on a Saturday morning, and he was early for his appointment.

He was also alone. Jackman, talking to him over the breakfast table, had said he wasn't coming. 'Ace, I'd only get in the way,' he'd said. 'You know all the yachty talk. You know about pullin' strings on sailin' boats. You're the one who goes cruisin' down in the Med.'

And Jackman had been generous too. He'd lent Wyatt the keys of his Range Rover, the keys of his motor-cruiser, not to mention five hundred quid in twenties.

'I'll get it back when this is over,' he'd said. 'But until that time, Ace, you int in no position to pay anybody back. What you got to remember is you're dead. No more talk of Dan Wyatt swannin' around Europe with his Biggles helmet. Any time you think different, just remember that guy in Southampton who had the pliers-job done on him.'

'Yes,' Wyatt had said.

'And another thing. Remember the way you used to play it when you flew jobs for me? You got a fake name on your passport, Douglas, right? So Douglas you are. You give yourself a fake address somewhere, which has to be an address you know well. And of course you have to be heavily into sailin' . . . So take some time and work it out.'

Wyatt had worked it out. And now, at nearly five minutes to eleven, he reckoned he was word perfect.

But the man he was here to meet was early too. Wyatt knew him from Jackman's description as soon as he came into the bar. 'Tall, around fifty, and wearin' a blazer,' Jackman had said. 'And nice, very nice, kind of cuddly with the gut he's got on him. Then there's this grey hair too, sort of distinguished and wavy, like British film stars used to have once.'

The man saw him and came over. 'Mr Douglas?' he asked. 'Hello, I'm Carver. How are you?'

'How d'you do?' Wyatt shook hands. 'Can I get you a drink?'

'No, they won't let you,' Carver said quietly. And in the same quiet voice ordered drinks from the bar fully fifteen yards away. It was a trick Wyatt had never been able to manage. And there were other things too, he remembered, that Jackman had said about the man. 'Don't ever think of him as a Jeremy. He's well-connected, he works three days a week, and he earns more'n you or I'll ever see.'

The drinks came. 'So you're a friend of Jackman's,' Carver

said. 'Very fond of the laddie myself. Refreshing's the word I'd use. Rather refreshing around here.'

'Yes, he would be,' Wyatt said.

'Between ourselves,' Carver leaned forward, 'a couple of stuffed shirts in the club are inclined to call him "one of nature's gentlemen" . . . Worst insult I think I could pay anyone in my life.'

And Wyatt quite liked him for that.

They sipped their drinks. Then Carver began probing, gently and politely, as Wyatt knew he would. 'Jackman tells me you're from foreign parts,' he said.

'Yes, Switzerland,' Wyatt told him.

'Oh, where?'

'Place called Horw, near Luzern.'

Which was the dark-haired woman's apartment by the lake. Wyatt felt a twinge of guilt about using it, but Jackman had told him to give an address he knew well.

'Luzern.' Carver nodded. 'And d'you sail on the lake? I mean, I gathered sailing came into it.'

'No, I get down to the Mediterranean when I can,' Wyatt said. 'I've got a boat down there.'

'Class boat?'

'Yes, a Moody 29.'

Which was Jimmy's boat, the little sloop Wyatt had sailed in last year, at Cannes.

'Very nice,' Carver said. 'Nice little cruising yacht. Though I had the idea you were interested in racing.'

'I was,' Wyatt said, 'three or four seasons back. But I had to give it up . . . Found myself on the wrong boat once, with the wrong crew. Managed to get myself in the way of a main-halyard winch.'

And he held out his right hand. Which was another story altogether.

A drink later, Carver was over by the bar's long window. 'Fine sight, aren't they?' he said. 'The Admiral's Cuppers.'

Wyatt saw he was looking at the ocean-racing yachts.

'Other people might call them Class I boats, but to us they're Admiral's Cuppers,' Carver explained. 'We like to think it's the big event in the calendar, the Grand National, if you like.'

'Yes,' Wyatt said.

'And, as I hear it from Jackman, you're over here to find out what the Admiral's Cup is all about.' The man smiled. 'So . . . Shall we make a start on the guided tour?'

They left the yacht club for the sunlight outside, and went round the quays to Jackman's cruiser. Wyatt took the wheel. Carver let go the lines and got the fenders inboard. Then he sat at Wyatt's side on the bridge cushions, smoothing his wavy grey hair back into place, and sipping at a large gin and tonic he'd brought up from the saloon below.

They went past the marsh-grasses at the river's mouth. And, once out in the Solent, Wyatt was surprised to find it was almost a Mediterranean day. Flat burning water drifted past, and haze was white under a cloudless sky. What made it England, however, was the smell of green fields and hedgerows. Land was all around them. And as they went further out, the island shore appeared, small cornfields and trees bent over by wind.

Carver looked out at the glare. 'One of the golden yachtpools of the world,' he said.

'You're not wrong,' Wyatt agreed.

'And there are others like it,' Carver went on. 'Long Island Sound, Nassau, Kiel, Rushcutter's Bay . . . What's more, in each of them you've had yachtsmen fighting it out for the past few months, selecting a team to come here for the Admiral's Cup . . . Big yachts . . . In a way it's like the old days when kings, emperors and tycoons were at the wheel.'

'Except that it's only tycoons nowadays,' Wyatt said.

'Yes, the kings have gone.' Carver nodded and sipped at his gin. But the drink, Wyatt saw, had little effect on him. Beneath his large stomach and chins there was hard rock. Not to mention a boardroom mind that brought out facts and figures with ease.

'The Admiral's Cup itself,' he said. 'Quite a modern pot, as these things go. Presented in 1957 by the Admiral of RORC, the Royal Ocean Racing Club, and four committee members. The idea being to juice up competition among British yachtsmen . . . Over the years the form of the Series has changed somewhat. In fact nowadays it's made up of five races. Three of them inshore in the Solent here, around the buoys. And two of them offshore, the Channel Race and the Fastnet . . . The last one, I don't have to tell you, being the biggy.'

Wyatt nodded. The sun beat down, the cruiser droned on through the haze, and the facts and figures continued.

Nineteen different countries were going to be Admiral's Cupping this year, Carver said, each with a team of three, making fifty-seven yachts in all.

By and large, the other countries had already chosen their teams. The Yanks, the Aussies and the Kiwis, for example, were already over here, tuning their boats and learning their way around.

The Brits still hadn't picked their three boats. They never did till the beginning of July, it being a home match.

What was most important to realise was that it was a team event. All yachts counted in all races. There was no use having just one fast boat out of the three . . . As was the case, or so Carver had heard it, with the Hong Kong laddies, the Swedes, the Dutch, and possibly the Bermudans.

Wyatt had been counting up. Eight different countries had been listed so far, and he turned to Carver. 'Tell me,' he said, 'is there a team from Corsica?'

'Corsica?' The man looked at him strangely. 'No. Why? Should there be?'

'Not as far as I know,' Wyatt said.

By now they were close to the island shore, with the bathing huts of Gurnard behind them, and the town of Cowes approaching. Carver pointed out Egypt Hill, the big houses where he said Royalty had stayed in the last century. He pointed out Cowes Green, and then the mass of grey stone battlements jutting out from the point beyond. Once it had been a fortress guarding Cowes harbour, he said, now it was the clubhouse of the Royal Yacht Squadron. To one side of it was a sloping lawn where a marquee stood among lopped trees. The most exclusive piece of turf in the world, Carver called it.

They rounded the fortress, and Cowes opened up in front of them, a town divided by an estuary. To their left were rows of moored yachts, to their right a stone balustrade above the water. And here there was elegance at first, from the Squadron steps to the end of Victoria Parade. But then old Georgian houses closed in, showing their backs to the harbour in a jumble of jetties and narrow waterways. Beyond were the corrugated sheds of the ferry terminal. And against the skyline the mean terraced streets of Victorian dockland, a slate grey in the sun.

'Charms it has but it hides them well,' Carver said. 'Couple of things you should know about British yachtsmen. They like getting wet and going without sleep for days on end. And they like eating terrible food and paying through the nose for it.' He looked at the shore and then pointed. 'But the Surrey Club should see us well enough . . . Go in to that jetty there, just this side of the ferry dock.'

They tied up and went ashore. The streets of Cowes seemed dark and narrow after the cruiser's white deck. And the hallway of the Surrey Club, Wyatt found when he got there, was even darker, an old mahogany colour. But Carver seemed at home there, he led the way straight through to the dining-room. He sat back in his chair and said they'd try the roast beef. It was pushed towards them in an old domed carving-trolley. And on the walls around were pictures of gaff-riggers and men in floppy hats, pictures of Cowes Weeks long past.

Wyatt found himself looking at them. 'Something that's not clear in my mind,' he said. 'Cowes Week and the Admiral's Cup, they're two separate things, aren't they?'

'Yes,' Carver said. 'Cowes comes round every August. But the Admiral's Cup takes place every other year.'

'But aren't they both at round about the same time?'

'Not really,' Carver said. 'The Cuppers get three of their races finished beforehand. Which leaves only two to come during Cowes itself.' He shrugged. 'Got to happen like that really. You must understand, there's a hell of a lot going on during the Week. Up to twenty-four races in one day. The Solent's choc-a-bloc with sails.'

'And the Admiral's Cup fleet manages to pick their way through all that lot?' Wyatt asked. 'A fleet of fifty-seven yachts or whatever?'

'They have been known to moan a bit,' Carver said. 'And moan about other things too, the overcrowding ashore, the lunatic tides in the Solent.' He spread his hands. 'But there's always been that. I mean, how do I explain the difference? . . . Cowes is fun-racing, champagne in the dawn, the Royal Yacht, that sort of thing . . . While the Cuppers are the world's best. And their sort of yacht-racing's deadly earnest.'

'The difference between professionals and amateurs then?' Wyatt asked.

'Professionals?' Carver stared at him. 'What are you talking about?'

'Aren't the Admiral's Cup crews professionals?'

'Good heavens, no,' Carver said. 'It's an amateur sport, strictly amateur . . . And thank God for that, say I, in a world where nearly all sport's been ruined by money.' He waved an arm at the old brown shadows of the dining-room. 'We're the last, if you like, the last to hold out. None of your floating billboards here. None of your yachts called *Charles Heidsieck* or *Gauloises* like they have in the round-the-world races. Our rules forbid it, I'm glad to say. And the reason? Television hasn't poked its nose into this class of racing. Not yet. And nobody wants it to either. Who wants to see a bloody great sail labelled *Wonder Bra* floating past the Squadron? Who wants power falling into commercial hands, as it has done with tennis and motor-racing?'

'Nobody, I imagine,' Wyatt humoured him.

'Nobody is right,' Carver said, calming down again. 'But since we're talking about Admiral's Cuppers, motor-racing's not a bad analogy . . . Not the present-day motor-racing, you understand, but days of yore . . . The Bentley boys. Laddies with their caps on the wrong way round. Laddies who paid for their cars, paid for their mechanics, and at the end picked up no more than ten bob in prize-money for their troubles . . . Except, for God's sake, here the Cuppers don't even pick up ten bob. All they're racing for is that two-handled pot.'

And Wyatt stared at him. 'I didn't realise,' he said.

'No. Nobody talks about money. It's boring.' Carver shrugged. 'All I'll say is there are different kinds of rich. There are racehorse-owning rich. There are penthouse in St Tropez rich. But then there are the ocean-racing rich. It's known as "the big man's game". You need an awful lot of it to play.'

Later, at around four o'clock, they were out in the cruiser again, crossing the Solent in a wide flat calm. But now heading in a different direction, towards Southampton Water and in particular the River Hamble. Carver said he'd heard quite a few of the Cuppers were based there. And he was right, because as they neared the river-mouth Wyatt once again had the chance to see 'the big man's game'.

Some half a mile away a thicket of sails was emerging from the Hamble, moving slowly in the very slightest of breezes. And watching them, Wyatt saw something that was almost uncanny. Three of the yachts – big yachts which should have been held back by their size – separated themselves from the smaller craft around.

They glided away as if they alone had wind. And, as they drew out towards the sun, they seemed to have patterns of dazzling fire on their sails.

'See what I mean about the AC boats being the world's best,' Carver said. 'That's what you get for your money. A hull-shape like that. Not to mention all the new thinking in sails.'

'Quite,' Wyatt said, not knowing what the hell he was talking about.

But at least the subject of sails had come up. And now, feeling his way carefully, he got back to the fleet of ocean-racers Jackman and he had seen on Saturday afternoon.

'Force Five, gusting Six it was,' he said to Carver. 'And when the yachts came past us there was a sail some of them had that was news to me . . . A spinnaker . . . And an unusual pattern it had, one three-pointed star set on top of another.'

'Yes, the Double Star,' Carver replied. 'I mean, as you probably know, the single star, the sail that's known as the Starcut Spinnaker, has been with us for years. But this one's part of the new thinking I was on about . . . It's for the laddies with hairs on their chest. High windforce sail. Spills the wind high. Supposed not to dig the bows down into the trough in big seas . . . Skyline Sails do it.'

'Who?'

'Skyline. They're a new loft, based in Lymington where we started out this morning. Recently their operation seems to have taken off in a big way. All happened during Calvi Week, or so they tell me . . . You've heard of Calvi Week? The Series they have in Corsica?'

'I've heard of it, yes,' Wyatt said.

'Anyway it seems their success is all due to one man. Their boss, the new whizzkid in sail-design . . . Name of Monroe.'

10

On the Monday morning Wyatt found out about the new thinking in sails.

He drove into Lymington, parked among its smart pink- and white-washed houses, and found his way to the library. There he passed the desks with the day's newspapers . . . each with its screaming headlines about the IRA bomb-attacks in London . . .

and came to the yachting-magazines. He read them. He read back-numbers too that the library had on file. And at the end of that time one thing, and one thing alone, was clear . . .

He was out of date. When he'd crewed on Jimmy's boat in the Med, he'd handled the sails, or 'pulled strings', as it was called. But now it appeared that that was exactly what he had been doing, pulling strings. Strings attached to pieces of cloth.

Because the new thinking was plastic. Ropes, it appeared, were now made out of a synthetic fibre called Kevlar. Sails, it appeared, were now made out of Kevlar or Mylar, or a combination of the two. And there was a third synthetic called Skimbar.

Plastic at any rate. Which would explain the dazzling pattern of fire he'd seen on the Admiral's Cuppers' sails yesterday, when they were against the sun.

But would explain little else. Because four of the five magazine articles that Wyatt read were highly technical. The fifth, however, was simpler. It traced the history of the firms who made sails . . . The sail-lofts.

It seemed there were three big international lofts in ocean-racing . . . Hoods, North Sails, and Bantings . . . And collectively they were known as 'the superlofts'.

But then there were smaller lofts too. And among them was Skyline, based here in Lymington as Carver had said. Wyatt took down their address. He walked over to the library-counter and found a town-map. He looked at it, went back to the car and drove on.

The map took him down to the river, but then got him turning left, upstream, away from the yacht club. And for a while he thought he'd come to the wrong place. Because he seemed to be in a dustbowl in the centre of an oasis. Gone were the fine pink and white houses of the High Street, gone too were the gleaming hulls of the marina-bays. Here were boatbuilders' and riggers', all of them deserted, all with a For Sale sign, and an air of decay. But then at the end of the lane he came to the one new building that was like a fortress holding back failure . . . Skyline Sails.

It was a single block, built of brick, with ribbed metal above. Two or maybe three storeys high, it was functional-looking, something like a sports centre in a new town. And the whole thing was big enough, Wyatt reckoned, to fit in squash courts, a table tennis room, and a sauna.

He parked and went in through the main doors. An open

staircase took him up past a tall window of tinted glass. At the top there were three offices, all empty. He walked on through double doors, and suddenly stopped.

He was standing at the edge of a vast area of floor, lightwood, like a gymnasium. Sunlight flooded it from wide windows. And running its length was a brilliant gash of colour, a shiny river of colour, fully sixty feet long. From Wyatt's feet it flowed away in torrents of red and yellow plastic. And what it was was a sail, one of the double star spinnakers.

It was a moment before Wyatt could take in the rest of that huge loft. Could see the square wells set into the floor along two of its sides, each containing a large sailmaker's sewing machine. And see too the group of men standing over in the loft-corner. Sailing men they were, tanned and powerful. And the one who turned and saw Wyatt sent a girl with a secretary's pad over towards him.

'Can I help you?' she asked.

'Yes,' Wyatt said, 'I want to buy a sail.'

She smiled and led him back down the corridor to the offices. She sat him down and made him a cup of coffee. 'Somebody'll be along in a moment,' she said.

Wyatt waited. The phone rang, and the girl picked it up, then pressed a house-button. Shortly afterwards a man's feet came softly, a tall very fair-haired man. 'I'll take it in my office,' he said. Then he saw Wyatt. 'You're not Admiral's Cupping, are you?'

'No,' Wyatt said.

'Okay if somebody else sees you then?'

'Fine.'

Wyatt watched him go through the connecting door, watched him sit at a desk there and pick up a phone. 'Monroe here,' he said.

And Wyatt was surprised that the boss of Skyline Sails should be a man in faded jeans and tee-shirt, under thirty years old.

'Jerry?' Monroe said down the phone. 'Hear you've got a problem.'

A man's voice answered.

'The main again?' Monroe asked. 'You want me to come out and take some video of you sailing? The leech, you say? . . . Jerry, you sure you've got the battens in the right way round?'

More from the man's voice.

'No, sure I'll come out, Jerry. The sail has to be right. If I have to bring it in and re-cut it every day, it has to be right.'

The talk went on, and Wyatt studied Monroe. The length of the man was coiled up in his chair, his worn yachting shoes against the desk. He was gaunt, and he was young and old at the same time. His fair hair was bleached white upon white. His face burned red on red, going back through layers of skin. And his eyes were red also, red-streaked from glare on water, somehow giving the impression they went back through layers of the man too.

Because there was a strange feeling about those eyes. Wyatt couldn't think what they reminded him of . . . Until he got there. A job he'd flown many years ago, a Yacht List job to Gibraltar, and a man he'd met there in a bar. A man who'd sailed solo halfway round the world. There'd been that same slow coal to his eyes, and maybe a little craziness too. Eyes that stared out at deep water and found it their only pleasure. Because that's what someone had called him . . . a deepwater man.

Now Wyatt's thoughts were interrupted by a hand that fell on his shoulder. He turned. A second man, younger than Monroe, was standing behind him. 'How d'you do?' he said. 'The name's Chas. I work for this shambles here.'

Wyatt shook the hand, and just in time remembered the name he had written on his passport. 'Douglas. Jack Douglas,' he said.

'Well, Mr Douglas. They tell me you want to buy a sail.'

'Yes, I do.'

'That's good news.' Chas beckoned him across the corridor to the office on the far side.

Wyatt sat down again. He explained what he wanted, and he didn't do badly. In fact he almost convinced himself . . . About the cruising yacht he owned, the Moody 29. How he'd sailed it down in the Med for years, but was now bringing it up to British waters. How he needed a new spinnaker because the old one was torn. And how he'd heard that Skyline was the only loft to come to.

Chas was pleased. He was pleased by a great many things, Wyatt saw. He was in fact a good deal younger than Monroe, with the lean body of a twenty-year-old. The deep tan on his face had only managed to bring out freckles and a schoolboy's chapped lips. And there was an innocence about him, an eagerness to talk to anyone who would listen about boats.

. . . This as he leaned forward, telling Wyatt about the sail he was going to sell him. The new cruising 'chute', as advertised in the yachting press. The idiot-proof sail that could be set without poles, could be set 'shy' with the wind almost abeam.

Wyatt let the technicalities drift on. He watched as Chas drew diagrams on a sketch-pad to explain them. And then he said, yes, it seemed to be the right sail for him.

'Okay,' the young man said. 'So what we do is we fix you up with a ride. We find a boat just like yours, a Moody 29. We kit it out with one of our sails. And then if you're impressed, we go on from there.'

'Fine,' Wyatt said. 'But are you sure you can fit me in? Right now, I mean, with all your racing customers around?'

'Sure,' Chas said. 'It's early days yet. Only a few of the Admiral's Cup teams are here at the moment, and the bossman can handle them on his own.'

As he spoke, Monroe's footsteps could be heard leaving the office opposite, and going out of the building.

'Monroe,' Wyatt said then. 'Somebody told me he was the new whizzkid among sail-designers.'

'He's good, yes,' Chas said. 'If you ask me, the best.'

'And somebody also told me,' Wyatt went on, 'that Monroe's sails hit the bigtime during Calvi Week.'

'Ye-es.' Chas shrugged. 'But it could have been any time.'

'What d'you mean?'

'Calvi just happened to come along when we got our act together,' Chas said. 'We got our new fabric, Skimbar, out of the factory then. And the right shape of sail to go with it.'

'So it wasn't planned?' Wyatt asked. 'Monroe isn't some big deal businessman? He didn't find financial backing at Calvi?'

'Monroe a *businessman*?' Chas burst out laughing. 'For heaven's sake, you saw the man. As I told you just now, he's the best. But the best with sails. He thinks, eats, and sleeps sails.'

They spent a couple more minutes talking. Then Wyatt got up to leave.

At lunchtime he met Jackman in a Lymington pub. And in the dimness of old oak beams they talked close.

'You want the bad news first?' Wyatt asked.

'Yes,' Jackman said, 'let's have it.'

'All right. I've put myself down for three hundred quid's worth of sail. I'm going to be short of money.'

'Three hundred quid's worth of *sail*?' Jackman asked. 'What the hell am I goin' to do with that?'

Wyatt shrugged. 'It's pretty. It's got nice patterns on it. Maybe your wife could cut it up for curtains.'

'Ace,' Jackman said, reaching for the roll of fifties in his pocket. 'I'm goin' to see this back, int I?'

'Sure you are,' Wyatt told him. 'I've got money put by.'

'Right. So now you tell me the good news.'

'Well, I'm narrowing it down,' Wyatt said. 'The guy we're looking for, it's not Monroe, I'm almost sure about that.'

'Why?'

'He's . . . Well, he's what you'd call a deepwater man.'

'Leave off with the Captain Birdseye stuff, will you, Ace?'

'All right.' Wyatt tried again. 'Monroe, he's sails, he's a sailman. There's this private battle he's got with the wind and the sea . . . What I mean is, he's crew, as opposed to being back in the owner's cabin with the gin and tonics.'

'Facts,' Jackman said. 'Just give me facts.'

'Okay, facts, straight from a kid I was talking to at the loft this morning,' Wyatt said. 'During the whole of Calvi Week, Monroe either sailed or worked in a shed he'd taken over as a sail-loft. He took English sailmakers out with him. He didn't want to have anything to do with the Corsicans. Didn't even eat their food, for Christ's sake. He went out there with a dozen packets of cornflakes and twenty pounds of steak . . . I mean, that's not the guy mixed up with big Corsican money, is it?'

'Doesn't sound like it,' Jackman said.

'But I tell you who is. Who it has to be in fact,' Wyatt said. 'One of the big money men, right? One of the millionaire yachtsmen who buy Skyline sails.'

Jackman nodded.

'Because there's another thing,' Wyatt went on. 'The lighter. The big Zippo lighter, remember? With the double star design? . . . Well, I thought it was steel, but it isn't. Seems it's silver, the real thing. And only nine of them have been given away so far. . . . No prizes for guessing who to.'

'The big deal customers,' Jackman said. 'The Admiral's Cup customers.'

'Right,' Wyatt said. 'And I'm due back at the loft this afternoon. This kid I was talking about is fixing me up with a boat-ride . . . And what I'm going to do is stay in that loft till I find out who these customers are.'

He returned to Skyline at around three o'clock. Monroe was still out on the Solent, but Chas was there. And he'd arranged the boat-trip, he said. It was on Thursday, in three days' time.

Wyatt followed him through to the loft itself, wondering what excuse he could find to stay. Then he saw that a new sail was being laid down. Men with foam rubber pads on their knees were taking precise measurements and marking out a huge curving triangle on the floor. Behind them on racks were long rolls of Skyline's patent fabric, Skimbar. Wyatt asked about it, and Chas showed him samples. They were shiny on one side, dull on the other, like very stiff carbon paper. Chas said they came in various weights, single or laminated, and were about as valuable as gold dust.

As usual the young man talked eagerly, with a breathless need to pass on facts. And Wyatt suddenly saw how he could stay around. All he had to do was ask questions.

'Is that an Admiral's Cup sail they're making out there?' he began.

'That's right,' Chas said.

'Well, how d'you know where to cut along the dotted line?' Wyatt asked. 'I mean, as I understand it, each Admiral's Cupper is a one-off, there's no other yacht like it . . . So where d'you start?'

And Chas, the walking encyclopedia, was away. 'With a computer,' he said. 'You see, we've got what's known as a consensus programme, and this gives us more or less a standard sail-shape and profile for an AC sail. So then we get the computer to adapt that to a particular boat. To the sail-plan suggested by its designer, to its degree of mast bend, and to the sort of water it's sailing over.'

Wyatt stopped him. 'The sort of *water* it's sailing over?'

'Oh, yes. Sails are designed round a particular race series,' Chas said. 'The computer's been programmed with different sets of weather-data. In some cases going back years.'

'And after the computer?' Wyatt asked.

'Well, that's when the sail-designer himself steps in,' Chas told him. 'He tailors a general design to a particular. Which means he either sails on the boat or rides behind it with a video camera, as Monroe is doing right now.'

'Which is going to show you what?'

'How to re-cut the sail. And sometimes we're talking about millimetres.'

'In a sail *that* size?' Wyatt pointed out at the loft floor.

'Listen,' Chas said, 'when we started work on this new spinnaker of ours, we put sails on two identical yachts. We had them going over and over the same course in wind-speeds from five to thirty-five knots. We swapped over skippers and crews. We even weighed skippers and crews . . . That's the only way to get an accurate picture for development.'

'It's something else, isn't it?' Wyatt said.

Beyond them in the loft now the sewing machines were whirring. Sail-panels were being sewn together and then laid in the outline marked on the floor. And there wasn't a straight line to be seen, Wyatt realised. It was designing and cutting in three dimensions.

Then he turned back to Chas. 'Computers. Not to mention all those man-hours,' he said. 'I mean, it's all very different from the story somebody was telling me yesterday.'

'Oh? Who was that?'

'Some yachtsman, in a club over at Cowes. What he wanted me to believe was that ocean-racing was a *Boy's Own* paper sort of affair. Like the old days of motor-racing. People putting their caps on the wrong way round, getting into their cars, and just driving.'

Chas shook his head. 'All sports have changed. They've got deadly serious all of a sudden, haven't they? Racing cars go round corners quicker. Yachts go faster . . . It's technology.'

And again he reached out for a pad and started sketching. 'Okay, you're a millionaire,' he said. 'You own an Admiral's Cupper, and you want to win. So I tell you the only way to win nowadays is to treat that fifty-foot-long boat of yours like a small dinghy.' He drew hull-shapes and sails. 'You make it plane over the water like a dinghy. You bend its mast like a dinghy. And you keep the hull as upright as possible, which has to mean a hell of a lot of sail-changes, doesn't it? As the wind-force varies?'

'A lot of sail-changes,' Wyatt repeated. 'Good business for you.'

'Good but tricky,' Chas said. 'Tricky to design for. And even trickier to sail the boats as they should be sailed.' He swung an arm round the loft. 'Which has to mean in practice that designers and crew are more or less the same people. Everybody here sails . . . Everybody.'

Wyatt looked at the men who were now marking out the shape

of the sail with long wooden splines. And suddenly he realised they were all as fit and tanned as Chas.

Then he frowned. 'Wait a minute,' he said. 'Your people here, they're all professionals, aren't they?'

'Yes.'

'But this yachtsman I was talking to yesterday . . . He told me the sport was amateur, strictly amateur.'

Chas looked at him. 'He was an English yachtsman, I take it.'

'Yes. Why d'you say that?'

'Because that's what an Englishman would like to believe,' Chas said, 'that Admiral's Cupping is all strictly amateur . . . Oh, of course, it's managed in the usual British way. Crewmen are paid to eat, paid to sleep at night, paid to walk down the quay to the yacht . . . Paid to do everything but sail.'

'I see.' Wyatt grinned. 'But how's it all work out? I mean, who sails for which yacht? Isn't there some scrambling there?'

And Chas grinned too. 'That's where we get to the *real* amateur part,' he said. 'For years, you see, it's been an accepted part of ocean-racing . . . Sail-lofts, riggers' yards, boatbuilders, they've all said to their customers, "Buy my stuff and I'll put a good man aboard your yacht".' His grin faded slightly. 'The only thing is, recently it's become much more serious than that. It's become a downright cut-throat affair.'

'How d'you mean?' Wyatt asked.

'It's the degree of what's going on. The number of yachts nowadays with so-called amateurs sailing on them,' Chas said. 'I mean, it's amazing how many hotshot helmsmen, ex-Olympic helmsmen, are suddenly being employed by sail-lofts . . . And I'm talking about the big international lofts here, the "superlofts" as they're called.'

'But why?' Wyatt asked.

In answer Chas took him over to the loft-window. He pointed out at the riggers' and builders' yards Wyatt had passed on his way in. Derelict, each with their For Sale sign . . . while Skyline's new brick walls looked down at them.

'Sometimes it's not easy to remember,' Chas said, 'I mean, working with ocean-racers and millionaires as we do, that there's a thumping great world recession going on. Because there is, and it's serious . . . Quite a few yacht-firms, big firms, are going to be out of business by the end of the racing season.'

'Racing season?' And Wyatt understood. 'You mean, it's all to do with racing? You've got to win? It's that important to win?'

Chas lowered his voice. 'It's not just important, it's essential,' he said. 'Win the Admiral's Cup, show well at Calvi and the Sydney–Hobart, and you sell sails all round the world . . . Every sort of racing sail. Right down to surf-boards.'

Wyatt nodded. 'But you're doing all right, aren't you?'

'Sure we are, because we keep up with the times, keep ahead of them even.' Chas's grin came back. 'We're the flavour of the month right now, got as many customers as we can handle.'

Wyatt left the window. He walked back along the edge of the lightwood floor. The big question was coming up now. And he tried to make it sound casual. 'So who are these customers of yours? I mean, the Admiral's Cup customers? . . . Or is it a well-kept secret?'

'No secret. The order book's there.' Chas pointed.

'Where?'

But suddenly Wyatt saw the answer. Because the huge sail was finished now, a river of shiny colour, just like the one he'd seen this morning. As he watched, four out of the five loft-men hauled the crackling plastic away, leaving just its triangular shape marked out on the floor. While the fifth man bent to the corner of this triangle, and wrote down the customer's name.

And there were other names, Wyatt saw, a great many of them in the maze of triangles on the floor. And a few minutes later, when Chas went out to take a phone-call, Wyatt noted them down.

He got to the library just before it closed. He took the back-numbers of the yachting magazines out again, and turned to the reports of Calvi Week. In particular the list of entrants.

This he put against the other list he had, of Skyline customers.

Which gave him just three names.

The first was a Swiss team-member, Helmut Prinzheim.

The second was a gentleman from Malaysia, called Kalicheean.

And the third was an Englishman, one of the trialists for the as yet unchosen British team. Michael Pedlar.

11

Days passed as Wyatt haunted the Solent in Jackman's cruiser, motoring and drifting in the sunlight. Days became a binocular view of the water where sails slatted across like screens on a distant theatre stage. More and more sails as the Solent gradually filled with yachts from around the world. And centre of stage, in the spotlight, were the three men he was after.

Or rather two.

Because Pedlar, the Englishman, was away on business in Canada. He was returning in time for the final British trials at the weekend. This Wyatt learned when he called at the Skyline loft again. Because a woman was there, a dark fine-looking woman of about thirty-five. Greek or Italian, Wyatt thought she was, although she wore English clothes.

It seemed she was Pedlar's wife. It seemed she knew Monroe well because she talked to him quietly, sitting on the corner of his desk. She was reading through a checklist of sails her husband had sent her. And the names – Number 1 lightweight drifter, and Dacron main – she pronounced charmingly, as if they weren't sails to her but trailing plants. Greek, Wyatt reckoned she was, Greek rather than Italian.

Then, when she'd finished the list of sails, she talked about her husband's arrival. He was due back on Friday evening, she said. He was going to drop his cases out at the farmhouse and then come straight on to the loft, she said. Which meant she was going to miss him because she would be over on the island, opening up the house in Cowes.

So Pedlar wasn't going to appear in Wyatt's binoculars until Friday. But the other two were, and he saw them often. Firstly Prinzheim the Swiss.

He was a tall man, nearer sixty than fifty, but with a wiry strength. At sea he kept his pale arms and legs covered. In fact he kept most of himself covered. He wore a wide floppy sailing hat, sunglasses with a trick plastic shield that came over his nose, and white anti-burn salve smeared on his lips. You could say he looked Swiss.

He sailed Swiss too, in straight lines he'd drawn on the water. There were no sudden swoops, no gambles. With his crew it was practice, practice over and over again. Beating up to a mark then setting a spinnaker, or coming in downwind and gybing. Everything done cleanly and with care. And fast.

Wyatt watched him afloat and ashore. On the Tuesday evening, for example, he saw him take his crew out to dinner in a smart Kombi bus. They went to the Bugle at Hamble, where they'd reserved a table. The crew all wore tee shirts with the yacht's name, *Tamburlaine*, across their chests. Their dark suntanned faces all had white triangles in their centre from the trick nose-shields they wore. They ate the food Prinzheim ordered, they drank the wine he ordered. And they drank when he drank.

All in all, Wyatt didn't think Prinzheim was his man.

And then, after dinner, he was sure. In the Bugle bar he talked to one of the crew, a quiet lad from Thun. And, leading up to it carefully, Wyatt asked about a certain Friday way back during Calvi Week, a day he personally was going to remember for the rest of his life. Because if anything was sure about it, it was that the horror – the killing of those three men on the anchor chain – had come somewhere between six and seven in the evening . . . But, as the Swiss boy told him now, Prinzheim's yacht had still been racing at that time. The fleet had run out of wind, *nicht wahr?* The boat hadn't finished until after eleven at night.

Which caused Wyatt to make other enquiries about that race. And after a while he learned that the Malaysian yachtsman, Kalicheean, had retired early and motored back to port around three. While the Englishman, Pedlar, had read the freak winds correctly, had come in among the leaders at four-thirty. Both, it seemed, were possibles.

Kalicheean now filled Wyatt's binoculars. And by that, he meant filled them. Wearing tent-like trousers and shirt, the man sat like some inflated frog in the stern of his yacht. Sat in perfect stillness, doing nothing . . . While all was chaos around him.

The trouble was that it was a big yacht, with a big crew. As far as Wyatt could tell there were Malays and Brits on board. And they didn't get on. There were shouts of anger, winch-handles waved in the air, men running in all directions at once. And from the crewman at the wheel a sawing-motion, a lack of any fineness of touch.

You could say Kalicheean's yacht beat a crude path over the Solent. In light airs it hung bedraggled, in anything like a breeze it swung from near-gybe to near-collision. It was completely outclassed by the company it kept. And, surrounded by slim blade-like hulls, it was a mess. There were the great gaudy dragons painted along its sides, in reds and golds and purples. There was the constant re-setting of sails and the constant tangle of ropes over the side. In fact the only part of it that was simple and of a piece was its owner, sitting there in spotless white, looking for the most part straight ahead.

Though there were times when he looked astern. Because Kalicheean didn't just have a yacht, he had a convoy. In his wake followed the largest Italian motor-cruiser Wyatt had ever seen. And aboard it were six of the best-looking girls he'd ever seen. Malay they were, and like porcelain. Their smiles moulded and dipped and glazed.

On the Wednesday evening, a sunset of pure gold, Wyatt came across Kalicheean's yacht sailing out past West Lepe. And for once it was sailing well, canted over to the land-breeze and bubbling through the water. While behind it came the Italian cruiser, keeping station. Wyatt turned in towards it, surprised to see none of the girls on deck looking at the fine sunset. Then he saw they were all in the saloon, smiling on, as they watched *Coronation Street* on TV.

Around the marinas and pubs Wyatt asked a great many questions about Kalicheean. The answer he heard most often was the single word you'd expect – inscrutable. Though there were other words you'd maybe expect too. That Kalicheean had made his pile out of girls and blue movies. That he'd made it out of gun-running. The only thing everyone agreed on was that a pile the man certainly had.

On the Thursday afternoon Wyatt turned up at Skyline for the boat-ride to test the new sail. And Chas had been as good as his word. He'd found a Moody 29, the same little sloop that Jimmy sailed down in Cannes. Wyatt felt pleasure at its familiar lines as he helmed the boat down-river to the Solent. Then Chas went below and brought up the cruising 'chute' in its bag. He set it without a pole, and it floated out in luminous panels of red and blue. It was a beautiful sail, idiot-proof, just as he'd said . . . And an hour later Wyatt had agreed to spend three hundred quid of Jackman's money.

Then, running back towards Berthon buoy in a south-west breeze, a familiar caravan loomed up behind them – Kalicheean's yacht, with the cruiser following astern.

Wyatt turned, watching the Admiral's Cupper as it came up fast, overhauling them. 'I've heard a lot of stories about that guy,' he said. 'None of them true, I don't suppose.'

'Don't suppose they are,' Chas said unhelpfully.

'Oh, come off it.' Wyatt turned back to him. 'You must know

about the man, he's a Skyline customer . . . Or are all your files confidential?'

Chas hesitated. 'They're meant to be,' he said.

'So does Kalicheean run girls, like they say he does?' Wyatt grinned.

'No, he doesn't need that kind of money,' Chas said. 'All right, if you have to know, the man's real name is Datuk Khaled Cheeanath. He owns huge rubber plantations in Malaysia. He also owns a very smart rubber-moulding process. And he makes about a quarter of the golf-grips in the world . . . Just think about it.'

Wyatt did, as the yacht surged past them, crowding on sail. Then the cruiser, catching them with its wake.

'Anyway, you're wrong,' Chas said a moment later. 'Kalicheean's not a Skyline customer. Not any more.'

'Not?' And for the first time Wyatt realised that the spinnaker the yacht was flying had no double-star design.

'He came to us and then he went,' Chas said. 'He bought a set of sails and only used them a couple of times.'

Wyatt stared at him. 'Why?' he asked.

'We couldn't make his boat go faster,' Chas said. 'Nothing wrong with the boat, it's brand new. Nothing wrong with our sails either. It's just his crew . . . I mean, we could've put a loft-man on board but it wouldn't've done any good. What he needs to do is get rid of half that shower and start again.'

'Yes,' Wyatt said, 'I've seen them at work.'

Chas sat watching as yacht and cruiser went away into the haze. 'I told you it was a serious sport, didn't I?' he said. 'But that man's the joker in the pack. I don't know why he goes ocean-racing. I really don't.'

'What d'you mean?'

'Well, there are always going to be one or two big-spenders, aren't there?' Chas said. 'One or two who buy sails they don't use. . . . Throwaway sailors we call them . . . But as for him, he should have an L-plate round his neck. He came to us far too late in the season to do him any good. And then suddenly we heard he'd moved on to one of the big lofts, Bantings, I think it was.'

Wyatt nodded. And then, suddenly, 'You said he came to you late. How late was that?'

'I don't know. Maybe three weeks ago now.'

'So it was only three weeks ago,' Wyatt asked, 'that he got one of those famous silver lighters of yours to light his fags with?'

'Yes.' Chas frowned. 'If you want to put it that way.'

Wyatt did. And the more he thought about it, the more he realised that Kalicheean was ruled out.

But there was somebody else who wasn't ruled out. Somebody who came very heavily into the betting. And this Wyatt learned about when the boat-ride was coming to its end.

They were returning up the Lymington river in the evening light, passing the yacht club, which was between them and the sun. And suddenly in the shadows Wyatt saw an Admiral's Cupper edging its way back into a berth. It was blue, with a low brute force to it, from the stub-angled bow to the sharp cut-off of the raked stern.

'That's Michael Pedlar's boat,' Chas told him.

'Pedlar's?' Wyatt frowned. 'D'you know, I don't reckon I've seen it around before.'

'No, it's been up at the yard. They've been doing things to the keel, as I hear it. Last minute gambles, before the final British team trials this weekend.'

'Is that right?' Wyatt said idly. Then he looked again. 'Wait a minute, isn't that your bossman Monroe? There? Standing on deck?'

'Yes, that's him.'

'But why should he be on board? I mean, if it's a question of work on the keel? Surely he's a sail-designer?'

'But he crews for Pedlar, races with him as tactician,' Chas said. 'And he looks after the boat while Pedlar's away.'

'Your bossman? Looks after somebody's boat?'

'Why not?' Chas asked. 'I told you all of us sailed . . . Anyway Monroe's an old friend of Pedlar's, he's crewed with him for years. And this year, you might say, he's got an extra incentive to stay on the boat.'

'What's that?'

'Didn't you know?' Chas was surprised. 'Pedlar's the business brain who got Skyline Sails up into the bigtime. He put money into the company just when we needed it. He hustled the new Skimbar fabric out of the factory well ahead of schedule . . . And he was the one who thought up the promotion deal with the lighters too. They had to be silver, he said, not steel. Expensive, and yet he was flashing them around during Calvi Week. Gave two or three of them away.'

12

That evening when the shadows were lengthening around the marina, Jackman came back on board the cruiser. He poured himself a drink and sat with Wyatt on the afterdeck.

'So you reckon you got it down to just the one guy, do you, Ace? Michael Pedlar?'

'I think so,' Wyatt said.

'And now what? I mean, Pedlar arrives here tomorrow night, and you're goin' to keep tabs on him, are you? Like, watch him all the time with binoculars?'

'Why not?' Wyatt said. 'I'm Jack Douglas, aren't I? Over here from Switzerland to follow the Admiral's Cup?'

'Oh, clever, very clever. I like that,' Jackman said. 'Particularly if he *is* the guy you're after, and he sees those binoculars of yours.'

'Have you got a better way?' Wyatt asked.

Jackman nodded. He took a quick look away down the deck, then lowered his voice. 'That Yacht List telex,' he said. 'The one that got you flyin' to Corsica in the first place? . . . Crack that and you crack the man.'

'How?' Wyatt asked. 'It's in code, remember.'

'Yeh, but even codes leave traces, don't they? I mean, that telex was docketed somewhere, a bill made out against a name.'

'No,' Wyatt said. 'There was no bill. I never made the pickup, did I? Never got as far as meeting the client.'

'The job's still docketed, on file,' Jackman said. 'And you want to know where? Yacht List Services down in Cannes, is where. And at Head Office, which happens to be in London, in the City.'

Wyatt looked at him. 'You've been doing your homework, haven't you?''

'No, not me,' Jackman said, 'but a good friend . . . Carver, the guy you were with the other day . . . City man, remember?'

'And he's found out things?'

'He's lunched a couple of people. Chums he calls them.'

'But,' Wyatt asked, 'd'you think Carver'll play when it comes to finding out a definite piece of information? Like that telex?'

'Reckon so. Couple of gins with a chum, int it? And then pickin' up a piece of paper by return . . . Happens all the time.'

'But will he play for *you?*' Wyatt insisted.

'I'll tell him some tale,' Jackman said. 'The sort he'd like to hear . . . Like there's this county surveyor I give the bung to, and who claims he never had nothin' off of me. And yet I hear the guy was down on this yacht in Corsica between certain dates.' Jackman grinned. 'Our friend Carver'll go for that. What's it he calls me, refreshin'? . . . *Refreshin'*, int that right?'

Evening became night. A long strip of yellow crossed the deck from the open companion door. A second light shone down on the cruiser's stern-ladder. And away through the darkness were the bright windows of the yacht club bar.

Carver arrived, a tall correct figure. He greeted Wyatt warmly, smoothing back his wavy grey hair, and then went down to the saloon with Jackman. The companion door closed. The strip of yellow went.

Wyatt sat there, listening to the voices from below. But then there was another voice, a young man's voice from the marina pontoon. 'Jacko?' it called out. 'Jacko?'

Wyatt went to the light at the stern. But it was a girl, a dark-haired girl, who was hauling herself up on deck. She wore a man's shirt and jeans. They were shabby, Wyatt saw, and the hands that gripped the chrome ladder were stained by cigarettes. Her face looked up at him, long and pale without make-up. She could have been eighteen or she could have been thirty, he thought, and she didn't care which.

Reaching the top of the ladder, she frowned. 'Oh, you're not Jacko,' she said. 'You're somebody else.'

It was a low voice, and careless. In the way the aristocracy were careless, Wyatt thought. Words came from her quickly, through teeth that were slightly crooked. And there was a hunger, almost an ugliness about her when she spoke, as if she were taking bites out of the air.

'Jacko, is he aboard?' she asked.

'Yes, but he's talking to someone.'

'He's got a woman,' she said.

'No, it's business.'

'He's got a woman.' She went past him, making for the companion door.

Wyatt went after her. 'Not right now,' he said.

She walked on. He reached out for her shoulder. She was surprisingly light to his touch, almost unsteady.

She turned then. 'I see,' she said. 'You're his lap-dog.'

'No, just a friend.'

'Oh.' She smiled very briefly, to show him it was false. Then she hitched herself against the side-rail, crossing one leg over the other. 'Who are you?' she asked.

'Douglas. Jack Douglas,' Wyatt said.

'And where d'you come from?'

'Switzerland?'

'Where?'

'Place near Luzern. It's called Horw. It's by the lake.'

'Oh.'

'Why?' Wyatt asked. 'D'you know it?'

'No.' She flashed the false smile again. And then, suddenly, 'Where d'you do your shopping?'

'What?'

'Where d'you shop? When you're at home?'

'I don't know. Different places . . . The Miniprix maybe.'

She looked at him, still hitched awkwardly against the rail. 'Very steep in Switzerland,' she said. 'My uncle, he had to build a cable-car just to get his morning papers. And before that they used to yodel the news up to him.'

'Is that right?' Wyatt asked.

'Yes . . . Though sometimes he made my aunt toboggan down the mountain on a chocolate bar.'

She started slipping down the ship's rail. And Wyatt understood. She was drunk.

'For your information,' she said then, 'there is no Miniprix in the German part of Switzerland. I don't think you live in Luzern at all. And I don't think your name is Douglas.'

Drunk, but sharp. Very sharp.

'And what's more,' she tensed herself, 'I think Jacko's got a bloody *woman* in there.'

She swerved past him and reached the companion door. She got it open. Wyatt tried to argue with her. But then Jackman was there too, helping him. And angry.

'Get her out of here,' he said.

'Out?' the girl's voice rose. '*Out?* Jacko, all I want is a couple of brandies. And lies. Tell me lies.'

'Alex,' Jackman faced her, 'listen, I'm busy. I got a meetin' on. It's man-talk.'

She tried to lean past him, to see who was in the saloon. Then she changed tack. 'Twenty minutes,' she said. 'I'll give you twenty minutes. After that you come and find me.' She pointed. 'I'm out in the bloody darkness there, on some boring yacht.'

Jackman sighed. 'Twenty minutes? Jesus, what's the time now?'

She unbuttoned her shirt, got out her left breast, looked at it. 'Ten past nine,' she said.

Jackman hissed his anger and got her shirt buttoned up again. 'Alex, do me a favour, will you? Just piss off.'

She looked at him. 'Piss off? You don't say that to a member of the aristocracy. You say, piss *orf.*'

She turned and walked away over the deck. And, carefully feeling her way down the stern-ladder, disappeared.

'Who the hell's that?' Wyatt asked.

'Alex,' Jackman said. Then he glanced behind him to the saloon. 'Let's hope she hasn't sodded the whole thing up.'

But she hadn't. Because half an hour later Jackman came back on deck, talking easily to Carver. He waved a hand as the man went away round the marina. Then he came back to where Wyatt stood.

'Fixed,' he said. 'He's goin' up the Smoke for us tomorrow. And we're goin' over to his place to get the answer Sunday evenin'. He's invitin' us to dinner . . . And *that's* when we should start nailin' your man Michael Pedlar.'

13

By six o'clock on the Sunday evening the final stage of the British Admiral's Cup team trials was over. And at half-past seven one of the competing yachts, a blue ocean-racer with a short stub-bow, returned under power to the Lymington marina. The man at the wheel reversed the yacht back into its berth. He did it expertly and fast, just as he did everything expertly and fast. There was a suddenness to Michael Pedlar that wasn't anger but enthusiasm. A hardness of eye that wasn't intolerance of slower people, rather that he surrounded himself with the quick. He was forty-seven years old, stocky, with the threatening belly and forward hanging head of the Anglo-Saxon. And he had the sleek sealskin hair of the public school man. Though the modern public school man – claret and shirtsleeves were more his line than winged collars or white ties.

The yacht docked. Two of the crew jumped ashore with lines, returned, and the white deck was marked by land. More crewmen came up from below. They were wet and chilled. The blue oilskin dungarees they wore were dulled by sea water. And their faces were dulled too – by disappointment.

They gathered round Pedlar, powerful men, nearer the age of thirty than twenty, and with the weight and muscle necessary for the job . . . Hal the bowman, Abe the coffee grinder man, Stan and Charlie foredeck gorillas, Greg the boat-bum . . . Eleven of them, including winch-tailers, navigator, and the tall thin-faced figure of Monroe.

Pedlar thanked them, and they answered with the flat voices of fatigue. Then they trooped ashore with sailbags over their shoulders. The marina-pontoons slapped underfoot as they walked, while at the rear of the procession Pedlar lengthened his stride to catch up with Monroe.

'No need to waste a night's sleep over the committee's decision,' he said.

'No,' Monroe said. 'We didn't make it.'

'Bloody shame.'

'It's that. Yes.'

They reached a Volvo estate parked on the hard. Both men were cold and they didn't linger with goodbyes. Pedlar got into the car, started the engine, and turned the heater up to full. By the time he'd reached the pink and white houses of Lymington, steam was rising from his body. And by the time he'd come to a drive-entrance some distance from the town, he was warm.

He drove between two lines of silky-muscled beech trees. At their end was a massive stone farmhouse that had once been a monastery. He parked and got out. The farm was on high well-drained land, and a breeze was lifting a skein of rooks from the beeches. Pedlar listened to their racket. He listened to the baying that came from the stables, the foxhounds there that he was kennelling for the local Hunt. And he listened to the creak of barley. It was all round the house, ready to turn now, green losing its edge and sweating like a horse's coat.

For perhaps a minute he listened. They were sounds that were important to him. Just as it was important to separate them, know them, and stand in their centre. As a boy he'd watched his father listening on this same spot. And the man had told him it brought the only real calm there was.

It had been true for his father, and perhaps it would have been true for Pedlar too. But during the past few years he'd spent too little time here, far too little. He frowned, trying to find his way back to the old calm of the house, needing it. Because today, out in the Solent, there'd been big disappointments . . . Big.

He picked up his sailing-bag and went in through the stone porch. The glass door beyond flared the evening back at him. Then there were the deep plum-coloured walls his wife had chosen for the hall, and his two children appearing suddenly at the far end. Sammy and Daisy, eight and six years old, were like small ghosts in the twilight. He was late, they had waited a long time, and their faces were pinched and white with fatigue. He went to them, bent down and hugged them, and felt the give of their tiny birdlike bodies.

'You taste of salt,' Sammy said.

'Yes,' he said.

Beside them were the presents he'd brought for them last week from Canada, the tooled Western-style saddle and the three-foot-high Snoopy. There was no need to ask if they were a success because the children were silent, treasure in their hands and in their eyes. For a while he crouched down and played, adjusting the stirrups to fit Sammy's legs, and making the Snoopy dance. It went on until Daisy yawned, suddenly and hugely. And under Pedlar's hands the Snoopy slid over and began to snore.

'Time for bed, is it?' he asked gently. 'Time to pull the Get Rid Of People lever?'

Daisy didn't answer. Then she remembered. She raised her white dress and showed the incongruity of brown school knickers underneath. 'My knickers are Aged Seven Years,' she said, 'and they fell down in prayers.'

Pedlar smiled and kissed her again. Kissed them both. Before Nanny appeared and took the trundling, backward-looking party upstairs. Then he stood up and turned to the other person who'd been there all the time. Katerina, with that dark Greek glow of hers in the English twilight, the pale lipstick she wore, and the eyes with the whirring of wings in them, pulling him close.

'You do taste of salt,' she said.

They walked, hand linked fiercely in hand, through to the drawing-room. This was the one room Katerina hadn't redecorated. Or perhaps he hadn't allowed her to. A long-case clock stood by one wall. In centuries past it had been the house's one correct timepiece, and a dozen different wallpapers had been carefully cut round it. Running the length of another wall was a dark oak mantel, where a row of brass roasting-jacks hung. The last of the red sunlight caught them as Pedlar crossed to the sideboard. He opened it, poured sherry, and took a glass back to Katerina.

She raised it and drank. Then she talked, but not of today's Admiral's Cup trials, warned off by his face.

'How was Canada last week?' she asked instead. 'You never really said.'

'Canada was fine.'

'You seem to have been going over there a lot recently,' she said. 'Not trouble, I hope.'

'No, not trouble. Bit of a kerfuffle, that's all. Kind of thing that crops up every now and then. We're almost over it now.'

'That's good.' She sipped slowly. 'And how was the flight back?'

'Not bad. Got to Heathrow too damn early on Friday morning, that was the trouble . . . But d'you know? Lyness was there to meet me. He got up at 4 am. That's a good friend.'

'He's a nice man, Martin Lyness,' she said. Then she leaned closer. 'But as it happens I tried to reach you last Wednesday evening. Tried to tell you the things a wife needs to tell her husband.'

'And I wasn't there.' Pedlar nodded. 'Wednesday. Let's see, Wednesday was when I managed to get a ticket to the opera.'

'Oh? What did you see?'

'*Rosenkavalier.*'

'Any good?'

'Fair,' he said. 'And *Rosenkavalier* has to be very good, doesn't it?'

'Yes, it does.'

He pulled her to him suddenly, caught the cool well of her scent, the softness of her hair. 'You've been very thoughtful,' he said, 'and you haven't asked me about the sailing today.'

'That's right.' She nodded. 'So how did it go?'

'We made a pig's ear of it,' he said quietly. 'A bloody pig's ear.

Came in eighth.'
'So you don't think . . . ?'
'No,' Pedlar told her, 'we haven't made the team. I know we haven't.'
'*Krima*,' she said in Greek. 'And it means a lot to you, doesn't it? You've been trying for, what, six years now?'
'Just happens that this is a very competitive year,' Pedlar said. 'Fifteen yachts trying for three places. Somebody has to lose.'
'Yes,' she said.
He put his glass down. 'I'll have a quick shower,' he said. 'I got cold out there, bloody cold . . . Be down when?'
'Dinner's at a quarter past eight,' she said. 'I asked for it early.'
'Okay.'
He stood in the shower, letting the warmth of it reach his bones, getting the chill out of them, the hours and hours of concentration at the wheel that the day had been.
A pig's ear was right. There'd been the chute they'd gone trawling with around Berthon, practically wrapped the damn sail round the keel. And then, taking a gamble at Hamstead, they'd grounded, hit bottom.
Somebody had to lose.
He closed his eyes. Then, faintly through the sound of the shower, heard the phone.
He turned the water off, put his feet into slippers, his arms into a robe. Then he padded across the landing, and through the curve of the banisters saw Katerina holding out the phone below.
'It's Hugh,' she said. 'The committee.'
For some reason he took the call downstairs with her.
'Michael?' Hugh's voice came through the phone. 'Just to let you know we were *almost* unanimous . . . You're in.'
'In?'
'Congratulations.'
'*In?*'
'Michael, we know you made a nonsense of it today. Can't think why your bloody lads weren't in the water, and your mast over the side. But, in a straight fight between your boat and Jeffrey's, you've been showing well. You're the kind of middle-rated yacht we want in the team. And we know you'll work those lads of yours arse-ragged.'
'Yes,' Pedlar said. 'Yes, I will.'
The phone was back on its hook. Katerina's arms were around

him. And her scent was there again. 'It's good, *good*,' she kept repeating.

But finally he drew away. 'It's only a game,' he said. 'It's only sailing a yacht round a few coloured buoys in the water.' And, kissing her fingers, he started back upstairs.

He passed the Morlands on the landing wall. He passed the tall vase of lupins standing on the monk's chest. Rust-coloured carpet gave way to the green carpet of the bathroom, and he was about to return to the shower when he swung round. He got the lavatory door open and reached the pedestal just in time to jack-knife over it, shoulders heaving.

14

A few minutes later a party of three people arrived for dinner at a house not far away. The Rolls Royce they came in crunched to a halt on the gravel, and Jackman got out from behind the wheel. His wife got out on her side, trailing a long glowing dress of pale blue. Wyatt helped her clear the skirt from the car door before he closed it. Then he followed her over the drive to where Jackman was ringing the bell.

The screaming started in the hall. It came from both women at once, Jackman's wife just inside the front door, and Carver's wife standing by the stairs, next to her husband.

Carver's wavy film-star hair had gone. There were cuts on the bald dome of his head. It had been completely shaved.

15

At half-past nine on the same evening a Volvo estate drew up behind the Lymington marina and parked. Pedlar got out. After a light supper he was feeling a great deal better. He walked round the Yacht Club and down the ramp to the pontoons. Then he stopped, looking at his Admiral's Cup team boat.

In the light from the yacht club bar the white deck seemed small, ridiculously small after the weekend's racing. It was difficult to believe now that twelve men had crouched there, had sat out to windward, moved in sudden bursts of frenzy, and sometimes moved as one.

Difficult to believe too that it had all gone on since last September. The finalising of the design, the building, the launch, the trials. The cold winter-sailing, and the winter-training too, hours of jogging on ice-covered roads.

Then the campaign for the Florida SORC Races in February. The campaign for Calvi Week at the beginning of June. And finally the campaign here, the big one, the one every other damn thing had been aiming towards . . .

Putting a Union Jack on the front of a shirt.

Well, he'd done it, he'd got there. Pedlar took a last look now at the white deck, the fat black winches and the huge steel wheel he'd gripped in his hands for so long.

Then at the name on the stern, painted in red on the blue hull.

Cry Havoc.

16

On the weekend before the Admiral's Cup began, the yachts came together. Slowly, like swans crossing a misty lake, they slid in from the rivers of the Solent . . . F 8304. I 482, KB 138 . . . French, Italian, and Bermudan.

They passed the iron piles off Sowley. They passed Black Jack, Spanker, and Prince Consort. Waters where for weeks they'd been darting back and forwards, learning the tides, cutting and re-cutting the sails, tuning rigging and masts.

Now they came in past the Squadron and moved up-river to Cowes. The rule book required them to be berthed there from the Sunday before the first race, and to stay there throughout the Series. Just as it required them to show racing numbers on their sails and on white canvas squares at their sterns . . . H 97, IR 783, KA 4190 . . . Dutch, Irish, and Australian . . .

And on that same Sunday afternoon somebody else crossed the Solent to Cowes . . . Wyatt, sitting on the deck of a Red Funnel steamer, his legs out, his eyes closed, warmed by the sun.

And he needed the sun. The past week at Jackman's house had been bad. The windows locked, the curtains drawn, bad. There'd been the sound of Jackman's wife slamming doors as she'd gone from room to room with her Siamese cats. Then her silences as she'd listened, afraid of every movement out on the gravel drive. In the end it had been a relief when she'd suddenly come at Wyatt and screamed at him to get out.

Jackman had put his case in the boot of the Rolls. He'd driven him to the Red Funnel terminal in Southampton. And they'd sat there for a while, looking out at the Royal Pier.

'You can see how it is, Ace, can't you?' Jackman said. 'It's just like the old days have come back to her, right past her french windows and her bleedin' flower-arrangin' classes . . . I mean, when she saw Carver like that. *Carver*.'

Wyatt nodded, remembering the man's strange white head and the razor cuts. 'Poor sod,' he said. 'How is he?'

'How *is* he? How would you be if you was some nice cuddly company director one minute, doin' a favour for a friend? And the next you had that done to you? I mean, Christ.'

'Yes,' Wyatt said.

'I tried to see him since,' Jackman went on. 'I tried maybe half a dozen times. But he won't have nothin' to do with me. And who's to blame him?'

'Nobody,' Wyatt said. 'But what I don't understand is how they got to him, straight to him, just like that.'

'It int difficult to see,' Jackman told him. 'Not now, I mean. And, Jesus, I blame myself . . . See, I asked him to get a certain piece of information about them that was right on their doorstep. Corsica, remember? And a certain date and time? Far too close to bleedin' home, that was.'

'So they didn't get to him through me, or anything?' Wyatt asked. 'I mean, I wondered about that, since I've been making the rounds . . .'

'No, Ace. They int lookin' for you, that's for sure. I mean, why look? You're dead, int you, far as they're concerned? They saw to that. But . . .' And Jackman leaned close. '. . . Since we're talkin' about you bein' dead, maybe there's somethin' I should tell you.'

'What's that?'

'You're on your own now, Ace. I can't help you no more. And the reason's simple . . . My missus, you saw how she was. I had to sit down and promise her I wouldn't see you again . . . So, all I'm sayin' is, go careful, all right? Real careful.'

. . . Careful. The word had no meaning for Wyatt as he sat back on the deck of the ferry-boat. There was the warm sunlight. There were the voices of trippers all around him, and the clang of the ship's telegraph as it closed in on West Cowes. Wyatt tried to fight off the feeling of the hot Sunday afternoon, tried to tell himself that the last time he'd come here it had been with Carver. And that then, for God's sake, the poor guy had had hair on his head.

But now, as the steamer pulled in, and Wyatt joined the trippers by the rail, he saw that Cowes wasn't the grey dock with the sheds and cranes that he'd last seen with Carver.

It had all changed.

The marina was just upstream of the ferry-terminal. And there at its entrance was a large notice saying 'Reserved For Admiral's Cup Yachts'. They were all now gathered inside, the hulls with the forward-raked bows and sterns, hulls that seemed to be moving forward when they were still. They were directly under the sun, and there was the hard gleam of porcelain about them. On their decks was a litter of sailbags and coiled lines. And their rigging and masts, fifty-seven masts, formed a shifting mass of gold wire against the sky.

Beyond were the sheds that Wyatt had seen before, sheds with the name of the marina, Groves & Guttridge, written across them. They surrounded a wide area of concrete hard and threw out a sound that at first Wyatt took to be the sound of the sea. Until he realised it was voices. Until, shielding his eyes, he saw the thick crowds where the village of trade-caravans had been set up. LEWMAR, BARON, INTERNATIONAL, EPIGLASS, he made out the signs. And then the signs of the two big mobile bars, 555 and CHAMPAGNE MUMM. They faced each other, and in the shadows between them two tides of drinkers met.

Then, away to the right and high up on a shed-wall, he saw the Admiral's Cup scoreboard. It was big, maybe twenty feet by twenty, newly-painted and shining in the sun. And on it were the fifty-seven yachts' names, grouped in threes by their countries' flags.

The circus had come to town.

Wyatt lifted his suitcase and followed the day-trippers ashore along a covered way. He found the Cross Keys, the pub just off the High Street, where Jackman had found him a room. It was open, all pubs were open, he found, from ten in the morning till midnight. He pushed his way through the bar and was shown up to a small chip-smelling bedroom. He didn't unpack. He listened to the current of voices moving down the High Street. Spanish he heard, and then German, Japanese, West Coast and Strine. After a while he went out to join them. He had a hunch they'd map out this town for him, even a hunch they'd lead him towards the man he was after.

The High Street, he found, was narrow and shadowy in the early evening. It ran parallel to the water but was hidden from it by shop windows and the shouting doorways of pubs. At one end were the gates of the Groves & Guttridge marina he'd seen from the ferry. Here the smell of fry came from a parked double-decker called the Burger Bus. And here too were men with tired faces and black hands, rigger and yard men, maybe, mechanics of those sleek yachts out in the sunlight.

Further along the High Street was style and the dim-lit windows of restaurants. And style too in the men walking the street. Crewmen they were, and by now Wyatt was getting used to their size and their fitness. On their tee shirts were yacht-names, *Estrelita*, *Cormorant*, *Ebo* and *Gertcha*, and they all seemed to be making for the same place, the bar of the Three Crowns. Beyond, men in dark blazers were going into the office of the Royal Ocean Racing Club. And from the narrow water-alleys between them came the smell of the harbour.

Then Wyatt stopped, frowning. It wasn't just a harbour-smell, he realised. There was more to it than that . . . Cowes, he realised, was different from Lymington, different from the Hamble or any other marina he'd seen. This was no modern parking-lot for boats, a square of wooden pontoons tied to a river-bank. Cowes was a yacht-town, and it was Carver who'd told him that. Carver who'd told him of the big yachts of times past, of the bosuns landing in these water-alleys here and dragging their crews out of the Three Crowns . . . That was what he could smell.

He walked on. The High Street crooked left then right, and rose to a crest. There was the striped marquee of the Mumm's Press Centre, the striped awning of Juliana's Disco. Both were silent. And beyond, downhill again, was the wideness of the Parade. Children were down there, holding Admiral's Cup balloons that gleamed silver in the evening. Past them the water gleamed too, a soft pink. And there was movement on it, the burble of powerboats, the slip of yachts.

Wyatt turned inland then, because an English crew came past him with Union Jacks on their shirts. They led him up a steep hill with town gardens on either side, and trees leaning over white walls. Wyatt followed and came to houses that had clothing hung up in the windows to dry. Crew houses. One of them full of shouting voices, and with a tall sail hanging down from attic to ground floor, showing where the party was.

And then the other kind of party. A quiet street with a row of calm Georgian houses, white-fronted in the twilight. There was the smell of cool courtyards about them, the smell of honeysuckle and the sound of champagne corks being eased out gently as they should be . . . And suddenly through the window of a tall Georgian room, a brass curtain-rail flashing as a door opened, and a woman coming in who was known to Wyatt, dark, fine-looking and Greek. She had two small girls with her. They crossed to a table where there were charts spread out. And by them a claret bottle with two glasses. The first man at the table – Monroe – Wyatt recognised. And the other, burly and burned, with dark sleek hair, he suddenly knew too.

Wyatt turned and walked away.

What he couldn't understand was why he felt no hate for the man, why he felt no hate for anything in this town. Perhaps it was because there was perfection here. Or because in other circumstances he might have been flying here on a Yacht List job. Dropping off a sailing-man maybe, or picking another up. Maybe even the man he'd just seen.

He came to the end of the street. He was high up. There was a golden haze out over the water, and it was as if he could see from one edge of a world to the other – Pedlar's world – from the man's house back down the street to that big farmhouse of his on the far Lymington shore. A world all on its own, just like the Mediterranean where Wyatt himself had sailed. Where the next harbour was just around the point, where there was always a next harbour in the haze.

Perfection.

Again he stopped. There was a steep road to his right, swinging sharply away downhill. Almost directly below him was the Squadron on its rocky point, its brass cannons ranged out at the water. And on the water a lone Cupper, practising late.

And then Wyatt saw what it was he hated, the one flaw there was here. It was the man at the wheel, that stillness he had, watching the sails, watching the water for any slight flurry of wind. That endless concentration.

He found he was rubbing the white scar on his hand where his thumb had been. He found himself remembering something that Chas, the young man from the sail-loft, had said. 'It's a power-thing,' he'd said. 'There's no accident that boardroom kings excel at this game. The men who can bend other men, bend the rule-book, bend nature.'

'Bend nature?' Wyatt had asked.

'Sometimes it gets bad out there. Sometimes it's no place for any except the best boat to be,' Chas had said. 'When those kind of seas rise up above you there's a certain green to them. And down where you are a darker colour, this dark black in the water around the rudder . . . And the guy at the wheel, he's making that black colour, without him it wouldn't be there. He's bending nature, making that money-man path through the water.'

Wyatt stood thinking a moment. And then he realised there was a wetness, a stickiness between his fingers. He looked down and saw he'd opened up a corner of the white scar, drawn blood. And hate returned to him, a cold unreasoning hate for the man who played the power-game too hard . . . for reasons Wyatt didn't yet understand.

But he would understand. There would be cracks in this world, this perfect world of Pedlar's. That much he knew.

17

The next morning bright colour took over from the greyness of the Groves & Guttridge yard. Eight of the Admiral's Cuppers had been lifted from the water and secured on timbers and chocks. Huge they were on the concrete hard, their mast-heads taller than the sheds around. And among them was the dark blue shape of *Cry Havoc*.

Pedlar stood beneath the hull, rubbing it down with wet and dry. To his right young Chas was playing a hose up towards the rudder skeg. Which made a thin stream of water course down Pedlar's arm and between his shoulder-blades, cooling him as he worked.

Then he heard a shout from behind him. He turned. A girl was standing there. She had fair hair and a lot of bright lipstick in the way girls had nowadays. And she wore a light denim suit that had a Press card pinned to its front pocket.

'Mr Pedlar, can you spare me a moment?' she asked.

'Glad to.' He went over.

She shook his wet hand. 'Jane Lambourne,' she said. 'You won't have heard of me. I'm not one of the regular yachting press.'

'But a great improvement,' Pedlar said.

'Thank you.' She smiled. It was a good smile, and she knew it. 'The thing is, I freelance, file a piece here, a piece there. And I wondered if I could ask you a few questions.'

'All right. Fire away.'

She got out a notebook. 'Well, let's ease our way into it, shall we? I mean, what are you doing right at the moment?'

'Dry-sailing the boat.'

'*Dry*-sailing?' She pointed to the hose Chas was holding.

'It means taking the boat out of the water before races,' Pedlar said, 'rubbing it down and slapping on a compound that makes it go faster. In this case we're using a graphite compound that reaches optimum effect in three days' time. Builds up a sort of slime.'

She didn't write anything in her notebook.

'Slime's not interesting?' Pedlar asked.

She smiled that good smile again. They both moved away as Chas worked the hose in their direction.

'What d'you think of *Havoc*?' Pedlar asked then.

'Not what I'd expected,' she said. 'Not what you'd call a beautiful shape, is she, out of the water like this?'

'No,' Pedlar said. 'In fact the best description I've heard of an Admiral's Cupper's hull is that it looks more like a jet fighter plane than a yacht.'

'Fighter plane?'

'All right, half a fighter plane,' he said. 'One that's been sliced lengthwise down the fuselage and then stood on its side . . . D'you see what I mean? Where the hull is there is the fuselage? The rudder is the tail-plane? And the keel is the wing?'

'Yes.' She nodded. 'Except that the wing, as you call it, looks a bit small in comparison to the rest.'

She wrote the word *missile* down on her pad.

And, judging by the way *Havoc* handled at times, Pedlar was inclined to agree with her.

'What are those lumps?' she asked then. 'Those bulges on the hull towards the stern? They seem to spoil the line.'

'"Ratings-bumps",' Pedlar told her.

'What-bumps?'

'"Ratings",' he said. 'Surely somebody's explained all that business to you?'

'They've tried,' she said.

'All right.' Pedlar sighed. 'How much d'you know?'

'Only that racing yachts come in different sizes, and they go at different speeds. Therefore a handicap system has to be worked out.'

'Fine,' Pedlar said. 'You're halfway there . . . What it's all about is that each yacht is handicapped according to its "rating". This simply means it's measured at certain points along its hull. And when these measurements are put together with certain other figures, the theoretical speed of the boat can be worked out.'

'Clear so far.'

'But then we reach the interesting bit,' Pedlar went on. 'By which I mean it's possible to trick the handicap rule, make it think the boat sails *slower* than it actually does.'

She looked at him. 'You mean,' she said, 'by cheating on these "ratings" measurements along the hull? By adding little bumps at the right places?'

Pedlar nodded. 'And by scooping the hull away in other places. Not to mention playing around with the sail-area, which all comes into it too.'

'Well,' she said, 'it seems quite simple the way you explain it.'

'But in practice very complicated,' Pedlar said. 'You have to remember that this year's rule-book has been updated by a computer to take care of last year's cheats. That this year's designers need another computer to take care of the new rules . . . And that yet another computer is needed to work out who actually won the damn races.'

'I see,' she said. 'All very butch.'

And it was Pedlar's turn to smile.

Later *Cry Havoc* was ready for the water. The big yellow yard crane that looked like a moon-walker came over. It slid its twin booms along the length of the deck. Thick webbing bands came down from them and were tightened round the hull. Then the yacht was carried bodily over to the narrow lifting-dock, where the crane ran its huge tyres out on either side of the water. *Havoc* was lowered, floated.

Pedlar, by now back on board, beckoned the girl to join him from the dock. She stayed by his side as he started the motor and steered out across the marina. The sun was high, there was a flat brightness to the water, and a bareness to the boat without sails. And, as the girl asked questions about what she could see around her, Pedlar was conscious of standing on a white moulded deck onto which were fitted pieces of stark black machinery.

'But are you sure you want to know about winches and things?' he asked. 'What about something gentler? The woman's angle?'

'*What* woman's angle?' She spread her hands. 'Look, it'd help if I knew the names of all the bits and pieces at any rate.'

'All right.'

He started with the cockpit. Not that it was a cockpit in the conventional sense, he said, not there to provide protection. It was more a shallow depression in the deck that allowed winches and lines to be handled at the right height. All races were won from the cockpit, he said.

In its centre was a large piece of machinery, a three-foot-high black column with what looked like a pair of bicycle pedals at the top. This was the coffee-grinder, the powerhouse of the boat, he said; it operated the winches through a system of linkages. And those things like bicycle pedals were not pushed round by foot but by hand. Four hands, two men facing each other over the machine. Hard work.

Next he showed her the winches themselves. There was a row of them on each side of the cockpit. Squat black milk-churns they looked like, the narrowing of their necks allowing for three turns of rope, winching in or giving slack. Further away on the deck were the sheet-tracks, which if you like, he said, gave various positions for controlling the sails. And nearer at hand, just in front of the wheel, was a black-mounted instrument panel. He pointed to its gauges in turn . . . Boatspeed, windspeed, direction of wind, angle of heel, depth-sounder . . . All self-explanatory, he said, though boatspeed was the most important. Boatspeed was what they were after, all the time.

Finally he came to the hydraulics system, with its levers and its four dials labelled After Runners, Back Stay, Baby Stay, and Vang . . . Without being too technical, he said, these were more or less concerned with bending the huge alloy mast into various profiles. And the effect of them was more or less the same – to keep the mainsail as flat as possible . . . Boatspeed, he said, came from a flat sail and an upright boat.

Havoc now reached an empty berth next to the British team yachts. Chas and another crewman made fast. Pedlar switched off the motor and suggested to the girl they look below. She went before him down the stainless steel ladder, and he watched her face as she looked round. There was always the surprise.

'You said racing yachts were like jet-fighters, didn't you?' she said as he joined her. 'But I didn't realise you meant inside as well.'

Because the interior of the hull was like a plane, a stripped-out plane. It was one long enclosed space down there, without partitions, and all the nuts and bolts were on show. There was the frame of shining metal, drilled out like an airframe, which Pedlar said absorbed the stresses. And beyond it the roughness of the hull, which he said was no more than a plastic skin to keep the water out.

The sparseness continued. Aft of where they stood were ten bare cots, canvas and tubular steel, hinged to lie flat against the hull sides. There was the navigation console with its hardware, its Sat-Nav system. Facing it was a small galley which was no more than icebox, sink, and stainless steel stove. And then – the one item Pedlar knew would surprise the girl most of all – the bare loo pedestal, with neither partition nor door.

'Primitive. Everybody says that,' he told her. 'But this is a racing machine. Everything's been stripped out to save weight.'

'Machine is right,' she said, looking around her. 'I'd hardly call this boat a "she".'

'No. Nobody does. And perhaps you'd realise why if you came out with us. In big weather there's a drumming and whining that sets up in the hull. It's brute strength, most of what you can see here.'

She took a step away across the floor – the floor which he told her was called the 'sole'. There were sailbags piled on it, and she sat down on them and started asking questions again.

'*Cry Havoc*'s a new boat, isn't it? I mean, brand-new?'

'That's right.'

'And would you say it was necessary to have a new boat? To do well in the Admiral's Cup?'

'You're going to have more chance, certainly,' he said. 'Seeing that technology's changing all the time.'

'So . . . Is it money that wins?'

'No,' he told her. 'That's a common delusion. It's not money, it's crews.'

'But maybe a little money helps,' she insisted. 'Or even a great deal? I mean, *Cry Havoc* is one of the most expensive boats around, isn't it? The latest in machinery? The latest in sails?'

He held up a hand. 'Let's nail this money thing once and for all,' he said. 'You can have the most expensive boat in the world, but if you've got the wrong crew you can still miss a racing mark by a mile on a misty day.'

'Granted, yes.' She paused a moment. 'But, I wonder, d'you think we could go back to the "ratings" business we were talking about earlier?'

'If you like.'

'Well, as I understand it from gossip in the Press Office, you've got a "middle-rated" boat, one that comes in the middle of the handicap system, a compromise design.'

'True enough.'

'And as I understand it too, there are a great many "middle-rated" boats around this year. Boats of a similar performance, if you like . . . And the important thing, I've heard, is going to be to leave these other boats behind at the starting-gun . . . get out of the ruck.'

'I've heard that too,' Pedlar said.

She leaned towards him, flashing that good smile of hers. 'Gossip has it that the British team have been looking for that extra-special "middle-rated" boat.' The smile grew wider. 'And gossip has it too that a certain very glamorous tycoon has been trying to make the British team for six years now, and that suddenly he's got himself the most expensive "middle-rater" money can buy.'

For the first time Pedlar didn't answer her. Instead he turned away, towards the yacht's galley. 'Little thing that might interest your women-readers,' he said. 'Rather clever little gadget we've devised to keep the mugs in their racks out in a Force Nine.'

Later he went round the marina, looking for Bill Wadey of *Ocean Racing* magazine. He found him with a group of other journalists in the 555 Bar, and he took him to one side.

'Bill, know anything about a little girl called Jane Lambourne?'

'Yes. Freelance. Quite a looker.' Wadey propped his comfortable middle-aged bulk against the bar-rail. 'Why?'

'Well, she's been asking me questions,' Pedlar said. 'And she seemed to know an awful lot more than she was prepared to admit to at first. About the "ratings game" and the rest of it.'

'I don't know,' Wadey said. 'Maybe she just kept her ears open in the Press Office.'

'You think that's all it is?'

'Yes.'

'Nothing more sinister?'

Wadey frowned. He put a hand on Pedlar's arm. 'Michael, what's the matter? Is something wrong?'

'Well.' Pedlar hesitated. 'Only the articles I've been reading recently in a certain yachting magazine that-shall-be-nameless. . . . About how yacht-businesses are going broke wherever you look. How the rich crazy world of Admiral's Cupping seems to be carrying on like some mad Nero, fiddling while Rome burns. How it would be better for ten men to race cheaper yachts than for one man to race a Cupper.'

'Yes.' Wadey turned then and pointed out at the marina. 'But you have to admit, all this has become ridiculously expensive of late.'

'Obscene's the word I've been reading,' Pedlar said. 'And why? I ask myself . . . God knows, I've helped the industry, haven't I? Building a brand-new yacht?'

'Helped a tiny part of the industry,' Wadey said. 'Very few yards can make a living building Admiral's Cuppers. You know that.'

'I do.' Pedlar nodded. 'So we're down to envy, is that right?'

'Let's just say there's a fashionable phrase, and it's something to do with the redistribution of wealth,' Wadey said. 'Me, I don't go for it.'

'Because it's your bread and butter?'

'No. My pleasure.' Wadey paused. 'Michael, you seem a bit hot under the collar. Why's that?'

'Simple,' Pedlar said. 'Nearly all of this Jane Lambourne's questions turned in the end to the subject of money. And perhaps I'm seeing things that aren't there. But it occurred to me . . . that dazzling smile of hers . . . perhaps it could just be in league with a certain yachting magazine that-shall-be-nameless.'

'Not a chance,' Wadey said. 'She's around here looking for a smart jetset column. That's all.'

'If you say so.' Pedlar shrugged. 'But, do me a favour, will you, Bill? If that magazine that-shall-be-nameless starts trying to publish figures, starts trying to put an actual price-tag on my boat . . . then just breathe in their ear, will you? Because I never talk about money to anyone, and I'll appear in print to that effect if need be.'

'All right,' Wadey said. And again he frowned, at a loss.

18

During the afternoon Pedlar's good humour returned. By three the day's checklist of work on *Cry Havoc* had been completed. And by three-fifteen Monroe and he were going back to Lymington in the rub-a-dub, the rubber raft with the Mercury outboard. At speed the two men flapped over the water, making for the Delta and then the Berthon buoys.

'First race is, what, three days off now?' Pedlar asked. 'So I suppose you'll have sold all the sails you're going to?'

'That's it,' Monroe said.

'And how's it look?'

'Not too bad. One or two people let us down finally, as far as orders went. But that's only to be expected.'

'Big boys were they? Big customers?'

'Couple of them, yes. In the end they stuck with the super-lofts, said they were safer, said their sails were proven . . . Ours could be a flash in the pan.'

'And that man Kalicheean?' Pedlar asked. 'As I heard it, he found his way over to the Bantings loft.'

'Right.' Monroe nodded. 'He and the entire Malay team are with Bantings. Buying up the shop there, apparently, from mains to storm trysails.'

'Kalicheean's no loss,' Pedlar said. 'Nor any of the Malay boats, from what I saw of them.'

'No.'

'But apart from them, what's the score?'

'By and large,' Monroe said, 'we've done complete suits for five boats including *Havoc*. And we've had maybe a dozen customers for the high-stress chutes in the Skimbar cloth.'

'Which is pretty damn good for a new enterprise,' Pedlar said. He looked ahead now as they slackened speed, nearing the estuary. 'And what d'you think?' he asked. 'Are these sails of yours going to win for us?'

'The loft could do quite well out of it, yes.'

'I didn't mean the loft,' Pedlar said. 'I meant the boat, *Havoc*.

Getting onto the team is only half of it. Winning's what it's all about. I didn't come all this way for anything else.'

Monroe turned to him. 'Come all this *way*?' he asked. 'For God's sake, man, that farmhouse of yours is no more'n a couple of miles from here, just outside the town.'

They went up-river and slid into the Lymington marina. Monroe tied the rub-a-dub up in *Havoc*'s empty berth, and they walked up the ramp to Pedlar's parked Volvo.

Monroe looked at it. 'Getting a new one of these, are you?' he asked. 'August the first? When the new registration comes in?'

'That's right.' Pedlar unlocked a door for him.

They got into the car, to be surrounded by the usual Volvo warning lights and buzzers.

'Fasten seat belts,' Monroe said. 'Handbrake on . . . School-fees due.'

Pedlar laughed. He drove off.

'Talking about school-fees,' Monroe went on. 'Your son, Charlie-boy . . . He broken up from Marlborough yet?'

'Yes,' Pedlar said.

'But he's not with you?'

'No.'

Monroe shot a glance at him. 'I heard he wasn't staying with you. I heard he wasn't even sailing at Cowes this year.'

Pedlar didn't answer.

'Bloody shame. That lad, he's the best helmsman for his age I ever saw. Better than you.'

'Yes,' Pedlar said quietly.

And Monroe caught his tone. 'So they got to him at last, did they?' he said then. 'Your first wife, your family . . . They warned him off.'

Pedlar turned from the wheel. 'We've been sailing together a long time,' he said. 'Leave it alone, feller, will you?'

Monroe nodded, stroking the side of his jaw where there was a small scar. A couple of seasons back he'd been hit by a mainboom. Since then he'd worn false teeth, which he took out for sailing. They were out now, and his face had a lean, bitter look.

'Your kind, you leave yourselves so open,' he said. 'You send your kids away to school. You send your gundogs away to be trained. And you hope they'll recognise you when they get back.'

But if the gundogs were away, the hounds from the local Hunt were there, howling from the stables as Pedlar and Monroe drove up to the farmhouse. And other visitors were there as well, the two-legged visitors Pedlar was expecting. Their cars were already parked on the drive. The Ford that Helmut Prinzheim, the Swiss yachtsman, was hiring. And the Daimler that belonged to Martin Lyness, a co-director of Pedlar's in the City. This was the man who had come for him early in the morning at Heathrow, when he'd returned from Canada.

Now, telling Monroe to go on in, Pedlar skirted the house, reaching the large walled garden at the rear. And, just as he'd thought, both men were out there, Prinzheim and Lyness, playing a two-ball on the silver square of the croquet lawn. 'What's this?' he called out to them. 'Turned up early to get some crafty practice in?'

'That's right, Michael,' Lyness said. 'It's all getting *rather* serious.' He pointed at Prinzheim, thin and white-haired, stooping over his mallet.

And serious it was, the croquet game, an annual event on Pedlar's lawn at Cowes time.

Prinzheim played, his ball going cleanly through a long hoop. 'It's not just this afternoon that I practise,' he said in the precise way he had. 'I have been working at my game since the spring. I have a Jacques Match Set now at home in Switzerland, and a lawn that I have laid down from English grass seed.'

'Sounds like it's time to start handicapping you,' Pedlar said. 'Sounds like it's time to make the Pimm's.'

Lyness walked with him back to the house. He was a large man, a bear of a man, with a slab of red hair falling over his face. He had a slackish mouth, and a voice that could cut across a grouse-moor. And perhaps, Pedlar thought, he was an anachronism. Perhaps he came from the time when there'd always been a Harrovian on the board, not to mention somebody who knew about claret. And perhaps too it was this old-fashioned quality that Pedlar admired so much in Lyness, a doggedness, an almost child-like fidelity. Certainly they'd been friends since childhood.

'So how are things in the big market-place?' Pedlar asked now. 'Getting on all right without me?'

'Extremely well, Michael. You've hardly been missed,' Lyness told him. 'Summers are much quieter affairs nowadays, aren't they? I mean, now we've learned how to parcel out the big international money-men. Frank takes the Germans to Wimbledon. Rodney the Americans to the Open. And I take the Japs to Scotland, of course, for the Glorious Twelfth.'

By this time they'd reached the paving stones outside the drawing-room. Pedlar stopped. He lowered his voice almost to a whisper. 'And the other thing?' he asked. '*Our* little thing? No more developments there?'

'None.'

'Well, let me know if anything happens. Anything . . . Even if I'm racing, I can be contacted within a matter of hours.'

They went through to the long cool kitchen. The makings of the Pimm's were laid out there on the scrubbed table. Slowly and deliberately Pedlar chopped cucumber, apple, mint, and tipped them into a cut-glass jug.

Then, as he was measuring out the Pimm's itself, the door opened. Katerina came in, followed by Monroe. Against the white tiles of the kitchen she was dark, slim, alive. There was an almost youthful beauty to her this summer, Pedlar thought, and it was enough to make him catch his breath. He went over and kissed her. 'Where were you?' he asked. 'With the kids?'

'No, they've gone out for the afternoon.'

'Out? I thought I hadn't heard their little Gestapo-like voices.'

'They've gone to tea with Pony Club friends,' Katerina said. 'I'm fetching them at six.'

'Well,' he smiled, 'at least it'll lend itself to more serious croquet. But first . . . the necessary ingredient.' He went back to the jug on the scrubbed table.

While the Pimm's was cooling, the four of them, picking up Prinzheim on the way, went out to see the hounds in the stables. They crossed the garden. Inside its old thick walls the smell was of lavender, of roses and sweet peas – order. Outside was the wildness of summer, long paddock grass, hogweed, and, up on the rise above the house, the dry breath of barley. A gravel track, white in the heat, led up towards it. And on either side were tree-stumps of old dark wood.

Prinzheim pointed to them. 'Tell me, Michael, weren't there trees here the last time I came? Big trees? Walnuts? What happened to them?'

'Disease,' Pedlar told him.

'So now they are cut down?'

Pedlar sighed. 'Very difficult decision to take,' he said. 'The forestry people told me I could fell them last autumn and sell the timber up to the first knot. Or just wait for them to die.'

'And are you going to plant more? Now, I mean?'

'What's the point?' Pedlar asked. 'If somebody's only going to chop them down again in three hundred years' time.'

'Three hundred years.' Prinzheim gave a sudden smile.

They reached the stable and opened the top door. The hounds were inside in the half-light. Their mouths were soft as they reached up. There was the smell of bad meat on their breath. Behind them a sheep-carcase hung from a hook, and there was blood on their flanks.

'But, Michael,' Prinzheim said. 'These are wild dogs.'

'Not the sort you put collars on,' Pedlar agreed.

'And you have them here through August? The hunters leave them with you for safe keeping?'

'The Hunt,' Pedlar corrected him. 'And they take them back when the season starts.'

'So how many seasons,' Prinzheim asked, 'do the dogs hunt?'

Pedlar, glancing at Katerina, tried to warn him off.

But Prinzheim wasn't to be warned off. 'Michael, how many seasons?'

'Three,' Pedlar said.

'And then?'

Again Pedlar tried to signal to the man. But Katerina got there first. 'Then they put them down,' she said.

'Kill them?' Prinzheim was shocked.

'Since they are wild animals,' Katerina said, 'and have been introduced to the taste of blood.'

Prinzheim said nothing.

Pedlar decided to lighten the mood. He turned and faced them all. 'Pimm's,' he said. 'Time for Pimm's and croquet.'

It was one of those perfect summer afternoons that eclipse a hundred others, Pedlar thought. The shadows reaching slowly out from the flint wall, the click of croquet balls, the moving from hoop to hoop with a mallet in one hand and a Pimm's in the other. Tea they had below the vine on the south wall of the house. Then evening came. The barley up on the hill took on the colour of grapes. And grape the sky, thick, musty, a haze that made the croquet balls carve tracks out of the dew.

Children's feet marked the dew as well. Sammy and Daisy, returned from their friend's house, ran barefoot in their nighties.

And while on the lawn they were respectful of their elders and worsers, away by the shadows of the swimming-pool they screamed like banshees.

Later when the girls were in bed, the men brought the cars round as they always did, parked them on the rise above the garden, and played on by the light of headlamps. The dew by this time was criss-crossed by lines. The play expert, the games long, and hard to finish . . . Until . . . At a certain moment Lyness was hesitating about trying the last hoop from a bad angle. While the other three were laying off, fully fifteen or twenty yards off, but sure by now of looping in and croquet-ing him.

'Go on,' Pedlar said. 'Take a chance, man.'

Lyness, bear-like, stood there.

And, flashing back suddenly through, what, four years, Pedlar saw another figure on the lawn. A slim twelve-year-old boy, tousle-haired, who hit a croquet-ball casually on the move, and didn't miss.

Four years back too, Lyness in almost the same position by the last hoop, lifting his big arms to the sky. 'But if I go on, Michael,' he'd shouted, 'that young boy of yours is going to knock all *hell* out of me!'

Young boy . . . Pedlar closed his eyes, felt pain.

It was one in the morning. Prinzheim, Lyness and Monroe were all asleep. Pedlar and Katerina were alone in the long bedroom over the vine. The window was open, the smell of stocks came in, and the summer moon.

'I saw your face out there on the lawn,' Katerina said.

'What?' he asked. 'When? When d'you mean?'

'Just before the end, when Lyness was trying to finish the game,' she said. 'I came out to ask about brandies, and I saw you.'

Pedlar didn't answer.

'You were thinking about Charlie-boy.'

'Yes.'

She looked round at him from her dressing-table. 'It's bad, isn't it, all of a sudden? With your family?'

'Getting to be,' Pedlar said. 'In this way at least . . . they have the clay to work with.'

'By which you mean Charlie.' Katerina got up, crossed the room. 'When did you last see him?'

'Three weeks after half-term.'

'And did he have any plans then? For the holidays, I mean?'
'He's sixteen years old,' Pedlar said savagely. 'He didn't know.'
'Was he just being polite?'
'Polite, Christ, yes.'
She sat by him, laid a cool hand on his neck. 'Is that why you've been away such a lot? Sinking yourself in work? Taking every fight on your shoulders? . . . The family?'
'In a way,' he said.
'Think of me.' She got up, went back to the dressing-table. She unfastened her watch. She put on lipstick.
Emma, his former wife, had always taken it off.
There was a smoke to Katerina, a dark smoke that had always awed him. A fierceness, as his mouth climbed the olive colour of her leg. And, as she moved slightly, a bellow that was him. A hammering on the square yard of soil that any person rented for seventy years. A bellow useless beyond the moment and entirely necessary. She had told him that. Told him again now as his mouth reached the fine dark olive branches that were her. *Her.*
Later they lay side by side, feeling the moon press into the room. And she spoke again.
'That family of yours. I'm not really complaining. I can see how difficult it is for you.'
'What is?'
'To see their weapons.'
'What?'
'English weapons. You have to understand, I can only compare them with Greek ones. In Greece, you see, we fight differently. We shout at one another. And if that doesn't work, we get a lawyer who shouts louder.'
'Lawyers,' Pedlar said. 'I tried them, remember? When I got divorced.'
'That's not what I meant. Greek lawyers shout, literally shout at each other. You can see them doing it all the way across the street to the courthouse. You see, it's all open there. Everybody knows what it's all about . . . Money or property, or women who play around after marriage, because the dowry-system prevents them playing around before . . . But here, everything is arranged secretly, behind closed doors. Money and property in that City of yours, divorce in the Inns of Court . . . Here you don't show anything. You don't expect other people to show anything. And honestly it wouldn't make the slightest difference

if they did.' She turned to him. 'Because, you see, Michael, you English fix each other in your minds.'

'I don't understand,' he said.

'You take a view of someone at a certain time . . . Your parents when you were young, your wife on the day you married her, your children at an age when they resemble you . . . And you fix them like that forever, in those roles.'

'I'm sure a lot of people do, to a certain extent.'

She sighed, *paw*, in the Greek way. 'Michael, I was at school here. I came out in Society here, whatever that means. But about those Society people I always remember thinking, these are not human beings but human beens.'

'B–E–E–N–S?'

'Yes.'

'Society people,' he said. 'You know you're talking about a few of the people I go around with.'

'I'm a foreigner, Michael. I don't wish to be rude.'

But he was ruffled. 'Well, shall we make a start with the people in this house? At the moment, I mean? . . . Prinzheim, Monroe, Lyness?'

'Prinzheim is Swiss.' She shrugged. 'Monroe, he's not of the class . . . There, I've said it . . . And Lyness, he makes me laugh, he makes the children laugh. In fact he's Lyness, the *only* one who's stayed really close to you since the divorce.'

He nodded. It was true.

'Honestly I don't wish to be rude,' she said again, 'but you know who I'm talking about. The people who fix each other always from the viewpoint of the past. "He's on good form", they'll say about somebody at a dinner-party. Always "on good form". . . . And the women, *panagia mou* . . . Last winter, every single woman I met in London had the headscarf, the flat patent shoes, and the kind of quilted jacket that Royalty have been wearing these past fifteen years.'

This last came out in a rush, word tumbling over word. And he knew without question she wasn't trying to be rude. But she had described his former wife exactly. Emma, uniformed, changing from uniform to uniform, breathless, at a rush. Emma exhausted by the invitations on her mantelpiece.

'The English disease isn't what they say it is,' she said then. 'It's just fear of change.'

He sat up on one elbow and looked down at her. Katerina,

summer woman, who sunbathed naked, without a mark of white on her body.

And that summer when they'd first met.

It had been at Vouliagmeni, the smart section of the coast near Athens. Pedlar had taken a villa. Katerina and her then husband had taken the villa next door. Every day their two caravans – nannies, children, beach-gear – had marched down to two separate beaches. Every day Pedlar had glanced across and told himself he'd like to meet her husband, a man who'd climbed swiftly up through the Praxitelis Institute and made far-reaching decisions.

Then they'd met. The two caravans had come together in a summer-house in one of the gardens. And it had been ridiculous. Ninety-four degrees in the shade, they'd all been overdressed, the canapés melting, the talk at best desultory . . . Until Pedlar had looked round.

'What was it you said?' he asked now suddenly.

'When?'

'That first time we met at Vouliagmeni.'

'I've told you before.'

'Tell me again.'

'I took one look at you and said, *afto eenay dikomou* . . . That's for me.'

19

Late the next afternoon, in the Cross Keys pub at Cowes, Wyatt had an unexpected phone-call.

'That you, Ace? How you doin'?'

'Jacko?' Wyatt said. 'Jacko, I thought you weren't meant to be contacting me. I thought you'd promised your wife.'

'I promised her I wouldn't *see* you, Ace. And I int seein' you now, well, am I?'

'No . . . So what's up?'

'Just wondered how you was gettin' along.'

'Well,' Wyatt said, 'as a matter of fact I was over on the mainland yesterday. Passed very close to your house.'

'Why was that?'

'Our man was over there in that big farmhouse of his,' Wyatt said. 'And three others were with him . . . Monroe, Prinzheim the Swiss guy, and somebody I didn't know.'

'Is that right?'

'Yes, they didn't come back here till late on this morning.'

'And what was they doin' all that time?'

'Playing croquet.'

'Croquet?'

'That's it,' Wyatt said. I watched them for quite a time from the hill above the house, and then from the garden. But I didn't see anything else.'

'Was that clever, Ace? Goin' into the garden like that?'

'Maybe not . . . But, Jacko, you didn't ring up just to hear about croquet, did you?'

'No.'

'What then?'

'Maybe I got a little information, Ace,' Jackman said. 'About things that are happenin' well behind the rest of it.'

'Is that right?'

'Yeh, but first . . . First I want you to think a few weeks back, to that guy who had the pliers-job done on him in the Southampton park. I mean, somehow that always bothered me, a thing like that happenin' in Southampton. Corsicans gettin' heavy so many miles away from home. Knockin' on doors down the street here.'

'Yes.' Wyatt waited.

'But then it bothered me a lot more when they got to Carver too. Because, Ace, that's golden doors they was knockin' on there. Golden doors with cherubs over the top and bleedin' great bunches of grapes. I mean, Carver, he's *connected*, both around here and in the City. That was takin' a hell of a chance, wasn't it? Them shavin' Carver's head?'

'Yes,' Wyatt said, 'agreed.'

'So maybe it was then they realised they'd handled it all wrong,' Jackman said. 'And they had to try a different way.'

'What different way? What d'you mean?'

'Hold on. I'm gettin' there, Ace. Just stick with Carver for the moment . . . Now why was it he got hurt? What was it he did?'

'Found something out.'

'Yeh, but more than that, much more,' Jackman said. 'He found somethin' out that went deep, right to the core.'

'All right,' Wyatt agreed.

'And how did he go about it?'

'Well,' Wyatt said, 'he lunched somebody. Somebody wearing the school tie. The City. All that.'

'Or, Ace, lookin' at it the other way . . . Somebody wearin' the school tie talked to Carver.'

'Same difference, isn't it?'

'No, not at all,' Jackman said. 'Listen, I was tellin' you about golden doors, wasn't I, with cherubs and all that? I was tellin' you about where it's really at, right up at the top?' He paused. 'And, don't you see, there's this gap that's opened up there? A gap that's got to be plugged?'

'Maybe,' Wyatt said.

'No maybe about it,' Jackman told him. 'Because now there's this information I got for you . . . It seems there are these new kiddies who've turned up in the country. New kiddies who're callin' the shots now.'

'What d'you mean?' Wyatt asked him. 'Corsicans? Is that what you mean?'

'I don't know, Ace. All I'll say is, if they are Corsicans then they int the backstreet touch like before. They int goin' at it with pliers and razors. They're people who wear suits and know which knife and fork to pick up. Like, we had the corporals and now we got the captains.'

Wyatt listened a moment longer, then he put the phone down. He walked through the bar of the Cross Keys and looked out at the street. It was nearly a quarter to six, he realised, the shadows were lengthening. And the Admiral's Cup crews were beginning to leave the gates of the Groves & Guttridge marina, away to his right, and come down the High Street in their groups of a dozen or more. Except that this evening they weren't strolling soft-footed down the pavement in tee-shirts and shorts. They were walking stiffly in polished shoes, wearing blazers and ties, their hair slicked down. And they were all going the same way.

20

'. . . welcome you all to what we sincerely hope will be a memorable Admiral's Cup Series,' the grey-haired man said.

It was the opening party, two days before the first inshore race. There was the marquee on the Squadron lawn, its panels raised to show the long white table inside. There was the microphone on the table where the grey-haired man was speaking. And facing him, in rows that stretched away on the sloping grass, were about eight hundred people, the crews, team-managers and ladies of the Admiral's Cup yachts. They stood respectfully, even the gorillas among them – the foredeck and winch men – shaved and shirt-cuffed and silent, with no more than two glasses of champagne under their belts.

And the Squadron achieved this sort of silence, Pedlar thought . . . Statuary, that was the word that came to him on this lawn. The lopped elm trees up at the top of the slope. The mown lines going down between the rows of motionless men. The marquee with its long table. And those other smaller tables and chairs below, facing the water. Older members of the Squadron sat there, stiff-backed, with telescopes at their sides.

Pedlar, like the rest of the eight hundred around him, was here only by invitation. He was not a member. The bad joke had it that Squadron membership required a K and at least one plastic hip. And to Pedlar it was a bad joke. Ritual was here more than in any other place in Cowes. And ritual meant a great deal to him, the worn stone steps that directed the feet, the buildings that were added to story by story.

Because here the stories were many and well-known . . .

Of the English king with the German accent, perhaps the last of the carefree kings, who had introduced women to the Squadron. Every year he and his current mistress had led the parade of fashionable beauties. While the townsfolk of Cowes had watched over the wall and kept silent. Gossip had not crossed the water to the mainland.

Of perhaps the best-known English yachtsman, an intimate of this same king, yet a man who had achieved membership only in his eightieth year. And the reason? Because he had founded a chain of food-stores . . . The German Kaiser had put it in a nutshell. One day on this very lawn he'd been asked where the king was. 'They tell me,' he'd said, 'he's gone boating with his grocer.'

Of the English society lady of the thirties, whose husband had been blackballed from the Squadron because she had dived from her yacht one Sunday during Cowes Week, wearing a red bathing-dress.

Of big yachts and bigger men. An ocean-racing man in particular whose card had merely read, 'T.B.F. Davis. East and

South Africa.'

And of the ending of the age of big yachts. In 1936 the British king known as the 'sailor king' had died, and ordered in his will that his great yacht *Britannia* be towed out into the English Channel and scuttled.

Ritual.

'. . . We trust that this year's Admiral's Cup will be hard fought. But that at the same time a spirit of camaraderie will prevail. And that in the end true seamanship will win the day.' The grey-haired man finished his speech at the microphone.

There was polite applause. Pedlar looked past the marquee and on towards Cowes Green. As in years past, townspeople were there in the evening light, watching the Squadron lawn. Then walking a few paces on, stopping, and watching again. Nothing, it seemed, changed.

Until . . . Until Pedlar looked further, out at the water and the slow procession of yachts passing by. And suddenly he felt alarm. Because some way past a grey-hulled ketch, overhauling it, was a yacht that shouldn't have been there. It was a motor-yacht, new, metal-built, about eighty feet long. It was closing in from the West, probably from Poole, where Pedlar knew it was based. But based only, because, as was clear from the flag flying astern, it was foreign-owned. And its owner was the last person in the world Pedlar wanted to see. Here. Now.

The yacht drew nearer. Pedlar's alarm grew. Then he saw a Squadron steward come out onto the lawn. The man went from group to group. People turned and pointed. At Pedlar. He was being called, he heard, ship-to-shore.

He followed the steward into the grey fortress of the Squadron. It was a white-painted room with a window out to sea, where he took the call. He knew at once who he was talking to, and he was curt, almost angry.

'I thought we'd left it,' he said, 'that you would contact me only when the Admiral's Cup was over.'

'Agreed,' the man said politely at the other end. Which was why he had no intention of meeting Pedlar personally now, nor of calling in at Cowes.

'Then why not reach me through Martin Lyness?' Pedlar asked. 'The usual way? The safe way?'

Because of the nature of the problem that had come up, the man said. The precise nature . . .

And Pedlar listened.

'All right, I agree,' he said then. 'It has to be done right away.' He thought for a moment. 'Tomorrow . . . Tomorrow's the last free day before racing begins.'

He put down the radio-phone. He walked over to the window. Somebody had left a pair of binoculars on the sill, and he focused them on the distant motor-yacht. The man he'd been talking to came out on deck and leaned against the rail. His hair was cut short, *en brosse*. He wore a tight-fitting suit. Both Pedlar and he had been talking in French.

21

'Racing begins tomorrow, and you've got to go to a business lunch?' Monroe asked. 'Is that right?'

'I can't get out of it,' Pedlar said. 'Something's cropped up that won't wait.'

'So what about the final things to be done aboard *Havoc*?'

'But they're very final things, aren't they? Just a short list,' Pedlar said. 'And Ronnie can look after that.'

'Okay, maybe you're right.' Monroe nodded. 'But what about the British team-meeting? At lunchtime?'

'I've cleared it with Hugh,' Pedlar told him. 'What's happening today is no more than a couple of gins, and a guess about tomorrow's weather. I mean, we've been all through tactics. We've had the pep-talk about sailing by the book, and not having Protests lodged against us. We've seen all the video there is of the opposition.'

'Maybe,' Monroe said. 'But while we're on the subject of the opposition, there are rumours flying around.'

'What?'

'Americans have been seen around the place. Hotshots. West Coast sailing men.'

'West Coast?' Pedlar asked. 'You mean, Krasker's changing crew?' He named the captain of the American team.

'No. Why should he? Why mess around with a winning bunch?'

'All right, Hoff? Or Ralphy?' Pedlar named the other two Americans.

'Not as far as I know.'

'Then they're probably over here to watch. Pick up some tips.'

'Very likely.' Monroe was sarcastic.

Pedlar moved away. He picked up his briefcase, glanced at his watch. 'Must be off,' he said. And then, lower, 'There's a chance Katerina might ring. Will you tell her I'm out? Playing sails?'

Monroe looked at him. 'So it's like last week.'

'Just like last week.'

'When you came back from Canada a day before time? And I had to back you up with that business about being out at the opera in Montreal . . . *Rosen*-whatever it was.'

'*Rosenkavalier*,' Pedlar said. 'I'm sorry it was German but it was what they were giving that night.'

'Yes, you'd know all that, wouldn't you?' Monroe said.

And Pedlar stared at him. 'What's the matter?' he asked.

Monroe hesitated. 'Today at lunch you're seeing Martin Lyness, am I right?'

'Yes.'

'And last week you flew back early to see him too?'

'Yes.'

Again Monroe hesitated. 'This under the table deal you've got going with Lyness, it's not going to sod up the sailing, is it?'

'No,' Pedlar said, 'it isn't.'

The helicopter came down from a clear blue sky. Soon it was below the hills surrounding the Wiltshire valley, and homing on the village in its centre. Thatched roofs, white walls, neat gardens rose up to meet it, and then the green square of the sports field that was to one side. The helicopter landed. Pedlar got out with his briefcase and crossed the grass to the waiting car. It was a perfect summer's day.

He was driven past the church and the post office to the Red Lion. Again it was a whitewashed building with a thatched roof. And white tables and chairs were set out on the lawn that sloped down to a small stream. Pedlar told the chauffeur he would be an hour. Getting out of the car, he saw Martin Lyness was waiting for him at one of the further tables. He waved and went towards him.

Lyness got up as he approached. 'Michael, good to see you,' he said. 'What d'you think? Weather like this . . . Shall we eat outside?'

'Sounds fine to me.' Pedlar sat down. And it was only now,

close to its bank, that the smell of the chalk-stream came to him. The air was very still. There was that dry edge to it that came with high summer. Not far away a combine was making the first turn in a wheatfield. And from the woods up on the hill came the *chorrock-chorrock* of pheasants calling.

Lyness, Pedlar saw, had not been in to the City. He wore a light brown suit and suede shoes. There were comfortable creases to his jacket, and he no longer fussed that slab of red hair out of his eyes. He was at home here. Lyness's sense of the order of things had always stemmed from the country.

Both of them turned as footsteps came across the lawn. A man in a chef's hat approached with two large salvers. One of them had a salmon lying slackly across it. The other a live lobster, its claws pegged.

'A day for the salmon, wouldn't you think?' Lyness asked. 'And shall we be abstemious and stick to the Blanc de blancs? They do an awfully good one here.'

The wine came, was poured, and brought a dew to their glasses. The salmon came, and they ate. They sat close over the small table; it was Lyness who talked, and Pedlar who smiled, often. He remembered Katerina telling him how Lyness could make both her and the children laugh. And it had always been his talent. Behind the clumsiness of a large man was an ear for mimicry that was quite delicate.

The meal over, Pedlar lit cigarettes. He blew out the match, crumbled the burnt tip of it away, and held the rest lengthwise between finger and thumb. Held it fiercely, hurting himself with the pointed tip.

A large man who was delicate, he thought. And years back, a large boy who'd been delicate. That side of Lyness had come as a surprise. It had emerged on their very first day together at prep school. They'd stood in the line of 'new bugs', alphabetically placed next to each other. In front of each of them had been their brand-new tuckboxes, made of white wood, unmarked. And right from the beginning Lyness, needing someone to trust, had chosen Pedlar.

The waiters came now over the grass and cleared the table. Pedlar turned and looked away past stream and wheatfield to the dark woods beyond. It seemed like calm English countryside, he thought. But nothing was calm English countryside, not any more. The restaurant where they sat, the village, its acres and sports field, were all owned by the Company. There were hospitality suites, there were holiday cottages for white-collar staff, and a Company cricket team. The reasoning behind all this was that agricultural land made good sense now that property prices were a lottery . . . And other people thought so too. The woodland up on the hill was owned by one of the largest trade unions in the country. Violently opposed to bloodsports, they let out the shooting there at four-and-a-half thousand a gun.

No, nothing was simple. Not any more.

The waiters went away, leaving the table clear. Pedlar, looking down at it, saw a crack in its wooden surface. He still had the match in his hand, and for some reason he wedged it into the crack. It stood upright.

Then he began.

'Martin,' he said, 'I've been talking to the Frogs.'

'That so?' Lyness asked.

'Yes. You see, they're over here at the moment, our Froggy friends. They want to stay right in the background, they tell me, but they want more control.'

'I see.'

Pedlar's hand went back to the match poking up from the table. He moved it backwards and forwards.

'Martin, why should I have to say this? We are dealing with people who need to keep certain events quiet. Absolutely quiet.'

'Of course.'

'And yet at the same time, a very important piece of information has got out,' Pedlar said. 'One that could have blown the lot of us sky high.' He took a deep breath and went on quickly, 'Martin, the Frogs have narrowed it down to source. They will have it that you're the one who nearly did for us.'

'Oh, come on,' was all Lyness said.

Pedlar's face didn't show anything. Again he moved the match between finger and thumb, like a lever.

'But they know, don't you see? They've sent me documentary proof. It's all here in my briefcase. The date, the time of a certain meeting.' He sighed. 'And what d'you think I said to them about that? What d'you think I *could* say? That perhaps you'd been naïve, trusted one person too many? Or, far worse, had old-fashioned values? Scruples even about what we were doing? . . . Martin, Christ . . .'

Pedlar bent forwards, looking closely at the match, the lever.

And from somewhere it came back to him, the remark he'd made to his daughter recently, the joke at bedtime, 'Time for bed, is it? Time to pull the Get Rid Of People Lever?'

He pulled the match towards him.

He talked for about five minutes. He hardly listened to what he was saying, and he looked at Lyness only once. And it was then, without either sound or movement, that he saw a man explode. Money burst from Lyness at every pore. And not just money. Because in the way that salaries were kept low nowadays, directorships and shares left the man too, school-fees, cars . . . house . . .

After that he didn't look at Lyness. He couldn't. All he could do was close his mind to everything except two clear thoughts . . . The Frogs were right in what they'd said, they had documentary proof. Therefore he was right to do what he was doing now.

When he'd finished he got up from the table and walked away. Sitting once again in the car he thought some image of Lyness would stay with him. But it didn't. In a strange way the image was stronger than that. It was of a tuckbox on the first day of school, new white wood, unmarked.

22

The morning of the first inshore race arrived, bright and cloudless, just like the day before. Wind was from the north-north-west, rising in strength the forecasters said, and backing to north-west by midday.

Well before that time, at nine in the morning, there was a growing note of excitement in the marina. The squeal of sail-trolleys going out to the yachts, the bark of fenders as men stepped aboard, the sound of voices straining too high. And by nine-thirty when the fleet began to leave, it was with a rush of motors starting up, one after the other.

Outside, bright sun danced as the flotilla brought its own chop to the water. Yacht hulls slid fast through each other's wakes, crewmen shouted across from deck to deck. While behind them the bow-waves of the Press and spectator craft were bigger, their wakes bigger in an effort to catch up. There was an urgency, it seemed, to quit the river and the grey Squadron guarding it, to quit the land.

Then there was haze, and the land fell back. For the first time each yacht became separate. Faces were close. Men leaned together in groups and talked softly.

Aboard *Havoc* there were two groups. Pedlar at the wheel had Monroe and Ronnie the navigator next to him. Ahead, leaning against the long boom, were the nine other crewmen. They stood tall against the glare, wearing rugger shirts that were hooped in dark blue and red, *Havoc*'s colours. And, as Pedlar watched, the men began to move. One by one they removed the rings from their fingers – dangerous when handling rope – and put on thick leather gloves. Then they started preparing the boat.

Winch-handles were brought up from below and placed in the deep plastic wallets below the winches. Wire-cutters and a sharp knife were taped to the black telescopic tube that was the vang. Sheet-leads were slotted into the tracks on deck . . . Though these last required a decision. 'Which genoa on deck, skipper? The light number one, or . . .?' Stan, one of the foredeck gorillas, called out.

Pedlar looked at the windspeed and wind-direction gauges in front of him. Rising now above twelve knots, he saw, and perhaps backing by a whisker to the north-west.

'Going to back early, isn't it?' he said to Ronnie. 'Well before midday.'

'Seems like it,' Ronnie said.

'More than seems,' Monroe said from behind them. 'I'd put money on it.'

Pedlar came to a decision. He turned once again to the foredeck man. 'Okay, we start with the light number one genny, and we have the medium single-ply handy.'

Monroe, tactician, who could over-rule Pedlar on matters of sails, nodded. 'Do for starters,' he said.

Stan put the sheet-leads in position. Charlie, the other foredeck gorilla, brought the genoa sail up from below. He unbagged it, hooked on the tack, and fastened the halyard to the head of the sail. Further aft, men were undoing the tyers that held the furled mainsail along its boom. Then there was little more to do. There was silence apart from the whine of the motor.

Haze was all round them at the horizon, blue shading into milky blue. Land was lost, and *Havoc* slowly entered a place that was all on its own out in the sunlight. In the distance were the motorboats that were tenders to the yachts, and the Press and spectator fleet. Closer was the Committee boat, the big blue motor cruiser, *Ocean One*, that was to order the course of the race. But all else was the dome of sky and mist, sealing off the rest of the world. There was the feeling of mysterious lines about to be drawn on the water, the feeling of a very private summer's day.

Almost immediately the Committee boat, *Ocean One*, made its presence felt. There was a crackle from the radio below, and a voice came up through the open hatchway. '*Ocean One* to Admiral's Cup yachts. *Ocean One* to Admiral's Cup yachts. Good morning . . . There will be a twenty minutes delay to the start, to allow wind direction to settle.'

Pedlar raised his binoculars, found *Ocean One*, saw the man on deck there with the anenometer, testing the wind. He was facing north-west.

'It's backing now,' Pedlar said. 'And they'll want a windward leg to start with.' He turned to Ronnie. 'So what time's high water?'

'Eleven thirteen,' Ronnie said.

'Then we'll have the tide with us.'

'Be a bulging start-line,' Monroe agreed. 'Interesting, yes?'

Pedlar swung the binoculars round. Among the distant craft dotting the water he found *Havoc*'s tender, saw Katerina and the two children aboard. There was time to motor over there for the last Good Lucks. But, he told himself, all the Good Lucks had been said.

He cut the motor. *Havoc* drifted into silence. Below the waterline, Pedlar knew, the bronze-coloured propeller would have stopped spinning. And, because of the way the boat was still carrying, both propeller-blades would have hinged back to the feathered position. Pedlar beckoned. Abe, one of the coffee-grinder men, stripped down to his shorts and went over the side on a rope. His hand looped a stout rubber band over the feathered blades, holding them in place. Then he was back on board, and towelling himself down.

Pedlar returned to the wheel. He brought *Havoc* round, head to wind. He waited till Abe was ready. 'Let's have some sails up,' he called out then.

The main went up to the rattle of halyard winches. Half the sky was blocked out, and *Havoc* became a yacht. Then the white genoa rose, flapping, in irons. The winches went into higher gear, took on the shrieking sound of fine metal links as the sheets were winched home. *Havoc* arced, swung, took her first leap forward. Hal the bowman was now in position. Ronnie in his, head and shoulders poking out of the main hatch. Ahead of him the foredeck gorillas crouched by the mast. Winch-tailers were in the cockpit. The other four men sitting 'birds in a nest', their feet out over the hull-side, the windward rail clutched to their chests . . . Positions . . . The yacht became a racing yacht.

Behind Pedlar, Monroe was playing hydraulics. A strumming went through the boat as he played backstay against babystay, mainsheet against vang. As he curved that huge mast back and flattened the sail. The boat canted slightly. Pedlar found neutral helm. And there was that hiss, that slick of water coming past, that arrival at the sum of nine months' calculations. Good calculations. Pedlar felt happy.

From the wheel now he could no longer see for'ard. His view was blocked by the foot of the great white genoa, flush with the deck. Hal, peering round the sail from his bowman's position, gave him directions. And Monroe too, standing against the stern-rail where he would be throughout the race. 'Bear off,' he shouted, which meant taking the wind wider on the beam. Or, 'Luff up,' which meant turning into the wind and losing speed.

These changes because now suddenly there was a column of yachts on the water. A column three–four deep, marching and countermarching like bandsmen, up-down, up-down, all on the same line. Some yachts they overtook. Others hissed at them suddenly on a closing course. And each avoiding action had its shriek of winch, cut off almost as soon as it began.

Pedlar knew why the column was so tightly packed. He knew from the feel of the yacht and the wind that a startline was settling, that a second start-boat was being manoeuvred into position by *Ocean One*. And it was no surprise when in a moment Monroe pointed astern. 'They've anchored,' he said. 'The line's there.'

'*Ocean One* to Admiral's Cup yachts. *Ocean One* to Admiral's Cup yachts,' the voice boomed out from the radio again. 'This is a course announcement . . . The course for today is Figure Two Red, Oscar Red, Yankee Green, Figure Five Red, Clipper Red, X-Ray Green . . .'

In the hatchway, his chart clipped to a board, Ronnie the navigator noted down the buoys. By the time the announcement had been repeated, he had his calculations done. 'Twenty-nine miles,' he said.

The startline was now there on the water, stretching between the two motor boats. For a moment now the yachts went away from it, bearing further offwind. For a moment Pedlar could see all fifty-six of them, sails like translucent ivory against the haze. Until they again re-formed in their column, up-down, up-down.

'Bear off.' . . . 'Luff up.' . . . The screams of winch as hulls came at them closer now, hissing in their spray. Otherwise there was just the sound of their own path through the water. And from far off the short bursts of engine from Press and spectator boats as they fought the tide to keep clear.

'*Ocean One* to Admiral's Cup yachts. *Ocean One* to Admiral's Cup yachts. The start will be in ten minutes. Ten minutes . . . Here is a timecheck. It is ten seventeen precisely . . . *Now*.'

Monroe and Ronnie the navigator both adjusted stopwatches. And then Monroe, craning higher, looked round. 'Make for the weather end,' he said.

They came about smoothly, seven men working as one. Then, with the wind freshening, they beat up to the north end of the line, and the distant cruiser there, *Ocean One*.

The top end of the line, to windward, was the smart end, Pedlar thought, where the air was clear . . . Unless it turned out not to be the smart end at all, because too many smart people were there.

Which was the case.

'Yanks. I see Yanks,' Monroe shouted suddenly. Then he bent close. 'They're the danger-boys today. Agreed?'

'In these conditions, yes.' Pedlar nodded.

'And not Doug, our hotshot Kiwi friend,' Monroe went on. 'Douggie who's been moaning about too little wind all week.'

'Right. I heard that wasn't as advertised,' Pedlar said. 'I heard he was set up for light airs.'

'So today Douggie won't like it,' Monroe said. 'He'll be in a sheep-shagging mood. There'll be trouble.'

They were nearing *Ocean One*, following a pack of other boats. Monroe was watching them. 'Krasker's there, and Hoff. That's two out of three bloody Yanks.'

'Keep with Hoff,' Pedlar said. 'He'll come back down again. He's the one to watch.'

They rounded the cruiser in a string of yachts. There was a puff of smoke from *Ocean One*, followed by the sound of the gun.

'Five minutes,' Monroe said louder.

The crew were tense. From now on they were under the rules

of racing, and they shifted position, felt the balance of the boat faster.

But other yachts were faster too. Up-down, up-down the line, and now there were near collisions in the haze. Sails were jittery, boats were nervous as they waited. Like greyhounds in the slips, Pedlar thought.

But there wasn't time for classy thoughts. Not any more.

'Four minutes,' Monroe shouted. Then, almost immediately, 'Hoff's gone about.'

'Ready about . . . Go!' Pedlar shouted.

Scream of winch and they swung round.

'Hoff's nosing in,' Monroe said.

And he was, creeping in towards the line, where now a whole group of yachts were in irons, sails flapping, waiting.

'Get out of it. It's too early. We want boatspeed, *boatspeed*,' Monroe shouted. And then, 'Hoff's going too.'

'*Go*,' Pedlar shouted.

A gust as they took the wind abeam, as they steadied, went down-line again.

Searching . . .

'Three minutes,' Monroe shouted. 'Decision?'

Pedlar nodded. He bore off and scanned the line of yachts, the thick shining mass of them, the pack of ivory cards he had to shuffle into the one good hand.

'That group there.' He pointed. 'A Canadian, then Kiwi Doug, then the others . . . The Canadians had a heavy night last night.'

'Agreed,' Monroe said. 'If anyone's going to bulge the line, it's them.'

'Okay, we try there,' Pedlar said.

But he wasn't the only one thinking like that. Hoff was thinking like that. And Hoff suddenly was *close*, his bow knifing across their stern, his curving genoa scraping past. For a moment surf boiled between the two hulls, and *Havoc* got dirty air. But only for a moment, because Pedlar brought her back and went for Hoff in his turn. On each deck men ran, handling the huge yachts like dinghies, each trying to out-manoeuvre the other.

'You're losing,' Monroe shouted then. 'Getting boxed in by that Belgian there . . . Decision?'

Pedlar looked round, saw the clear space back from the line. 'We lay off and do it the hard way,' he said. 'Quick gyber. Come in behind the gun. Starboard the buggers.'

He called the shots, swung the wheel. A broad reach took them away.

'Two minutes,' Monroe said. 'Ronnie?'

Ronnie measured the widening gap between them and the line of yachts. 'Two hundred yards,' he said.

Pedlar waited, waited for Monroe.

'*Go!*' the man shouted.

The gybe, the big one in this wind-strength . . . The huge mainsail was clawed in. Until with a snap it went. The boom smacked over. A wrench to the whole boat as they went round. The genny was sheeted in, fast . . . And they were making back for the line.

'Point high until I say Go,' Monroe said. 'Then go like fuck.'

Pedlar was blind. The genoa was a dazzling screen of white ahead of him, with just Hal's dark head craning round.

'One minute . . . Fifty seconds . . . Forty seconds . . . Thirty seconds . . .' Ronnie's calm voice counted down.

'*Go!*' Monroe shouted.

Pedlar came round, took the wind, felt *Havoc* suddenly leap forward.

Around the white genoa the press of other sails came up fast.

'Can we still starboard the buggers?' Pedlar shouted.

Yachts on starboard tack had preference, were given way to . . . provided there was 'water', sufficient room for port-tack yachts to change course.

'Have we got water?' Pedlar shouted.

'Twenty seconds . . . Fifteen, fourteen, thirteen . . .'

'Luff up!' Hal shouted.

Pedlar, blind, did so.

Huge dazzling canvas was all round them.

'You've got Hoff!' Monroe shouted. 'Maybe you've got the whole . . .'

'Off! Bear off!' Hal shouted.

'. . . Eight, seven, six . . .'

'Water!' Hal started shouting.

'Water! Water! Water! Water!' The chant came up from the crewmen sitting out.

1 And they had 'water', Pedlar could see past the genoa now . . . Hoff and his crew, he saw, spinning round, surprised.

'Water! Water!'

The Yanks gave water.

And beyond them the white sails, the pack of ivory cards shuffling into the one good hand.

Douggie the Kiwi, barging his way through, was caught. The Canadians caught him, bulging the line with the tide, forced him over.

Then they too went over. Early.

Because then came the bang of the start-gun.

Then the second bang, recalling Douggie and Canadians.

And then Hoff the Yank, still legal but looking two ways at once, joined the snarl-up.

Shouts and screams from the yachts. Collision. A Bermudan skipper, Pedlar saw, swimming after his boat with a broken arm.

And *Havoc* was through.

Sudden silence. A line of sails in the haze to left and right. Long line, calm now, kicking just a little. White veined canvas dwindling down to confetti white.

Space too, because of the tangle that was behind them. Space to find clear air. Space to see the yachts down-line that had found a hole in the wind, and to keep well away from it.

The fleet settled. The big-rating yachts went away of course, the yachts that would be pulled back later on handicap. The big Frenchman stole two hundred yards, and tacked as soon as the big Irishman tacked behind him. There was a glint of fire from his spreaders as he crossed the path of the sun.

Pedlar's race was a different race, with the middle-raters. He couldn't tack yet, couldn't yet lay the first mark that was far off, hidden in the haze. But he knew he had to put in the tack as early as possible, steal as many degrees as possible to windward.

On the shining surface of the sea they entered that grey area of calculation. Ronnie kept producing figures from his hatchway. Monroe kept taking bearings on other yachts with a hand-compass. And then he said, 'You're looking good on the leading Yank. Move when you're ready.'

Pedlar called it, and they went about onto the port tack. Everybody sat out on the port rail then, everybody that was except for Monroe and the winch-man on the genoa sheet. They sat as far aft as possible, keeping the weight back, the spray pattering on their oilskins. And there was silence again. Nobody said anything to Pedlar, not a word.

Crouching at the helm, he felt the boat and the sea. He felt the hiss and rise of the waves, and the crash and rise of the bigger waves. Then he began to see the bigger waves coming and he pinched in to meet them. And he saw more . . . The patter out on the water that was a gust, the different shape to the waves that was a hole in the wind . . . The creasing of the genoa just before it lifted to spoil the wind-slot. The 'tell-tale' ribbons on each side of the sail that had to stream out without touching the canvas . . . The instruments, wind-direction, boatspeed, and compass . . .

All these things he saw at one and the same time, though his thinking brain told him that was impossible. But it wasn't his thinking brain he was using. It was balance, it was forestalling the changes, it was pinching more in the gusts and laying off more in the lulls. It was hearing Monroe playing hydraulics and sails behind him. Hearing the winch-clicks as the sheetman moved at Monroe's command. It was feeling wind and water on his cheek, crouching till cramp set in. And being part of the spray, of that sun-frosted day.

Knowledge came into it too somewhere. Knowing that a six-knot tide was running with him over this part of the water. Knowing that the Solent, that great basin underneath him, was still filling, and that holes of wind could lie out in its centre at high water . . . Knowledge, but mainly instinct, as he did two things – tried to make a knot more boatspeed than anyone had the right to expect – and tried to claw the boat little by little to windward.

The first to justify his place in the British team. To be able to pull clear of the other middle-rated yachts.

And the second to be able to lay the mark that was still far off in the haze. To make sure that the final starboard tack down to it was as short, as controllable, and as safe as possible.

Because – there was no getting away from it – at the first mark of an Admiral's Cup race a few years back, a helmsman had died of a heart-attack.

Just for a moment, nearing the end of that first leg, Pedlar allowed himself to think of the size and power of the boat he was trying to control. A yacht of almost two tons, canted over, crashing through the spray under full mainsail and genoa . . . While ahead now was the mark, the tall rusting metal buoy. And beyond it, close, far too damn close, was the spectator fleet, being shouted at by *Ocean One* to move back. A village of boats there on the water. About half of them in the way if anything went wrong.

And there to his left was the line of big-rating yachts, careering in on port tack. While Pedlar again was about to try the starboard manoeuvre.

Monroe was taking bearings. 'Okay,' he said.

'Ready about,' Pedlar called.

Foredeck gorillas, grinder-men and tailers took up positions.

'Go!' Pedlar called.

They came about. Stan hauling the leech of the genoa round the mast. Grinder-men screaming home the sheet.

And now they were slicing straight in towards the line of yachts.

Okay, fine, Pedlar thought, fine to play dinghies back at the startline, to throw the big yacht about. But here, at speed, coming diagonally in across the big-raters, and with the crush of spectator boats beyond them. Here was where it all counted. Only Stan was for'ard of the mast now, hooking the spinnaker to its halyard and sheets. Only Stan. And the reason was simple – one man out on the foredeck took off one knot of boatspeed, two men two knots. You put them out there as late as possible, a hundred yards away, eighty yards away. It was like outbraking race-cars into a corner. Except that here the cars were coming across you on another track.

Eighty yards. Pedlar called. Men moved. Charlie rigged the spinnaker pole. Aft in the cockpit sheetmen waited.

Monroe, at Pedlar's shoulder, was measuring by eye. 'Get in before the big Eyeteye,' he said. 'No pissing about. You can take him where it's still legal.'

Legal meant over two boat-lengths from the mark itself. Legal meant calling for 'water' at that distance. And getting it.

Provided nobody lost their nerve.

Pedlar took her in. In to the crash of surf. *Havoc* he inserted at right-angles into a fleet coming hair-raisingly fast. 'Water! Water!' was again the shout. *And* the rest, the words you'd expect.

They cut in front of the Eyeteye. Screams. And that bow knifing straight at them for a long second. Just fucking frightening that bow, Pedlar thought. And then he bellowed, '*Go!*'

A lot of men ran. A lot of things happened as the boat

swung out and round that mark. The spinnaker, a snake of coloured cloth, darted up outside the white genoa, visible through it like a shadow play. Then the snake burst the rubber bands that held it, and gushed out to become a vast balloon of colour. Only for a second, that was. Because *Havoc* caught dirty air, and the balloon threatened to collapse. But sheet and pole caught it. The spinnaker filled again, and kicked the boat away from the spectator fleet to safety.

Almost at the same moment the big white genoa came down. Stan and Charlie threw themselves on it, gorilla-fought and clawed at the cloth, bunching it aft to the sail-hatch behind them. Wind caught a fold. Charlie was lifted, almost to the side, but held on. If the sail had hit water, had 'trawled', they'd have lost speed.

Men came aft. The deck was clear. Ronnie gave a course that would take them in towards the island and the better tide there. Other people were taking the same course, Pedlar saw, the fleet was splitting in two. A Malay boat he saw just behind him to his considerable surprise. Well, the bugger had got lucky on the first leg and now was following one of the local boats. Some did that. Some just tagged on – and got lost in the tricky tides inshore.

A simpler leg now, downwind. A different feel to the boat, and for the helmsman less to do. Monroe was now beside him, playing the spinnaker sheet delicately like a fly fisherman. And Pedlar took the chance to glance back.

A rusty metal buoy in the water. Sunlight, spectator boats, and, when seen from this distance, a file of racing yachts coming calmly in. Just as calmly, it seemed, they swapped white headsail for coloured spinnaker, and went round. Blue sky, Pedlar saw, blue water and a summer's day.

But he was still shaking, still seeing the bow of that big Eyeteye yacht coming at him, still seeing the things that could have gone wrong. But they hadn't. Racing at this level meant an absolute trust in other people – absolute. In race-car terms it meant twelve different feet on the accelerator or brake-pedal. And it was this sort of tension, this sort of expertise that Pedlar couldn't turn his back on. It was given to very few yachtsmen in the world, he knew. And he knew too that he, Michael Pedlar, was now part of their number.

23

At around six-thirty that evening the sun began to dip towards the Groves & Guttridge sheds. Between the 555 and Mumm's mobile bars the shadows began to lengthen. And a thick crowd of crewmen stood there, sucking at cold lager cans after a day spent on dry boats. Then they turned and looked up at the Admiral's Cup scoreboard, high in the sunlight above them, as the day's results were posted.

After one race the Aussies were in the lead, it seemed; their yachts finishing third, eleventh, and nineteenth. The Yanks were second, Hoff having made up time after a bad start. And the Brits were third, Pedlar making his contribution there with a good twelfth place.

But the big surprise came lower down in the order.

The Malaysian team had come in sixth.

A great many people, looking up at the scoreboard, began to put one or two things together . . . The Malaysian team's sudden switch from Skyline to Banting's Sails . . . Banting's, who were one of the big American superlofts . . . And finally the rumours that had been flying around, of American hotshot crewmen being seen in Cowes.

Questions were asked. It was discovered that the Malaysian skippers weren't as advertised on the race-programme. Each of the Malay yachts, it was discovered, had three Californian hotshots on board . . . Banting's employees . . . sailing as helmsman, tactician, and navigator.

On the whole people took this in good part. It was agreed that some of the finest sailing men in the world came from California. And maybe it was a shame that only three United States crews could represent their country in the Admiral's Cup . . . Okay, so the Malaysian team was now christened the American 'B' Team. The three Malaysian skippers were christened *Datuk* Rod Newbolt, *Datuk* Bill Liebermann, and *Datuk* Lew Lutowski. These gentlemen were later found in the bar of the Three Crowns. They were asked how much they were being paid in this, the most amateur of amateur sports. They grinned fatcat grins, sat on fat back pockets and replied that, like the rest of the Malay crews, they were getting by on a handful of rice a day.

The three gentlemen bought a great many drinks as the pub filled up. Good humour prevailed. If a Malay called Kalicheean wanted to give a few Yanks a good sail in a good race, where was the harm in it? A couple of hotshots on a boat couldn't work miracles with a learner crew. The Malays were never going to climb higher than sixth place.

The Admiral's Cup continued. There was racing again the next morning. And, as was to be expected with a fleet of fifty-seven yachts, a few injuries showed up. Crewmen appeared with legs or arms in plaster, and were replaced by substitutes.

But then it was seen that the Malay team was having more than its fair share of injuries and substitutions. It was seen that on each Malay boat there were suddenly six Californian hotshots . . . all of them Banting's men . . . sailing as helmsman, tactician, navigator, two foredeck gorillas, and a cockpit boss . . . It was seen that all the Malays had to do, in fact, was to turn a winch-handle when they were told, or lean over the boat's side when they were told.

Evening came round again. The sun dipped towards the Groves & Guttridge sheds. The racing results were posted again on the Admiral's Cup scoreboard. And good humour vanished . . . Okay, the Aussies were still leading, and the Brits had now moved up to second place. But the Malaysians, or American 'B' Team, were now third, beating the official American team by nine clear points.

Good humour vanished from the faces of the race-organisers too. Because at the same time as the scoreboard was changed, something else happened out in the marina. A sail was hoisted. It rose above the deck of Kalicheean's yacht, and on it the word KALO gleamed huge and golden in the sunlight. KALO too was written on the caps of the Malay/American team who squatted below it. KALO was across the slinky silver catsuits worn by Kalicheean's six model-girls. And across the white shirt of the smiling Malaysian businessman himself.

The camera-call was for six-thirty. A specially chartered hydrofoil had brought pressmen across from the mainland. They had each been given a promotional pack, compliments of Kalo, the company who made a quarter of the golf-grips in the world. But this the pressmen ignored. They were here only for pictures – of the Oriental who looked set to beat the teams of the Western world at their own game.

Pedlar sat with Helmut Prinzheim in the oak-panelled bar of the Surrey Club.

'The pity of it is, it's all legal,' Pedlar said. 'In harbour the man's allowed to hoist what sails he likes. It's only between start and finishing-gun that he's not allowed to advertise.'

'And his crews are quite legal too,' the Swiss said in that precise way of his. 'The rule-book clearly states that an entrant must have a crew composed of fifty per cent of his country's nationals. The other fifty per cent can come from wherever he wants.'

'Which, as I don't need to remind you, Helmut, was a rule designed to help the smaller countries like yours. Or Bermuda, or Hong Kong.'

Prinzheim nodded.

'But,' Pedlar went on, 'what nobody in their right mind imagined was that one man would enter an entire team. Three yachts loaded down with foreign nationals. The problem is the *scale* of the thing.'

'No, the problem is different. It's a corner being turned. Commercialism coming into yacht-racing,' Prinzheim said. 'Kalicheean, don't forget, heads a vast business corporation. Our sport is about to go the way of all the others.'

'But will it? Can the man get away with it?'

'In purely racing terms, he can,' Prinzheim replied. 'His yachts are brand-new, among the best there are. Two of them are sister-ships of other yachts in the fleet . . . And nowadays, these hotshot crews, as they're called, can drop onto a good boat at almost a day's notice, and . . .'

'Win?' Pedlar asked. 'Were you going to say win?'

There was silence between them.

'I'm not sure,' Prinzheim said then. 'All I feel is that this state of affairs has been coming for a long while.'

'How d'you mean?'

'Michael,' Prinzheim leaned forward, 'people always ask if money wins yacht-races, on't they? And we always say no. We say that perhaps we spend a certain amount on boats and sails, but money doesn't win. Good crews win.'

'And now,' Pedlar said, 'money buys good crews.'

'Suddenly, yes, over the past season or so.' Prinzheim nodded. 'Last season, for example, I bought my new yacht *Tamburlaine*. A yacht which I found so complicated in the matters of hydraulics and sail-changes, that I needed two professionals on board to help me.'

'Well, everybody's the same, aren't they?' Pedlar asked. 'I mean, if they're honest about it?'

'Precisely . . . I don't make any secret of the fact that I have two Englishmen on board, one from a rigger's yard, and one from your sail-loft, Skyline. You have two men from Skyline . . . The Americans, the Germans, the Australians have professionals from their countries. Usually between two and three men.'

'But not six,' Pedlar said. 'Or, let's face it, eighteen men in one team. Eighteen of thc world's best.'

'Agreed. But to return to my yacht *Tamburlaine*,' Prinzheim said. 'When I launched her I experienced that pride . . . you must know it well . . . of looking at a boat that is beautiful because it is almost perfect. That deep shine of a racing yacht's hull. That shape that makes of the water a single curving wave. And then, when I sailed her, I felt the excitement that you know well too. Except that it was not like the excitement of other years. It was less. Because there were two professionals on board who knew more about their chosen field than I did.'

'What?' Pedlar frowned. 'What on earth's wrong with that?'

'Simple. I can see that the next boat I order from the yard will need three professionals. The next, four . . . In fact I can see a time when I will have to remove myself from the yacht altogether and follow it in a motor boat, like the man Kalicheean.'

'Helmut, you're getting old.' Pedlar stood up.

'Perhaps.'

'This division of labour of yours doesn't worry me at all,' Pedlar told him. 'I like experts around me, always have . . . No, what worries me is something else altogether.'

'What's that?'

'The thing I mentioned to you just now . . . Winning . . . Knocking the hell out of a commercially entered team.'

'Of course. Winning. How very British.'

Pedlar smiled and left him. But, walking out of the club, the memory of another conversation came back. The time he'd talked with Monroe, when they'd motored in towards Lymington in the rub-a-dub.

Winning, Pedlar had said. *That's what it's all about. I didn't come all this way for anything less.*

All this way, man? Monroe had asked. *What are you talking about? Your house is only a couple of miles out of the town here.*
But Monroe had misunderstood.
Pedlar had come a long way. An awful long way.
Lyness knew all about that.
And so did one or two others.

24

Wyatt, the hunter, was on a cold trail. For the past two days – race-days – Pedlar had followed the same routine. He'd jogged with his crew in the early morning, gone out to sea with them by nine-thirty. He'd raced, spent the evening in a huddle with the rest of the British Team, or worked out tactics with Monroe.

And Wyatt was not one step nearer finding out what made the man tick.

Two days ago he'd thought he had been. Because then at midday Jackman had rung. 'Ace,' he'd said, 'I got another bit of news.'

'What's that?'

'Well, you remember me tellin' you about some guys once before? Guys recently arrived in the country? Wearin' suits and knowin' which knife and fork to pick up?'

'Yes.'

'The word is they talk Frog, Ace.'

'What d'you mean? Corsican Frog?'

'There int nobody can tell that exactly, but it don't make no difference. What it is, Ace, they operate on the French mainland, but they're part of an organisation that's much bigger. Transport. They run this direct route across France from one end to the other. Regular shipments. Contract work.'

And Wyatt had only to think for a moment. 'France,' he'd said. 'France being between where we are now and Corsica.'

'You got it.'

'So there's traffic. But which way's it go? Into this country? Or the other way, out to Corsica?'

'In, Ace, it comes in. Nobody picks up the Queen's Award For Exportin' nowadays, not so far as I've heard.'

'All right then, is there anything else you've heard, Jacko?'

'No, I just give you all I got. But it could be enough, couldn't it? There could be somethin' there you could make stick.'

But there hadn't been. Because last night Wyatt had gone into the Three Crowns, the pub the crews used. And there he'd found the young man from Skyline Sails, Chas . . . Wyatt had bought him a drink, talked of this and that, and gradually moved the conversation round to Corsica. In particular any shipments made out to the island or back by Michael Pedlar.

There'd been just the one, at the time of Calvi Week. Pedlar had sent *Cry Havoc* out to Corsica by container. Once there, the container had been left on the dock and used as a workshop between races. Then it had been brought back at the end of the Week. And it had been just the one return-trip. Nothing since. Nothing like the regular shipments Jackman had talked about, the contract work.

Dead end, and Wyatt hadn't been able to get any more news out of Chas. Because at that moment Californians had come into the pub, members of the famous American 'B' Team. Talk had started. Then it had become more than talk. In the end the fight had only been prevented by a group of Australians buying a huge round of drinks at the bar. 'Come along now, girls. A pint of Pommy piss. Drink up, girls.'

Tonight at roughly the same time, nine o'clock, Wyatt was once again in the Three Crowns. To find all the crews had gone. They were away in their quarters, it seemed, getting in an early night. More, they were going to be away now for the best part of three days. Because tomorrow was going to see the start of the next event in the Admiral's Cup Series . . . the two hundred and twenty mile course that made up the Channel Race.

It should have come as no surprise to Wyatt that with the going of the Admiral's Cuppers, the town would change. That for the next week of the year – Cowes Week – it would be given over to the people who'd made it what it was. But even so he was surprised by the speed at which it happened.

Earlier this evening the Royal Yacht *Britannia* had anchored out in the roads. The sound of twenty-one guns had boomed out from the shore. And a naval cutter had appeared, bringing a tall man to the Squadron steps. A man who wore a blazer, who talked to people quietly, and as often as not made them laugh.

As if by magic those twenty-one guns changed the sound of the streets. Because now suddenly the accents of the world – Yank,

Kiwi, Belgian, Japanese and Strine – were gone. In their place was a different accent. And a different uniform – men in blazers and women in Guernsey sweaters.

During his days of flying an air-taxi around Europe, Wyatt had tangled with the English upper classes at times. And in truth he rather admired them. In his experience they were mean with money. They dressed badly. They didn't exactly disfigure themselves with water. And far from starting two drinks behind the rest of the world, they were at least four ahead. There was a lunatic rage about them that he liked . . . how to explain it? . . . Where had he read that you couldn't understand the English gentry without understanding cold mutton and draughts?

But with the gentry too there were always the other kind. The kind who were the imitators, who made themselves felt, or rather *heard*. It only needed a dozen or so of them in a roomful of people to take over. . . . And this evening there were just such a dozen, standing next to Wyatt in the bar of the Three Crowns. Only in loud voices they changed its name to the Three Crines. They looked the bar-menu up and down and said, nay actually, they'd have the smaked trite.

Wyatt was trapped in their centre. And it wasn't the loudness that got to him so much, nor the exaggeration. Just the precision of the words, the self-conscious precision, never a stray vowel. It was ya for yes, nay for no, and vey for very. It was gorn for gone, and rind for round. It was villidge but never village, garage but never garridge. . . . Dear God, Wyatt thought, Father, Son, and Haley Gaste.

He sat lower and lower on his bar-stool, and his irritation grew. Really, he told himself, he had nothing against these people. It was just that he'd reached a dead end. The trail he'd been following, cold as it was, was now obscured by different trails. Nor was there any chance of picking it up again before Michael Pedlar returned from the Channel Race.

Wyatt finished his drink and came to a decision. It was time to quit this town and try elsewhere . . . Jackman's house, for example, he was going to put his foot in Jackman's door again. Somehow he was going to talk his way past the man's wife. And somehow find out more about certain men in suits, recently arrived from France.

Putting down his glass, he left the Three Crowns. He walked down the High Street in the flicker of headlights, the press of people. And he was just making for the Cross Keys to pick up his suitcase . . . when somebody tapped him on the shoulder.

'Hallay,' a dark-haired girl said. '*Orfly* nice.'

Wyatt looked down at her. The long face, the tousled hair, the nicotined fingers. Girl or woman, impossible to tell which.

'Daint you remembah?'

'No,' Wyatt said. But then, 'yes.' Because you didn't forget Alex that easily. Not when you'd last seen her on Jackman's boat, taking out her left breast, looking at it and saying it was ten past nine.

'Came here to meet you, ac-tu-ally,' she said. 'Found you *rather* easily.'

'You're here to meet me?'

'Ye-es. Hape I've gort it right.' She nodded. 'Last week was Let's Be Bloody To Christopher Week, far as I can remembah . . .'

'Christopher?'

'Some man.' She flapped a hand. 'Oh, somewhere.'

'And this week?'

'This week,' she said, 'is Let's Find Jack Douglas Week . . . Jack Douglas, not-his-real-name, from Switzerland, not-his-real-address.'

She pulled herself up and kissed his mouth. He tasted spirits.

'Bit pissed,' she said, 'as usual. Sorry.'

He didn't answer.

'Point is,' she went on, 'found you *rather* easily as I said. Reason's quite simple. You're the ainly man in this bloody tine wearing a leather jacket.'

And he was, Wyatt suddenly realised. It was the jacket that Jackman had brought for him, a long time ago now it seemed, on the morning he'd left the clinic.

Alex was watching him closely. 'Vey bad move,' she said, 'walking rind like that. Vey conspicuous . . . For a man, that is, who used to fly parcels of knocked-orf money for Jackman. In the good old Borny and Clyde days.'

Wyatt stood quite still. Headlights passed him, and the shuffle of people on the pavement.

'Bit of a bosh-up really, the leather jacket,' she said.

'Will you stop all that stuff?' he asked her.

'What? Abite Jackman? The flying and the money?'

'No, the bosh-up stuff. All that rubbish. You didn't talk like that the last time we met.'

'Sorry,' she said in her normal voice. 'It's this bloody tine, I mean town . . . But I think you should get rid of the leather jacket, don't you? Seeing as how you used to rob banks?'

His mind racing, he allowed himself to be led over to a shop. It was a men's outfitters, still open, still brightly lit. Inside he stood in front of a mirror and tried on the two dark blue blazers that an assistant found for him.

Alex decided on the second one. She did it from close range, smoothing the material over his shoulder and down the line of his sleeve. Then she found his right hand. He let it go limp as she raised it for inspection, touching the scar where his thumb had been.

And he knew what she was then. Years back with Jackman there'd been one or two around like her, society girls who found the East End irresistible. Boxers and villains they found irresistible, particularly with the sweat on them after work.

Wyatt's mind was still racing, and still getting nowhere. He realised Jackman must have talked about the old days. Jackman who never talked, who was like a stone when it came to giving out information. So why . . . ?

The assistant went away for a moment. Alex turned back to Wyatt and caught him unawares. 'I heard you were quite a wild boy at one time,' she said. 'Jackman told me you were quite a wild boy. Is that right? I mean, did you ever kill for him?'

'No,' Wyatt said.

But she was searching his face. And she was sharp, very sharp. 'You've killed,' she said . . . And then, in a louder voice, as the assistant came back, 'We'll take the one he's wearing. And will you wrap the leather jacket?'

Wyatt emptied its pockets and watched the jacket being wrapped in tissue and put in a carrier bag . . . Jackman had to have a reason, he thought, to throw this girl at him. *Had* to. Everything the man did was planned.

The assistant came back with the carrier and a written out bill. Wyatt paid. Then he turned to Alex. She was looking at her watch.

'It's getting late,' she said. 'Shall we gird up our bollocks and eat?'

The restaurants they passed were packed, with queues waiting just inside the doors. But there were other places, Wyatt saw now. Between the old dark buildings of the High Street there were striped canvas tunnels, lit up, and leading to shouting marquees. Two of them, Juliana's Disco and the Press Tent, he remembered seeing before, unlit, on his first evening in the town.

Now Alex led him to a third. It was at the end of one of the narrow alleys that went down to the waterfront. There was an entrance that said Island Sailing Club, and a man on guard there turning away non-members. Alex had club-badges. She took Wyatt on down a slope to a glowing marquee. It seemed to be pitched on a concrete hard above a jetty. Because there was water on two of its sides. And beyond, alongside the jetty, a line of small boats moored.

They went into the tent. It was brightly lit, the tables were crowded, but there was no queue at the food counter. Alex piled her plate with rare beef and salad, she piled her glass with brandies. Then he followed her outside with a tray. They sat on the jetty. The noise of the marquee and its glow were behind them, the water black at their feet. Alex ate quickly, her mouth close to her plate, and drank quickly too. She said nothing until she'd finished, then she stood up. 'How d'you feel about walking a girl home?'

'Where's home?'

She pointed up above the bright candy-stripes of the marquee, and above those other marquees that wound caterpillar-like among the dark houses. 'Up there,' she said, 'on the hill.'

It was a street of Georgian houses that looked down on the far side of the town, on the Squadron lawn and the dark Solent. Alex, a little ahead of Wyatt, stopped by the pillars of a cream-painted porch. She found her keys. Then she shrugged out of her clothes, all of them, and let them fall to the pavement. 'Will you come in for coffee?'

25

The kitchen had a high ceiling. There was the smell of old wooden draining-boards and old wooden plate-racks. There was a big unlit Aga, and above it, hanging from the ceiling, one of those long clothes-airers that was raised or lowered by a double rope.

Alex put a whistling kettle on an electric ring. She found coffee and sugar, and then her nakedness was lit as she opened the fridge door and found milk. It was a woman's body not a girl's, Wyatt decided, a woman of about twenty-five, with two folds of skin appearing suddenly over a thin belly as she leaned forward.

The kettle whistled. She made coffee and handed him a cup. Then she led the way out to the hall. They passed a dining-room with a polished mahogany table and chairs. On one of them was a pair of oilskins and a sailing bag.

'Those yours, or is anyone else here?' Wyatt asked. 'Maybe I should know.'

'There's a girl, and a boy-friend of hers. Friends of friends,' she said vaguely. 'Only they've been in when I've been out, and out when I've been in. I haven't the foggiest who they are.'

He followed her white body and the black soles of her feet up the stairs. She led him past a first landing to a second, then down a corridor that got longer as the ceiling got lower.

'My father always bought houses with long passages,' she said, 'so that children could play in them.'

Finally there was a door she pushed open and a light she switched on. Inside was a bedroom that had pale colours. Wyatt couldn't have said what the wallpaper was, or the material of the curtains. But it was a young girl's room, with a young girl's collection of beach-stones and shells. And the lightweight case that lay open on the floor was a much later invasion, years later, now.

She kicked the case shut. She sat on the bed and patted the eiderdown for him to sit beside her. He did so. She sipped at her coffee, then got up suddenly and switched off the light. Returning to the bed, she spoke softly. 'This killing you did . . . Tell me about it.'

Wyatt had been expecting that, and he'd been expecting to lie. Now he didn't know if he could. 'It was just a thing that happened,' he said.

'What sort of thing?'

'It got me waking up at nights for months afterwards,' he said. 'In the end I tried not to sleep.'

'Why?'

'You don't want to know.'

'Yes, I do.'

Wyatt was silent for a moment. 'All right,' he said then. 'I was doing a run for Jackman, and it was late on in the game. By that I mean, people were beginning to get the message about us.'

'People?'

'The Law. That kind of people.'

'Oh.'

'Anyway, on this particular trip I wasn't taking the money directly into Switzerland, but to a field in France, not far from the Swiss border. And I was using a plane that was new to me too, an Auster, high wing, fixed undercarriage.'

'What's the significance of the wing and undercarriage?' she asked.

He ignored her. 'I found the field I was making for, circled it, and everything was normal. I landed, got out of the plane, and it was then they came at me, police and cars, just like the movies. So I got back in the plane and started up, but one of these people managed to get the passenger door open. I slammed it shut. He was bounced away. There were cars and all hell coming at me by this time, and I took the plane away fast . . . It was only when I was getting up in the air that I knew the weight was wrong. He was still there, this guy, hanging on to the undercart.'

She no longer sipped at her coffee.

'Even if the Law hadn't been back at the field, I couldn't've landed. Anywhere, I mean. The way this guy was hanging from the wheel-strut, landing would've killed him . . . I flew. I tried to set the plane up so that I could get across to his side, get the door open, and maybe reach out for him. But every time I got that damn door open, the plane flipped out of control. Twice we nearly started the spin that would've killed us both.'

He paused. 'Oh, he turned blue slowly, his hands and then his face. He unhitched his belt and got it round the strut, got it buckled again. He took off his tie and knotted it round one wrist. I . . . I flew the plane. He got bluer and bluer. Then the cold took his strength away. The belt slipped right up past his elbows. He was just hanging by that knotted tie round his wrist.

'An . . . an old plane, an Auster, with no auto,' he went on. 'Jesus, by this time I was trying to fly the bloody thing with one foot while I reached out for him. Crazy, because we dived and he fell. I could see his face every time he turned over. Then he went into the mist.'

She put down her cup and his. She took his right hand, his right hand where the scar was, and he thought, so fucking help me, this one's weird and I'm scared.

But it was a mistake, the right hand. She dropped it immediately and found the left, holding it and waiting. He breathed out a long slow sigh of relief. All along he'd seen her as a person doing the opposite of what was expected, a person kicking out in all directions, but mostly at her own kind. Once or twice he'd seen her pale unmade-up face as young, very young. Once even the image had come to him, he didn't know from where, of a choirboy going into a cathedral alone and lighting a cigarette, watching the column of smoke rising to the high vaulting above.

There was no more talking as they lay together now on the narrow bed. Maybe it would have helped if there had been. Because the thing wasn't a success. He had the impression that her body was separate from her, that she'd used it too often as a tool. She gave him caresses that must have worked for previous men. Then she made movements pleasing herself alone. Finally, and by far the worst, she made her body neutral, like a blank key.

When it was over, or half over, or what the hell over it was, they lay side by side awkwardly. 'Don't for Christ's sake give me a progress report,' she said.

'I won't.'

'The way I carried on this evening, I was surprised you stayed with me,' she said. 'Even more surprised when you walked me back here.'

He nodded.

Though he wasn't. Surprised, that was. Not now, not by anything. He understood why Jackman had talked, why he'd let those few facts slip out about the old days. Why in fact he'd given the girl a taster he knew she wouldn't be able to resist.

Wyatt sat up. Beyond Alex the room began to take shape in the light from the street outside. And it was a street Wyatt knew, he'd been here once before. The house opposite belonged to Michael Pedlar, a man who'd been coming here summer after summer. Just as this girl had, judging by the collection of beach-stones and shells in her room.

So she would know Pedlar. And Jackman would know she knew him. Jackman who did nothing that wasn't planned.

He woke, late and suddenly, to the bang of a gun. He got to his feet. The gun had been outside the window, a starting gun. Sails were going away across the Solent.

Wyatt looked round. He was stiff, he'd slept on the floor. But the bed, he saw now, was empty. Finding his clothes, and the new blazer, he dressed. There was a bathroom with cold water that didn't want to turn hot. And then there were the three floors of the house, rambling, with passages darting up and down between different levels . . . which he searched, looking for Alex.

He found her on a small square roof, sitting in the sun and watching the sails. He sat beside her. There was a puff of white smoke from the Squadron below, and then another bang. It was the Channel Race, he knew that. And he knew too that of the hundred-and-fifty or so yachts starting, the Admiral's Cuppers were bringing up the rear. Theirs was a private race in a large fleet. They would start last and finish first.

After last night it was a relief to feel the warm sun and say nothing. To watch the Cuppers now as they fought and darted for position behind the line. And then, as the cannon boomed again, cross. It was a downwind start in a good breeze. The fleet fanned out, setting tallboys and bloopers as well as spinnakers. And in no time at all, it seemed, the sails were gone. The Solent stretching blue and empty to the mainland shore.

Talk was necessary then, but Alex didn't look at him as she spoke. 'About breakfast, I don't know if there's any food in the house.'

'Okay, I'll go shopping,' he said. 'And it's nearly twelve, so which d'you want? Breakfast or lunch?'

'Whichever.'

He bought lunch. In a good delicatessen in the High Street he found cheese and warm bread. He found peaches and grapes next door. And in a wine-merchant's he took two bottles of Mumm's from the shelf, then made it three.

She saw the champagne as he brought it up onto the roof in an enamel basin with ice, and left it in the shade.

'What's this?' she asked. 'Trying to improve on last night? One-point-eight or whatever it was on the Richter Scale?'

'No,' he said.

'Then it's Drake's Prayer.' She sighed. 'The continuing of the same until it be thoroughly finished.'

'Look,' he said, 'it's a sunny day and it's warm, and there's wine.'

26

The light was grey out in the Channel, with occasional smears of sun towards the West. Blue water was now grey too, the calm of the Solent giving way to that longer rearing feeling of the sea. And the wind was backing, with the promise of storms and thundery rain.

Pedlar was at the wheel. He was staying there till the first mark at Poole Fairway. It was important to him, important to treat an offshore like an inshore race. The crew would be sitting out long hours in the spray. And when those off-watch slept below, they would be moved from port to starboard bunks at the change of tack. Every movement, every yard of water gained, counted.

Because there'd been mistakes. In the boiling surf of the Shingles they'd ridden tight as they could to Hurst Point. The beach had been within spitting distance, and they'd had sails collapse in the chop of water there. Boats around them had pulled away.

Across the deep water to Poole, the wind had been north-east, five to six. Blooper and tallboy had come down, and the Double Star reaching chute had been set. Set shy, and other spinnakers they could see were in the same curving shell. Those ahead luminous against the fading sun, those astern with an onion-skin sheen to them against grey clouds . . . And there were a lot of Cuppers astern now . . . Including the Malay boats, Pedlar was glad to see. That famous Double Star chute was giving *Havoc* speed. Waves were beginning to bunch up and hiss under the hull.

At Poole there was only time to glance at the crumbling chalk cliffs. In seas that were tight and lumpish now, the entire fleet of smaller classes seemed to have come together. Maybe ninety, maybe a hundred yachts were trying to round the mark at the same time as *Havoc*. 'On through,' Pedlar called out to Hal the bowman, 'as if they weren't there.'

'As if they weren't there,' Hal repeated.

Most knew there was an Admiral's Cup race on. Most got out of the way. But in slapping grey waves where bows were pointing to sky one moment, rudder to sky the next, there was a coming together of boats. The dull crash of hull against hull. The harness jingle of spars and rigging at impact.

Havoc was lucky. Pedlar hit no-one, saw no protest flags hoisted, and then took the run of the sea on the beam. The spinnaker was handed. The genny shrieked up and was sheeted in. Pedlar left the wheel, stiff and beginning to see flash-dots from concentrating so long. He made his way up the sloping deck to where the crew were sitting out. And for the first time saw the bigger picture of sky and sea.

There were grey rain-squalls, he saw, out to the east of them. They were gathering, darkening. Even now he thought he could see where the storm-head would appear. And even now feel the hesitation from both *Havoc* and helmsman about the course.

He went below. He pulled down one of the port bunks and lay on it, his cheek against cold canvas. He didn't sleep. He knew the boat too well. Every change of sound or motion alarmed him. Everything was wrong with course and sails. They were losing boatspeed.

Then from above he heard Monroe's voice. 'No, come round. Head round. Steer one-three-five.'

And Pedlar knew. The storm-head was forming.

That old cry, head for the big winds, the boatspeed. 'Steer for the black cloud.'

27

Maybe it was the champagne. Maybe they'd drunk too much on that small square roof. But the light at Cowes had changed. It seemed grey and metallic, as if through tinted glass.

Other things had changed too. The yacht-races were going off in a different direction from this morning. There were many classes, Cowes Week classes, of small two- and three-man yachts. And, starting close by the Squadron, they seemed to appear from the rooftops below. The boom of the cannon got each race away. Each was a white line tacking out across the Solent, then thickening to a white square. To be followed by another white square, and another. Merging together like folds of paper leaving the town.

And this had to be the champagne . . . It seemed to Wyatt that the folds of paper were like those coming out of a hurdy-gurdy. Each new bang of the cannon pushing out another fold. And the organ was the town below him, its pump and rasp the pump and rasp of parties.

While singing the words of the song was the girl, Alex, lying on the roof beside him.

Strange words.

'That boom of the cannon,' she said. 'I remember it every year. One year, I remember, I was walking on the beach with my mother, though she never walked me as a rule. Anyway I was dawdling, lagging further behind, and she was getting angry. Suddenly she turned to me and said, "You're plain. You're the plainest thing I ever saw." . . . I lagged further behind. Tears ran down my cheeks, and I saw this dead fish on the sand. I picked it up and stroked it all the way home.'

Another boom, another verse.

'There were nannies. Lots of nannies. One of them I remember when I was catching 'flu or something, when I was feverish. Anyway I spilt my hot milk. The cup and saucer I was holding seemed to be spinning round in circles. And this nanny said, "I know a foolish girl who's pretending to be ill." . . . Years later we had to go and see her when she was old. No more than old. She had fits and had to be strapped in bed. And I can remember thinking, now I can hold her nose and make her drink hot milk. But I didn't.'

Another verse.

'It's very different now. When I was young, the house in Scotland was very big. It had old lino and old paintwork, all kept beautifully clean by servants. Now people don't have servants. They just keep having new. New wallpaper and new paint. It seems very important to them, this paper and paint. But I don't trust anything a sixteenth of an inch thick. I don't trust people a sixteenth of an inch thick . . . It's as if I'm stateless now.'

Another verse, with a smile.

'To give you an example of this stateless business . . . I was told that my father ate meat and potatoes, never any vegetables. . . . And the first man who ever took me out in London ordered broccoli. I thought he was queer, and I never saw him again. This happened quite a lot.'

Another verse, with a sad smile.

'I never knew my father really. And after the telegram came from the War Office, everything changed. The house in Scotland had to be sold. My mother had to learn to drive a car. And whenever she got to where she wanted to get, she always looked for some passer-by to park the car for her. She said it was perfectly ridiculous, you were never taught how to park in one of those little gaps, just reverse round corners.'

Another verse, with a much sadder smile.

'I told you about my mother saying that to me on the beach, didn't I? About me being plain? . . . I didn't really blame her. She was beautiful then, and she wasn't good with children, only with the outside world . . . Anyway I knew what she meant. That I looked like my father.'

'Your father?' Wyatt asked.

'She was angry with him because he'd got himself killed,' she said. 'We were only angry *because* he'd got killed. He was good with the inside world. But he was a soldier too . . . I was five when the telegram came. It had happened somewhere. Cyprus, Malaya, oh, I don't know where. I never bloody *listened* to where.'

She was crying, and at the same time leaning over and rubbing one fingertip on the lead of the roof. Then she showed it to him, a round circle of grey dust.

'*Mon vieux homme est un homme de poussière*,' she sang very softly. '*Il porte le chapeau d'un homme de poussière. Il a tué trois mille Allemands. Et qu'est-ce que tu penses de ça?*'

Maybe it was the champagne. Maybe they'd drunk too much. But maybe that was why things now became clear. About her. About what she needed from him. And what she gave.

It had been a long time, Wyatt told himself, and he'd forgotten beauty. Beauty had last crossed his path months ago, in an apartment looking down on Lake Luzern. And maybe it was a cold thing to say, but in his experience there were few women who were beautiful at first glance. While there were few women who were *not* beautiful at fiftieth glance, close to in bed . . . Yes, it was a cold thing to say. He stroked the soft white line of her neck that was suddenly warm. He stroked her shoulder-blade that was no longer sharp. And, hardly touching her, he stroked her eyelids while she slept.

Her beauty was calm, a calm she'd never shown him before. Perhaps, he thought, it wasn't going to last long. Perhaps it was the calm of a netted bird, exhausted while it slept. But when she awoke there was calm between them both now, as slowly they turned towards each other and began again.

Time was slow too. But it played tricks. There was, for example, the knock on the door, and a girl's voice saying, 'Alex, it's nine in the morning, and we're just going out sailing.'

And in the next second the same knock, the same girl's voice, 'Alex, it's seven in the evening, and we're going out to drinks.'

A night and a day had gone by, she told them.

28

The storms, the rain-squalls and the circling winds had come and gone. And now, returning to the lee of the English coast, the wind had slackened, north-east Three to Four.

Pedlar was on the canvas bunk again, not sleeping again. Two hours at the wheel, two hours off. And the deck-watches putting in two and four. They were all tired after thirty-five hours at sea.

The damn race they'd lost last night, at CH1, off the French coast. Suddenly there'd been light winds and calms there too. Only a dozen yachts had rounded the mark before the tide turned, slamming the gate against the rest of the fleet. *Havoc* had arrived an hour late. They'd dropped the kedge anchor. The lights of maybe fifty other yachts had drifted in with the tide then, and kedged too. An Aussie boat had laid up close. The Aussie crew had seen Stan the foredeck gorilla, crouched in pain, his leg splinted. Stan who'd gone up with a knife to free the heavy double-ply reacher in the darkness. And fallen.

'Only two things fall out of the sky,' the Aussies had called across the gap of water, 'birdshit and fools.'

Then more lights had come up – in convoy – the Malay Team.

. . . Now, twenty hours after CH1, Pedlar lay on the canvas bunk, knowing that one of the Malay boats had slipped through. And that a second had been tailing *Havoc* along the English coast, putting in tack for tack as they'd rounded the Owers, Nab, and Horse Sand. Was still there now as they were making for Gillicker and the finish of the race.

Pedlar was expecting Monroe's voice from the deck above. And it came. 'Somebody give a shake to the watch below,' he said. 'We'll be crossing the line in twenty minutes. It'll look better if the guv'nor's at the wheel.'

29

Alex turned to him. 'Now that we've been properly introduced,' she said, 'tell me something.'

'What's that?'

'You're using a fake name, and you've got this fake Swiss

address . . . What are you up to in Cowes?'

Wyatt had thought about this, thought about it a lot. And he'd come to the conclusion it would be better to tell her at least part of the truth.

'I'm looking around,' he told her.

'Why?'

'Because people pay me to look around,' he said. 'Nowadays, that is. Now that flying's given me up.' And briefly he pointed to his right hand with the missing thumb.

'You mean, that stops you flying?'

'Yes,' he lied. 'Doesn't look very good on the medical report.'

'I see.' She nodded. 'So what sort of people pay an ex-flyer to look around?'

'Industrial people. People maybe interested in a particular company.'

'A spy. An industrial spy.' She clapped her hands.

'No, just an investigator.'

'But why here?' she asked again. 'In Cowes?'

Which was the tricky part, the part he'd thought about most of all. . . But, he'd reasoned, Jackman had sent Alex to him. And he'd done that because she knew about Michael Pedlar.

'I'm doing a little nosing around a certain man,' he said. 'His name's Pedlar.'

He watched her carefully but she showed no alarm, just surprise.

'*Michael* Pedlar?' she asked. 'But, he's big, isn't he? I mean, in company terms, international? . . . Canada? Australia? South Africa and the rest of it?'

'That's right.'

'But, you mean, he's in trouble?'

'Who said anything about trouble?' Wyatt asked. 'Perhaps somebody wants to do business with him, in a big way, I mean. Perhaps they want to check out a few facts.'

'And that's what you're doing now?'

'Yes.'

'So how far've you got?'

'Well, you know,' he shrugged, 'a bit here, a bit there.'

She was silent a moment. Then, 'D'you want any help?' she asked suddenly.

'What?'

'Michael Pedlar has a house opposite to ours. I know him, of course. And perhaps I know people who . . .'

'No,' he told her. 'No, thanks, I can manage on my own.'

And he waited.

'Companies,' she said then. 'Companies mean money, don't they? And if it was me, I'd say the best way to find out about Michael Pedlar was to find out about his money.'

'Is that right?' he asked idly.

'Yes. And there's a chance I could help you there. In one respect, anyway . . . As it happens, I know a few yachting journalists. And one of them in particular, well, you could say he's been making a bit of a nuisance of himself this season, putting quite a few people's backs up. The thing is, he's actually had the nerve to appear in print, mentioning the kind of money that certain yacht-owners have been spending.'

She took him to the Mumm's Press Centre. It was in a large Victorian building, overlooking the Press Tent that Wyatt had seen before. Alex led him inside. There was a hallway with a stripped pine floor, and a noticeboard with a mass of clippings pinned to it. Beyond was a bare room with typewriters on long trestle tables. About half a dozen journalists were at work there, and Alex went over to one of them, sitting on his own in a corner.

Wyatt waited by the door. He noticed that all the day's papers were there, spread out on a table. He picked one up and saw that there'd been another IRA bomb-attack in London. Bad, it seemed, more than bad, a Cabinet Minister had been gravely injured. And the front page of the paper was full of questions . . . Where had the bomb come from? What were the police doing? Why did they claim, as they did claim, to have sealed off all sources of explosives in the British Isles?

Wyatt read on, thinking how crazy the world was becoming. News, he thought, was just finding someone to blame nowadays. The poor sod of a Cabinet Minister wasn't dead yet, so he wasn't news. And those IRA bastards certainly weren't.

Then he looked up. Alex was beckoning to him. He went over and sat between her and the man in the corner. A man whose name, he learned, was Maitland. And a man who was going to take him back to the private sun-filled world of ocean-racing.

'Mr Douglas?' He held out a hand. 'I hear you're interested in yachts. And in particular yachts and money.'

'That's right,' Wyatt said.

'Well.' Maitland shrugged. 'Really, I suppose you could say the money side of it's a bit academic this year.'

'Why's that?'

'Oh, come on now. You've got a man called Kalicheean, haven't you, entering three yachts? A whole team? And of course he has to be well out in front, as far as emptying the piggy-bank goes.'

'Yes, that's true,' Wyatt said.

'But then, second in line, comes a man I hear you're rather interested in . . . Michael Pedlar.'

'Pedlar?' Wyatt raised his eyebrows.

'Yes, it is a bit of a surprise, isn't it? I mean, usually, as you know, the Yanks are reckoned to be big spenders. But this season a Brit seems to be leaving them well behind.'

'Why d'you think that is?' Wyatt asked.

'Difficult to explain, off the cuff,' Maitland said. 'But I'll try . . . Michael Pedlar comes from an old family hereabouts. His father was very big in ocean-racing, had a large yacht with a famous name . . . Now, all this was long before the present-day Admiral's Cup, of course. But it looks as if Pedlar's trying to fill his father's shoes. For six years now he's missed getting into the Admiral's Cup Team. It means a hell of a lot to him. I don't think you or I can really understand how much.'

'In terms of money, you mean?'

Maitland nodded. He began ticking off on his fingers. 'Okay, we start with the hull of his yacht. *Very* exotic hull, I might add . . . Then we go on to rigging and hydraulics, pinching no pennies . . . Sails, which can't be a big item, since he's a director of Skyline Sails. But there again, can be a big item *if* you happen to know the size of his investment with Skyline, which I do.'

He ticked off another finger. 'Then we come to carting the yacht about. Marina-berths . . . Crews. Crews' hot dinners. Crews' wives' and girlfriends' hot dinners . . .'

'Aren't we getting a bit small here?' Wyatt asked.

'*Small?* We're talking about a man obsessed,' Maitland said. 'A man trying to hog the limelight this year to impress the Admiral's Cup committee . . . Listen, I don't just mean crews' hot dinners in England, from last winter onwards . . . I mean the SORC Series in Florida, shipping the whole roadshow out there. *And* to Calvi later on . . .' Again he paused, frowning. '. . . Therefore, total cost . . .'

Wyatt waited.

'Total cost in round figures would be nearer a third of a million than a quarter,' Maitland said. 'And don't forget that's just for jollies, for hols.'

30

It was the evening of the Squadron Ball. Out in the roads the lights of the Royal Yacht, and the frigate next to it, hung in the darkness. The naval cutter was once again by the steps, where black water was making white spray. And inside the gateway of the Squadron itself a lit canvas tunnel led over the grass, around the back of the castle, to the marquee on the far lawn. Evening shirts and powdered shoulders gleamed in the light for a moment, before entering the tunnel and moving on.

Alex and Wyatt watched from near the steps. Then they walked on, rounding the point outside the castle wall. They came to the curving row of brass cannons pointing out at the Solent. They drew level with the lights of the marquee on the lawn, and the sound of music. Then they reached the wide gusting darkness of Cowes Green.

Alex stopped, pointing up at the large houses among the trees of Egypt Hill.

'It's that one there, with the big lit-up window,' she said. 'D'you see it?'

'Yes,' Wyatt answered. 'But you really think she'll help?'

'I'm not sure, but I think so,' Alex said. 'You see, she doesn't like Pedlar at all. She's related to his first wife.'

'What's that supposed to mean?'

'You'll see. If you get on with her, if she likes you.'

Wyatt had to leave it at that. They walked on, nearing a road that went from the shoreline up the hill. Alex stopped in the light of a street-lamp.

'I'll go back now,' she said. 'She told me she wanted to see you alone.'

'Why's that?'

'She's got her own way of looking at life,' Alex said. 'She's an old woman, nearly eighty now.'

'Nearly *eighty?*'

'Don't worry about her age. She's as bright as you or I, brighter

. . . And when you see her, think back to the days of the big yachts, the "J" Class. Think of the women parading up and down the Squadron lawn before the war. Because that was her time. She was a raving beauty then.'

One wall of the large drawing-room was a plate glass window. It was a room that was overheated in the summer night. And the woman who nodded at Wyatt when he came in was tiny. She had a tiny voice, a squeak, barely audible. She moved slowly warding off objects with arms that were matchstick-thin. For a moment Wyatt watched her. Some people's skin hung in folds as they aged, he thought. But hers was tight and gnarled, tanned the colour of tree-bark. And she was afire with diamonds.

'Mr Douglas? Mr Jack Douglas?' she asked.

'That's right,' Wyatt said.

'Alexandra phoned me about you. Would you sit there?'

He sat, in a hardish chair, facing the window and the dark Solent.

'I'd be grateful if you wouldn't smoke, Mr Douglas. But would you like a sherry?' Her hand pointed to a bell-push on the wall.

'No, thanks.'

She came closer, very slowly, and sat in a second chair at his side. Wyatt had been expecting a faded beauty, a woman with a painted mask of a face and blue-dyed hair. He'd been expecting an old cluttered room, with pictures of great people and great yachts of the past. But there was none of that. Both she and the room were strangely modern. There was a large modern telescope, expensive, mounted on a tripod by the window. And the only wall he could see was bare apart from a large steel crucifix.

She saw him looking at it. 'Are you a religious man, Mr Douglas?'

'No, I'm afraid not.'

'Doesn't matter. But, as it happens, I began life as a convent girl. And youthful impressions do linger on. At a very young age I remember the nuns taking us all over to France, to Lisieux it was, in the north. They were installing a new saint there, St Theresa of the Infant Jesus, in the church. . . . Let me see now, were her miracles before or after her death?'

Wyatt shook his head, sat uncomfortably on the hard chair. The tiny voice squeaked on:

'I think most of her miracles would have been after. As far as I can remember, she promised to send roses down from heaven. . . . I can't help thinking the real St Theresa would have thought her a right little so-and-so.'

Wyatt smiled, then laughed softly. The woman nodded in agreement.

'Religion's not what it used to be,' she said. 'A few years ago I met the bishop. The suffragan bishop, is that one up or one down from the real thing? . . . Anyway he was in his gardening clothes, definitely not wearing gaiters. And when I was introduced to him I clung on like mad until I'd kissed his ring. I like my religion with all the frills, you see. Can't stand these human clerics.'

There was an end to her talk suddenly. It was as if a wall had come down in the room. Something had changed.

'I gather you wanted to talk about Michael Pedlar,' she said then.

'Yes, that's right.'

'Well,' the tiny breathy voice went on, 'it just depends whether we can do an exchange.'

'Exchange?'

She leaned forward slowly and got up, refusing his help. Then with a flash of diamonds she beckoned him to follow her over to the window. He did so. She pointed at the telescope, and he looked through it.

He was surprised to find it wasn't lined up on the water but on a large Victorian house, set in grounds on the far mainland shore. Though through the telescope it wasn't far. The house, its lit windows, drive and parked cars were close.

She motioned him to move back, and then pressed a button on the tripod. There was the hum of an electric motor. The telescope moved through a horizontal arc, then through a shorter vertical arc, and stopped again. Wyatt looked again and saw another large house. The process was repeated, and he saw a third.

He looked at the old woman then. At the glitter of her eyes which was suddenly as bright as her diamonds. At the telescope. And at the lights of those distant houses drawn up like battleships across the water.

'I told you I started life as a convent girl,' she said. 'And perhaps you know that just a few years later I was standing on the Squadron lawn. That was quite a jump. I knew at the time it was important to . . . know certain things. Just as it's still important to know things now.' Her eyes never left his face. 'D'you see what I meant when I talked about an exchange?'

He nodded.

She led the way back to the chairs. They both sat down. 'Now, let us see if your information about Michael Pedlar,' she said, 'is worth my information.'

Wyatt hesitated. Then he found himself telling her all he knew. Beginning with the day he'd flown to Calvi on the Yacht List job, and leaving out nothing since.

When he'd finished, she nodded. 'Yes,' she said, 'I think that fits in. I think it fits in very well.'

She was silent for a moment, twisting the diamond bracelet on her stick-like wrist.

'You will have seen,' she said then, 'that my telescope is focused on houses. Large houses belonging to people who've lived in them for a long time. They have land. At night there is quite a large area of darkness around them before the lights of the world begin. The world may change, in fact, but the houses do not.'

He nodded.

'However there is one house,' she said, 'that is out of the reach of my telescope. It's some two miles the other side of Lymington. A farmhouse, very old . . . and very important to what I have to say.'

'Pedlar's house,' Wyatt said.

'You've called there?'

'Not exactly.'

She wondered about that for a moment, but then went on. 'As it happens,' she said, 'I used to call there quite often. There were many invitations to balls and parties in the days when Michael Pedlar's father was alive. He took a lot of pleasure in showing me round the house. The long-case clock for example in the drawing-room. And the wallpapers that had been cut round it for generations back, because it was the only accurate timepiece in the house, and could not be disturbed . . . Do you follow my meaning?'

'Yes.'

The tiny voice, the squeak, went on . . .

'So now we move to the time when Pedlar's father died. Michael moved into the house because he was the oldest son, and almost immediately he got married . . . To a niece of mine, incidentally, a very favourite niece, and I can't say that I was unconcerned in the match . . . Anyway it was a big wedding. Most of the county were there. The reception was in the house, of course, and the barley field above it had been let to grass just so that the newly-weds could take off by plane.'

She hissed in her breath. Her head moved into the light suddenly, and that glitter came back to her eyes.

'Sixteen years and two children later, Michael broke up the marriage. He found this Greek harpy while on holiday, and he brought her back to live with him in the house. That was bad enough for all of us, as you can imagine, but worse was to follow. At that time he was using the house for no more than three months of the year, and yet he let the Greek re-decorate it in her own wild colours. He let her dig up the asparagus bed and replace it with a swimming-pool . . . And most recently, and by far his greatest outrage to date, he has allowed her to cut down an avenue of walnut-trees that has stood for three hundred years.'

She leaned towards him. 'Perhaps you can't understand the importance of all this. How it can eat into the soul. How big it can become. How the house that has always been the centre of the family is now denied to us all . . . Michael's younger brothers, for example, feel that they are dispossessed. His ex-wife, my niece whom I pushed into marriage with him, is now desperately trying to re-claim her children . . . Michael's mother even, feeling herself to be the head of the family once again, is now trying to take back the reins . . . This she is managing to do, however. Happily she's a woman fifteen years younger than myself, and a fighter . . .' She paused, and bowed her head gracefully. '. . . So I, being old and feeble, can leave it all in her hands.'

Old and feeble, my God, Wyatt thought. Again he had that feeling there was something modern, young even, about the woman facing him. And somehow the feeling that she'd never aged, just changed at some time into her present shape. But what shape? He couldn't think what it was she reminded him of. Until suddenly he knew . . . A stick-insect, peering out at the world with glittering eyes. A slow-moving, tropically-heated creature that would live for ever.

Nothing surprised him about her any more. Not the information she had at her fingertips. Nor the grasp she had of complex business matters . . . Because now she began to talk money.

'I mentioned Michael's mother, how she has been able to fight back,' she said. 'And there's an irony here. You see, Michael has always been the clever one. He has the business brains. It's been in his lifetime that the world-wide corporation has come into being . . . Canada, South Africa, Australia . . .' Again she paused. '. . . But the important thing to remember is that actual control still lies with the original company. It's in the family's hands.'

Wyatt's eyes widened.

'Control, in fact, still rests largely with his mother,' she went on. 'Her shares, when put together with his brothers' and sisters', can easily outvote Michael's. Nothing finally is in his name. The house . . . that farmhouse we were talking about . . . is not even his.'

He stared at her.

'Now, obviously a working arrangement can be arrived at, given two requirements,' she said. 'One is the family's goodwill. And the second depends on a stable business climate, world-wide.' She shrugged. 'As for the first, goodwill is non-existent. Frankly, things have reached the stage where the family are trying to squeeze him out. . . . And as for the second, I don't have to tell you about the recession, do I? That juggling between different currencies has become extremely difficult? That transactions have to take place at exactly the right time, and no other?' Again she fixed him with her eyes. 'But that's precisely what *hasn't* been happening. Because, d'you understand, the family have been refusing to sign cheques when asked. They've been refusing to do a great many things when asked. And they've managed to bring about what you might call a very considerable time-lag.'

'And so we come to the heart of the irony,' she went on. 'Which is that in the long term Michael Pedlar's world-wide business is extremely viable. Only in the short term is it in trouble . . . On paper, I mean. You have to understand that this is a paper fight . . . But, it's true to say that at the end of last year things began to go badly wrong for Michael Pedlar. And true too that the man is now only hanging on by his fingertips . . . And can you see why? Can you think of any vast financial commitment the man might have taken on all those months ago? At the end of last year?'

And Wyatt understood. 'Building a very expensive racing yacht,' he said. 'And mounting a very expensive campaign for the Admiral's Cup.'

She nodded, pleased. 'And do you have any idea how much such a campaign could cost?'

'Yes,' he said, 'I have.'

'All right. Do you know how money of that size can be found?'

'No.'

'Well, obviously it can't come from private sources,' she said. 'And I won't go into details, but let us just say that a yacht . . . even a racing yacht . . . can be termed a company asset. I mean, the Inland Revenue are in no position to deny it, are they? In a very real sense the yacht is an advertisement, a way of telling the business world how successful the company is . . . That's *if* the company is successful.'

'Which it wasn't, at the end of last year,' Wyatt said.

'Precisely . . . And so, faced with the necessity of having to give up his yacht, his obsession, Michael Pedlar for the first time in his life did something that wasn't clever, not clever at all.'

'What was that?'

'Well, he wanted to take care of a large chunk of the yacht's expenses, agreed?' the woman asked. 'And so he cobbled together as much money as he could from his Canadian companies. He "pushed it throught the books", as they say. And this money he invested in a sail loft, Skyline Sails.'

'But why was that so stupid?' Wyatt asked. 'As I heard it, Skyline look set to do very well.'

'Long term! Long term!' Her claw-hand clutched at his wrist. 'As I explained to you before, all Pedlar's troubles are *short* term!' She paused, out of breath. 'And, d'you see, what nobody can understand is how he's able to realise short money from a sail-loft, a gamble. Because all yacht-firms are gambles nowadays. Everywhere you look, another one of them is going to the wall.'

'Yes,' Wyatt said.

'But now,' the woman went on. 'Now you come along with stories about Corsica and the Mediterranean. Stories which fit in with a certain little rumour I've been hearing recently.'

She was close to him now. Her dry breath was on his cheek, and the scratch of her diamonds on his wrist. 'Listen . . .'

31

It was dawn. The chain of bulbs outlining the Royal Yacht and the frigate had gone out. And beyond them the sky in the east was whitening.

On the Squadron terrace there was still a gunmetal grey. Pedlar, his evening shirt beginning to crumple, leaned against the stone battlements. From inside the fortress now there was beat music, the ballroom black and cavernous, given over to the young. Pedlar turned and looked at his wife, sitting on the terrace by his side. Katerina seemed dark and happy in the pale light. Happier than he remembered seeing her at any other Squadron Ball. Perhaps she was no longer apprehensive about meeting so many of his first wife's friends. Or perhaps pleased that he himself was something of a celebrity in this, the Admiral's Cup year.

He bent to kiss her and realised she had just put on new scent. He wondered if it was a signal that she wanted to leave. 'Tired?' he asked her.

'No, not really.'

'Only Hugh, Hugh-of-the-committee I mean, asked if we wanted to go and have breakfast with him.'

'Breakfast? Where?'

He pointed. 'That ketch moored out there. D'you see it? The good-looker, Fowley-designed . . . Almost in line with the Royal Yacht.'

'Ketch? Fowley-designed?' she asked.

And he smiled. 'All right, it's the big white boat, with the two masts.'

'Fine,' she said. 'Fine by me, if you want to go.'

'It'd be nice.'

They said their goodbyes and walked away along the deserted Parade. At the far end, Hugh's Riva speedboat was waiting by the jetty. They stepped aboard, it rose in the water, and a moment later they were out in the wider morning, out past the shadow of the land. The tall white ketch grew larger. They bumped against its varnished side-ladder, and then they were in a different pool of sound, another party.

There were perhaps a dozen people in the yacht's long cockpit. They were drinking champagne and eating a breakfast of kidneys, bacon and mushrooms. Hugh stood up. He made a space for Katerina next to him, and then began talking to her in that quick way he had. Temporarily there was no other space that Pedlar could see. He took his breakfast and moved slightly away along the deck to sit on the saloon housing. The first shafts of sunlight were warming the water around him. Mist was rising in thin curls. Back on shore he could see the lights of the Squadron and the couples still sitting out on the lawn. While closer at hand there was laughter from the yacht's cockpit.

Idly Pedlar supposed it was the sort of scene that would have appeared in a Martini commercial on television. Except that the television director would have made his characters young and lean, with white film-star teeth. And the breakfasters aboard the yacht certainly weren't that. You would call them middle-aged only if you were feeling charitable. But among them was a QC, an Admiral of the Fleet, and an ex-Prime Minister.

Pedlar, hungry suddenly in the early morning air, ate his way through the kidneys and bacon. He put his plate down, and at the same time admired the whitened teak planks of the deck. He'd always admired the traditional workmanship that went into a Fowley-designed yacht.

Then he looked up. The man himself, Roger Fowley, was coming along the deck towards him. He sat down, champagne-glass in hand.

'I was just looking at the finish you put into these boats of yours, Roger,' Pedlar said. 'Marvellous work.'

'Yes, the yard always do me proud,' Fowley said.

'S'pose you've sold a good few in your time.'

'Quite a few.' Fowley nodded, looking at the bubbles in his champagne.

'And what've you got on the drawing-board at the moment?'

'Oh, a bit. You know, a bit. Including one cow of a boat. Dreadful thing it is.'

'Dreadful?'

'Sort of a Chinese junk-thing. That's the nearest I can get to describing it,' Fowley said. 'American customer told me that was exactly what he wanted. I told him it'd go over on its ear.'

'And will it?'

There was a silence that seemed strange to Pedlar. And then Fowley said very quietly, 'It'll go over on its ear.'

'What d'you mean?'

The man put down his champagne-glass, spoke from behind his hand. 'Michael, the damn junk-thing's a waste of time. But it's the only sure order I've got at the moment. The only one that's certain.'

Pedlar was surprised. 'Oh, come on, Roger. You're a household name, up and down the land.'

'Maybe,' Fowley said in the same soft voice. 'But people aren't ordering. The rich, unlike the poor, aren't always with us.'

Pedlar realised he was serious. And then he realised something else. Because Fowley was leaning close. 'Michael, the reason I came up the deck towards you,' he said, 'was I thought I'd ask . . . I mean, since you'd put money into Skyline, Monroe's firm, I wondered if . . .'

There was another silence. Then Pedlar too spoke from behind his hand. 'I take it all this is strictly between ourselves?' he asked.

'Strictly.'

'All right, Roger. Let me just say I'd like to help you, like to very much. I think you're the best there is . . . But the fluidity situation is bad at the moment. And I mean bad. There's a time lag thing working very much against me. The next few months, as they say, are going to be a bit iffy.'

Fowley looked at him, and believed him. 'Sorry I spoke,' he said.

'Doesn't matter.'

But the man was still frowning. 'You said the next few months were going to be iffy,' he said. 'But if that's so, how are you going to get away with the Skyline thing? A long term gamble like that?'

Pedlar hesitated a moment, then decided. 'Skyline's different,' he said. 'Since you ask, Skyline's down on the books for quick gains.'

'But how? I mean, a small firm like that up against the big superlofts?'

'It's something that came up at Calvi,' Pedlar said very quietly. 'One of the reasons I went there, in fact . . . You see, Calvi's a new date in the yachting calendar, isn't it? And there've been complaints about the way it's been organised? So, to cut a long story short, the people out there are looking for help. To put the Week firmly on the map, I mean.'

'Help?' Fowley asked. 'Your help?'

'Well, really, I s'pose, I'm talking about facilities,' Pedlar said. 'What's happening is that we're going to set up a second Skyline loft out there. We've negotiated a friendly tax deal, and a more than friendly real-estate deal. Skyline's going to be the first sail-loft based on the marina there. And as such it's going to mop up a lot of that Mediterranean gravy.'

'But . . .' Fowley was surprised, very surprised. '. . . You're talking about Calvi, isn't that right? And, I mean, I've heard of scores of people who've tried to get into that development and failed . . . Michael, the Corsicans, they're gangsters, aren't they?'

'So I'm told,' Pedlar said.

32

Wyatt sat on the narrow bed in Alex's room. It was nearly midday; they'd got up late as they always did. And he was staring fixedly out through the window at Pedlar's house across the street.

Right, you bastard, he was thinking, I've got you now. I know you're in with Corsicans. I know why you are. And I know the kind of deal you're offering in exchange. . . . All I need now is proof.

Behind him on the bed Alex stirred. She reached out for his arm. 'How did you get on last night?' she asked.

'Last night?'

'With the old lady up on Egypt Hill . . . You never really said.'

'Oh, fine, fine,' Wyatt said absently.

'And your client? The man you're working for, getting information for? D'you think he'll do business with Pedlar now?'

'Client?' he asked.

Suddenly she hit him, hard, across the back of the head. She hurt him, and she hurt her hand. 'What the hell was that for?' he asked.

'You know, I really wanted to believe!' she shouted at him. 'This cock-and-bull story of yours! I really wanted to believe it!'

'What are you talking about?'

Her arm went back again. And she hit him again, hard, every time she shouted. '*Jackman* sending me over to see you! Jackman telling me about you and the *old* days! Jackman, who's never told me *anything* before! And it was for a *reason*! I was being *used*!'

Wyatt backed out of range. Just once in your life, he told himself, remember when you're dealing with a woman who's bright. A woman who catches on fast, thinks fast, and acts very, very suddenly.

So all right, he told himself, put it all back together again. Make it work again. Do it now.

But he was too late.

Because as he started to dress, as he started to pick up his small change and belongings from the dressing-room table . . . she reached across and snatched something away.

'What's this?' she asked.

'A penknife,' he said.

'Is that all?'

'No, it's a Swiss Army penknife.'

'From Switzerland?'

'Obviously.'

'I mean,' she said, 'was it bought in Switzerland?'

'Yes.'

'And given to you perhaps? As a present?'

'Yes, as a matter of fact.'

'By a woman?'

'No,' he said, 'by two young kids.'

She looked down at the knife again. 'Not two young kids with a good-looking mother?'

He frowned. 'No,' he said. 'Why?'

Suddenly she went to the window and threw the knife out. Following her, he was in time to see it land in the street below.

'If it wasn't given to you by two young kids with a mother,' she said, 'then you won't run outside and get it.'

He hesitated a moment. Then he went down to the street and picked up the knife.

She was waiting for him, hands on hips, when he returned. 'Jackman didn't only tell me about the old days,' she said. 'He was really quite chatty.'

'Was he?'

'Yes. I don't suppose he thought it mattered when I asked him about Switzerland . . . I mean, why, for example, you gave me that phoney Swiss address.'

And he knew what was coming.

'What he said was,' she went on, 'that you'd been living in this apartment in Luzern. That you'd been, well, shacked up there.'

'Yes,' he said. 'Why? Does it worry you?'

'I'm not sure.'

She turned then and pointed down at the bed. 'You know, that first night I had the impression I wasn't much good in the sack. . . . But you know something else too? I somehow had the impression I couldn't put a foot right with you.'

'It could be true,' Wyatt said, 'and I'm sorry.'

But the worst of it was that she was calm now, no longer

shouting. 'I can take being used,' she said, 'even in bed . . . But what I can't take is being compared to anyone else in bed. Being compared to them, I mean, and *losing*.'

She walked past him to the door and opened it.

'Where are you going?' Wyatt asked unhappily.

'I don't know. The mainland maybe. Stay with friends.'

He pointed to her suitcase. 'Aren't you going to pack?'

'I never pack,' she said.

That night Wyatt had a lot too much to drink. He went round the pubs, and, about an hour before closing, found himself back in the Three Crowns.

It was as if events had turned full circle. Standing by the bar again was the ya-mob, the ya and nay and vey-good-mob. Chas was there too, he saw. And next to him this real looker of a girl, with russet-coloured hair and a wide smile.

It was only her voice.

'But I'm bind to say,' she was telling Chas, 'that I ainly gay ite with your yay-heave-hays, your actual crews.'

'And I'm not crew, is that it? No Union Jack.' Chas pointed to his chest. 'So I don't stand a chance?'

'Nay, darling,' she told him. 'You ainly follay orn behind the yacht, dain't you? Twiddling the wheel of the mater-bait?'

And it was too much. Wyatt asked for a translation.

'Motor-boat,' Chas said. 'I'm in charge of *Cry Havoc*'s motor-boat, her tender. I follow the races, the inshore races that is, and I take the family and V.I.P.s out to watch.'

'Just a jolly aild shafer, really.' The girl nodded. 'Orfly sorry and all that.'

'But what is this motor-boat?' Wyatt insisted, the drink getting to him. 'I don't understand.'

Chas looked at him then, and talked him through it slowly. 'Remember that first day you came to the loft? Remember Monroe went out in a boat? To take some video of a sail?'

'Yes.'

'Well, *that* motor-boat. It belongs to Michael Pedlar. And both he and Monroe have been using it for recutting sails . . . Though,' Chas shrugged, 'sometimes we used to joke about how long Pedlar stayed out in the damn' thing. Out at sea, I mean . . . Must have been halfway to France most of the time.'

33

The next morning Wyatt went down to the marina. His hangover was bad, it still seemed to be yesterday, and Alex still seemed to be with him. She was there as he passed the gents' outfitters where they'd bought the blazer. There by the Island Sailing Club where they'd eaten supper. And there as he walked out now onto the marina-pontoons. Because she'd told him they were never called that. Here at Cowes they were known as 'the trots'.

And it was down on 'the trots' that he saw the motor-boat Chas had been talking about. And he saw too why he hadn't noticed it before. It wasn't in the Admiral's Cup bay, but the next one, moored stern-to, almost directly opposite *Cry Havoc*.

In spite of his hangover, Wyatt looked the boat over appreciatively. There was no resemblance between it and the Italian eggbox of a boat that Jackman owned. This was a Broom cruiser, about forty feet long, taut-looking, and with good fast lines. There was an open wheelhouse, set low and neatly into the fairing of the main saloon. There was the feeling of power and strength from the cold-moulded deck and hull. And there was a price-tag that went with the boat, Wyatt knew. He'd come across a few of them during his Yacht List days in the Med. They belonged to the man who wanted a fast big-sea boat . . . Like Pedlar maybe, he thought, getting across to France and back in a day.

Then suddenly Pedlar appeared, leading his crew down the ramp from the Groves & Guttridge yard, with sailbags over their shoulders. And as Wyatt watched, other crews appeared, more and more of them over the next ten minutes. Soft-footed, with that aggressive fitness of theirs, they swarmed onto the Admiral's Cup yachts. And in the bright sunlight they worked quickly, singling lines, removing mainsail covers, and starting engines. Until the whining, spitting sound seemed to stretch over the whole marina . . . It was the day, Wyatt realised, of the final inshore race.

As on other days the yachts all seemed to leave together, making for the dazzling water with crews standing black on their decks. Then the spectator boats and tenders began to follow on behind. Wyatt watched them, until he turned once again and looked at the Broom cruiser. He saw that Chas was aboard her now, getting her ready for sea. And the party he was taking out with him was arriving too.

First came the goodlooking Greek woman, Pedlar's wife. She had the two children with her, and they ran ahead, climbing the cruiser's steel ladder and calling out to Chas. Then a second group arrived, bigwigs as far as Wyatt could see. There was the man he thought he recognised as the British Team Manager. There were other men he'd seen with Pedlar before. And finally someone whose face he knew from newspaper pictures – a former British Prime Minister.

They stood grouped together on the afterdeck. The Team Manager helped Chas let go the warps and get the fenders aboard. Then with a burble from the powerful marine diesels, the cruiser carved a gentle wake around the far marina and slipped away.

The harbour seemed silent and empty suddenly. Wyatt stood alone. He knew there was nothing more he could do until the boats returned this evening, and he went back into the town to work on his hangover.

He slept most of the morning in his room. He had lunch, and then he climbed the hill above the town to the green of a park. There was a line of oaks, and he lay down in their shade. Somewhere out on the Solent, he knew, tall sails were fighting their own mysterious battles. But he didn't think any more about them. And he didn't think about Alex.

He must have slept again, because suddenly the sun was getting low. He went back down to the town and through the gates of the marina. There were shadows now around the trade-caravans and mobile bars, but sunlight out on the concrete hard. And in its centre was a strange machine. Wyatt looked at it for some time before he realised it was a pair of jockey's scales, with a small seat on the one side that balanced a weight-pan on the other. Except that there were no weights. Just, standing by the machine, crate after crate of Mumm's champagne.

The sun dipped lower and further to the west. The jockey-scales were still sunlit, but so now was the Admiral's Cup scoreboard, high up on its shed wall. Gradually a crowd began to gather, spilling out from the bars towards the concrete hard. Wyatt stood with them, and began to learn a few facts. Today's race – the third inshore race – had been sponsored by Mumm's. And the winning skipper, it seemed, was to be presented with his weight in champagne.

The fleet began to come back. Yachts and spectator-craft made rough water of the marina as they swung in through its entrance. Then, crew by crew, the teams joined the crowd around the jockey-scales. And the word was that Hoff, the American skipper, had finished first. While Michael Pedlar had come second, had, as people said, 'got a gun.'

Later the results were put up on the Admiral's Cup scoreboard. There was no letter P for Protest after the winning yacht's name. Hoff's first place was confirmed.

A gap in the crowd was made, and Hoff was found, a large man in Bermuda shorts. There were cheers and catcalls as he sat on the scales. Cheers and catcalls as the champagne bottles rose higher. Hoff watched them, grinning. And he was still grinning as the champagne lifted him slowly off the ground, as the photographers' flashguns flashed. Then he was on his feet, passing bottles round to his crew. In the last of the sunlight there were milk-white fountains of champagne. The crowd fell back from the spray, and began to disperse.

Wyatt edged his way closer to a certain group of people he'd been watching. In their centre the former British Prime Minister was shaking Michael Pedlar by the hand. He was thanking him for the day spent out at sea. And in return inviting him to supper in two days' time, early in the evening, before they all went on to the Corinthian Ball.

The dark woman, Pedlar's wife, looked pleased. But suddenly she was far less than pleased when her husband politely refused. He was sorry, he said, but a problem had come up. There were now only four days remaining before the Fastnet Race, he said, and he'd had to set aside three of them for a business trip. Business, he said, couldn't just come to a halt.

The former British Prime Minister agreed, shook his hand again, and moved away. Pedlar then turned to Chas who was standing close by, and gave him a list of instructions . . . And it was these last that made Wyatt walk quickly off to the pub where he was staying, and get on the phone.

'Jacko?'

'That you, Ace?'

'Jacko, I took the chance and rang you at home. I mean, is it all right? Your wife, is she there?'

'She's out, Ace. Out at some Siamese cat-lovers' meetin'. Some stuff like that.'

'Okay, well, listen, Jacko, there was something I wanted to know . . . You remember when we talked before? You remember telling me about certain people? Certain men in suits who'd come into the country recently?'

'Yeh, Ace. What about them?'

'Well, are they still over here? Still in the U.K., I mean?'

'No, Ace, they've gone. This business they came to do was fixed. All taken care of, as I heard it, in a couple of days. So they went back again, the end of last week.'

'Back to Froggy-land?'

'Right.'

'Okay then. So tell me this,' Wyatt went on. 'That operation you said they were running from Froggy-land . . . the deliveries, the contract work . . . is all that on again?'

'Yeh. Back to regular shipments. Business as usual.'

'You're sure about that, are you, Jacko?'

'Positive.'

'All right then,' Wyatt said. 'Then I'm going to have to do something . . . I'm going to have to get hold of a plane.'

'A *plane?*'

'Yes. You can fix me up, can't you? You've got friends with smart yachts. You must have friends with planes.'

'What if I have, Ace? You think one of them's going to lend it to you? Just like that?'

'Why not? I'm a commercial pilot. I'm not going to crash the bloody thing.'

'You're also a commercial pilot who's dead, Ace, remember?' Jackman sounded angry. 'You'd have to be crazy to fly under your own name.'

'Maybe,' Wyatt told him. 'But then again, maybe not. Not if it's worth the risk.'

'What risk? What is all this?' Jackman shouted down the phone. 'I mean what *gives* with you wantin' this bleedin' plane?'

'Simple, Jacko. Quite simple,' Wyatt said. 'You told me just now that the shipments coming in from Froggy-land were starting up again.'

'I did. And they are.'

'All right. So listen . . . Just now, on the quayside here, I heard a man called Michael Pedlar turn down a *very* smart invitation to dinner.'

'What are you talkin' about?'

'And after that' – Wyatt ignored him – 'I heard Michael Pedlar say why he wasn't going to be at this dinner party . . . Because he's going away, on a three-day business-trip.'

'What?'

'And after that,' Wyatt continued, 'I heard Pedlar giving out with instructions. They were to do with this fast motor-cruiser he owns. He wanted the big service done, he wanted it test-run, and he wanted it filled up with fuel . . . Because tomorrow, Jacko, what's happening is that Pedlar's starting out on his three-day trip. In the motor-cruiser. Out in the Channel. On his own.'

'Ace,' Jackman said tiredly, 'all this could be very big news for you . . . Me, I'm lost. So why don't you start again? At the beginnin'?'

Wyatt did. And as he spoke, Jackman became more and more interested. 'All right, Ace, I int promisin' nothin',' he said then. 'But I'll see if I can fix up a plane for you. Just see about it . . . But there's other things too. What you got to do first, see, is plan it all out very thorough at your end. And then come over to the mainland here. I mean, none of this is goin' to be easy.'

34

But it turned out to be easier than expected.

Shortly afterwards Wyatt went to the Three Crowns, where *Havoc*'s crew were celebrating their second place in the day's racing. Chas was there in a corner of the bar, and they talked. And among other things Wyatt learned that the Broom cruiser was going to be serviced early tomorrow morning, up-river in Cowes. Then it was going to be given a quick test-run and brought back to the Groves & Guttridge marina by midday. This, because Pedlar wanted to start out before midday, with the last of the ebb-tide.

Wyatt had heard enough. He left the Three Crowns, walked to the Hydrofoil Terminal, and bought a ticket for Southampton. He had over an hour to wait before the next scheduled service, and so he made his way to a chandler's in the High Street and bought certain items. Then he went out in the darkness of the marina to the Broom cruiser, and used the certain items to do a certain small job.

The Hydrofoil he caught with five minutes to spare. Twenty-five minutes later he was over the water in Southampton. And Jackman he met in a pub half an hour before closing, as arranged. It seemed Jackman had got lucky. Using the name of a friend, who was a member of the Hamble Flying Club, he'd managed to get a three-day booking with a club plane.

But there was more to it than that. There was a second man with Jackman, leaning up against the bar. A man called Sinclair. And Wyatt wasn't sure about Sinclair. He was a large man who seemed overweight. But he wasn't. His face was fatted rather than fat – there was just recent good living there. And underneath was something that Wyatt remembered from the old days. Something wired up to the violence of city streets.

'What's he doing here?' Wyatt asked. 'A heavy?'

'Him? No, he runs a flower shop,' Jackman said.

Wyatt sighed.

'No, listen, Ace,' Jackman went on. 'I thought it best we had him with us on this caper.'

'Oh, you did?' Wyatt asked. And then, suddenly, '*We? . . . Us?*'

'Oh, yeh, I'm comin' as well. Told my missus I was goin' to be away on business up in the Smoke.'

'But, why?'

Jackman put an arm round him. 'You could need the two of us along with you,' he said. 'I mean, if you find in Froggy-land what you expect to find in Froggy-land . . . Well, it int goin' to be no church picnic, is it?'

The next day at twelve the three of them met in the same pub. Just after twelve the phone out in the passage rang. It was a man Jackman had sent over to the island on the car-ferry early that morning. He was ringing from the call-box in the Groves & Guttridge marina . . . Pedlar had just left.

Twenty minutes later there was a call from the small island town of Gurnard. The man, following the Broom cruiser along the shore road, said Pedlar was heading West.

There were two other calls. One from Yarmouth. And the final one from Totland out near the Needles. Pedlar was standing well out to sea, and coming round now to the south-west.

'Right. Once he gets out of sight of land, he heads for France,'

Jackman said. 'So what we do is drink up here and get over to the Hamble Flyin' Club quick.'

'No, we don't,' Wyatt told him. 'We take our time here. We go and have a long lunch somewhere, followed by coffee. And then we get over to the Flyin' Club slow.'

'But, that'll take us till, what, Ace? Three-thirty in the bleedin' afternoon?'

''Course it will,' Wyatt said. 'But why've we got the plane? To search a dirty great big area of sea off the French coast, all right? . . . And how long d'you think it's going to take that cruiser to get there?'

'I don't know.'

'Well, at top whack, keeping up a steady twenty knots,' Wyatt said, 'it's still not going to be in that area before five, five-thirty.'

'That's if it gets there,' Jackman said. 'If it's headin' for France at all.'

'That's it.'

They had the long lunch. They had the coffees. Then they drove slowly to the Hamble airfield. And the club-plane, Wyatt was glad to see, was an old Beechcraft that looked well-maintained. But still he made sure. He got Jackman to sit in the pilot's seat and waggle the controls, while he felt the play in rudder and flaps. And he ran up the engine for a few minutes. Then, satisfied, he went over to the clubhouse. He had a moment's doubt about showing his commercial pilot's licence, made out in his real name. But he did so. He filed a flight-plan. And they got up in the air.

The plane felt like a canvas and string job after the Piper Saratoga he'd last flown. But in a way he liked it, feeling every gust, every kick through the light-handling column. And, far more to the point, it was good to fly again, to know he *could* fly, the missing thumb on his right hand taking away none of his feel.

They passed over the bright white sails of Cowes Week. They overflew the island and went straight out to sea on a heading for the Cherbourg peninsula. Not that Wyatt thought the cruiser would make for a large port like Cherbourg. But he intended to start his search seventy-five miles east of the peninsula, and then make sweeps westward.

But first of all there were routine matters to be taken care of, the nuts and bolts of flying . . . He found the weather-stations in the book, and checked with them in turn to update his weather-chart.

'What you doin' then, Ace?' Jackman asked. 'Showin' off? Flyin' the airline way?'

'No,' Wyatt said. 'A plane moves quickly, and the weather moves quickly. It's when they're going in opposite directions that things can change all of a sudden.'

And, as if to bear him out, forty miles out across the Channel the weather did change. The sun of the English south coast was gone, and the colder front that hung over the French land-mass began to reach out towards them. The sky became white and the sea grey. There was the occasional tanker below, cutting through the waves like a black chisel. But few yachts.

'So where's this cruiser of yours?' Jackman asked.

Wyatt didn't answer. He came round on the compass to the west, and then began making the long sweeps he'd planned. Nothing. Just grey sea, with every now and then a sail. Not a motor-cruiser in sight.

And nothing either from Sinclair, sitting in one of the rear seats. Wyatt leaned close to Jackman and spoke softly, 'Doesn't say much, does he?'

'I don't know,' Jackman answered. 'I remember him askin' for a large Scotch. When was it, just before lunch?'

'So he did.'

'What it is,' Jackman nodded at the slab of a man behind them, 'he's a thinker.'

The search sweeps went on, up-down, up-down, each leg covering fifteen miles of sea. They began to close in on the Cherbourg peninsula, its fields grey, then silver-grey in the breaks of cloud. Finally they drew near to the huge sprawl of Cherbourg itself.

And then Wyatt saw it, the Broom cruiser, about ten miles out, thundering over the water in a white line that smudged out the wave-tops. And he'd been wrong about it not making for a large port. It was heading straight for Cherbourg.

He altered course. 'That's the boat,' he said to Jackman. 'That one down there.'

'How d'you know, Ace? You int goin' close enough to read the name.'

'No, and I'm not going to. Not going to scare him off.'

'So how d'you know that's him? Pedlar?'

'Oh,' Wyatt said offhandedly. 'That's a Broom cruiser. Anyone can see that.'

'You're jokin'.' Jackman raised his voice. 'I mean, listen, we come all this *way*.'

'Jacko,' Wyatt grinned at him, 'it's a Broom cruiser . . . and the only one in the world . . . with the top of its radar-scanner painted in red lead paint.'

Jackman looked again at the scanner, spinning round on top of the short stub mast. And it was. Red.

'I did it last night, after dark in the Cowes marina,' Wyatt said. 'All the crews were ashore then, in the pubs.'

'You did?'

'Seemed like a good idea at the time. I mean, who's going to look up on top of the radar-scanner? Highest part of the ship?'

Wyatt flew on, in a wide half-circle out to sea, until he was certain the cruiser was putting in to Cherbourg. Then he turned to Jackman. 'Look for an airport, shall we?'

They went into the town by taxi. And there was a strange feeling to Cherbourg, a feeling that summer had gone. A white haze was everywhere, with a chill to it as evening approached. And yet there were tanned bodies, bright bikinis . . . people shivering on the beach, and on the quays that curved around the yacht-pool.

And it was here that they saw the Broom cruiser, moored among the masts. There was no sign of Pedlar aboard, no sign of anyone as far as Wyatt could see, the boat seemed locked up. He leaned forward and got the taxi-driver to stop. 'Right,' he said, 'this is where I get out.'

But Jackman stopped him. 'Don't be crazy, Ace. Listen, as I heard it, you been hangin' around Pedlar for, what, three weeks now? So what happens if the guy looks up along the quay and sees you here in Cherbourg?'

'I don't know,' Wyatt said, 'but is there a better alternative?'

'Sure there is.' Jackman got a diary from his pocket. 'I come prepared with Froggy phone-numbers, int I? I done my homework.'

'What d'you mean?'

'Friends of friends,' Jackman said. 'And in this case, what's the French for *soixante-neuf? Amis?* . . . There's people over here waitin' to go to work. Waitin' to do our watchin' for us.'

'And you trust them? These people?'

''Course I do. Same way they trust our people, back home.'

'And how d'you talk to them?'

'You do the talkin'. I mean, you can, can't you? Do it easy . . . So what happens first off is we find a hotel. Then you get on the blower. And the Froggy machine starts hummin'.'

Finding a hotel though, it seemed, in the first week of August, wasn't going to be easy. The taxi-driver took them to a few that were full. Until finally they had to settle for the big one, the one that handled the liner-passengers. The Sofitel.

They drove a little way out of the town again. Out past the entrance to the harbour, which was a straight channel with sloping stone walls, and a flashing light at the far end. And there, on a narrow spit of land, with the sea on one side and the sheds of the liner-dock on the other, was the Sofitel. It was a concrete block all on its own, like some immigration centre out in the haze.

Maybe Wyatt was tired after the flight, but he didn't have the feeling he was back in France. The interior of the hotel was modern and predictable. There was no smell of France, just air-conditioning – no sound of France, just whispers and ghostly muzak. And through wide plate glass windows, haze that was darkening, was becoming sea-mist. And the flashing red of the harbour light, on-off, on-off.

They took two rooms. And then Wyatt, using Jackman's phone-numbers, got hold of a local man called Lefebre. Lefebre spoke a pinched northern French that Wyatt wasn't used to. He was very precise, and he said, yes, he would initiate enquiries. Yes, he would find out about an Englishman called Michael Pedlar, who he was with now, and what he was doing in Cherbourg . . . He promised answers to all these questions, and said that he would be at the Sofitel within two hours.

He came within three. He was a small man with a schoolmaster's manner. And he made notes with a silver propelling-pencil as he talked . . . But, it was strange, he said, there was truly very little information. Yes, a Broom cruiser had come in, and an Englishman had come ashore. But as to any records of the name Michael Pedlar – reliable contacts in the Customs department were suddenly keeping quiet. And it was the same with normally reliable contacts in the town. Michael Pedlar had quite simply vanished.

This was far from normal in Lefebre's experience. In fact he would go as far to say it was unique to come up against such silence. Almost as if a large agency were here at work in Cherbourg. A large agency that had come in from outside . . .

But, Lefebre repeated, he would continue with enquiries. He would maintain surveillance of the cruiser, and have a fast boat ready on a twenty-four hour basis in case the cruiser left harbour. With the silver propelling-pencil he wrote down his phone-number. And said that in any case he would call immediately there was news.

Lefebre left. Jackman, Sinclair and Wyatt sat in the bar and drank slowly. There was mist outside, and the *tock-tock* of fishing-boats coming past . . . They sat in the restaurant with a three-language menu and cellophane-wrapped rolls. There was silence outside, and the red flashing light of the harbour . . . They sat in one of the bedrooms upstairs. Still the mist, the silence, and the flashing light.

But at eleven-thirty something happened. Sinclair spoke for the second time in Wyatt's hearing. He said, 'I'm gonna send down for a bottle of Scotch.'

It came, and he drank faster. Jackman drank faster too, from a brandy-bottle he had in his case. From the window Wyatt watched the two of them, sprawling on the beds with their shoes off.

'Get better tomorrow, Ace,' Jackman said.

But it didn't get better tomorrow. There was the white haze again. There were the masts of yachts coming past as they left the harbour. And breakfast was once again in three languages with cellophane-wrapped rolls.

By eleven o'clock Wyatt couldn't take any more of the waiting. He rang Lefebre and met him in a café by the yacht-pool. The Broom cruiser was still locked up, and Pedlar hadn't returned. Lefebre had nothing more to report. Wyatt went moodily back to the Sofitel.

He found that Jackman and Sinclair were once again in the bar. And Jackman, it seemed, had got himself an English couple to talk to, sitting at a table over by the window.

They were a Mr and Mrs Goodhew from Solihull. They were both in their late forties, obviously well-heeled, and were cruising along the coast, they said, in their British built motor-sailer.

Jackman made the introductions, and the four of them chatted for a while over the window-table. It all seemed harmless enough. . . . Except that Wyatt should have known. He just should have bloody *remembered*.

'We're just pottering along from harbour to harbour, really,' Mr Goodhew told him. 'Stopping where we fancy. Living from day to day.'

'Of course we've done the coast before,' Mrs Goodhew said to Jackman. 'And in Cherbourg we always call at the Sofitel for drinkies and lunch.'

'Oh, yes?' Jackman said to her very quietly. 'And have you had it in lately?'

35

Jackman didn't get his face slapped. He just got a surprised grunt, and then lighting-up time around the eyes.

So how did he pick them? Wyatt asked himself. How did he always *know*?

Take this one, for example, Mrs Goodhew . . . All of forty-seven, jangly with bracelets. And attractive, my God, if you liked thin birdlike women, dressed in bright birdlike colours. Not to mention the orange lipstick, and the vivid suntan that had to have come out of a bottle.

But against that, Wyatt supposed, was Jackman's need. And the fact that she was the only Englishwoman in the place . . . Which was why he now went to work, arranging the table so that Mrs Goodhew and he were at one end, Mr Goodhew was at the other, and Wyatt and Sinclair were in the middle, running interference.

Then there were two different conversations, one coming from each side of Wyatt.

'How it is,' Mr Goodhew said to him, 'I run my own engineering firm. Industrial tools. Precision stuff.'

'He's going broke,' Mrs Goodhew said to Jackman. 'Straight for the wall. And he's tranquillised up to the eyeballs. A real bad case of the Bendy Bunnies in bed.'

'Nowadays management's an eighty-hour week,' Mr Goodhew said to Wyatt. 'Keeping one jump ahead of the Vatman, not to mention the unions.'

'Saturdays,' Mrs Goodhew said to Jackman. 'I can get him to leave off the tranquillisers on Saturday nights. But then I've got to negotiate. Apply in triplicate, and go through the bloody works-committee.'

'Say what you like, it's nice to get away,' Mr Goodhew said. 'Nice to leave it all behind and head out to sea.'

'Biff, biff, biff against the waves in that bloody motor-sailer of his,' Mrs Goodhew said. 'And no sun. No sun ever since we've been over here. All my suntan comes out of a tube. Bronzer Pour Elle. Bought it in Quimper.'

'Does her good to get away,' Mr Goodhew said. 'Her a power of good.'

'Different last autumn,' Mrs Goodhew said. 'I had a luxury sight-see of Rome, on my own. *He* couldn't understand why I wanted to go on my own, of course. But I saw the Coliseum in curlers, St Peter's Rome in curlers. Oh, those waiters Italiano in the evenings.'

'Something about the British and the sea,' Mr Goodhew said. 'Seafaring nation, I suppose. In the blood. Must be.'

'Bloody fool, he is,' Mrs Goodhew said. 'Tripped over a boathook on our first day here. Broke his ankle. He has to have a plastic carrier-bag tied round it on the boat . . . Plastic carrier-bag on his leg, and he stands there like Jack Hawkins in *The Cruel Sea*.'

And Wyatt saw then why Goodhew needed a plastic bag on the boat. The man's right trouser-leg was split round a large white plaster-cast. He stood up, put his weight on it gingerly, and hobbled out around the table.

'My shout,' Goodhew said. 'Who's drinking what?'

'Here, let me do it for you.' Wyatt tried to help him.

'No, my shout.'

He reached Mrs Goodhew, and she held out her glass. 'Gin and Sin for me,' she said. And then, as he limped away, 'Bloody fool. Will you just look at the bloody fool.'

Which was when Jackman turned round, his mouth close to Wyatt's ear. 'Ace, you got to help me,' he whispered. 'You got to take care of him for the next hour.'

'Take *care* of him?'

'Feed him drinks. Keep him happy. Just for the next hour.' Jackman hugged himself at the thought of it. 'Jesus, her mouth when she slags him off,' he whispered. 'Did you *see* that mouth of hers?'

It was a relief when Mrs Goodhew swallowed down her Gin and Sin, stood up, and said she had to go out shopping. A relief when Jackman said he'd go with her to carry her things. They left . . . And Wyatt fed Goodhew drinks for half an hour, fed Sinclair drinks.

Then Sinclair spoke, for the third time in twenty-four hours. 'Borin' in here,' he said. 'Gonna getta bottla Scotch sent up to the room.'

And Wyatt had to think hard about that. He didn't want Sinclair left alone too long with any bottle, but at the same time he'd said he'd keep Goodhew happy for the next half hour. Finally he decided to move the party upstairs, and he asked for whisky to be sent up to Room 402.

But the door of 402, when they reached it, was locked. And the waiter, standing outside with the bottle on a tray, wasn't getting any answers as he knocked.

No prizes for guessing why.

Wyatt took the tray on to 403, which was the other room they were using. He sat Goodhew down, gave him large measures of Scotch, and Sinclair small . . . And then he heard the fun and games coming from next door. Loud fun and games.

There was a radio by the bed. Wyatt turned it up to full volume, and kept filling Goodhew's glass. And maybe it was the Scotch, or maybe it was the tranquillisers the man was taking, but Goodhew began to smile in a dopey way. He propped his plaster cast up on the bed and started talking about the Small Tool Industry.

The half hour went by. There was no sign of the fun and games slowing down next door. Then the phone rang.

'Ace,' Jackman's voice said, 'Mrs Goodhew's finished her shoppin', but she's decided to get her hair done.'

'She's decided to make an *appointment* to get her hair done,' Wyatt corrected him. 'So you'll be twenty minutes longer. I'll pass on the message.'

He did so. The fun and games got louder again next door. Goodhew finished talking about the Small Tool Industry and got onto family holidays at Littlehampton.

Twenty minutes later the phone rang again. 'Ace, we're at the shoe-menders. Mrs Goodhew's just snapped the heel off her shoe.'

'So you'll be ten minutes,' Wyatt said loudly. 'Okay, I'll pass it on.'

But he couldn't pass anything on now. Goodhew was asleep, still with that dopey smile on his face, while the fun and games went on in the next room.

The phone rang again. 'Ace, we're at the apothecary's, and our bleedin' postillion's been . . .'

Wyatt slammed the phone down.

He didn't answer it when it rang shortly afterwards. Nor when it rang a second time. But the third time he picked it up.

It was Lefebre. He'd been trying to contact Wyatt for fifteen minutes. The Broom cruiser had just left harbour. He, Lefebre, had a fast motor-boat ready and wai . . .

Wyatt ran to the balcony door, opened it, stepped out. The cruiser was a small white shape out in the haze, Michael Pedlar no more than a dot at the wheel. And the wake was a curving line, pointing round to the West.

The motor-boat that Lefebre had handed over to them was a Riva 34, fast, capable of a good twenty-nine knots. Though Jackman at the wheel wasn't opening up the big GM motors to anything like that speed. But still they were thudding along between grey and white, twilit water and haze. And it was dangerous. Even more dangerous as patches of mist, thick over the shoreline, came out to meet them.

Wyatt and Sinclair were hanging on to the grab-rail in the cockpit. And Wyatt was angry. 'Reckon we've bloody lost Pedlar,' he shouted above the roar of the engines. 'Reckon we can just kiss him goodbye.'

'Ace, I got me trousers on, got into that taxi round the harbour a second after you,' Jackman shouted back. 'I mean, who was it never answered the bleedin' phone?'

Wyatt gave up. It was useless. And useless too chasing after Pedlar. All they had on the man was that he was heading west. Though maybe keeping inshore as they were, where the haze was thickest.

They smashed on over the water. Mist rolled up ahead of them, huge fat fingers, curling and white. They knifed through them, and there could have been a fishing-float, damn great fishing-vessel even in their path . . . Dangerous. Useless and dangerous. Wyatt was just about to call the whole thing off . . . When suddenly there was the Broom cruiser two hundred yards away, low in the water, making half their speed.

Jackman yanked back the throttles, swung round on a parallel course, offshore. But mist closed in around them, a long dense stretch of it. The cruiser was lost to sight again, and all they could do was stop the motors altogether, and listen.

There was the slap of water under the hull. Then the low drone of the other boat's engine. And it was steady, Wyatt was sure of it, keeping to a constant bearing.

'Coming towards us?' he asked Jackman.

'No. Goin' away. Goin' inshore.'

'You certain?'

Jackman held up a hand. After a while he spoke again, 'Yeh, inshore. Hear that? He's cuttin' back on the motors now, feelin' his way in.'

Wyatt listened. He nodded slowly. Then he reached into the locker ahead of Jackman and found the chart. He looked at it for some time. 'How far d'you reckon we've come west of Cherbourg?' he asked.

Jackman frowned. 'Ten sea-miles? Fifteen?'

'Could be here then.' Wyatt pointed at the chart. 'It's about the only landing-place I can see.'

'Where?'

'Here. This bay that starts wide and narrows in. With the jetty right inside at the far end . . . Pedlar could be making for that.'

'But we got to be sure, Ace. Well, int we?'

Wyatt nodded. 'Okay, head due north out to sea and see if the mist lets up. See if we can pick up some bearings.'

They went out. Mist quickly thinned to haze, and then became a sky darkening towards evening. And suddenly there were pinpricks of light, French coastal lights, flashing and occult. Wyatt identified two of them from the chart. He took bearings with a hand-compass. He got a fix.

'We're here,' he said. 'And it *is* the bay with the jetty.'

The mouth of the bay was little over half a mile across. There were shoals along its eastern shore but Wyatt fixed them in his mind, and he worked out the state of the tide from the tables. Finally he gave Jackman a course that would take them in through the deepwater channel, and leave a good margin of safety on either side.

The man started edging them in, blind as the mist thickened again, his eyes never leaving the compass . . . Suddenly the white rocks of the shore were ahead. There was a graunch from the boat's hull. Jackman gave a burst of throttle. They just scraped clear. He swung the wheel and found darker water again, the channel. He cut the engines.

'Ace,' he was shaking, 'I'm strictly one of your Sunday drivers.'

Wyatt breathed out a long sigh. 'Okay, we anchor here, in the mouth of the bay,' he said. 'And we do it with a light kedge-anchor and some rope. We don't want the sound of any chain going out.'

Jackman nodded. He went round the cockpit to the foredeck. Wyatt turned and looked at the Riva's square stern. There were high-angled davits, with an inflatable speedboat lashed to them. He looked more closely and saw the boat had paddles as well as its outboard motor. Which was the smart way to get in to the shore, he reckoned, slow, but quiet.

He had the inflatable lowered into the water by the time Jackman returned. 'I get it,' the man said. 'All ashore that's goin' ashore.'

Wyatt didn't answer. He looked at Jackman a moment, remembering the business of this afternoon, with that Goodhew woman. And remembering the compass course just now that had nearly got them on the rocks. Jackman looked grey in the mist, he thought, and maybe a little old. Maybe he was losing his touch.

Then there was Sinclair too. Sinclair who'd been drinking steadily back at the hotel. And still had the bulge under his jacket that could be a Scotch bottle.

'Reckon I'll take this one alone,' Wyatt said.

'Alone?'

'Yes, for the moment . . . Listen, Jacko, I'm going into that bay up there to take a quick look around. I'm going to stay out of trouble, find out what's happening, and get back here. None of the rough stuff you were talking about before.'

'Oh, do us a favour, Ace.'

'No ifs, no buts. Just give me an hour and I'll be back.'

The man shook his head angrily. But he stayed on deck as Wyatt got down into the inflatable and paddled away. Then, still angry, Jackman crossed to where Sinclair was standing at the rail, looking out at the mist. It was coming in patches again across the mouth of the bay, coming in strange white shapes . . . And, Jackman realised, there were other shapes too. Black shapes. Clouds of fat black mosquitoes, attracted by the boat's lights. Jackman flailed at them for a while. Then he moved closer to Sinclair. 'Any of that Scotch left that was at the hotel?'

'No, it's finished.'

'What you got then?'

''nother bottle. It was in the boat here. Froggies left it for us.' Sinclair handed the bottle over.

The mist was thicker the deeper Wyatt rowed into the bay. He lost his bearings, then realised he must have turned in to the shore. There was the scrape of pebbles against the inflatable's bow, a beach, with rocks above it. Wyatt got his feet wet as he pulled the boat up out of the water. Then he started walking, keeping always within about twenty yards of the shore. And maybe it was his imagination, but he had the feeling the evening was becoming lighter. Until he realised it wasn't imagination. There was whiteness all around him, on the beach and on the rocks. A white dust, like snow. And, like unmelted snow, floating out on the surface of the water.

The white dust grew thicker underfoot. He came to where it took over from the beach, where it rose up in what he took to be a smooth man-made embankment. His footsteps crunched up it. And at the top were railway tracks, old and rusty.

Wyatt didn't understand. All he knew was that the mist was thinning the higher he climbed. And he went on, up another white embankment, and over another rusty railway track at the top.

Suddenly he was out of the mist. It hung below him like a thick white pool around the walls of the bay. And the landscape above him was equally white and strange. It rose in tiers, embankment after embankment, climbing up to the black sky. Each of them had its railway track. And away in the centre of the bay was the track that linked them, rising steeply up the slope. There was a diesel locomotive here and tipper-trucks, silent and covered with the white dust. And beyond them black iron buildings, white-streaked too.

Wyatt moved closer, keeping the rise of an embankment between him and the buildings above. He saw cars parked up there, and what seemed to be a single-decker bus, none of them with lights. He saw no movement, but he heard voices. And it was these last that made him freeze. Because they were speaking French, but a particular kind of French. A kind he'd last heard on a boat-trip that had ended with an anchor chain.

Corsicans.

Jackman, leaning against the rail with Sinclair, knew he should ease up on the Scotch. He had one last bite of it, handed the bottle back – and then heard the hum of an engine behind him. He turned. A city of lights, it seemed, came out of the mist, came alongside, and let go its anchor with a roar of metal.

'Ahoy there,' Mrs Goodhew called from the deck of the large motor-sailer.

'Jesus,' Jackman said.

A seaman held the two hulls together. Mrs Goodhew stepped aboard. 'Saw you trying to give us the slip at Cherbourg,' she said. 'Came out and followed you on the radar.'

'Jesus,' Jackman said again. Thinking if she'd seen them on the radar, what about Michael Pedlar?

Mrs Goodhew came up to him. She put a jangly arm round his neck. 'Do something,' Jackman said to Sinclair. 'For Christ's sake, do something.'

But Sinclair didn't open his mouth. He went away into the shadows with the Scotch bottle.

And things were happening too fast. Mrs Goodhew's other hand slipped under Jackman's belt.

'Listen,' he said to her. 'Christ, Evelyn, this int no place for you to be.'

'I'm not sure about that.' Her hand moved.

Sweat stood out on his face. 'Evelyn, there's things goin' on, oh Christ . . . You got to get out, oh Christ . . . In another ten *minutes* . . .'

Her hand moved again. She looked down at it, smiled. 'Bingo,' she said. 'I thought it would be Bingo.'

'Christ.' Jackman found himself being pulled onto the larger yacht's deck. 'Christ, be *careful* . . .'

'Ten minutes, like you said,' she told him. 'Then I'll be away.'

She led him down the yacht's companion ladder, switching out lights as she went. And there was only one sort of reasoning going on in Jackman's mind now. 'What about your old man?' he asked.

'Two tranquillisers in his last Scotch. He's asleep.' She pushed him in through a dark cabin door.

But Goodhew wasn't asleep. There was the sound of another door opening along the passage. 'Evelyn,' his voice came sleepily, 'I was woken up . . . These mosquitoes, great big mosquitoes, coming in through the porthole.'

'Shut the porthole,' she called out to him, 'and use some of the insect repellent cream.'

'That, oh, yes.' There came a yawn. 'Where is it?'

'On the locker-top between our bunks,' she called out. 'I saw it there, next to my suntan stuff.'

'Yes.' He yawned again.

'Get back to bed,' she told him. 'I'll be right there.'

There was the sound of his cabin-door closing.

'Bloody fool,' Mrs Goodhew said.

Wyatt was feeling his way along the foot of a white embankment. He was down in the thick mist again, using it for cover. Ahead of him, and on a lower level, there was a yellow glow. Worklights, he reckoned, worklights down by the water. The jetty he'd seen marked on the chart.

He edged nearer, and heard voices again, talking in that same rough Corsican. There were footsteps too, shuffling on the white dust, then on the creaking boards of the jetty, and finally onto what had to be the fibreglass deck of the Broom cruiser . . . A lot of footsteps going aboard the cruiser . . . Wyatt remembered the bus he'd seen earlier by the sheds. He put it together with the sound of the shuffling queue below him. But didn't come up with any answers.

He moved still nearer. The lights were brighter now, each one with its separate glow. He was directly above the jetty, but still could see nothing. Until, picking his way carefully down the slope of the next white embankment, he almost walked into the back of a man.

The man turned. They saw each other, the second before Wyatt moved. Then he was back up the slope again, sliding, slipping, and jumping the railway tracks at the top.

He took another slope, another railway track, another slope. Trying to make the man behind think he was going away from the water. Then he doubled back, ski-ing the slopes and jumping the tracks. Making for the thickest of the mist, the water, and the beach where he'd left the rubber inflatable.

But he got lost. He went past it. Because suddenly the Corsicans were behind him, a whole pack of them now, and they'd found the rubber boat . . . and things began to happen that Wyatt just didn't believe. Firstly the mist began to thin out here near the mouth of the bay. Secondly the Corsicans looked round at the water and pointed . . . And thirdly Wyatt saw what they saw. The lights of some bloody great yacht moored alongside the Riva.

Wyatt sank to his knees. He knew what was going to happen, and it did. The Corsicans pushed the rubber boat out into the water and hauled themselves aboard. And, in line with the lights of the moored yacht, there was the flash of razors.

Mr Goodhew woke up in his cabin. He was feeling bad, very bad. It was night, the cabin was dark, and he couldn't see the time from the alarm-clock by the bunk. But he didn't switch on the light. Evelyn would be angry if he woke her, and he remembered her saying she was coming to bed. He looked out through the closed porthole, saw the lights from above. And decided to take the clock up on deck.

His plaster-cast clumped onto the cabin sole. And he almost tripped over it as he started moving. The carrier-bag, he realised, the one he usually wore around the plaster, had fallen down to his toes. He was about to kick it off when he realised Evelyn would be angry if he went on deck without it. She always was. But, try as he might to pull the plastic bag up, he couldn't reach it.

Mr Goodhew thought for a moment, then found a wire coat-hanger in a locker. With its hook he managed to get hold of one of the carrier bag's handles. He pulled it up. And started for the deck.

Reaching it, he was surprised to see a rubber inflatable coming towards him over the water. There were men aboard, men he didn't know. One of them, crouching in the bows, grabbed at the yacht's rail and hauled himself up. Mr Goodhew was amazed to see a cut-throat in his hand.

. . . What saved Goodhew's life was that he was standing there with a plastic bag on one leg, held up by a coat-hanger in his right hand. In his left was an alarm-clock. And his face was streaked like a Red Indian's with suntan paint from a tube.

The man with the razor, his head just over the yacht's rail, froze in amazement. Which gave Sinclair time to see him from the deck of the Riva, Sinclair time to vault the rail, come running, and, on the move, kick him hard across the Adam's apple. The man made no sound. He fell back clutching his throat. Other men grabbed out to keep the inflatable alongside. But Sinclair toe-capped their knuckles one after the other, and at the same time started shouting.

Jackman appeared, pulling on his trousers. He saw the inflatable and the Corsicans drifting away. He jumped across to the Riva's foredeck and let go the anchor-rope. He shouted at the seaman on the motor-sailer to get his anchor in. Both yachts' engines fired at once. Side by side they went fast out of the bay.

Jackman looked round at the other deck. He saw Mrs Goodhew appear, saw her husband turn to her.

'Man tried to kill me,' he said.

'Bloody fool,' Mrs Goodhew said.

36

The night and its dangers had gone. The plane from the flying-club at Hamble was going back over the English Channel. With Wyatt in the pilot's seat.

'Very funny, yes,' he said. 'Terrific. I mean, when I saw that woman's yacht out there, lit up like the QE2.'

'Ace, how was I to know she was goin' to come along? Nobody in this world could've seen that.'

'Nobody in this world would've got involved with that Goodhew woman,' Wyatt said. 'That freak.'

'Good mouth,' Jackman said. 'Good mouth on her, though.'

Wyatt didn't answer.

'Ace,' Jackman leaned towards him. 'Ace, Christ, I'm sorry. I mean, how it used to be in the old days, a few laughs and then strictly business . . . I sodded the whole thing up for you, dint I?'

Wyatt adjusted the trim, flew the plane on.

'Dint I?' Jackman insisted.

'No.'

'No what?'

'No, you didn't sod it up,' Wyatt said. 'I mean, for a while I thought you'd done just that. What with those loony Goodhews, and the Corsicans going out to them in the rubber raft . . . Not to mention me having to leg it, Christ, way along the coast to the east. Then cutting inland, and *then* walking for three hours along this road until I got a lift back to Cherbourg.'

'Yeh, Ace, you told me.' Jackman nodded. 'But then why is it, after all that, you reckon I dint mess you up?'

'Simple,' Wyatt told him. 'Because without you, without that Froggy organisation you tapped, and the Riva speedboat . . . I wouldn't ever have got to that bay where we anchored.'

'And?'

'Well, inland there, when I went ashore,' Wyatt said, 'it was strange. I didn't understand what it was all about at first . . . the white dust everywhere, the railway lines, the tipper-trucks and the sheds.'

'Me neither,' Jackman said.

'Until,' Wyatt went on, 'until I realised it was the answer to the whole thing.'

Jackman shook his head. 'You're jokin', Ace, int you? . . . Int you?'

'No,' Wyatt said. 'Listen, you bought an English paper this morning at the Sofitel. So what was in it?'

'All about this Cabinet Minister snuffin' it,' Jackman said. 'The one who was in the bomb-attack in London.'

'And?'

'Carnation Jack came in twenty to one at Epsom.'

'I mean, on the front page,' Wyatt said. 'The piece about the Cabinet Minister dying.'

'Well, it was all on about the bombers. Questions from MPs,' Jackman said. 'Askin' how the Law can claim to have cut off all sources of IRA explosives in the British Isles.'

'They don't *claim* they have,' Wyatt said. 'They have. It's as simple as that.'

'What d'you mean?'

Wyatt pointed back behind him.

'I don't get it, Ace.'

'All right. These sources of IRA explosives in the British Isles. What would they be?'

'Workin's,' Jackman said. 'Dams, motorway tunnels . . . Quarries . . . Mines.'

'Think about white dust,' Wyatt said. 'Think about railway lines, tipper-trucks, sheds.'

'A mine,' Jackman said. 'That place with the jetty was a mine.'

'And the Broom cruiser was there. And Pedlar was there.'

'No,' Jackman said. 'Not the man himself. I mean, doin' work like that.'

'We had a man watch him leave Cowes in the cruiser,' Wyatt said. 'We followed the same cruiser over to Cherbourg. And we followed it on to there.'

'But why take that kind of risk? I mean, him?'

'That's what I thought,' Wyatt said. 'That's what I was getting stuck on, all the time I was walking away from that place last night . . . But then I thought, for Christ's sake, he's the most likely. For Christ's sake, the Law's been watching routes into the U.K. for months now. And *he's* the one who's going to get through. Big man. Yacht-owner. Racing for his country. Union Jack on his shirt . . . Not to mention that cruiser of his, out in the Channel at all hours.'

'You're tryin' to say it's him, him personal, doin' contract runs for the IRA?'

'Think back. Think it through,' Wyatt said. 'First we heard about Corsicans expanding into Europe, right? We heard about them taking on European partners. We heard about Pedlar doing a deal with them. We heard about regular shipments . . . But our *mistake* was to think the shipments were coming from Corsica. They're not. It's just a business operated by Corsicans, out of France. And Pedlar's the last link in the chain. The big link.'

'*Pedlar?*' Jackman still didn't believe it.

'Listen,' Wyatt said to him, 'we believe it when we hear about an American car-manufacturer smuggling drugs, don't we? We believe it when one of the king-pins of the Vatican bank is found hanging under a London bridge . . . We just don't believe it when it's an Englishman.'

'Ace,' Jackman said, 'a Cabinet Minister's dead this morning . . . That's Pedlar killing his own kind.'

37

Michael Pedlar was exhausted, at the end of his strength. He steered the Broom cruiser up the river to Lymington and turned into the marina opposite the yacht club. He reversed into his berth and left the throttles at Slow Astern while he stepped onto the pontoon and put a line round a bollard. Willpower alone made him put out a second stern-warp and a spring, before he switched off the engines and let his head fall forward on the instrument panel.

It had been a long trip, a very long trip solo. But, he knew from experience, there was only one way of dealing with the kind of people he'd been seeing. . . . They told you they wanted you personally, and you went. They spoke all the time in their strange brand of French, and you forced yourself to understand. And you did all that because you wanted what they were offering badly enough . . . Which, Pedlar supposed, in the end had to be money.

And it surprised him to admit to that. Never in his life had he felt the lurch of excitement that other people felt about money. To him money was just figures on an account-sheet, black on white. If they were good figures he felt no sense of achievement, just a sense of carrying on with a plan that had begun generations before. Anyway, as far as his personal spending money was concerned, there'd always been enough.

He straightened up now and walked down the four steps that led to the deck saloon. Two years ago money had bought this expensive sea-going cruiser with its grey carpets and fitted teak. Two years ago it had been an expenditure easily justified. It was only recently – and suddenly – that money had caught him out.

Standing in the saloon, he realised it smelt of hot oil, of long engine-hours. He knew he was supposed to lift the trap-door in the grey carpet and check the engines daily, check the oil every hundred sea-miles or so. But he'd done neither, he'd been too tired. . . . In any case other people would see to it all now. The shipyard who usually looked after the boat.

He went down two further steps into the teak-fitted galley. He put on an electric kettle and made a cup of Nescafé. He drank it slowly, leaning against the bulkhead. Then, without moving his body, he stretched out his arm with the dirty cup. The feeling of tiredness was still with him. If he could reach the steel sink with it, he thought, he'd flick the tap on and wash it up. But he couldn't. He left it on the draining-board . . . Other people would take care of that too, he told himself. Leave the whole thing.

He closed his eyes and thought about what he'd say to Katerina when she came to pick him up. It was going to be difficult to return to mundane affairs after the past two days.

But, as Katerina drove him out of Lymington in the car, there was nothing mundane about what she had to say. In fact she had surprising news. She mentioned the name of the ex-Prime Minister. Apparently his security-man had turned up that day to inspect the farmhouse. And the man himself, it seemed, was arriving later on to spend the night.

'Spend the night?' Pedlar asked. 'But he's never stayed with us before.'

'*Ochi, agapi mou.*' Katerina shook her head. 'But in the circumstances . . . Of course everyone wishes the circumstances were happier.'

'What circumstances?' he asked.

'You mean, you haven't had time to read the papers?'

'No. Why?'

'Maurice Haverham has died,' she said. 'The Minister, you remember, who was in the bomb-attack.'

'I know who he is,' Pedlar said. 'I was at school with him.'

'Well, he lives . . . lived,' she corrected herself, 'in a village in the New Forest.'

'I know that too.'

She caught the coldness of his voice. 'You're probably tired,' she said. 'But of course the funeral is to be in his village church. And of course an ex-Prime Minister is expected to go.'

'So he's staying the night?'

'Yes. He's still in Cowes at the moment. It will make an easy trip for him. And he was very apologetic about inviting himself, but he said there was the security-angle to consider. Everybody seems to be very security-conscious at the moment.'

'So they should be,' Pedlar said.

'Anyway,' Katerina went on, 'he thought you and I would be going to the funeral too.'

'S'pose so,' Pedlar said. 'S'pose we must.'

The ex-Prime Minister went into the church early, to take his place in one of the front pews. Katerina and Pedlar waited outside in the sunlight, as other people arrived. And the thought came to Pedlar that it was going to be a smart funeral. None of your smell of cleaning fluid. None of your Moss Bros.

There were a great many people from school that he knew. And a great many he hadn't seen for years. It was uncanny how little they'd altered. The intent of the faces was still there. It was only round the edges that they'd changed, the folds of skin or the hair, added or subtracted like those Identikit pictures in the newspapers.

'Terrible business,' they all said. 'Cut down in his prime like that.'

'Dreadful,' he said.

'Those bastards with their bombs.'

'Bastards, yes,' he said.

Even Pedlar's ex-housemaster, a man with mutton chop whiskers and a rich creamy voice that had floated down from the lectern in chapel . . . Even he said it, 'Bastards.'

'Bastards, yes,' Pedlar said.

Katerina and he went into the church. They sat towards the back. From the bell-tower above came the sound of the funeral knell. And through a half-open curtain to Pedlar's right was the bell-ringer, a man with squeaking shoes. He was doing the job correctly. A toll every thirty seconds or so. A toll for every year of Haverham's life . . . Seventeen . . . squeak . . . Eighteen . . . squeak . . .

Pedlar thought of Haverham at school, a thin boy, white, with thin glasses. He thought of him bent over his 'fort' in Upper School, which was his desk, piled as always with the sheet after sheet of paper that he covered with his neat round hand. Haverham working, always working. While others came and went, smelling of the Fives Courts or the Snug at the Castle Inn.

Twenty-seven . . . squeak . . . Twenty-eight . . . squeak . . . The London house early one evening. Pedlar in the bath, and Emma his first wife coming in with the phone. It was Haverham . . . Was he speaking to Pedlar? Pedlar M? Who had been in B2 house at school? . . . Haverham had moved into London after long years away in the Civil Service. He was going through the phone-book for Old Boys.

Thirty-seven . . . squeak . . . Thirty-eight . . . squeak . . . A dinner party. Haverham not only thin now, not only spectacled, but dry. With a dry wife and a large house in Westminster that he seemed to flit across as if afraid of. Dinner, flowers, cigars had all been brought in by caterers. They'd finished eating by ten. Addresses had been exchanged and written down in diaries, as if after an accident. Then Haverham had left for the House.

Forty-two . . . squeak . . . Forty-three . . . squeak . . . Haverham in one of the Sunday colours. His face grey with nerves and fatigue. The dispatch-boxes he said he brought home and worked on till all hours.

Forty-five . . . squeak . . . Forty-six . . . squeak . . .

Behind Pedlar the second leaf of the church door was opened, coffin-wide.

Forty-seven . . . squeak . . . Forty-eight . . . squeak . . . Forty-nine.

Silence.

So Haverham had been forty-nine years old.

Young for a Cabinet Minister. Very.

In the late afternoon Katerina and Pedlar walked up on the slope above the farmhouse. The barley-field was white stubble now. The year had been taken.

And not just the year, Pedlar thought. Today had been a strange day. Leave had been taken, people had said their goodbyes one after the other. First Haverham. Then the ex-Prime Minister. And finally the children, Sammy and Daisy . . . Although they were only going for a week. Sammy to Pony Club camp. And Daisy, just six years old, to a make-believe camp on a friend's lawn.

But the upshot was that Katerina and Pedlar were alone for the first time in months. Alone and walking across a wide field. And she was in a strange black mood, a Greek mood. He wondered if it was to do with the children leaving, and he asked her.

'*Ochi, katholou.* Not at all.' She shook her head. 'I know where my children are. I can reach them.'

They walked on, then stopped near the crest of the field and looked back at the house.

'Michael,' she said suddenly, 'I have always had money of my own. I have always bought. Last week, for example, I bought a dressing-gown for seven hundred pounds . . . Is that right?'

'What d'you mean?' he asked. 'Morally?'

'No. Right for me to spend that amount.'

'Yes,' he said. 'No problem.'

'So it isn't money,' she said, and walked on.

He caught her up, took her hand. 'What isn't money?'

They had stopped again. The tiled roof of the farmhouse was below them. The smooth lawns inside the flint wall, the long paddock grass outside. And the baying of the foxhounds from the stables.

'*Etsi toe speeti eenay*,' she said. 'It's the house. It's our position here. Our way of life.'

'What is?' he asked again.

She turned to him. 'Michael, I would have to be a fool not to know that your family were only contacting you through solicitors, and sometimes QCs. A fool not to know why you were travelling so much on business. Why you were returning with a face that was paper thin, crying out for help.'

'What?'

'Only you don't cry. No sound comes out of your mouth. It is the English fight. Without tears. Without friends.'

'Katerina, what's *prompted* all this?' He put his arm around her, gripped her hard.

'Nothing. No reason,' she said.

'But there has to be.'

'No.'

'All right.' He thought a moment. 'Now listen, I'm meant to be going back to Cowes tonight, aren't I? . . . So come with me, please. I don't want to leave you here alone. Not like this.'

'To Cowes?' she asked. 'To watch you prepare for your famous Fastnet Race?'

'Yes.'

'No,' she said, 'I don't like the Fastnet. It's deep water and it's dangerous.'

'But that's simple too. Don't come near the yacht. Just relax, have a few people in to the house.'

'No,' she said. 'No, I don't want to.'

He frowned. 'I don't understand. Why so definite?'

She didn't answer.

'I mean, I thought you liked Cowes this year. I thought that at the Squadron Ball . . .'

'It was after the Squadron Ball,' she said suddenly.

'What was?'

She hesitated, but then went on. 'You remember we were sitting on Hugh's yacht early that morning? Having breakfast?'

'Yes. Yes, of course I do.'

'And you remember you were sitting a little away from me? Sitting further towards the mast? Talking to that yacht-designer?'

'Yes.'

'Well, it was then . . . Then I heard a conversation I wasn't meant to hear. It came up from below, I think. From the cabin below.'

'What did?'

'A man was talking about Martin Lyness,' she said. 'Lyness, your friend since schooldays. The *only* one of your old friends in fact who has stayed close since our marriage.'

And he knew what was coming next.

'Why did you get rid of him?' she asked. 'Why did you take away his job? His house? His car? His children's schools? In that awful English way?'

'Because, in that awful English way, that's how salaries are paid.'

'You haven't answered my question. *Why* did you get rid of him?'

He hesitated. 'Business,' he said. 'It happens in business. One is forced to place a huge amount of trust in those most intimate. And sometimes one . . .'

'One?' Her voice rose. '*One?*'

'All right, what do you want? Old-fashioned words? . . . Martin Lyness betrayed me. He threatened the entire structure of our business operation, could have left us with nothing. And he knew exactly what he was doing.'

'He knew? Are you quite sure?'

'At the time he did, yes. But whether he'd thought the whole thing through . . .'

'Michael!' Her arms came up. She beat at the air with her fists. 'There is nothing, nothing, *nothing* dishonest about Martin Lyness!'

He didn't answer. He waited for her fists to fall to her sides, again, to unclench.

They did, and her breathing slowed. 'Business, just as you told me,' she said. 'That sordid family fight you keep silent about. But Martin was a victim of that, wasn't he?'

Again he didn't answer.

'So . . . a friend gone.' She turned back towards him. 'But what did you feel? When you got rid of him?'

'Bad. Bad for a while,' he said. 'But then I knew it was necessary.'

'Necessary,' she repeated.

They faced each other in the failing light. He knew he had to steer the conversation on, away from Martin Lyness. 'What is it about today?' he asked. 'I mean, why do you brood about this for so long and then bring it out today?'

'Because Martin Lyness is only part of it,' she said.

'Part?'

'Yes.' She nodded. 'The other part is this morning. When we were in church, I mean, at Haverham's funeral. I was watching your face then.'

'What?' He was alarmed by this new path her intuition took her down. 'What's the connection? I don't see it.'

'Simply this. The death of Haverham didn't seem to affect you at all. And yet he died horribly, in a bomb-attack.'

'He was in it for that kind of risk,' Pedlar said. 'They all are nowadays.'

'But Haverham was also at school with you, just like Martin Lyness was. I mean, again I have to ask you, what did you *feel?*'

'Not a great deal,' he said. 'In all honesty there wasn't much to feel. Haverham wasn't a desperately attractive man. Not desperately liked.'

She turned and walked on, away from him. He caught her up.

'I have the feeling,' he said, 'that like Haverham, I'm not desperately attractive at the moment. Not desperately liked.'

'Your feeling is correct.'

'But once?' he asked. 'Once upon a time, as they say in the stories?'

'Once upon a time it was impossible for a silly emotional Greek woman to resist a calm cool Englishman.'

'I see.'

'But,' she swung round suddenly, 'is this calm and this cool everything? Or is it even worse than that? Is it cold and hard? . . . Michael, I just don't know. Your act is so convincing.'

'It's always been convincing,' he said with total honesty. 'I've never known why people are taken in by it. Never.'

They continued walking, a space between them now.

'Let me try and talk about this clearly, just like you,' she said after a while. 'It's very possible that I'm at a disadvantage. I mean, I've only known you since our marriage. While everybody else around here . . .' She shrugged. 'So tell me. What were you like years ago, for example? What were you like at school? What would Martin Lyness or Haverham have thought about you?'

'Well, probably,' he said, 'that I was one of those irritating people who were always getting their names up on the Honours Board. I mean, I got Form Prizes, scholarships. And there were the sports teams too . . . cricket, boxing, Eton Fives.' He shrugged, embarrassed. 'I don't want to take any credit for it. Things just came very easily to me, that's all. It never seemed to be my hand that was racing across the paper in exams. Or my hand that could make a cricket ball move in the air.'

'I see,' she said. 'But then, after school?'

'Well, there was Cambridge, I don't know if you mean that . . . And, well, there just came a day when I was told to forget all about Dante and Baudelaire, Goethe and Eliot. And go out into the big world and start printing pound notes.'

'Working for the family, is that what you mean? In the family business?'

'Yes. Really it was expected of me. I suppose I was the bright one of the family.' He shrugged again in embarrassment. 'And business was easy. Business people weren't all that bright. And those who were, well, there was never any of that Mercantile Honour I'd been told I'd come across. Greed's the word, really. Understandable too . . . But in a way I was successful because I never took money seriously. And I've never been affected by people who do.'

She stopped walking again and turned to him. 'Affected,' she said. 'In your whole life, Michael, has there been anything that's really affected you?'

'Yes.'

'What?'

'Two things,' he said. 'The first is our marriage. Truly I never really questioned who I was until I met you.'

'Sounds like a bad song.'

'Maybe. You don't believe me?'

She didn't answer. 'And the second thing?'

He pointed back down to the farmhouse. 'D'you see the drive down there? Outside the front door? Well, my father used to stand there quite a lot. Just stand . . . And he also stood up here on the field where we are now. He would look out to the south.' He pointed. And she saw now, from the crest of the field where they were standing, the sails out in the Solent, white against the dark strip of land that was the island.

'People say I'm obsessed about yacht-racing,' he said then. 'Obsessed about getting into the Admiral's Cup Team after trying for so many years . . . I don't think it's really true.'

She waited.

'My father, you see, he raced in the days of very big yachts,' he went on. 'There were thirty crew, and they could all be lying flat on the weather deck to reduce windage. There was a mainsail boom to that yacht thicker than the trunk of a tree. And my father would be at the wheel, hauling at it, sometimes up to his knees in white water . . . Once I saw the mast torn out of the yacht. Always, as a very small child watching from another boat, I was terrified.'

'Yes,' she said.

'And in a way now,' he said, 'sailing has come back to the same thing. Plastic sails, carbon fibre materials, hydraulics, they allow the boat to *race* whatever the weather. They can take anything the sea can bring, and it's boatspeed, boatspeed all the time.' He paused. 'I can tell you, which is true, that ocean-racing is the most intellectually demanding thing I've ever done. And the most physically exhausting. But what I should say too is that it's the most frightening.' He reached out for her hands again. 'I'm over that fear now. I'm no longer the small boy watching my father's yacht. And the proof is that some of the finest sailing men I know, the crew on board *Havoc*, want to race with me. And race hard . . . to win the Admiral's Cup.'

She was watching him, biting her lip.

'Silly, isn't it?' he said.

She didn't answer. She started back down the hill again towards the house. She said nothing as they went through the gate of the stubble field. As they went past the long paddock grass and the stables where the hounds were baying.

He stopped her at the gate in the flint wall. 'Katerina,' he said. 'The Fastnet Race begins on Saturday. It's going to occupy all of my time for the next six to eight days . . . So tell me,' he pulled her towards him, 'am I risking anything? Leaving you here alone?'

38

'Jacko?'

'Yeh, Ace. Where are you? Where you ringin' from?'

'Cowes. I've been over here since this afternoon. And . . .'

'And what?'

'Well, something strange . . . Pedlar came back to Cowes too this evening, quite late on. From his house in Lymington. But he didn't come in the cruiser, he came over in what they call the rub-a-dub, the rubber raft with the big outboard.'

'What's strange about that, Ace?'

'Only that when he went *into* Lymington, he had the cruiser, remember?'

'Yeh, course I do. So where is the damn cruiser then?'

'Back here at Cowes,' Wyatt said. 'It's been in the yard up-river here half the day. Being serviced.'

'*Again?*'

'That's what I thought. I mean, the boat was only out at sea for two days . . . So I asked someone I knew over here. Guy called Chas, who works for Skyline.'

'And?'

'Chas said Pedlar didn't look after the boat properly when he was away. And it started running hot or something. Anyway somebody had to give it a test-run, and then bring it back to the yard here to be looked at.'

'Doesn't sound very likely, does it, Ace?'

'No.'

'So what you goin' to do then?'

'Have a look,' Wyatt said. 'Later on tonight. Much later on, when everybody's left the yard.'

It was midnight, and the shipyard on the east side of the River Medina was dark. Wyatt climbed the fence and crossed to the large boatshed at the top of the concrete slipway. He walked right round the building. All the doors he came to were locked. But then he saw the metal outside staircase, and the small door at its top that he supposed led through to the gantry. It was open. He went in.

He waited in the darkness. Waited until he could identify the sounds – the wind creaking a ventilator fan, and the shifting links of the chain-hoist in its path. Then he flashed the torch. The Broom cruiser was below him on its cradle. The first thing Wyatt saw was the top side of the radar-scanner that he'd painted red. And the second thing was the cruiser's white deck, footmarked by the shoes of yard-men.

He went a little way along the gantry and then down a ladder. The cruiser seemed massive now, towering above him. Wyatt climbed up onto its deck, and followed the footmarks down from the open wheelhouse to the saloon. The footmarks continued, on a plastic sheet that had been laid over the saloon's grey carpet. But they didn't lead to the trapdoor in the carpet, the one that was the inspection-hatch for the engine. Nor was the plastic sheet folded back around the trapdoor.

Wyatt swung the torch-beam round. He saw that the footmarks were clustered around a bulkhead, one of the main structural bulkheads of the cruiser. It formed the rear wall of the deck-saloon, and of the narrow galley that was on its starboard side. And it formed the front wall of the stateroom, set lower down in the hull and taking up most of the box-like stern.

A structural bulkhead, nothing unusual about it. Until, with a length of string, Wyatt began measuring the interiors of the lockers that were fitted on either side of it, in deck-saloon, galley, and stateroom. Then he found the lockers were shallow, and the bulkhead far thicker than it looked. Four feet thick, in fact. In a cruiser forty-two feet long.

Wyatt looked inside the lockers more closely. He saw no obvious way of getting into the cavity that had to be concealed behind. No fastenings or studs. If it hadn't been for the footmarks on the plastic sheet, he would never have looked at it in the first place.

He went back on deck, and down the ladder to the boatshed floor. He flicked the torch round it, then searched in outward-moving circles until he reached the shed-walls. Nothing that shouldn't have been there . . . Workbenches, toolracks, light and heating switchboards, hoist controls . . . Then in a store-room he came across a load on a wooden pallet. It was square, wrapped in black polythene, and stencilled HALDANE CROPSPRAY PLC.

Cropspray? In a boatshed?

The load was held in its square shape by a metal frame. Wyatt got out his Swiss knife. With its screwdriver he undid eight screws and lifted the top section of the frame clear. He unfolded the black polythene wrapping, and underneath saw grey wooden boxes with rope handles. They had serial-numbers on them that included Continental sevens and ones.

For some time Wyatt worked with the screwdriver again, unscrewing the lid of the topmost box. Removing it, he found thick egg-box style wrapping designed to protect the shipment from the heaviest of knocks. And the shipment, he discovered, was made up of thick clear plastic bags. He took one of them out. Through the plastic he could see two cartons, each the size of a milk-carton, and made of waxed card. They had bases and sides, but no tops. And inside them he could see a grey malleable substance like putty. Oily putty. Because a trickle of clear viscous liquid had seeped from the cartons, and left traces on the inside of the plastic bag.

He knew what it was, the grey putty. And, more to the point, he knew its source could be identified. Because on the cartons were serial-numbers . . . ORL 739882, and ORL 739883.

He put the plastic bag to one side on the store-room floor. He replaced the lid of the wooden box, the polythene sheeting and the metal frame, until the pallet-load was exactly as he'd found it.

Then, holding the bag in one hand, he climbed ladders and walked gantries until he was once again at the door high up on the shed-wall.

Looking back a moment, he swept the torch-beam once again round the shed. It came to rest on the cruiser finally, the white deck and the black footmarks. And inside him was the smallest suspicion, that it had all been just a little too easy.

'Jacko? It's seven. I get you out of bed?'

'No, Ace, I been up, gettin' the missus off.'

'Off? Is she going away?'

'Yeh. Eight o'clock. Goin' off to some bleedin' horse trials or somethin'. Takin' the Range Rover of course.' Jackman yawned. 'And she's only after me to use her Mini today and not the Rolls. Save petrol.'

'No, don't bring the Rolls,' Wyatt said.

'What's that, Ace? Don't bring it where?'

'Red Funnel Terminal, Southampton. Nine thirty-two arrival,' Wyatt said. 'Bring the Mini so nobody'll remember you.'

'Why should they remember me?'

'Because I've got proof that might be very important to certain parties,' Wyatt said. 'Two cartons. French serial-numbers all over them. Gelignite.'

'Eh?' Jackman's voice was suddenly wide-awake. 'Gelignite? . . . Two? Two cartons?'

'Yes. They're packed together in this plastic bag. I didn't open it to be on the safe side.'

'What d'you mean, *safe side?* How's that bleedin' stuff go up anyway?'

'No need to worry, Jacko. You have to have a smaller amount of explosive to set it off. By that I mean a detonator. What it does is cause the necessary shock-wave that makes the whole lot go off bang.'

39

A man called Lefebre had been ringing the Sofitel for two days now. Yesterday he had been told that Mr Jackman's party had left, without saying whether they were returning or not. Today he had been told that there was now no vacant room in the hotel, and it could be taken that Mr Jackman's party was not coming back.

Lefebre, with his neat schoolmaster's mind, tried to think of some way of contacting Jackman in England. But it would have to be through a friend of a friend, the way he himself had been contacted. And in this case Lefebre was reluctant to deal with people he didn't know. Because the information he had to pass on was delicate. It was traceable. It involved serial-numbers.

Also the information was unusual to say the least.

It concerned the agency, the outside agency that had been working with the Englishman, Michael Pedlar, in Cherbourg. Because in the end, information had come Lefebre's way, as he'd known it would. And it had come in the usual manner, through an informer. Predictably either a man who was underpaid or frightened. In this case frightened.

The man was a barman in the town. He was in the habit of working at small extra jobs of a certain nature, and two evenings ago he had taken on just such a job. At a mine, some twenty kilometres away along the coast. He had worked there before, and he was ready to reveal now that he'd worked for Corsicans.

Two evenings ago Corsicans had picked him up, together with other men, in a small bus. They'd gone out to the mine, and had worked, as on other evenings, loading boxes of gelignite onto an English cruiser. They had concealed the gelignite in a bulkhead on the cruiser, under the Corsicans' supervision.

Halfway through the night's work the Corsicans had made off into the mist, chasing some man they claimed to have seen. They hadn't found him, but they had seen an English yacht moored out in the bay. There'd also been an inflatable raft on the beach. This the Corsicans had taken. They'd gone out to the yacht, but hadn't been able to board it because the English yachtsmen there had proved very aggressive. And had subsequently taken the yacht out to sea.

Returning to the mine, the Corsicans had been unable to decide whether the English yachtsmen had merely been very angry holidaymakers, or a group of people with more sinister intentions. Therefore a plan had been decided on. The Corsicans had made up the explosives-shipment as usual, taking gelignite from the mine's lock-up store. But two boxes had been taken from a secondary store, and these they had placed on top of the shipment. It was planned too to leave these boxes on top when the shipment reached its English destination. And to leave them there for a day or two, in case anyone came nosing around.

Lefebre had not understood. Nor had he understood his informant's fear.

But the point was, the man said, that these particular boxes had serial-numbers prefixed ORL. They came from a stock of old gelignite. Gelignite had a shelf-life like many other commodities. It deteriorated. And when that time came it lost small amounts of explosive in liquid form. This acted as a detonator, made the gelignite highly unstable. And, once removed from its protective wrapping, was liable to go up at any moment.

40

In the passenger saloon of the Red Funnel steamer, Wyatt realised he hadn't travelled among crowds for some time. He had been in small aircraft, cars or yachts, and wasn't used to queues, to fighting for a seat, or to groups of rowdy children.

All of these were now around him in the passenger saloon. He sat squeezed up on a long curving bench seat. Facing him, away over the lino-tiled floor, a long queue stretched to the cafeteria counter. Closer at hand a troop of Cub Scouts were sitting at tables. They were fighting, and they were already starting on their packed lunches at nine in the morning.

One of them, Wyatt saw, must have been in the cafeteria queue. With grease running down his chin, he was chewing his way through a bacon sandwich. It smelt good. It reminded Wyatt he'd been up half the night, and was tired and hungry.

He got up, put the Woolworth's carrier-bag that held the gelignite down on the bench seat, and joined the queue.

It was slow. The smell of frying bacon came only gradually nearer. Looking back, Wyatt saw the Cub Scouts getting rowdier, saw one of them snatch off another's cap and dart away with it to the bench seat. The Woolworth's carrier fell. Wyatt went over and picked it up.

Jackman seemed huge standing by the Mini. The interior of the car, as he opened the door, was filled with smoke from his cigar. Wyatt sat beside him, hugging the Woolworth's bag on his knees.

'That it?' Jackman asked.

'Yes.'

They drove for some time without talking.

It was a hot August day, hotter than any there'd been recently. Jackman left the city on the Ringwood road. It became dual carriageway, and he cursed the lack of power in the Mini engine. They went on to the Lymington turning and then passed through tall dark pines that shredded the sunlight.

'So what's it look like?' Jackman asked, turning from the wheel.

Wyatt opened the Woolworth's carrier and showed him the sealed plastic bag.

'Two in there, you say then, Ace?'

'That's right.'

'Well, maybe that's best. Maybe we're goin' to need more'n one try at gettin' it to the Law.'

'What d'you mean?' Wyatt asked.

'You ring the Law and tell them to pick up some gelignite, what they goin' to do? Maybe send a bomb-disposal team and blow it up, right?'

And Wyatt hadn't thought of that.

They reached the outskirts of Lymington, and Jackman's driveway. He turned in, gravel flying up from the wheels. And he parked at the side of the house, between kitchen and garage.

Jackman stubbed his cigar in the ashtray and they got out, Wyatt carrying the Woolworth's bag. 'What I mean is, Ace, what's their procedure? They get a call. All the red alarms go. They cordon off the area, press a button, and wallop, get it out of the soddin' way . . . Or . . .' He poked a finger at Wyatt. '. . . Do they photograph the stuff first?'

'Photograph it?' They were walking across the gravel towards the kitchen.

'Take pictures. Get this serial-number of yours on file. I mean, if they do that, we're quids in.'

'They would photograph it. Bound to,' Wyatt said.

'Yeh . . . Depending on the area, of course. Where you left it, I mean. You'd have to choose that so they'd have time to go to work. No panic.'

'Right.'

Jackman walked slightly ahead as they neared the kitchen door. 'Two in that bag? Two cartons?' he asked again.

'Yes.'

The man stopped, turned, blocking Wyatt's path. 'Okay, Ace, I know you said it was safe. But let's not piss around . . . We take one in the house, okay, and work out what to do with it. We leave the other in the car.'

'Don't know why you're nervous,' Wyatt said.

But he put the Woolworth's carrier down on the drive. He took the plastic bag out of it, opened its seals, and held out one of the wax-paper cartons of gelignite. 'Here.'

Jackman backed away. 'No, you keep hold of that, Ace. Out in the open like that, just in its carton, it bothers me . . . I'll take care of the other one, the one that's still in the bag.'

Jackman took the plastic bag and walked away across the gravel to the Mini. And maybe he was nervous, or maybe the Mini's door stuck, but he managed to smack the bag, hard, against the side of the car. He stood quite still a moment, sweating. Then he put the bag in the car and came back. They went into the house.

'Our main bother, as I see it,' Jackman said then, 'is where we put the stuff before the swift phone-call to the Law . . . Street, no good . . . Park, no good . . . It has to be somewhere out in the country, all right? Somewhere by a B-road. A B-road where nobody int goin' to go.'

'Okay, I'm with you there,' Wyatt said. He put the wax-paper carton down on the kitchen table.

'Sticky, innit, Ace?' Jackman bent close. 'Sticky stuff comin' out of it?'

'Seems to be,' Wyatt said. 'Weeping? Haven't I heard that expression somewhere before? Weeping gelignite?'

'Weepin'?' Jackman said. 'Soddin' pissin' out. Look at it on the table there. I mean, that carton must have, what, quarter-inch, half-inch of liquid in the bottom?'

'Maybe,' Wyatt said.

'Ace, you sure it don't mean trouble?'

'You have to have a detonator,' Wyatt said. 'I told you.'

'If you say so.' Jackman started for the hall door. 'Okay, I'll go and get a map, Ordnance Survey. We find ourselves some small B-road out in the country.'

He went away through the hall door, leaving it open. And, almost immediately, one of his wife's Siamese cats came into the kitchen. It leapt up from the tiled floor and started prowling along the work-surfaces. Wyatt watched it. Outside in the hall he heard Jackman rummaging through a table drawer. 'Here, got it,' he said. 'Reckon this has to be the one.'

Wyatt looked at the Ordnance Survey map as the man came

back. 'No,' he said, 'that's Ringwood.'

'But it'll do, won't it? I mean, dump the stuff out of the area?'

'No, let's keep it local,' Wyatt said. 'Short car-ride. Less chance of being seen . . . Where are the other maps? Out in the hall-drawer?'

'Yeh, Ace.'

Wyatt went out, then stopped halfway across the hall. 'Right or left drawer?' He turned back, saw Jackman by the table, saw the Siamese cat jump up onto the table, saw it knock over the carton of gelignite, saw it land base-down on the floor.

Wyatt frowned. He walked on to the hall-table, found the local map in the right-hand drawer, brought it back. He picked up the carton, put it back on the table.

Then he saw Jackman was shaking. 'Okay, Ace, I believe you. This stuff don't go off wallop. But, listen, I'm goin' to put the soddin' cat out anyway.'

He picked up the animal and went through the outside door. Beyond him, across the drive, was the parked Mini. And it had to be a trick of light but there seemed to be a steady blue flickering inside the car. Then half of Jackman's arm, and Jackman's hand, still holding onto the cat, passed Wyatt with the blast coming into the kitchen. There was yellow flame. There were breaking windows. Machine-gunning gravel.

Immediately black smoke, billowing outwards like some huge flower. Wyatt ran outside, through smoke and bits of falling-clanging Mini car. He saw Jackman, lying on his side. His left arm was meat. His left leg was meat. And bone the left side of his face.

'Jesus! Jesus! *Jesus!*' Wyatt shouted.

He bent to Jackman. The man was still alive. Blood was pumping dark onto the gravel. Wyatt moved him as little as possible. He took off his own belt, got it tight, tight, around the man's trouser leg at thigh-level. He ran back into the kitchen. He found a standard lamp. With the Swiss knife he cut off the flex. Went outside. Put a tight tourniquet around the stump of the arm.

He was still alive.

Running, Wyatt went back into the kitchen. The phone was going to be dead, he told himself. But it wasn't. He dialled 999, asked for police and ambulance. Said there'd been an explosion. Gave the address.

He ran outside again. Jackman was still alive. He ran back into the kitchen, saw the carton of gelignite still on the table. Again he ran outside. Jackman was still hanging on.

The faintest whooping of police sirens. Wyatt checked Jackman's breathing again. Then he knew what he had to do. He went back into the kitchen. He grabbed the kitchen roller-towel from its rail. He wrapped the carton of gelignite in it, then wrapped it in a second towel he found in a drawer, until it was a soft bulky parcel. Gingerly he took it outside with him. Jackman was breathing in the same shallow way. There was a wide hole in the drive where the Mini had been. The sirens were nearer.

Holding the towel-wrapped parcel carefully, brushing his way carefully past clawing branches, Wyatt went away through the trees on the far side of the lawn.

41

'Mr Windlesham? Mr Arthur Windlesham?'

'Yes. Who wants me?' the man said down the phone.

'My name's Wyatt.'

'Who?'

'We met, Mr Windlesham, earlier this summer on a racing-gallop. We watched a racehorse of yours being exercised.'

'Did we now?'

'Yes, I was with a man called Jackman. He did most of the talking.'

'Oh, you were with Jacko? Yes, I remember . . . How is he then, Jacko?'

'Not very well. Not very well at all,' Wyatt said.

He explained, and it was very difficult to do, over the phone.

There was a long silence. 'What the fuck d'you want me to do?' Arthur Windlesham asked then.

'Listen,' Wyatt told him. 'I didn't know who to ring. I didn't know how the hell to find any of Jackman's friends. Then I remembered your name. And I got your number from the book.'

'So?'

'So I did all I could for Jackman, all I possibly could. I fixed him up without moving him. I rang the Law . . . But there was this second carton of gelignite, there on the kitchen table. And what could I do? I couldn't leave it there for the Law, could I? Not with Jackman lying right by it, *involved?* Not with it looking exactly like it was?'

'No,' the man at the other end said. 'No, you couldn't.'

'Thank Christ for something.' Wyatt breathed out slowly. 'Now, listen, I have to know what to do. I'm out in the country, calling you from a phone-box. And three hundred yards away down this lane is the gelignite, in a ditch. I can see it.'

'You can *what?*'

'See it,' Wyatt repeated. 'But as I said, I have to know what to bloody do. I have to find out from somebody, somebody in the business who knows about gelignite . . . I mean, I've got to make it safe, haven't I? Before I do any more phone-calling? To the Law? . . . What d'you want me to do? Kill more people?'

There was another long silence.

'Call me back in ten minutes,' Arthur Windlesham said. 'I'll see if I can get you a number to ring.'

Wyatt called back. There was a number to ring. And he began to learn a few facts about gelignite . . .

Weeping gelignite, for example, could not be detonated by rough handling. As the man now told Wyatt, he could stand at the wicket in Southampton cricket ground and hit sixes and fours with the stuff all day, and nothing would happen.

Weeping gelignite, in fact, produced a clear liquid. This was highly unstable. It turned into gas in a warm confined space. In a hot confined space it could even ignite. Maybe in a small parked Mini on a hot August day. Maybe, but doubtful. Much less doubtful would be a spark, or a cigarette somewhere . . . A cigar even better . . . A big cigar stubbed out in a small ashtray, a dead cert.

Dead cert, Wyatt thought. But he didn't say it. What he said was, 'For Christ's sake, tell me what I do now.'

And the man told him. He was to walk to the nearest grocery store and buy rubber gloves and plastic freezer bags. He was to wear the gloves so that he would leave no fingerprints. And he was to put the carton of gelignite into a freezer bag and knot it so that it was airtight. Then he was to put it into a second freezer bag and do the same. Then a third.

And then he was to ring Arthur Windlesham again. In two hours' time.

Wyatt walked to a nearby village. He bought gloves and plastic bags. He returned to where he'd left the gelignite and made it safe. Then with forty-five minutes in hand, he waited, hidden from the road by a hedge, until it was time to phone Windlesham.

There was good news. 'Jackman's still alive,' Arthur Windlesham told him. 'He's in Intensive Care, fighting, and fighting good, they say. They give him a sixty-forty chance now, say he's built like the proverbial brick shit-house. But, of course, he int goin' to walk for a long while, nor use his left hand . . . And . . .'

'And what?' Wyatt asked.

'He int exactly beautiful.'

Wyatt was silent for some time.

'When will they know?' he asked then.

'Know what?'

'If he'll pull through?'

'By tonight.'

'I see.' Wyatt nodded. 'And . . . And what am I supposed to do?'

'With the gelignite, you mean?'

'With the gelignite.'

'Well, I hear as how you were told how to make it safe,' the man said.

'That's right.'

'Okay. So what you do is the followin' . . . Have you got money?'

'Yes.'

'You get a hire-car. You drive well away from any town. You take the gelignite to some country field. It has to be a field where they done the ploughin', and where they planted the winter wheat or barley. A field they int goin' to disturb till next spring . . . D'you know how to look for a field like that?'

'Yes,' Wyatt said.

'Okay. Well, you got the gelignite in plastic bags, all knotted up, right? And what you do in this field is you dig a small hole, you got me? And you bury it . . . And you mark it good too. Then you ring me as soon as it's done, and tell me the exact spot where it is.'

'And what will you do?' Wyatt asked. 'Ring the Law?'

'Not yet,' the man said. 'First some thinkin's got to be done. About how to keep Jacko out of it, I mean. Maybe we wait until he wakes up before we can do that. So's he can see one of us. So's he can decide.'

'Can I see him?' Wyatt asked. 'I mean, how soon . . . ?'

But the man interrupted him. 'You don't see him at no time, my son. You're goin' to be exactly the last person in the world to see him, if you want my opinion.'

Wyatt nodded slowly. There was a click at the other end as Arthur Windlesham rang off.

42

It was after midday. Pedlar, Monroe, and Hal the bowman were aboard *Cry Havoc* in the marina. The start of the Fastnet Race was now only twenty-eight hours away, and they were rigging a safety-line along the length of the yacht, from cockpit to forestay. This was a line to which crewmen would clip their safety-harnesses whenever they worked the deck in rough weather.

Monroe looked up from the wire-splice he was making at one of its ends. 'Reckon there's a fair chance we'll be using this damn thing,' he said.

'You think so?' Hal asked.

'More'n a fair chance, yes.'

And Pedlar knew what he meant. It was too hot. The air was too still. And the western horizon was like smoked glass, darkening every time he looked at it.

He bent back to his work. But then something came into his mind, something Katerina had said to him last night, when she'd refused to come back here with him to Cowes.

'*You'll be preparing for your famous Fastnet Race*,' she'd said. '*I don't like the Fastnet. It's deep water and it's dangerous.*'

Dangerous? . . . He worked on, securing the safety-line to the deck . . . Rubbish. You just had to be well-prepared. Know what you were about.

But then, maybe ten minutes later, another part of that same conversation came back to him, something he himself had said. At the end. When he'd been worried about her, not she about him. '*The Fastnet's going to occupy all of my time for the next six to eight days*,' he'd said. '*Am I risking anything? Leaving you here alone?*'

Risking anything? . . . Again rubbish. He trusted her absolutely. Without question.

But if so, why? . . . When Monroe and Hal knocked off for a

beer at one o'clock . . . Why did Pedlar go to a call-box and ring the farmhouse over on the Lymington shore?

The phone rang for some time. Then the nanny answered. She said that Katerina wasn't at home. She had gone out at about half-past eleven, saying she would be back for lunch.

'Lunch?' Pedlar asked. 'But isn't it lunchtime now? I mean, well after one o'clock?'

'Yes,' the nanny said.

And again, no cause for alarm. Katerina, Greek, was notoriously relaxed about appointments. She was just late for lunch.

So then why did Pedlar now go and find Monroe in the 555 Bar? Why did he tell him a lie? That he'd left something back at the farmhouse, and was going across the Solent to fetch it?

No reason. But he went down to where the Broom cruiser was moored, opposite to *Cry Havoc.* He took it slowly out of the marina entrance. And then, faster, went over flat gunmental water to a darkening sky.

The silky beech trees flicked past him along the length of the drive. The sky was suddenly darker, much darker, away to his left. But it wasn't weather, it was the farmhands burning the stubble in the cornfields. Three men he could see, working with pitchforks, outlined by yellow flame. Then black smoke trailing away downwind, around the grey stone walls of the house. Pedlar parked and got out. The crackle of the straw-burning was loud, drowning the sounds of the countryside. But even so something was missing, something he couldn't put a finger on at first. Until he realised – there was no howling of dogs from the stables.

He went into the house. The sound of burning stubble was muffled now. But there was another sound, a woman crying. Pedlar ran down the hallway. Then flattened himself against the wall. Six lean foxhounds swung out of the shadows ahead of him. They passed, knocking over a standing vase with a crash. He spun round. The dogs were gathered, milling, near the front porch. He shouted at them. They paid no heed. He went towards them. In a pack they moved out on to the drive.

The woman's crying was still there.

Pedlar went through to the dining-room with its longcase clock. He reached the kitchen. The nanny was there, sitting at the table, weeping.

'What's the matter?' he asked.

'Those dogs. Those wild dogs.'

'Foxhounds, yes. How the hell did they get out?'

'Mrs . . . Mrs Pedlar let them out.'

'She *what?*'

The pack of dogs came in again, nosing into the corners of the kitchen. Pedlar tried calling again, but they didn't recognise human voices. He tried to grab out for them, but they wore no collars. They just slipped past him, lean, intent on their hunt.

He threw a chair. Startled, they went out again in a pack. 'Now,' he said to the nanny, 'let's get this right . . . Mrs Pedlar let the dogs out?'

'Yes . . . Yes, just before she went off.'

Off. The word was there between them, like a red warning light.

Pedlar tried to keep his voice calm. 'When I spoke to you before,' he said, 'on the phone, I mean . . . You didn't say she'd gone off. Just out.'

'Yes.'

'And you said she was coming back for lunch.'

'Yes.'

'But she didn't, did she? And what's more you knew she wasn't going to. Isn't that right?'

'Yes,' she said softly.

'All right then. Where's she gone?'

There was no answer.

'Where?'

'She didn't say where.'

'Didn't *say?* I don't bloody believe it.'

The nanny started crying again.

Pedlar went towards her. 'You're trying to tell me she left no phone-number?'

'That's right.'

'But she wouldn't do that. She just wouldn't . . . What would happen if Sammy had an accident, say, at Pony Club Camp? Or if something cropped up at the house where Daisy's staying?'

'Then,' the nanny said, 'then I was to . . .'

'The number,' Pedlar said. 'Just give me the bloody phone-number.'

She cried louder.

Pedlar softened his voice. 'Make yourself a cup of tea,' he said. 'And sit down and drink it.'

She went to the fridge and opened it. Then the dogs came back. They fought round her and past her, got muzzles and paws into the fridge, pulled out milk-bottles, meat, eggs. The nanny screamed. Hounds were snapping all round her.

And Pedlar let it happen. He let the mess of eggs, sausages, bacon build up over the kitchen floor. Let the hounds slide and snap, milk on their long lean flanks. Let the woman's hysteria grow.

'The number!' he shouted suddenly. 'My wife's blasted *phone*-number!'

And just as suddenly she gave it to him. Though he had to hear the figures three times before he understood them correctly.

He kicked the dogs away then, slammed the fridge door shut. And, holding the nanny's shoulders, spoke softly. 'Go up to your room,' he said, 'and shut yourself in.'

She went away up the back stairs. He stepped past the snarling dogs and returned to the hall. He went into his study and closed the door. Then he picked up the phone, dialled.

Katerina answered. 'I thought it might be you,' she said.

'Yes.'

'She gave you the number?'

'She was surrounded by bloody foxhounds. They got everywhere. Into the fridge.'

'Poor Nanny. I'm sorry. Truly sorry.'

'But you let them out?'

She didn't answer.

'Let's leave that for a moment,' he said. 'But I have to know. Where are you now? What is this damn number I'm ringing?'

Again she didn't answer.

He made his voice calm then, slow and calm. 'All right. Just tell me one thing,' he said. 'Why?'

'Why?'

'That's right.'

'Because it all came to a head this morning,' Katerina said.

'What did?'

'Everything . . . You see, I had a visitor. A woman, an old woman, a relation of yours.'

'A woman?'

'She came out of an overheated car,' Katerina said. 'And she made me switch on an electric fire. This morning, hot as it was. She was very old, eighty or more. She had arms like dried up sticks. And she was covered in diamonds.'

Pedlar knew who it was. 'Oh, Christ,' he said. 'Oh, Jesus Christ.'

'Yes,' Katerina said. 'She told me many things. Things she thought I should know.'

'I'll bet she did.'

'What's more she was right. They were things I should know.'

'But are you sure they were *true?*' He found he was shouting again. 'I mean, if you knew that evil old woman . . .'

There was a pause.

'True, yes, I think so,' Katerina said then. 'She told me about money, for example. She said you were in serious money trouble. Very serious. Because of your yacht.'

'Is that right?'

'Yes. And she said you had been trying to wriggle out of this trouble by doing a deal in Corsica, with Corsicans.'

'I have done a deal in Corsica, yes.'

'With gangsters?'

'I call them that for a joke.'

'There have been deaths in Corsica,' she said. 'In and around Corsica . . . Three men killed on an anchor-chain, for example . . . That's a joke?'

'I don't know what you're talking about.'

'D'you deny then that you've been having meetings? Recent meetings, with French-speaking people?'

'No, I don't deny it,' Pedlar said. 'But they're Canadians.'

'What?'

'Canadians. From the French-speaking part of Canada,' he said. 'Katerina, I don't know what the hell this business about Corsica is. As far as I'm concerned, Corsica's just a small deal, on the edges, to help pay for the yacht's expenses . . . My real troubles, from start to finish, have been in Canada. *All* of them.'

'I don't believe you.'

'I'm sorry. But even you must admit, I've been over in Canada a hell of a lot recently.'

She thought a moment. 'It's quite simple,' she said then. 'If it's Canada, if your meetings have been with Canadians, then you must have proof.'

Pedlar hesitated. His head sank onto his chest. 'No . . . No proof,' he said. 'These people . . . How do I explain it? . . . These people don't work like that. They . . . they don't leave any tracks behind them. Nothing on file, I mean. And . . .'

'D'you mean we're back to gangsters again?' Katerina asked. 'Or just people you call gangsters, for a joke?'

'No,' Pedlar said, 'of course not gangsters. But these people, some of their activities have been looked on as, well . . . *nearly* criminal . . . They move fast, without tracks, as I said. And when I meet them, they always insist I'm, well, on my own.'

The dogs came back then, in through the study window. They leapt lean and slaver-jawed onto the sofa, then under a nest of tables. The tables went over. The lead of a small lamp went too, pulling it down. A hound was trapped. Snapping and snarling, it splintered a chair-leg. The room became wreckage.

'Don't hang up!' Pedlar shouted. 'These bloody dogs . . . *Don't hang up!*'

He left the room, slamming the door behind him, and racing upstairs to the bedroom. He snatched up the bedside phone. 'Are you there?'

'Yes.'

'Where were we?'

'Hearing you stammering and stumbling about your Canadian friends,' she said. '*Very* unlike you. In fact I didn't believe one word you said.'

'No,' he said. 'No, let me explain. Let me try and go about it another way . . .'

'Don't bother.' She cut across him. 'Because there's something you can't talk your way round. And that's the sacking of your friend, your oldest friend, Martin Lyness. Stripping away his job, his house, his . . .'

'We've had all that,' he said.

'No, we *haven't!*' And she swore at him in Greek. 'We haven't had Martin Lyness! Because, as I learned today, you sacked him for one reason, and one reason only! . . . You were dealing with these men we were talking about, the Corsicans, call them gangsters, call them near-criminals, call them what you like! . . . And Martin disapproved of what you were doing, disapproved utterly! So he told people about it! People you didn't want him to tell! . . . And that's true, *true*, isn't it?'

'True. Yes, all right, it is.' Pedlar slumped down, deathly tired. 'True in broad outline . . . Except for one thing, the thing I've been trying to get you to understand all along . . . Not Corsica. Never Corsica for one moment, but *Canada!*'

'Canada, of course,' she said sarcastically. 'I forgot.'

'Canada, yes, don't you understand, where the company should be showing huge profits!' Pedlar was shouting once again. 'But where on paper the whole think looks godawful! And why? Because the family, *my* family, have gone back on decisions, have refused to sign cheques, and cut off *all* short-term money! And what did you expect me to do in return? What *could* I do in return, but call in people who know how to deal with this kind of fight? . . . Canadians, and, all right, fly-boys, pretty bloody nasty boys! And, all right, pretty bloody nasty things have been happening over in Canada! Salting the mine, mickey-mousing the order-books, getting short-money in *any* damn how!' He paused, out of breath. 'And it's true, just as you said . . . Martin Lyness couldn't stand the heat. He did pass on information. But he passed it on to where it really mattered, to the worst possible place, the *family!* . . . And, Katerina, I don't have to tell you, do I? About this family of mine? How they've been trying to destroy me for the past year? Destroy my home? And destroy you? *You* as well?'

'The record's stuck,' she said. 'You just repeat the same things over again, Canada and the family, Canada and the family. And I don't believe any single . . .'

The pack of dogs came in again, while Pedlar watched. And while he watched, they ran their snouts into the open drawers of Katerina's dressing-table. They pulled out scarves, handkerchiefs, stockings and underwear. They went into the open wardrobe, came out with his pyjamas and shirts. They were on the bed . . .

Slowly he put the phone down.

Driving away past the line of beech trees again, he saw the thick black smoke was still there. But now it was coming at him from a different quarter. Men were burning the lower stubble fields, down by the road. The black clouds seemed to be following him, the clouds of war. It wasn't over, he told himself. It hadn't even begun.

43

Wyatt waited in the saloon of the Broom cruiser. He'd got in through the for'ard skylight that had been left open in the heat.

He'd shut it behind him. And now he waited.

Footsteps came along the Lymington marina. Footsteps sounded on the deck. A key opened a door. Pedlar appeared.

Wyatt smashed a fist into him, knocking him down. He picked up the keys, locked the doors. Then he went round the cabin, pulling down the metal blinds over the windows. There was a strange slatted light.

He stood in the centre of the grey carpet, looking down at Pedlar. 'We're locked in,' he said. 'There are just these four walls now, and the two of us.'

Slowly Pedlar got to his feet. His eyes never left Wyatt. 'I've seen you, haven't I?' he said. 'Here in Lymington and at Cowes? Watching me?'

Wyatt didn't answer.

'It's that hand of yours.'

'What is?'

'That right hand. The thumb that's missing. That's how I know you.'

Wyatt held it out then, the white scar where his thumb had been. 'You want to talk about it?'

Pedlar shook his head, as if he didn't understand.

'All right, I'll tell you,' Wyatt said. 'I lost this thumb of mine when I was down under the sea. I was trapped down there, handcuffed to an anchor-chain with three other men. They died . . . But you wouldn't know anything about that, I suppose?'

'No,' Pedlar said. 'No, I wouldn't.'

'Just like you wouldn't know about a couple of other things,' Wyatt went on. 'This cruiser, for example, this Broom cruiser. And a trip you made in it two days ago. Over to France and back.'

'What?'

'A trip I know you made. Because I followed you by plane.'

'To France? France and back?' Pedlar frowned. 'But that's impossible. I took the boat along to Torquay. And there I . . . I saw certain people.'

'Who?'

'Canadians, if you must know, Canadian associates. I don't think I have to tell you any more.'

'No,' Wyatt said. 'Because you never made the trip. You went over to France, as I said. And I know that because I painted the top of your radar-scanner red. Which made it very easy to pick the boat out from the air.'

'*What?*' Pedlar was genuinely shocked.

'And there's more,' Wyatt went on. 'That little French trip of yours brought back a certain cargo. A cargo that did an awful lot of harm. For example it nearly killed a very good friend of mine.'

Pedlar stared at him. 'I don't understand a single thing you're talking about,' he said.

'No? . . . All right then, we'll try it this way.'

And Wyatt settled into the crouch, chin tucked well into left shoulder, the crouch that had been second nature to him years ago when he'd boxed light-heavy in the RAF. He felt almost bad about it as he closed in on Pedlar. Bad, because his hands were weapons. He'd had seventeen light-heavy bouts, and lost one.

While Pedlar, ridiculous as he shaped up, was all public school. Was all chin up and hands held high . . . It was only a question of moving within distance, Wyatt knew. Moving well within distance and taking that first probing punch from the other man. The punch he was going to throw out of distance, leaning back. You took it, and still you came on, hitting as you came on, low, never straightening the arm.

Pedlar's high probe came out. Wyatt moved in, set up with his right. And he didn't see it. There was just an explosion in his head, and he was on the floor.

That had happened too, before. So all right, more careful this time.

But the same explosion. The same left hook, coming from nowhere, which he never saw. He picked himself up again.

And then again.

It wasn't a long fight. Because at some time back in that public school of his, Pedlar had done a lot of boxing. He was good, very good. And, more than that, for a man of his age he was very, very fit.

Which, Wyatt told himself as he lay on the floor for the, what, sixth time . . . he maybe should have known.

'I don't think there's any point in prolonging this,' Pedlar said, panting.

The calmness of the man.

'What I do think there's point in doing, is talking.'

The *calmness*.

'And why there's point in talking,' Pedlar went on, 'is because a great many over-emotional things have been said this afternoon.'

Wyatt got to his feet. His knees felt like jelly. He sat down on the grey settee.

Pedlar leaned back against the locked companion door, watching him. 'I always find it better, at a business discussion,' he said, 'to get right back to the beginning. To get all the way back to the first things, and start from there.'

Wyatt was still amazed, at the precise voice, the boardroom manner.

'So what's the start-point going to be?' Pedlar asked him. 'You tell me.'

Wyatt thought for a long moment. Then he gave in. He held out his right hand with the jagged white scar. 'This,' he said. 'This has to be it. It was done to me by Corsicans. They took four of us out in a boat, off the coast of Italy. They shackled us to the anchor-chain and threw us over the side.'

'Us?' Pedlar asked.

'Yes. There were three other men and myself. I'd flown them out of Calvi airport earlier.'

'Earlier,' Pedlar said quietly. 'Earlier. D'you see what I mean? . . . That couldn't have been the start of the story then, could it? You have to tell me what you were doing in Corsica. Why you were with these people in the first place.'

Wyatt hesitated. It was getting too close to his real name, and to the company he'd once run, Custom Air.

'We can't help each other unless you tell it all,' Pedlar said.

So Wyatt told it. Right from the beginning. From the Yacht List telex, in fact, that had come into Cannes on that Friday morning months ago.

And Pedlar looked up. 'Yacht List telex?' he asked. 'You mean, from Corsica?'

'Yes.'

'And a Friday, you say? Would that have been in early June? The fourth of June?'

'Yes,' Wyatt said.

'You're sure?'

'Quite sure.'

'All right, this telex, would its number have been . . . .' The man reeled it off. '. . . YL06040130?'

'I don't remember,' Wyatt said. 'I can't carry figures in my head, not for months.'

'I can,' Pedlar said. 'It's my job.'

'And?'

'That was a telex that always bothered me,' Pedlar said. 'It was charged to my account. I queried it. I never found out who'd sent it, of course, owing to the anonymity of the system . . . But it was confirmed by Cannes, and by head office in London. So I had to let it go.'

'You mean, you didn't send it?' Wyatt asked.

'No.'

'Can you prove that?'

'Yes.'

'How?'

'Simple,' Pedlar said. 'The code number on a Yacht List telex shows the date and time of transmission, doesn't it?'

'That's right.'

'Okay, let's break the number down . . . YL, Yacht List . . . 0604, sixth month, fourth day, equals fourth of June . . . Friday the fourth of June.'

'Yes.'

'And finally, 0130 means what it says . . . One-thirty in the morning.'

'Yes,' Wyatt said again.

'Or in other words,' Pedlar told him, 'definite proof.'

'What?'

But the man didn't seem to hear him. He seemed to change tack. 'You say your name is Dan Wyatt?' he asked. 'You used to run a firm called Custom Air? You flew the Yacht List?'

'Yes.'

'So, would you know another Yacht List pilot, called Harry Tambay?'

'Yes. Well, I mean slightly. I know his name.'

'All right,' Pedlar said, 'what we've got to do is find some way of getting you to a phone. An international phone.'

'Why?'

'Why?' the man repeated. 'Because, don't you see, I couldn't possibly have sent that Yacht List telex. At that particular time I was up in the air with Tambay. He was flying me.'

'*What?*'

Pedlar sighed. 'My life has been pretty damn complicated recently,' he said. 'I've been hopping airplanes when I should have been sailing yachts. At Calvi and at Cowes . . . And early that Friday morning I was coming back from a meeting with certain people. Just in time to sail in the Calvi Offshore Race, which started at ten o'clock.'

Wyatt stared at him.

'Ring Tambay and he'll tell you,' Pedlar said.

44

Pedlar moved quickly. He took Wyatt with him in the cruiser over to Cowes. He got the use of a friend's office in the town there, just off the High Street. He sat Wyatt down at the office phone and told him to call anywhere in the world, and keep on calling. Just so long as he raised Harry Tambay.

Then, alone, he walked back to the Groves & Guttridge marina. He returned to the Broom cruiser and stood once again in its saloon. He needed time to think, and he needed a cup of coffee to start him thinking. He went down the two steps into the galley, made Nescafé and drank it slowly, leaning against the bulkhead. Then, still leaning against it, he reached out with the dirty cup to the stainless steel sink. He put it under the tap and flicked the water on.

And suddenly he remembered.

Two days ago he hadn't been able to reach the sink, hadn't been able to wash the cup – from exactly the same position.

Pedlar thought about that. Then he started looking at the bulkhead, the big structural bulkhead that divided galley and saloon from the after stateroom. He began opening lockers and taking measurements.

Day had become evening. The western sky was now a dark blue gunmetal, the same colour as the sea. And Pedlar was low on the surface of the sea, crouching down in the rub-a-dub, the rubber raft, with just his head peering over its grey float.

He was out in deep water, out past the Needles. Spray was beginning to lip into the raft, a swell was building up, a dark stormhead coming. And though a minute ago Pedlar had not been able to mark the line of the horizon, to see exactly which was sea and which was sky, now suddenly he could. Because two white lines appeared on the water, luminous white, strange against the gunmetal blue. They were the wakes of two approaching boats, two identical Broom cruisers. The one that

Pedlar had followed out from Cowes, and the other that must have come from France. The white wakes curled in question-marks as the cruisers circled each other, as they closed, came together. A dark figure from one changed places with a dark figure from the other. That was all that happened. And then the wakes separated again, the Cowes boat on to France, the French boat back to Cowes.

There was more to it than that, of course. There had to be, Pedlar knew. The changing of the boats' names on the way back to harbour. And the shipyards, the yardmen who had to be involved somewhere along the line. But, he knew too, the thing was possible, more than possible. Whichever cruiser was berthed at Cowes had only to leave the marina for an hour or so . . . even for a test-run, a test-run after a service . . . had only to head for the open sea at a steady twenty knots, and the changeover could be made well away from prying eyes.

Pedlar turned for home. And the shocks began to come . . . the size of the operation first of all . . . People were always accusing him of having a boardroom mind. And perhaps it was true. But the fact remained . . . to buy a second Broom cruiser, just like the one he himself owned, was going to cost somebody eighty-seven-point-four thousand pounds.

Then more shocks came, much bigger shocks, and thick and fast. About that dark figure, the man who'd changed over from boat to boat. He'd been too far away to recognise. But now as Pedlar headed back towards Cowes, as the rubber raft lurched from wave to wave, his mind lurched too, from step to step. And finally he had to admit it . . . In all the world there was just one person it could be. One person who had the opportunity, the inside knowledge, and the contacts.

And to think about that man in those terms was impossible. Utterly impossible.

Why? Pedlar kept on asking himself. *Why?*

By the time he returned to the marina at Cowes he'd given up thinking. He had to, it was a difficult enough task to moor the rub-a-dub in the slapping waves and the spray. The wind had risen still further. Darkness was coming early, with a rush. There was the shriek of wire rigging, and the bark of fenders between wildly rolling hulls.

A great many hulls. Hulls that were moored alongside eight or ten deep. It was the night before the Fastnet. Privately-entered yachts had come in from France, Germany, the Low Countries, even from as far afield as the United States. Because the Fastnet was the 'biggy' as they all said, the hardest ocean race in the world. In addition to the Admiral's Cuppers there were going to be over two hundred and fifty other yachts starting, in other classes. And with such a large fleet the problem, as always, was finding experienced racing crews.

Pedlar walked along the trots. In the shadows to the right and left of him were dancing bowls of light. Yacht-cockpits. And in each of them owners or skippers were trying to sign on new hands.

'You say he can navigate?' Pedlar heard.

'It's what he tells me.'

'But can he navigate offshore?'

'Yes, offshore.'

Then, where the trots neared the concrete hard, he came to a struggling queue of young men. They had tired stubbled faces, lit by the swinging lamps overhead. They had duffel-bags, and were holding out crudely-lettered placards, itemising their past experience on yachts . . . The Fastnet hopefuls. The kids who'd come on foot from God knew where, trying to hitch a ride in the race.

Pedlar went up the ramp to the hard itself. He came to the crowds that were around the mobile bars . . . Kids again, eking out their last pence on lager, hoping to hear talk of the yacht that needed crew . . . He walked past them, and on towards the Groves & Guttridge yard office. He knew what he had to do. Phone the Authorities. Tell them about what he'd just seen out at sea. Tell them what he knew, and what he could only make wild guesses at.

Then he stopped. He turned back towards the crowds and pushed his way through to where they were thickest. And, once there, he looked up.

Above him, high on the shed wall, was the gleaming gold lettering of the Admiral's Cup scoreboard. And the news it held was no news to Pedlar. The American Team was in the lead. The 'American B Team', or Malays, were lying second. The Brits were third. Twenty-seven points behind.

But, as far as the scoring system for the Admiral's Cup went, the Fastnet, the 'biggy', counted triple points. The Brits could still win.

Pedlar knew how stupid that sounded. Yesterday he'd asked Katerina if it was stupid . . . winning, helming one of the yachts in the winning team . . . She hadn't answered.

Perhaps it was stupid. Perhaps the whole thing, the nine months that had made up his Admiral's Cup campaign, the six years prior to that when he'd tried to put a Union Jack on his chest . . . Even the small boy frightened by his father's huge yacht years ago . . . Perhaps it all meant nothing. And he was, as people said, a man obsessed by that glittering scoreboard above.

But the fact remained, he now made a decision. He put off going to the Authorities . . . put off doing anything that would threaten his freedom of movement . . . until the end of the Fastnet Race.

45

It was the night of the Cowes Week fireworks. For an hour or more in the twilight a crowd had gathered on the Victoria Parade. The first-comers had been able to lean against the stone balustrade, in the spray there, but with the best view out over the water. But gradually they had been pressed tighter and tighter against the stonework as the road filled up behind them. The road and the bandstand on its far side, where the band was playing selections from light operas. Then the bandsmen left, and the crowd took their places, standing on chairs and on railings, filling the orchestra pit. While above, the balconies of the yacht clubs were like plush theatre boxes, peopled by glowing cigarette-ends and quiet voices.

Night fell. The street-lamps went out, and still the crowds thickened. As did those other crowds out on the water. They were aboard yachts. More and more yachts making the short trip out from the marina, until they were like a second town out there, their masthead lights dipping and swaying in the darkness.

Nearer at hand, between the yachts and the Parade, were the dark pontoons where the fireworks waited, the rockets, starbursts, and set pieces. And where men in fireproof suits waited too, glancing at their watches.

The mortar shell, the red spark that hurtled up into the night to explode with a sky-splitting crack, opened the display.

Wyatt heard it. He was in the office just off the High Street, where Pedlar had left him. And where he'd been for three hours now, phoning halfway round the world as he tried to find Harry Tambay, air-taxi pilot.

Finding a taxi-flyer was hard enough at the best of times. Finding Tambay at the moment was almost impossible. Because apparently Tambay had struck it rich, he'd moved up into the King Lear bracket. And with those kind of jet engines pushing him along, he was burning up an awful lot of sky. Wyatt followed the trail. He rang airline after airline. And those fake-cheerful, fake-comforting voices of the girls on the switchboards pushed him on from Italy to Germany to Denmark. And finally over to the far side of the Atlantic, where the real money was.

Tambay was flying steel-men around the United States. They moved fast. There were loops and false trails in Wyatt's information, but in the end he got hold of Tambay's flight-plan, Minneapolis to Des Moines, E.T.A., roughly two hours ago.

And that was the hitch . . . No more than a slight hitch, those fake-cheerful voices assured Wyatt . . . But it seemed Tambay had been diverted. It seemed a freak storm had hit Des Moines. More than an inch and a half of rain had fallen in twenty-four hours.

Wyatt tried the diversion-airports. He tried a long list of them, one after the other. And Tambay he eventually ran to ground at a small airfield in Omaha.

But even then he didn't get the information he was after, not straight away.

Because firstly there was Tambay's shock, his stunned reaction to the flight he'd just made. That storm he'd had to avoid, over Des Moines.

A hurricane, the real thing, hailstones as big as golfballs, Tambay said. Christ, it was something else, flying in the States. There was a hurricane season, for Christ's sake. In the early Fall these things blew up in the Great Plains. They cut a trail of destruction across the country, and left by the eastern seaboard. Then, how it went, was they crossed the Atlantic and blew themselves out in the Bay of Biscay . . . The only trouble was, Tambay said, this particular hurricane had been the exception. It had moved so fast, the weather men had only time to get it down on the map as a depression . . . a depression, Jesus.

Wyatt had to wait, had to let the man talk it out of his system. But then the time was right and he could ask the question, the sixty-four-dollar question . . . About a certain flight Tambay had been booked for, way back in the beginning of June when he'd been flying the Yacht List in Europe. A flight into Calvi, arriving early in the morning.

Had his passenger been a man called Pedlar? Michael Pedlar?

Tambay said he'd have to look at his diary. It was in his flight-bag, just outside in the corridor.

Four thousand miles away Wyatt waited. As he did so he heard the crack of another firework rising up from the Cowes Parade. He saw it burst into a star high overhead, saw that star split into further stars, and those stars split yet again. Until bright silver light flooded the room.

Then Tambay came back on the line. 'Night of third–fourth June,' he said. 'Yacht List. One person into Calvi . . . And the guy's name was Pedlar. Just as you said.'

Ten minutes later another starburst exploded in the heavens. Another star which became further stars, which each split again in their turn . . . Four times . . . And the crowds along the Parade counted the number of times, 'One! . . . Two! . . . Three! . . . *Four!*'

The night became silver. The sky was unzipped. And a new sky, dropping to the horizon on every side, gave the crowds a feeling of rushing through space. A feeling of the world tilting and swinging. All old perspectives lost.

Michael Pedlar stood in a street in the town. It was lit like day, and he was watching a certain door. It opened. His wife Katerina came out. She was putting on her watch, and it was then that he knew. Because the watch was a Vacheron, one of her proudest possessions. It was waterproof, shockproof, every proof bar one. There was just one act in her life that she preferred to perform completely unencumbered.

Perform completely unencumbered . . . The coolness of his mind, Pedlar thought. Why couldn't he think like others? Why couldn't he think, fucking cow? Fucking whoresmelt of a ditch-fucked fucking . . . ?

But he couldn't. The coolness of his mind centred on just one thing.

The irony.

That she had left him because of his supposed dealings with criminals, with pay-offs and killings. And she had gone to the very man who was responsible.

Irony. Because she didn't know, of course.

But Pedlar did. Above him the starburst was still falling in the sky. It was still day, bright, ice-cold. And his mind still ice-cold too . . . The thinking that had got him this far . . . The phone number he'd rung this morning to speak to Katerina . . . Finding out who that number belonged to . . . Who the man was, in fact, inside that house right now.

The only man in the world it could possibly be, as Pedlar had realised before. But what he hadn't realised was what the man wanted.

Answer, everything. Pedlar's money, his business . . . his wife.

Because the motive was plain too now.

Hate.

And, looking back over the long days of summer, Pedlar could see what had been in front of his eyes. *Why* that hate had seeded itself, why it had rooted and grown. He could even see the times when it had grown. The precise times.

In the night sky the starburst faded. Light went from the street.

There was a gap in the firework display, a pause while the next sequence of maroons and set-pieces was made ready.

In the silence a man walked down the ramp of the Groves & Guttridge marina, and out onto the trots. He passed the queue of young men there, the Fastnet hopefuls with their crudely-lettered placards. But unlike them, the man wasn't soft-footed. The sound of his footsteps was the sound of stout leather shoes. He was more at home on the turf of racing-gallops than in yacht harbours. He owned a racehorse, he was a friend of Jackman's, and his name was Arthur Windlesham.

Arthur Windlesham walked past the rows of Admiral's Cup yachts. They were deserted, their crews all away at the fireworks. And the one yacht in particular he stopped by was deserted too. It had a long blue hull, and the name on its stern was *Cry Havoc*.

Clumsily in his leather-soled shoes, Arthur Windlesham stepped aboard. He raised the companion-hatch and went down the steel ladder to the long enclosed space below. He stood there a moment. In his left hand he held a torch, and in his right a plastic bag. It was tightly knotted. And inside it were two other knotted bags.

Because, earlier in the day, Windlesham had been to see his friend Jackman in hospital. And he'd been amazed. Jackman wasn't just going to live. He wasn't just very much alive . . . Burning out from the terrible hospital bed of dressings and drips was that violence of his that Windlesham had often seen in the past.

In a few whispered sentences Jackman had told Windlesham what he was to do. He was to go to a certain field and dig up a certain plastic-wrapped bundle. And he was to take it to a certain yacht in the marina at Cowes. Because the man who was down to pay for the gelignite explosion was the man who'd been down to pay all along . . . Michael Pedlar.

Now, on Pedlar's yacht, Windlesham swung the torch-beam around him. It settled on a pile of blue sailbags up near the bows. Windlesham chose one of them. He saw it had a Skyline trademark on it, and a label that meant nothing to him . . . storm trysail, it said . . . Windlesham unknotted the sailbag. Then he unknotted the three plastic bags around the gelignite, just as he'd been told to, allowing it to breathe. Finally he put the gelignite into the sailbag, and tied the knot at its throat once again.

Returning to the quayside, he found the darkness above him was raining silver stars. Starburst after starburst was spreading out to fill the sky. And from the distant Parade he could hear the crowds counting the bursts. 'One! . . . Two! . . . Three! . . . *Four!*'

Arthur Windlesham watched. Tomorrow, he told himself, there was going to be a bigger firework display aboard a yacht called *Cry Havoc*. Much bigger.

The fireworks were over. The final set-piece, with its royal coat of arms, had brought applause from the Parade, and from the balconies above. And now, out on the dark water, the town of yachts was dispersing. Before they left, however, they were mounting a display of their own. White smoke lay around their hulls, thick and curling. Maroons rose from them to the sky, trailing more smoke as they went. And then from high above, carried quickly away on the rising westerly, the red distress flares came down.

46

The next morning there was a meeting of the British Team in Michael Pedlar's house. Hugh the Team Manager was there, as were the three skippers and the tacticians. And the problem was sails. The rule-book allowed each yacht to take thirteen sails on the Fastnet. Thirteen and no more. It was deciding on horses for courses.

The weather chart was on the table in front of them. And the real question-mark was not the present westerly gale. That would blow itself out quickly, everyone agreed, moving on round the shoulder of the self-same high that was to the south. No, the real question concerned this high. It seemed to be receding even further south. And a deep low, far up in the Arctic circle, seemed to be moving in from the north-west towards Iceland . . . The north-west, people said. A lot of rubbish could come in from there.

All of which meant that Pedlar had a problem on his hands. Because he was for taking the pessimistic view, the view that the high windforces would come. In that case, he said, the storm sails would be needed, the small 'pocket handkerchief' sails. And first on his list was the smallest of them all, the storm trysail . . . While Monroe said that was cautious thinking, old-fashioned thinking. He was against taking the trysail. In its place he wanted the 'bullet-proofer', a sail that was part of his own brand-new thinking for high winds. All right, a slightly bigger sail, a riskier sail, but a sail he'd designed for one purpose only, dammit . . . Winning . . . And winning was what it was all about, taking *Cry Havoc* to the limit. Because the yacht was strong. It was the best. It could handle anything the sea threw at it.

Sails . . . Pedlar knew they were Monroe's department. But he knew too that final questions about the boat's safety were his. He shelved the decision temporarily.

Towards the end of the morning he left the house. He walked down the High Street and called in at the chandler's. His chart of the Western Approaches, he knew, had been torn, and he needed to replace it. The man behind the counter sold him a new one. He seemed worried. Fastnet morning, he said, and as grey a one as he could remember. But what he could never remember was selling so many charts of the Fastnet Rock. Who were all these people? he asked Pedlar. What did they think they were going on? A joy-ride?

Pedlar went on to the Groves & Guttridge yard. From the top of the ramp he looked down at the trots. In the Admiral's Cup marina all was calmness. Boxes of provisions, wet-weather gear, sailbags, were being ferried aboard. Crewmen were preparing the boats for big weather, fitting life-lines, taping wire-cutters and knives at strategic points, securing anything that could move.

While away in the visitor's marina it was as if an army were in retreat. Packing-cases and tinned food littered the decks there. Crewmen, unfamiliar with their boats, moved awkwardly, still feeling their way around . . . Though, as Pedlar knew, it wasn't an army in retreat, but advancing. There were now only two hours to go before the smallest class of yachts went out to the start. Well before the Cuppers were due to take their gun at 1400.

1340. Twenty minutes to go. And the motion of the sea was too uncomfortable, the wind gusting too strongly back from the start-line, for Pedlar and Monroe to have much of an argument. *Havoc* was still under engine, the Broom cruiser was still alongside, and the argument was still about sails. Following Monroe's instructions, the storm trysail had been removed from the yacht, and the 'bullet-proofer' handed over in its place. But Pedlar was uneasy. The latest weather chart looked as if it could turn bad on them in a few days' time. Really bad.

He compromised. One of the number 2 genoas was taken off, and the storm trysail was handed back from cruiser to yacht. Monroe took it with bad grace. And his frown deepened when he saw that the throat of the sailbag was tied, for some reason, with a very un-seamanlike knot. He re-tied it. The sail was passed down below.

The cruiser fell back over grey water. Pedlar watched it unhappily. This was like the start of no other race. There was no exciting waving from his children on the motor boat's bridge. And no waving, excited or otherwise, from Katerina. For the hundredth time in the past few hours Pedlar wondered where the hell she was.

And for a moment too he wondered about somebody else. Because the tall figure of Chas wasn't there in his usual place, behind the cruiser's wheel. But then Pedlar remembered. There'd been another injury among *Havoc*'s crew – stupid injury – Dallow, one of the winch-men, had fallen off a chair at a party. And Chas, next in line on the waiting-list, had finally got his chance to race on the yacht.

Pedlar gave orders. He got the mainsail up and took a single reef. He got up the heavy genoa. Then, in irons like the rest of the fleet, *Havoc* waited. There was too much white spray about, too much short chop to the water, to dart around and play silly buggers. And anyway there was only one choice for the start. Wind and tide favoured the island shore. And that's where Pedlar was going, close in for a couple of tacks, to knock hell out of the waiting Press boats.

They left with the gun. They followed Hoff, creaming and hissing in his wake. Hoff's sails ahead meant that Pedlar was steering blind. But Hoff was running interference for them too. Which helped, because there were screams and shouts as the American knifed past the anchor-chains and square sterns of the motorboats. And Pedlar followed, close on his tail, putting in tack for tack. He didn't look round until he noticed that the Press boats were thinning out, and that on the last one were photographers he recognised. 'Good luck,' they shouted at him. And, Pedlar reflected, that was going to be the last he was going to hear from the outside world for, what, five days? Seven days? More?

Out past the Needles, *Havoc* began to take the westerly gale full on the nose. There was a second reef in the mainsail now, the smaller number 3 genoa was set, and no longer was there a line of crewmen in dripping oilskins, sitting out 'birds in a nest'. They were below, leaving just Pedlar, Monroe, and a winch-man in the cockpit.

It was stuffy below, and warm, with the hatches battened down. Nine men there were in that long enclosed space, all of them grouped on the windward side of the hull to keep the yacht balanced. Four men were lying aft on the tubular steel cots. Ronnie the navigator was at his console, his chin sunk down in his hands. And the remaining four, including Chas, were sitting on sailbags piled up on the cabin sole.

Chas moved. And the sailbag that had been under his feet escaped. It pitched across the leeward side as the yacht rolled. Chas went after it. He noticed it was the storm trysail, and he noticed it had a bulge inside its tightly knotted throat. A bulge as if it were inflated. He pulled the bag back underneath him and sat on it. There was a hiss like escaping air. And an acid smell. Ammoniac.

At the same moment Archie the cook leaned towards him. 'Your watch is due on deck in a few minutes . . . Hot soup put you on your feet?'

Chas nodded. Archie turned, steadied the steel stove on its gimbals, and lit one of the burners.

Around Chas there seemed to be a strange blue flickering in the air.

And . . .

The hatchway above their heads opened. A blast of cold Channel wind flooded the hull. 'Weather's showing signs of easing,' Pedlar called down to them. 'Let's get some sails on this thing and go racing.'

47

The Fastnet fleet had set off four hours ago. Wyatt was sitting in the Cross Keys, the pub where he had a room. He drank a pint or two in the public bar and did some thinking. Then he went up to lie on his bed and think some more.

He'd come a long way, he thought, to find a certain man. He hadn't found him yet. In fact all he really knew was who the man wasn't . . . Michael Pedlar.

And yet Pedlar was caught up in it all somehow. More than that, Pedlar was worried, dead worried . . . Or why would he have stuck Wyatt in an office last night, and staked him to phone-calls around the world that must have cost hundreds of pounds?

Pedlar was worried, all right. And the simple answer had to be that a wealthy man, head of a large business empire, had one hell of a motive to clear his name.

A far stronger motive than Wyatt's, in fact. Which meant that Pedlar had to be the man to stick close to, the man who in the end had the power to sort the whole thing out.

But Pedlar was away in a yacht-race. And it didn't take a genius to work out that a yacht-race started in a certain place, and finished in a certain place. In this case, the finish was at Plymouth, in anything between five and seven days' time.

So, Wyatt told himself, the only thing he could do was to wait it out for the next four days, and then go to Plymouth on the fifth.

That settled, he lay back on his bed, loosened his tie, and told himself he could sleep against the voices in the public bar below. And he managed it. Until suddenly there was just the one voice, calling to him up the stairs. He was wanted on the phone.

Going down to the hallway, Wyatt tried to work out who it could be. The only person he could think of who knew his number here was Jackman. But Jackman? Phoning from a hospital bed?

It wasn't Jackman. It was a voice Wyatt knew very well.

'Can you come over?' Alex asked. 'Now? To the house? Right away?'

He walked up to the street on top of the hill. He passed the row of white Georgian porches and stopped outside Alex's house. It was now evening, but he could see no lit windows, just a light through the glass transom of the hall. He pressed the bell once, with no answer. Twice, with no answer. Then he tried the front door. It was open. He went in.

Alex was standing at the far end of the hall, alone, under the light. It wasn't cold but she was shivering, and she had a coat draped round her shoulders. There was a strange hump in the coat at the back of her neck. She walked towards him, bumping against the wall. 'Hallay,' she said. '*Orfly* nice.' Then she fell. The coat slipped from her. There was a knife between her shoulders, a knife in her side, and a knife in her arm.

There was movement then, away by the light. Three darkish men there with razors. The hall was red rage. Wyatt was at them, seeing no razor as it caught his fist, sliced his arm. Seeing just the jaw, close, right inside his distance. He knocked the man's head off, felt breaking bone. The man fell against another, who went back through a doorway, off balance. There was still the third, who cut Wyatt's other arm with a circling movement. Steel was nothing. It was kill. He was in behind the circling movement, through, hitting low, twice, very very hard. The face was a skull, sucking for breath. And Wyatt turned for the one who'd gone in through the door. Who now made his mistake. He backed.

It was the kitchen where he'd been with Alex before. The fridge, the kitchen range, and the big scrubbed table. And on the table a pile of tins, yacht provisions maybe. Wyatt grabbed them up. He threw straight for the temple, straight for the mouth, the eye. It was kill, kill. Joy at the spurt of blood.

At the end of it only one of the men was still moving. But Wyatt was taking no chances. He stood like a madman in the centre of the kitchen, and within seconds saw the First Aid locker on the wall. He wrenched it open, found a big roll of surgical tape. The three men he dragged to three different corners of the kitchen, sat them on the floor, and taped their wrists high above their heads. One to the rail of the kitchen range, one to a water pipe, and one to the heavy gas-stove.

Then he was running back for Alex, sick with fear. Fear that became horror and relief all in one moment as he found out what they'd done. The knives were through the skin of her body. They'd grabbed up folds of skin and pierced them. She was breathing, alive.

He left her then, locked the front door and pulled the heavy wooden shutters across the front windows. At the back of the house he found a scullery door, which he bolted. And next to it some sort of maid's sewing-room that also had the heavy shutters . . . It was all he could think of to do. Before he carried Alex carefully into the kitchen, laid her on the table, and pulled the knives from her.

The pain opened her eyes. She screamed. He realised suddenly that he was dripping blood all round her on the scrubbed table from his hands and arms, the flapping cuts. He went back to the First Aid locker. He disinfected her wounds and bound them up. Then his own, hauling the flaps of skin together, and winding the surgical tape as tight as he could. Her eyes were open again, he saw. She was staring at the three Corsicans strapped up in their corners. 'Are there any more?' he asked her. 'Any more?'

He had to ask three times before he found out there were four more men outside. They'd arrived in two cars.

Her eyelids were fluttering again. He carried her out of the kitchen, locked its door, and laid her gently on the hall floor. There was a phone on the table beside her. He picked it up. It was dead.

He leaned against the wall then and thought. They'd got to

Alex, that much was clear. And they'd set Alex up to try and get him. And they were going to succeed, no doubt about it . . . With four men waiting outside. The second wave.

He went up the stairs two at a time and looked out. At the back of the house a man was waiting below him in the alley. But the scullery door Wyatt had bolted was heavy. As were the wooden shutters of the room next door. Safe enough for the moment.

He went to a bedroom window at the front. There were cars parked along both sides of the street. But only one car that had cigarette-smoke rising up from half-opened windows. It was a hire Ford, and it was parked just to the left of the Georgian porch below, where one of those old cast-iron overflows crossed the pavement to the gutter.

Wyatt was in trouble, he knew that. All the houses he could see were unlit, their occupants probably away on the Fastnet Race. Nor was there any movement down on the street. Just a deserted pavement with those cast-iron channels crossing it from each house.

Then he thought, or rather began to think, about those overflow channels. In particular the one directly below him, leading out to the gutter where the hire Ford was parked. An overflow meant a down-pipe. And he saw it then, moulded and ornate, going down the front wall of the house. With his eye he traced it up to its top. The gutter it drained was up on that small square roof where he'd sat with Alex that afternoon, looking out at the yachts.

Yachts. This was a house of yacht-people . . . The tins of food on the kitchen-table . . . The oilskins he'd seen in the dining-room when he'd been here before . . . He went down through the house again quickly now, passing Alex in the hallway. He found the cellar-door, the cellar-light, and went down brick steps.

There was an old patched lug-sail hanging up from a hook. There were oars, collections of rowlocks strung together with twine. There was rope of all descriptions, from thin nylon to old unlaying manilla. And, over in the corner, the thing that Wyatt had expected to find . . . An outboard motor, fastened by its clamps to a workbench. And below it on the floor, a can.

There was petrol both in can and outboard tank. Wyatt mixed it and took the now three-quarters full can up with him to the hall. There was an unread *Daily Telegraph* on the table there, and he took that with him too, up through the three storeys of the house, to the small square roof. He found the gutter just inside the parapet, and the grille where it drained into the downpipe. He emptied the can into the pipe, and far below, saw a black stain spreading out from the gutter to reach both near-side tyres of the Ford car. He took a page of the *Daily Telegraph*, lit it, and held it to the grille.

There was a *woomph*. He nearly had his hair burned off by the bowl of yellow flame. Then it was less. Then it was turned inwards, crackling its way down the inside of the downpipe. He saw yellow flame cross the cast-iron channel in the pavement. Saw it reach the black pool of liquid in the gutter by the car-tyres. They'd have time to get out, he thought, if they were quick.

Wyatt was quick, leaping down three flights of stairs, bundling up Alex in the hall, and carrying her on, to the lower scullery door at the back.

Shouts and separate explosions he heard now from the front of the house. And closer to him, just outside the back door, a man's footsteps going away down the alley. Wyatt counted up to five seconds. Then he unbolted the door and ran, with Alex over his shoulder, the other way.

He ran always downwards, through alleyways and narrow streets, towards the waterfront. He reached its stale breath, and then found a jetty with a line of dinghies moored alongside. He lowered Alex into one of them, and cast off.

Out on the dark water her eyes fluttered open. She looked round. 'Are we . . . ? Are we going to the boat?' she asked.

'Boat?'

'The family's. Family boat,' she said.

'*Your* family's boat?'

'What else?'

He thought quickly. 'Is anyone using it? Right now, I mean?'

'No. Why should they? They never do.'

Her eyelids were beginning to close again. 'The name of this boat? What's its name?' he asked.

'*Primavera*,' she said. And passed out again.

He found the *Primavera*, a smallish chunky Fairey motor-yacht, about ten years old. He broke a padlock, got Alex aboard, and took her below. Then he cast off the moorings and motored away into the night, past the lights of the Squadron. And for the first time since he'd got to Alex he had the chance to think.

The Corsicans had finally come after him, he thought, which

was something he'd been expecting for a long while. And he'd been lucky, he'd managed to fight his way clear because they'd under-estimated him, and because the battleground had favoured him as well . . . But they would come again. And the next time they would choose the weapons and the ground.

He motored on, keeping bow to spray and peering ahead in the darkness, wondering where the hell to make for. Until suddenly he realised. He was in the safest place there was, for the next few days at any rate, until the Fastnet finished . . . The Solent in early August. Miles and miles of water, and hundreds upon hundreds of yachts milling about through the holiday fortnight.

Needle in haystack time.

48

A little later on the same evening, *Havoc* was creaming along in a good south-westerly Five to Six. Hatches were open, as they had been since the gale had eased, and Pedlar had a happier crew on his hands. It wasn't just that in bad weather, clothes and footwear became sodden. It was that modern fibreglass hulls, with all the hatches battened down, began to sweat. After a while it was impossible to touch anything below deck that wasn't dripping wet. And the usual petty irritations began. The mugs of cocoa that slid and tipped over. The smell of other bodies in the confined space.

But then, one complaint that wasn't usual. It concerned the smell of gas. This, however, Pedlar just couldn't believe. From what he'd heard it was a bitter, ammoniac smell, not like Calor. And in any case he'd had the galley-stove and its system checked over before the start of the race.

All complaints had finished however when the gale had blown itself out. They'd opened the hatches then and gone racing again. And in the growing darkness they'd passed the lights of yacht after yacht. Over seventy-five yachts Charlie, one of the foredeck gorillas, had counted. Nearly all of them smaller-class yachts of course. But it meant *Havoc* was making boatspeed.

And boatspeed they needed. Because the tide that had favoured them so far was slackening. Within the next two hours, Pedlar knew, they had to reach Portland Bill, and round it before the tide finally turned and slammed the gate against them . . . The only chance, as Pedlar knew too, of finishing up where it counted, among the leaders.

But they didn't reach Portland Bill before the tidal gate. In those two hours the wind fell still further and veered towards the west again, dead on the nose. And so, with the merest glance at Monroe, Pedlar made the only decision possible. They went rock-hopping.

It was night. They were very close inshore in almost slack water. And in the pitch black there were two bowls of light out over the bows. Two men there had torches trained down into the water. They turned and shouted every time a rock appeared ahead. And, from below deck, Ronnie shouted whenever the depth-sounder registered less than three metres . . . But even so there were rocks that slipped through. Jagged graunching noises that slid the length of the hull.

It was a godawful strain on the eyes of the men for'ard. And a godawful strain on the nerves of Pedlar at the wheel. He had to fill the sails, catch every eddy of the inshore wind to keep way on the boat. He had to stay clear of the foul tide in deep water, and at the same time pray he wasn't steering up a blind alley of rocks onto the beach. Which would put them out of the race.

Once he thought he'd done it. Once the torches swung violently back along the sides of the boat, and they were surrounded by rocks. Monroe and Charlie raced up the mast then, right up to the second spreaders, and swung with all their weight to kick up the keel. There was a lurch. They lodged for a moment, luckily against soft gravel, and were free.

Then, abreast of Portland Bill itself, there were long minutes when they seemed to be going backwards, *were* going backwards. But at the last moment the wind suddenly backed towards the south, and filled, giving them their first edge on the tide.

They were round. They were heading for open sea again, the wind stronger the further they left the land behind. And astern of them they could all see the growing township of lights on the water. The mass of yachts that had been forced to anchor, to kedge.

They were up among the leaders now, Pedlar knew it for a fact when Ronnie caught the radioed positions of twenty or so other

Admiral's Cuppers, the American 'A' and 'B' Teams among them . . . This, as *Cry Havoc* was beating against the same steady south-westerly towards the Lizard.

The Lizard. Just a point of land, two short words on the chart, Pedlar thought. But a full night and most of a day's sailing on from Portland Bill. It was now early on Sunday evening, and from below he heard Ronnie at his radio again, taking down the 1750 shipping forecast. And he waited with impatience for the man to appear on deck.

'How is it?'

Ronnie glanced at the chart in his hand. 'Bad news, I'm afraid. Winds light and variable, falling away tomorrow to winds light and bugger-all. Visibility poor to bugger-all as well.'

'Oh,' Pedlar said.

'So tomorrow could be a day of rattling and rolling,' Ronnie said. 'Drifting round in circles.'

'Yes.' Pedlar sighed. 'But what about the glass? No movement there?'

'No.'

'And no sign of anything coming in? Anything, I mean, from the north-west?'

'No.'

'That's good,' Pedlar said.

'Why?' Ronnie asked him.

'Because at the team meeting, don't you remember, it was thought the bad stuff might come in from the north-west?'

'Yes, but . . . it's not like you to be scared of a bit of weather.'

'No, not usually.'

'Then why now?'

'Well, you remember that gale when we left Cowes? When we were battened down? Hatches closed?' Pedlar shrugged. 'Well, a couple of people came to me with tales of leaking gas. Only a couple of people, and they were the professional moaners. I didn't set much store by it at the time.'

'But you do now? Is that what you mean?'

'Frankly, yes,' Pedlar said. 'Because since then there've been quite a few others who've come up with the same story. Quite a few, really. And what I've had to do is take damn good care to keep the boat ventilated.'

'Mmm . . .' Ronnie was thoughtful. 'Well, I can't see anything on the weather chart to upset that.' He held it out so that Pedlar could see. 'Look, there's no change. The high down here to the south, centred over the Azores, is stationary, all right? It hasn't moved further south as they thought it might at the team meeting . . . Which means that this low everybody was worried about, the low up here in the Arctic circle, hasn't come in any further either. It's stopped over Iceland.'

And Pedlar, following the man's pointing finger, saw that the deep low . . . Low X as it was called . . . had indeed come to a halt where the man said.

'So the only other thing we've got . . .' Ronnie's finger moved on. 'Is this tiny depression here, Low Y, coming in over the Atlantic.'

'Yes.' Pedlar glanced at it briefly, the cluster of isobars. 'Tiny, as you say. And miles out to sea . . . Nothing to worry about, is there?'

49

In the landlocked pool of the Solent it was high summer, one of those August afternoons of haze and blue and flat calm. And Wyatt, at the wheel of the *Primavera*, was leaning back and steering one-handed. While with the other he ate a tinned meal that Alex had prepared.

She lay in the sunlight beside him. There were just the patches of white Band-Aid on her body now to remind her of last night. She lay without pain, and more importantly without fear. And he wondered if it was time to bring up the subject of Corsicans.

He did. A shadow crossed her face, but she talked. 'I don't know how they found me, or why,' she said. 'I truly don't.'

'Well, maybe it would help,' he said, 'if you told me everything that happened to you yesterday.'

'Yesterday.' She sighed. 'I suppose, yes, it would have been yesterday morning when I read in the papers that there'd been an explosion at Jacko's house. That he was badly injured.'

'Yes,' Wyatt said softly.

'And, you see, I was fond of Jacko, very fond of him. So when I heard he was at Southampton Hospital, I jumped in a car and drove down there.'

Southampton Hospital, of course, Wyatt thought. The

Corsicans would have been watching the place. Once they'd learned who'd been injured in the gelignite explosion, they'd have waited there to see who turned up.

'Not that I got to talk to Jacko, as it happened,' Alex went on. 'The Nursing Sister wouldn't let me. She said that Jacko had seen one visitor already and that it had exhausted him . . . So then, I don't know, I left a message for him. And I went on over to the island, to the house in Cowes.'

And the Corsicans would have followed her there, all the way, Wyatt thought. Followed her and seen she was alone in the house.

'There was this ring at the doorbell,' Alex said then, her voice rising. 'These three men. They came in. And they did . . . what they did . . . They seemed to know about you, you see. They seemed to know about a flyer with a thumb missing from his right hand. They wanted me to phone you, get you over to the house . . .'

And even that was clear, Wyatt thought. Clear now. For God's sake, he'd left enough traces. Flying that trip over to Cherbourg. Using his own pilot's licence, his own name . . .

But he was forgetting Alex.

Her voice was rising even higher. 'I told you I don't know how they got to me, or you. And I don't *want* to know. I don't want to think about it *ever* again.'

He pulled her towards him with his free hand. He held her tightly. 'It's over,' he said. 'All over. I promise you that.'

'Over? How d'you *know?*'

In answer he pointed at the flat water and haze that was all around them. 'Because they can't find us, not here on the Solent. And we're going to stay out here, for days if necessary . . . Or anyway till the food runs out.'

She quietened then. Gradually her body stopped trembling. And they were close, her hair brushing his cheek, as they droned on through the late afternoon.

By Alex's side, trapped under a seat-cushion, was a piece of paper. It was a crude weather-map, drawn by Wyatt earlier when he'd caught the 1750 shipping forecast. And he'd meant to crumple it up and throw it away. But he hadn't, because something in it had caught his eye. Something that had taken him back, a long way back to a long-distance phone-call he'd made . . . To Harry Tambay, air-taxi pilot, over in the States.

It concerned Tambay's hurricane, the one he'd nearly flown through over the city of Des Moines. Hailstones as big as golf-balls, and the rest of it . . . Hurricane-time in the States, Tambay had said. They tore a path out over the eastern seaboard, he'd said, crossed the Atlantic, and blew themselves out somewhere down in the Bay of Biscay.

Now Wyatt picked up the piece of paper again and looked at it. And again he saw the thing that bothered him, the lone cluster of isobars, the small depression, Low Y. It was nearly halfway across the Atlantic, coming eastwards, almost on the 48th parallel of latitude. Could in fact be heading for the Bay of Biscay . . . And while Wyatt couldn't see it as Tambay's hurricane, he did remember something the man had said. The damn thing had moved so fast across the States, he'd said, that the forecasters there had only time to get it down on the charts as a small depression.

50

At dawn on the third day of the race *Cry Havoc* was some forty-five miles to the north-west of the Scillies. Becalmed. It was going to be a day of rattling and rolling, just as Ronnie the navigator had said. A day of drifting round in circles in the Atlantic swell.

But the next few hours proved Ronnie wrong. The figures in his weather-log spoke for themselves . . .

0530–1030. Winds light and variable. Settling south, Force Four, by 1115.

1230. Wind south-west, Force Four to Five.

1330. Wind south-west, Force Six.

Twenty-five minutes later the shipping forecast confirmed the Force Six, and Ronnie took the news up on deck. *Havoc* was now heeling over, reaching under a number 3 genoa, and with a single reef in her mainsail. The haze and blue sky of the early morning were gone. There was a clear whitish light. And on the faces of the men of the deck-watch broad grins. It was good sailing, fast sailing, and they were on the rhumb line for the Fastnet Rock.

Ronnie's face alone was tired. Ronnie alone hadn't spent a

moment in his bunk since the dawn, and Ronnie didn't sleep when he couldn't find answers. Now he looked around the horizon and saw even more that he didn't understand . . . To the south-west, where the wind was coming from, there were high almost crystalline towers of white cloud. But to the north-west, a point or two off *Havoc*'s bow, was blackness. Black metal, layered in the tight leaves of some vast metallic spring.

Pedlar had seen it too. Just as he now saw Ronnie's drawn face. 'What's happening there?' he asked. 'Nothing in the forecast, is there? Up by the Rock?'

'No,' Ronnie said, 'it's the same as here. Fastnet reports south-west Six.'

'And the glass?'

'Steady, as it has been all along. No change.'

'I don't understand it,' Pedlar said.

'Me neither.'

But Monroe did. Understood what was facing him, and what it meant in his terms. He had Pedlar up-helm a point or two, had the winch-men trim the sails. And he didn't even have to come out with it, that old racing cry, 'Steer for the black cloud.'

Ronnie watched for a moment. Then he stared once again at the weather chart in his hand. And whatever it was that was escaping him.

. . . In fact it was something he couldn't know about, nobody could know about, for the next few hours . . . Low Y, that tiny depression, was nearing the eastern shore of the Atlantic. It had overtaken the stationary Low X, up in the Arctic circle. And, caught by the spiralling winds of the larger depression, was suddenly changing course. Was making for the coast of Ireland, forty miles to the north of the Fastnet Rock . . .

The black cloud made for them quicker than they could make for it. Though Pedlar didn't see it at the time, lying on his bunk for his four-hour watch below. When he was woken, however, he knew at once there was a far worse motion to the yacht. He pulled on his wet weather gear and safety harness, lurching against the bunk-frame as he did so. Then he made his way for'ard to the navigation-desk and wedged himself against it. Ronnie sat forward over the chart. There were livid circles under his eyes.

'The glass has fallen?' Pedlar asked.

'Yes, but only by a millibar or two,' Ronnie told him.
'But that's crazy.'
'Nonsensical, in the circumstances.'
'What,' Pedlar asked, 'are the circumstances?'
'South-westerly Seven, gusting Eight, gale Eight imminent.'
Pedlar looked at him for a moment, before hauling his way up the vertical steel ladder to the cockpit hatch.

The howl of wind and rain, the greyness of sea, were suddenly all round him. And south-westerly gale Eight had to be right now, he reckoned, buffeting at them, lifting white spray from the wave-tops. He looked aloft. *Havoc*, he saw, now had three reefs in her mainsail, and the heavy reacher was set. But still in the gusts the yacht was laying over with a lurch that brought a tightness to his throat. He clipped on his safety-harness and fought his way aft to Monroe at the wheel. 'We're over-sailed,' he said.

'Never. Never on your life.'

'How can you be sure?'

'Because Hoff's up there ahead.' Monroe pointed. 'And he's carrying exactly the same canvas. You can see him in the lulls.'

And in the next lull Pedlar did see the American, his reefed mainsail and small genoa, some quarter of a mile away on the starboard bow.

But gradually the lulls became fewer, the gusts longer, and though it was still day it seemed like night. At the wheel, Pedlar now had Ronnie poke his head out of the hatch every twenty minutes or so to tell him about the state of the glass. The man kept saying that it wasn't falling but steady, kept saying the same word, nonsensical, over and over again. But by this time Pedlar had other things to think about. Great curling waves were coming in every so often on the port beam. Waves he managed to luff up into before sliding down their backs. Except for the one or two he missed. The one or two that sent *Havoc* rolling over on her beam-ends, bringing crashes from below, and the shouts of men.

Finally he made the decision he'd put off for so long. He called Ronnie on deck. 'All right, we batten down,' he said. 'Hatches screwed down, ventilators closed . . . And, Ronnie, for Christ's sake, no smoking below. Smoking or cooking . . . That damn' smell of gas, remember?'

Almost immediately the large Plexiglass-covered main hatch, just ahead of Pedlar, was screwed down. Leaving him and the watch on deck, alone and huddled in the darkness. While the waves coming in on the port beam were higher, their crests beginning to topple in sudden corridors of spray. And the howl of the wind rose.

A gale, strong gale, the full Force Nine. The handle of the Plexiglass hatch spun, and Monroe came on deck with extra men. They fought and cursed, getting the main and headsail off the yacht. And then Monroe hauled himself close on his safety-harness, for a conference.

It was hardly what you'd call a conference. Pedlar only had to mention the two words, storm trysail, and Monroe shook his head. The 'bullet-proofer', he said, *his* sail. It would see them through a Force Nine, and anything that came later.

Anything did come, and fairly quickly. Driving rain and gusts, huge gusts, Force Ten on anybody's scale. They laid *Havoc* flat. Or rather the first few did. After that, with Monroe's help, Pedlar was able to ride them out. And he saw that both Monroe and the 'bullet-proofer' were right.

. . . In the event, rounding the Rock, the Fastnet Rock, was something that was meaningless. As a racing-mark, that was, a goal they'd had in front of them for hundreds of sea-miles. Rounding the Rock was seeing the loom of a light through the rain and darkness. Was danger. From the rock itself, and later from the lee shore of Clear Island beyond. Was changing sail. Was fighting and clawing their way to windward. Because they were against the wind now, the south-westerly gale, taking it on the starboard bow, and up-helming in the gusts.

Until suddenly that word cropped up again, *nonsensical*, shouted in Pedlar's ear. Ronnie was crouching by him, saying the glass had dropped, had rocketed down a full half inch while they'd rounded Fastnet.

Pedlar shook his head. Nonsensical was a word that had no place in the darkness, the rain, or the building waves. But what happened next had no place at all. In the whole of his sailing-career he'd never seen anything like it.

While he watched, the wind shifted from south-west to west. Then on through north-west to north-north-west.

A hundred and ten degrees.

In a matter of *minutes*.

* * *

They were running before it again under the 'bullet-proofer'. Gusts and savage squalls were piling up astern. And by now the big waves were piling up too . . . Big? They were vast. Those that Pedlar could see behind him in the driving rain. And those he could only guess at from their approaching roar. They came late and suddenly. They swung the stern of the boat up before he had time to pay off the wheel. They smashed white water around the men huddled in the cockpit. And they hurled *Havoc* down, bow-down, into the black pit opening below.

Then suddenly it all went wrong. All was madness. The big waves came in a chain. The black pits were deeper, deeper . . . Until, hurtling downwards, the scream built up in Pedlar's throat. Because he knew. The yacht was going to pitch-pole. Nearly two tons of yacht, that was, going to somersault forwards and topple mast-first into the black. But, as he watched, white water rushed on, out and around the beam of the boat. Was colour, red and green momentarily, in the navigation lights. Then flew on, past the single sail they were carrying.

The 'bullet-proofer', with its trademark of a double star. Danger signal. Shrieking at Pedlar now.

'Jesus Christ, that sail's too much!' he shouted in Monroe's ear. 'We've got to get it off her!'

'Off? You're crazy!' Monroe shouted back.

'The trysail! The storm trysail! We've got to set that!'

'Why, for God's sake, man? With the bullet-proofer we have way! We can steer! We're *racing!* Why d'you think I designed that sail?'

'What?' And fear gripped Pedlar's heart . . . The man beside him was laughing.

'High area of *lift* on that sail!' Monroe shouted. 'High area of lift on *all* my big wind sails! . . . We're pushed down, we come up again! *Every* time!'

Until the wave, the wave that Pedlar just didn't bloody believe. It wasn't an approaching roar, just a roar. A wall, Jesus, a wall of water behind them. Towering. Sucking them up. He was looking vertically down into the black. *More* than vertically. They were . . .

Monroe smashed him away. Pedlar fell, one hand for his safety-line, one hand for the ship. Monroe had the wheel. They swung up and round. And the man no longer tried to surf with the wave, he surf*boarded* it, an ocean-racing yacht lipping sideways, traversing that wall. Then at the last moment, with the sail threatening to collapse, Monroe dived for the pit. Down. White water the length of the deck. Until they nosed up again. Up.

Monroe was laughing.

Pedlar inched his way forward, spun the locking-wheel of the hatch, opened it, and unclipped his safety-line before going below.

It was a mess down there. Sailbags, bedding were strewn the length of the hull-space. Men were white-knuckled, hanging on. Men were sick. And the air wasn't just foetid, Pedlar discovered. There was a bitter ammoniac smell. Gas.

Then there was Ronnie's face, a skull, as he sat wedged behind his desk.

'Maydays,' he said. 'I've been picking them up. A dozen or more.'

'What?'

'They're away to the east of us. Smaller class boats, they are . . . Force Eleven over there.'

'*Force Eleven?*' Pedlar's mouth dropped open. 'But that's hurricane time.'

'Nearly,' Ronnie said.

51

Earlier it had been a strange evening in the Solent. Summer it still was, but with a chill to the haze, a dull metallic colour. And now at ten o'clock, half an hour after dark, a metal shine to the water too, against the lights of the Hamble quays.

Because, after two days' cruising aboard the *Primavera*, Wyatt was putting into the Hamble River. Not that it had been the tinned food that had given out finally, but the diesel.

And the risk of putting in was minimal, Wyatt told himself. Up-and down-river were the lights of moored yachts, scores of them. And hundreds of yacht-families on board, eating, drinking, or moving from craft to craft.

The Hamble waterfront too was packed with people. Jetties, dinghy-park, and the High Street sloping up past the Bugle Inn. Wyatt took the *Primavera* over to the fuelling-dock. It was closed, but a notice hanging on one of the pumps said the attendant could be found in the Bugle bar.

It seemed a harmless idea to walk over to the pub with Alex.

Harmless to find the man in the crowd there, give him the boat-keys, and say they'd be back at the fuelling-dock in half an hour. Harmless enough to linger over a drink.

Maybe they'd been away from the boat for forty minutes, maybe three-quarters of an hour, when Wyatt led Alex back down the outside steps of the Bugle.

And stopped.

Because there, down past the lights of the High Street, and the strollers on the hard, were four men. Four dark men, small, in dark suits. They were at the entrance to the fuelling-dock.

Wyatt hauled Alex back out of sight. 'How?' he asked. 'How, out of all the yachts in the Solent, did they manage to find us? Just forty minutes after we'd docked?'

'I don't know.' Her face was pale.

'Wait a moment.' He tried to think it out. 'When they followed you before, it was from the Southampton Hospital to your house in Cowes. Right?'

'Yes.'

'And you took the ferry to Cowes? The Red Funnel?'

'No,' she said, 'the boat.'

'You mean, the *Primavera?*'

'Yes. It was round at Bursledon. And . . .'

'So they know the boat. Why didn't you bloody tell me?' he demanded.

'Because you didn't bloody ask.'

He looked out round the Bugle steps again. And began to see more black suits in the different pools of light. Three men by the dinghy-park. Two more looking down at the slipway. Another three . . .

'Too many,' Wyatt said. 'Just too many this time.'

'So what do we do?' Alex asked.

But he was still looking, at the lights of the waterfront, at the buildings around him, even in desperation up at the night sky.

Then he seemed to decide. 'You have two choices,' he said. 'I can leave you here now. Or we do something very, very illegal.'

'Don't leave me,' she said. 'Don't leave me alone.'

'Right.' He nodded. 'We walk slowly. We keep walking slowly. We do everything nice and easy.'

And they did walk slowly, up the High Street, and then turning to the left in the darkness, out of the village. They went along a main road, by a grey metal fence that seemed endless. Then it did end. In a wide gateway with a barrier.

Wyatt led the way round it. There were the black shapes of buildings, then hangars, then small planes parked in a row. One of them the elderly Beechcraft, the Hamble Flying Club plane he'd taken to France and back.

'Still walk slowly,' he said. 'Wait for me to break the door-lock. Then jump up into the damn' thing and keep low.'

She did as he said. They crouched together, below the plane's instrument panel. 'Easy as hot-wiring a car,' Wyatt told her.

He had ignition. He had full tanks. And he had half the minimum time of engine warm-up. Then he was bumping the plane out over the dark field, not looking back.

'Where are we going?' Alex asked.

'They expect me to fly the Channel,' Wyatt said. 'Anybody in their right mind would expect me to fly the Channel. So that's exactly what I'm not going to do.'

'Oh?'

'No. You see, there's a small airstrip in this country. One we used to use in Jackman's day. Small. Safe to land at.'

'But at night?' Her voice rose. 'Safe to land at night?'

'It's high summer,' he told her. 'First light's, what, not too long after four am?'

'And it'll take that time to get there?'

'Oh, yes. It's a few hours off,' he said. 'Away to the north-west.'

52

Force Eleven.

The wind was neither roar nor howl, but an endless banshee shriek. Looking up from the troughs, the walls of the waves were sheer, toppling from a pitch black sky. But up on the walls, in the wind, everything was white. Sea and spray, a shrieking driving white.

Or red.

The red of distress flares.

Pockets of red Pedlar came to now. Unbelievable sights he saw . . . Surfing a monster crest, the sea red below him. And in that sea a small ketch reeling under bare poles. A ketch that swung broadside to a wave, broached. Not broached, *fell* off the wave.

And afterwards, the hull upside-down, just the fin of the keel. Men trailing from it in the water, yards from it, dragged along by their life-lines. And more men, the rest of the crew, trapped in that upside-down hull . . . Trapped for a minute, a minute and a half . . . Until, hit by a second wave, the yacht righted. Deck, stump of a broken mast, and the killer-tangle of wire rigging, snaking out in the spray.

Or the wider valley of red. The long, long trough lit by the maroon. And three boats. One a massive sea-going tug, escort to the fleet. The second a sloop, abandoned, swinging tattered sails. The third a rubber liferaft, circular, like a circular tent . . . The raft, kicked like confetti by the wind, neared the ocean-tug. Scrambling nets and hands were ready . . . But the wave . . . Snatched up from the tug's waterline to its bridge-rail, the raft flipped over. Upside-down, it went away. Flipped again, right side up. But too far away. From a gap in the raft-tent a hand waved. And then disappeared, over the next red wave-crest.

Unbelievable sights. But Pedlar was a spectator. Monroe was at the wheel. And, unbelievably, red meant no distress in Monroe's eyes. Red meant danger. Boats in the way that could drag them down. Because Monroe was still racing.

Force Eleven . . . Again and again Pedlar checked it on the instrument panel. Again and again he checked that the height of those waves was higher than the masthead, sixty feet, when they were below. And from below, each time, he knew he was going to die. But Monroe, laughing, knew different. There was the dizzying vertical rise, the teetering in the blast of white spray, and then the dizzying drop on the far side.

Nothing worse could happen, Pedlar told himself. Nothing worse could possibly come.

Until it did.

He thought he was dreaming at first. He looked up, up to the sky, and saw clouds racing. But in the opposite direction to the Force Eleven wind.

Opposite?

And then he saw what came next. Saw waves coming in the opposite direction to the waves they were sliding down. Walls of water coming against walls. Joining. Rearing up. Forming solid blocks of water. Sheer. On both sides.

'Waterspouts!' Monroe bellowed in his ear. 'That's what we called them anyway! Saw it all once before! *Bloody* great storm in the Med!'

And these waterspouts, these solid blocks of water, he climbed. Climbed and scrambled his way down on the far side.

A spectator, Pedlar watched Monroe. Watched him glance up at the spray high above, swing the wheel, get way during the sickening rise up into the white. Then lose way, lose steerage as the stern kicked up and the rudder broke surface . . . Lose *way?* The man lost everything suddenly. Smashed *Havoc* headlong down into the pit. Smashed every join in the hull, it seemed . . . Until, miraculously whole, the yacht shook itself free.

It couldn't go on, Pedlar knew. No man could keep up that kind of concentration. And in the next trough, waiting for the next wave, he shouted, 'We have to get this sail off her! Get rid of the bullet-proofer!'

'That again?' Monroe snarled at him. '*That?*'

'The proofer's too much! There's too much speed!'

Monroe shook his head. There was the sickening lurch upwards again. And the juddering, nose-down dive.

As they came out. As they just clawed their way from the hole in the water, Pedlar shouted again, 'The storm trysail! We're setting that!'

'You want to die?' Monroe screamed. 'Where's the bloody *lift* with that sail? I told you all that *before!*'

'Less boatspeed! We'll be okay with less boatspeed!'

Monroe shook his head.

'The trysail!' Pedlar shouted again. 'Safety of the yacht's mine! We fly it!'

A sudden lull of wind, and Monroe stated it as a fact, 'Okay, you want to die.' He handed over the wheel.

With the taste of bile, of hot fear in his mouth, Pedlar took it. Desperately he looked around him at the walls of water. Then saw Monroe unscrew the watertight lock of the main hatch. Go below.

At the foot of the steel ladder, Monroe's eyes smarted. It was that smell. That acid smell. And he saw others were affected by it too. Close to him was a crewman, Chas, his eyes running. Then Monroe saw different. Chas was crying, was badly bruised about the head. And, dazed, the boy reached into his pocket for cigarettes, for matches. He lit up.

There was a sailbag by Chas. The one Monroe was looking for. The trysail. He saw the neck of the bag was inflated like a balloon. He saw Chas throw his match down by it. And then the strange blue flickering that surrounded the bag, like a halo.

Monroe saw it, the flickering. And two lightning thoughts flashed through his mind . . . He didn't know the hell why it was there on the yacht . . . *He just knew it exactly for what it was.*

He grabbed up the bag. He took the three steps back to the steel ladder. He went up to it, tore at the watertight lock. The blue flicker was all around him.

From the wheel Pedlar saw the hatch open, and the man outlined in fire. Monroe hurled the bag. Its flickering arched away. It lipped just to the far side of the wall of water *Havoc* was sliding down.

Sky was jagged light. Was tons of water. Was a sixty-foot mast and wire rigging crashing down.

Was *Havoc* falling sideways off the wall. Turning over.

53

Pedlar felt a bone-shattering jerk. His eyes opened. He was in ice-cold water, streaming out at the limit of his life-line. Hal, who had been the sheet-man on deck, was next to him. And there was the tangle of wires and broken mast, snaking out through the spray towards them.

The spray curled, swinging rigging and spars to one side, away. Pedlar and Hal sucked in air. Then kicked, hauled in on their life-lines . . . Hauled in to what? *Havoc* was just a fin keel poking up from the sea. And how long? How long, for God's sake, had the yacht been over?

In the capsized hull water poured upwards from the open hatch. The massive steel stove tore free from its gimbals and fell downwards. Floorboards, sailbags, the batteries of the yacht's engine came raining down . . . More water came in. The air-lock tightened. There was a singing in men's ears, and they became dazed. Charlie, foredeck gorilla, moved slowly. The steel stove rolled, found him, dragged him down.

Ninety seconds, a hundred seconds, Monroe was counting.

Then with a thunder of spray, another wave. The hull righted. And the process was reversed. Stove, floorboards, batteries, joined now by half a ton of water, pitched down towards the bilges.

Monroe got to the main-hatch, screwed it tight. Then he got to Charlie, who had one arm and one shoulder crushed, was dying.

Up in the cockpit, Pedlar and Hal hauled their way aboard. They found big Abe, the coffee-grinder man. He'd been trapped on deck, his lungs filled with water. Hal tried squeezing the water out of him. Tried mouth-to-mouth. He failed.

The ten of them still alive were below. And there was a new sound now. The strange drumming and whining of a fibre-built hull. A hull trying to fight off an enemy that was too great. It brought fear to men who normally kept down fear. Men covered in engine-oil and cuts, wading up to their thighs in slimy, litter-strewn water. Seamen, but now conscious of the thin fibreglass skin between them and three hundred metres of sea. A skin, a husk, again dropping sideways down a sheer wall.

Again rolling over.

The capsize was different this time. This time Monroe, Ronnie, and two others had the big steel stove lashed against the yacht's frame. This time it was the engine-batteries, bedding, and lockers of tinned food that fell around them . . . And the sailbags, sodden, choking, trapping men underwater with weight piled on weight.

Fifty seconds, sixty seconds, sixty-five . . . The yacht rolled back.

Men came together. And the working-party was larger now. Pedlar, shocked, teeth chattering with cold, joined it. He helped pump bilges, secure anything that could move, examine the seam of hull and deck for damage . . . All the time listening to the eerie whining of that hull . . .

And to the one terrified voice.

Pedlar didn't blame Chas. He was injured. He was the youngest, the least experienced. He was the most afraid . . . But his was the voice that said the obvious. They had no mast, no radio, no engine, no mechanical pump . . . No hope.

Chas was the one who hauled his way up the steel ladder, who opened the main-hatch, got to the cockpit. And by the time they'd reached him, he'd already cut the lashings of the life-raft and pulled the toggle.

By then there was only one decision left for Chas, for all of them. The life-raft, CO_2 gas hissing into it, was becoming a huge orange shape, a circular tent. It was filling the cockpit, then flapping up and out with the wind, then threatening to spike itself on the cable-ends in the spray.

By then just the one decision . . . Either to cut the raft free and let it go . . . Or climb in.

Chas climbed in. Monroe was silent. Pedlar was silent. There was the roar of another approaching wave, and Ronnie said, 'We abandon?'

Spray hissed round them. They swung up, swung round, then down again. And, in the long trough, Pedlar made sure that the life-raft was held securely to the yacht's side. He made sure that each crewman in turn unclipped his safety-line from the yacht, then immediately re-clipped it inside the raft. He made sure that life-jackets, torches, rocket-flares, and a container of water were in their places. He got the crew over the side one by one.

Until Monroe. And Monroe shook his head.

Pedlar stared at him. There was a long, long moment. Then, the roar of another wave coming, Pedlar cut the line. The raft went away. Both men stayed.

54

Havoc was still sailing. Monroe had rigged a jury sail, a small triangle of canvas, to the stump of the mast.

Sailing?

Nothing was real any more. Reason had gone, and with it physical fact.

It was a dream-like world. The shriek of the wind seemed less, seemed to be waiting, sharpening itself on jagged teeth. Waves were waves no longer, but rocky screes. Water was rock. Shale clattered down its slopes. Clattered onto the deck and the two men in the cockpit . . . Dream-scape. The sky now a red bowl above them. As, with the creak of hellfire, black sky fell back.

'The eye of the hurricane!' Monroe shouted. 'Slap bang in the middle of the bugger!'

Canyons there were, red canyons. And Monroe found ways

through them and up onto rocky crags. Found ledges where cliffs divided and cracked. Found bluffs and overhangs, inches from the ravines.

But strangest of all was the slackening of the wind. It was distant, somewhere out beyond the canyons, circling.

Until there was something even stranger . . . Monroe's voice, his mouth pressed close to Pedlar's ear.

'You stayed,' he said.

'Yes.'

'Because you knew it was me? Me working with the Corsicans? You found that out?'

'Yes.'

'And, British-bloody-British to the core, you had to see it through?'

Pedlar didn't answer.

'When did you find out?' Monroe asked.

'The day before the race began,' Pedlar told him. 'When I saw you with the two Broom cruisers, out past the Needles.'

'You saw that, did you?'

'Yes. And then later I was sure, when I saw my . . . when I saw Katerina come out of your house-door.'

Monroe nodded strangely. 'I've driven your car,' he said. 'I've sailed your yacht, and I've screwed your wife.'

Red cliffs. Red canyons and falling shale. It was all a dream.

And dream-like too, there was the other thing, the telescoping of time . . . Because Monroe's words couldn't have come out in the way that Pedlar remembered them later. There must have been short angry bursts as the man edged *Havoc* up onto the sheer red cliffs. Or longer hate-filled tirades as he threaded his way through the canyons.

But it was the hate that Pedlar remembered most clearly. The hate he was sure of.

'I mean, you know why I did what I did?' the man shouted. '*Why?*'

'Yes,' Pedlar told him.

'Christ knows, you bloody should! Christ knows, the reason's right here, *here*, in this bloody race. And it was all spelled out for you, wasn't it? Just a couple of hours ago?

'Yes.'

'All those buggers firing distress rockets!' Monroe pointed astern. 'Abandoning their boats. Leaving them floating in the water! In the way! The bloody *way!*'

Red of distress rockets, Pedlar thought. Danger in Monroe's eyes, he thought.

'Those buggers they don't see how it is nowadays! They don't see what modern boats are about! Christ, it's not racing-yachts that get into trouble nowadays, it's racing-*men!* Christ, I've jumped two-tonners clear out of the water! Two tons of yacht with daylight under the keel! A bloody *spinnaker* set in a Force Nine!'

'Yes.'

'What d'you mean, yes? You don't know anything about that, do you? You, or any of your bloody blazer-brigade! Your club-wallahs! For Christ's sake, what *you* do in a Force Nine is try to ride it out! Or in other words, wait-to-bloody-die!'

'Yes.'

'Crap! Out of date crap!' Monroe shouted. 'How many times do I have to tell you? You race! You *race*, you have *way*, you have *control!*'

'Yes.'

And then later, perhaps five minutes later, Pedlar didn't know . . .

'You're just like the bloody rest of them, aren't you?' Monroe shouted at him. 'The rest of the bloody blazer-brigade! . . . You sail a desk seven months of the year! You sail a cheque-book three months of the year! And you sail a boat for just two!'

'Yes.'

'So how can you know?'

'Know what?'

'That you've paid for just about the best boat in the world! One that'll take on *anything!* That you've paid for just about the best sails in the world too! Sails you try to leave behind on the bloody *quay!*'

'Yes,' Pedlar said. 'Yes.'

And then, later . . .

'But you go on, blazer-man! You march on, puffing out your blazer and saying you've made the British Team! Saying you're bloody good! You must be bloody good, because a bloody good crew sails with you!'

'Yes.'

And Monroe's rage grew. 'But that's what it's all about, the whole thing, don't you see? . . . You're no good! No damn good at all!'

'Yes,' Pedlar said.

And then . . .

Monroe's face close, very close, strange. 'That doesn't come as a surprise?' he asked. 'I thought that would come as a surprise? . . . I mean, when did you know?'

'That evening before the race,' Pedlar told him. 'That same evening when I saw . . . Katerina come out of your door. I saw a lot of things then. I looked back over the season, the racing, and I knew.'

'That it was me calling the shots?' Monroe shouted. 'Me saying, "Try this end of the line," or "Ready about," or "You're looking good on the Frenchman so turn the bloody yacht around"?'

'Yes,' Pedlar said.

'Christ, there are things you just about bloody get away with! You just about bloody cut a dash round the buoys! The inshore races where it's safe! Where it's all slide-rule and boardroom stuff!'

'Yes,' Pedlar said.

'But not in the deep water! Not out *here*!' Monroe went on. 'Christ, half the offshore races you spend blithering and bleating! Half of them you spend down on your bunk, wittering your guts out! And at the finish, Christ, how many times do we have to shovel you up on deck? Sit you behind the wheel to cross the line?'

'Yes,' Pedlar said.

'Some say it's sea-sickness, some exhaustion!' Monroe shouted. 'But it's none of that! Just plain crawl-on-your-belly fear!'

Pedlar looked up, met his eyes. 'Yes.'

And then . . .

'I've driven your car, screwed your wife, sailed your yacht,' Monroe repeated. 'But the thing is I've never *won* with your yacht!'

'What?' And in that mad world, that telescoping of time, Pedlar understood. That the dream was moving on, was becoming a new dream. And he sat forward. He began to watch Monroe more carefully, and listen to him more carefully. Because he had to know. What it was that lay behind the man's hate. What it was he'd missed so far.

'Winning! Christ, we were all set up to win, weren't we?' Monroe shouted. 'Early on in the season, I mean, things looked good! For *my* sails! The sails *I'd* designed! . . . At Calvi that was, remember? But it was at Calvi that you started to go missing! Started flying off on those business trips of yours! . . . Christ, man, you never put in the *time* behind the wheel! You were never *going* to win!'

'No,' Pedlar said.

'And it was there at Calvi that it happened, don't you see? You flew off? I was on my own? And late one night these people came to the loft. People with money, an awful lot of money . . . Christ, man, that real-estate deal that was set up there, did you really think it was for *you?*'

'No,' Pedlar said. 'No, not now.'

'Right! I mean, just look at it. Was it *you* who stood to gain most? *You* with a new sail-loft built for you in the Med? *You* with a brand-new marketplace dropped in your lap?'

'No.'

'Right!' Monroe repeated. 'Right on all counts! *I* was going to take over the business! . . . And all these people wanted from me in exchange was so little! Just a few short trips in a motor-cruiser!'

'Few short trips?' And Pedlar was shouting too, appalled. 'What about the boxes you were carrying? The gelignite? The killing?'

'Killing, yes!' Monroe swung round on him. 'Killing your kind! The blazer-brigade!'

'*What?*'

And the final understanding . . .

'Your kind!' Monroe almost made as if to hit him. 'Christ, man, I've been there at your side for months and months now, haven't I? Closer to you than almost *anyone* else in the world! And yet still to you I'm just Monroe the sail-man! Monroe the deepwater man! Monroe who only knows about racing boats! For Christ's sake, you just haven't the faintest *idea*, have you, what it is I hate about you most of all?'

'No.' Pedlar shook his head. 'No.'

'All right, I race for you!' Monroe shouted on. 'And how do you pay me? Not in money, in handouts! In dinners! Hot bloody *dinners!* . . . Sit there, Monroe, you say! Pass the wine to Prinzheim, you say! Monroe, Prinzheim's glass is empty!'

'What?' Pedlar asked, lost.

'A fucking *amateur* sport!' For a moment Monroe lost control. 'You and your kind decided that! You made up the rules, as you always do! You turned it into this game, this *private* game!'

'But?' Pedlar was still lost. 'But what's wrong?'

'*Wrong?*' Monroe swung an arm round at the sea. 'Listen,

Christ, where we are now is out in a yacht-race, right? And, Christ, if you win, it's the dinner-table again, and champers all round! If you lose, it's awfully bad luck! . . . But if *I* lose, my *business* goes under!'

Again he lost control. But he seemed to know it now. Seemed to guard himself. And, leaning close again, spoke softly. 'A yacht-race,' he repeated. 'Which means a couple of hundred yachts out at sea. But, and this is what I'm trying to tell you, how many thousand men back on shore? . . . How many boatbuilders? Riggers? Sailmakers? . . . You've seen them all around the Solent. And something else you've seen . . . How many of them going bankrupt? How many up for sale?'

A lull, a strange lull under that strange sky.

'Your rules, your private rules, they're played out. They've gone wrong,' Monroe went on softly. 'It's all changing, here, now, in front of your eyes.'

'What?'

'This yacht-race we're in.' The man nodded at the sea. 'I mean, who's well-placed? Who's up among the leaders? No, who's going to win? . . . Win, I guarantee it?'

Pedlar shrugged.

'No idea? All right, I'll help you . . . Which is the team we've been hearing so much about? For weeks now? The new team? The bloody Orientals? From Malaysia? The team you blazer-boys hate so much because they *bend* your rules?' His words were quicker, his voice rising again to a shout. 'Christ, they use advertising money! They make no secret about it! They advertise golf-grips! On their sails! *Awfully* bad form! . . . And what's more they've got professional crews who can run the *arse* off you blazer-boys!'

He was half-standing now, hurling his rage to the sky. 'And that's just *one* team! . . . Christ, next year there'll be *six!* And the year after that, *sixty!* By then a *hell* of a lot of people will be making sails for them! *I'll* be making sails for them, in the new loft I'll have down in the Med! . . . More important, I'll be *winning* with my sails! Because I'll have a professional, not you, a dead weight, a *sack* behind the wheel!'

Half-standing he was, still shouting up at the sky.

Red bowl of sky . . .

But now suddenly changing to black. Suddenly shriek of wind, white spray, and the walls of water returning.

And for the first time ever on a boat, Pedlar saw Monroe off-guard. Saw it in slow motion. The boat rearing up on the wave. Starting to roll on its beam-ends. Monroe slipping. The cable-ends curling. Coming in. Reaching for him in the spray.

In the rush of the returning hurricane, the mad motion, just Monroe's feet were on deck. His feet. The trunk of the man, his head, were below water, held under by the mass of cables. And Pedlar tried to save him. Tried desperately. Grabbed up cable-cutters and cut his way through strands. Getting nearer all the time to the tangle that held the man down.

But he cut wrong.

With a shift of the boat the tangle gathered. In a sudden octopus it wrapped round Monroe and took him down. Through three hundred metres of water. To black.

55

Flying the small plane, Wyatt had the range of hills behind him now. He'd managed to clear them in the rising gusts of wind. But ahead it was worse. Ahead that strange orange colour he'd noticed to the dawn was now being blotted out. By the high circling thunderheads. And the black, the deep black that was between him and the ground.

Now he knew the worst. He couldn't run. The plane, small and old-fashioned, was past running. And he could see what was waiting for him, the whole thing.

Low Y, that so-called small depression, had swung round yet again, had come eastwards. And Wyatt had committed the unforgivable sin. He'd been so busy checking on maps and memory, thinking his way back to the airfield he'd used years ago . . . that he hadn't toured the radio wave-bands, hadn't updated his weather-map.

'You mean, we're going down *there*?' Alex was horrified. 'Into *that*?'

'Yes.' He smiled at her. 'Nothing to worry about. There's level ground mapped as a hundred and twenty feet above sea-level. And the ceiling of visibility's a hundred above that. Yards to play with.'

. . . The first part of which was true. But the second part, just wishful bloody thinking. Looking at it now, he reckoned the ceiling down there could be thirty feet if he was lucky. Sod-all if he wasn't.

The circling towers of cloud reached out for him. And the blackness below him was larger, fatter, like a great whale, grinding and heaving its innards. He put the nose down, went in.

'Why are you whistling like that?' Alex asked. 'I've never heard you . . .'

Then the first of the big bangs hit them. The first that slammed them upwards and to port. He managed to ride it, managed to end up, what, two hundred feet away from where he'd started? But then there was more. The bucket-drop downwards. The plane that was beyond his control. Rivets, yes, rivets popping from the metal.

Lightning. The wall they flew through. Harry Tambay's bloody hailstones, big as bloody golf-balls as the man had said. Solid wall. Wyatt pushed on down . . . a hundred and twenty feet above the deck, hundred and ten, hundred . . . Rocket-lift up to two hundred and forty. Then down again . . . a hundred feet . . . ninety . . . eighty . . .

Black, *black* ahead . . . seventy . . .

A tree sliced past one wing.

Sixty . . . *Still* black . . . He pushed down.

Madness.

Trees, hedgerows . . . Level with them . . . Then gone in spray and hail.

Madness. He remembered it as he'd seen it. Inched down.

'Are we all *right?*' Alex screamed.

He put it down. They bounced. Kicked up . . . *Up* . . . But he'd seen it . . . a field.

He crabbed down, torn at by side-gusts.

'Undo your safety-belt!' he shouted at Alex.

'What?'

'*Undo it!*'

And she undid it.

Kicking high on one wheel, they hit deck again. A big gust, but he held it, held it on the deck.

'Thank Christ,' Alex said.

He checked the speedo. Eighty miles an hour . . . seventy . . . sixty . . .

Again she said it, 'Thank Chri . . .'

Suddenly he reached across her, got the door open, pushed her out.

Alex fell heavily, hurt herself, lay stunned. She picked herself up in a howl of wind and rain. The plane was just ahead of her, engine screaming, but hardly moving on the ground. Then it kicked up. Just kicked up on its tail. Was batted back, straight at her. She fell again. The tail-plane carved a great gouge from the field just by her. Like a cross it went on. Like a cross hit a tree and exploded. Flame was torn from it, a long shrieking tunnel of flame.

Utterly spent, Alex stood there in the rain. She watched the long looping flame that was yellow. Watched the centre-bowl of it that was white, around the metal of the fuselage. No-one could live in that, she knew. No-one.

Then a sound came behind her. Wyatt was there, limping heavily. She screamed.

'But I jumped just after you jumped!' he shouted. 'Jesus, what did you expect? With a sixty mile an hour wind against us! Sixty bloody miles an hour!'

And she seemed calm. To an onlooker she would have seemed calm. Even to Wyatt as he talked on. There was a town and a railway station close by, he said. And a train was necessary now. They had to get back down south. To Plymouth. Plymouth was where the whole story would end.

But her calm was only on the surface. Inside she was still screaming. 'No, you go to Plymouth!' she shouted suddenly. 'I go in the opposite direction! *Any* opposite direction there is! I mean it, I mean it, I *mean* it!'

And she walked away. Walked until both he and the yellow fire were swallowed up by the rain.

56

Maybe the gale had lessened. Maybe it *was* a gale now, and no longer Storm Force. But Pedlar didn't believe it. The walls of water seemed just as high. The wind, while no longer backing as violently as before, just as strong. The troughs as black. And, up on the walls, still the screaming driving white.

No, he believed it was just as strong. But, without Monroe now, he managed it. He managed the routes up and down, managed the traverses of walls even, just as Monroe had done. It was as if the man were still there.

Or simply because Pedlar believed. That the boat *was* the best in the world, could take on anything. That the triangle of sail ahead of him *was* necessary. That, as the man had said, he *had* to have way, steerage, control.

Until he began to believe something else.

It was news, and it came to Pedlar only gradually. It was there in those vertical walls he scrambled up, and careered down on the far sides. There in every one of the yacht's three-hundred-and-sixty-degree rolls. Because there were those too, and he saw them coming. He kept close to the stern of the boat as it went over. On a shortened life-line he fought the white spray and kept clear of the snaking, twisting cables. Then, as the boat righted, he gathered his strength and hauled his way back on board.

What it was was knowledge. Monroe's knowledge that had been passed on to him. And his own. He knew, for example, that the sea could kill him at any moment, and that he was afraid. But he knew too that he had to live with that fear, let it work for him, sharpen his mind, force him to think ahead. And stay alive.

And if stay alive, in these the worst seas he had ever known. If stay alive unaided, on his own. Then . . . whisper it . . . he was good.

And if . . . whisper it . . . good, then a whole new understanding came to him. Of the flaw that ran down the centre of Monroe's shouted argument, cracked it apart.

Because if good, if not a *sack*, as the man had said, behind the wheel. Then he could race against other good men, behind other wheels.

Yacht-racing was simple. It was man and boat against sea and man and boat. Only the rules were complicated . . . And let them change, Pedlar shouted exultantly. Let a thousand professional seamen sail a hundred boats. Let them come from America or Malaysia or Timbuktu. Let them have the names of golf-grips plastered all over their sails. If the buggers are good enough, Pedlar shouted, *then* they'll beat me.

Exultation faded, of course, and tiredness took its place. Tiredness, and then bone-ragged brain-dimming exhaustion. And still Pedlar hung on . . . Until he saw the skies were lighter, were grey. Until he saw the waves take on a longer, rolling motion. And the spray no longer lift white from their crests.

It was then that he saw something else too. A large black spider on the deck ahead of him . . . The shadow of a helicopter.

57

Plymouth was a grey town, a town of disaster. The sound of it was everywhere. From radio and television shops the news-bulletins blared out. Smaller shops too had transistors hung up in their doorways. And groups of people drifted from doorway to doorway, listening in silence as the list of missing yachts grew.

Other news there was too, more muted news. Because a race had been run after all, and a race had been won. By and large the big boats, the Class I yachts, had survived the storm. The Malaysian Team, for example, had brought all their yachts through, had finished high on the leaderboard. And theirs was the cup, the Admiral's Cup, silver and shining just a few days ago, but now tarnished by tragedy.

Because tragedy it was. At the last count two hundred and eighteen yachts had retired, been abandoned, or sunk. And fifteen crewmen lost.

Among the groups of people listening in the shop-doorways was a lone figure, a limping figure. Dan Wyatt, who himself had survived the storm in a light plane, was as affected as anyone by the radio-bulletins. But as time passed, as he learned more, there was one particular item of news that affected him even more strongly.

It concerned *Cry Havoc*. *Havoc* was in the headlines. It was one of the few Admiral's Cup yachts to have been abandoned, and the only abandoned yacht in the British Team. Moreover it had happened in strange circumstances. Newspapers told of an explosion dismasting the boat. They told of a gas-pipe coming adrift from the cooking-stove. This, at any rate, was the story given out by Michael Pedlar. The man at present still in the sick-bay of the Naval Air Station at Culdrose.

And yet Wyatt had heard differently. He had spoken with *Cry Havoc*'s crew, already flown back from Culdrose to Plymouth. In particular he had spoken with Chas. And Chas had talked about a sailbag. He had talked about a blue flickering flame coming from the mouth of this sailbag. A flickering flame the like of which he had never seen before.

But Wyatt had. And while Wyatt didn't understand how gelignite could have found its way on board *Cry Havoc*, he knew where it would have come from. Just one of two sources – the shipyard in Cowes where it had been stored – or Jackman. And the odds were on Jackman. Retaliation.

But yet Michael Pedlar's story was of cooking gas. And the reason for this was clear. Due to the Press and television coverage of the Fastnet tragedy, Pedlar was now a household name. And the last thing he was going to do at the moment was talk about criminal connections, about gelignite, about an attack that had led to a Cabinet Minister's death.

Or, for that matter, talk about an air-taxi pilot called Dan Wyatt. Get him off the hook.

Wyatt, a man with a name he was afraid to use, a passport he was afraid to show, limped through the grey streets of Plymouth. In his pocket was a cold metallic object, a Swiss Army penknife. He remembered the two children who'd given it to him. He remembered their apartment overlooking Lake Luzern, and he remembered their warm, dark-haired mother. And what was becoming clear to him was that he was unlikely to see them again.

Because alone, he couldn't take on Michael Pedlar. Not the man's version of what had happened, not his power, and certainly not the way he was going to put the lid back on top of the whole rotten business.

A Naval helicopter brought Pedlar into Plymouth. A police car took him into the town and through the streets to the Grand Hotel. There were crowds waiting for him there on the pavement. And a press conference he knew too, waiting for him inside the hotel.

He crossed the pavement. It was all going to be too easy, he told himself. There was now no link between Skyline Sails and organised crime. Monroe was dead. And Monroe too, in the eyes of the Press, was a hero. A brilliant sail-designer. A huge loss to the world of ocean-racing. And a man of courage moreover, who had done everything in his power to save *Cry Havoc* . . . So let it all rest. Let the whole affair be forgotten about, ended.

He went into the hotel. To the warmth inside it, and the smell of graceful living . . . Smell . . . It was a strange thing, but in the past when Pedlar had returned from long sea-trips, he'd always found that his sense of smell had been scoured. Found that women, for example, suddenly trailed lingering rose-arches of scent behind them. And now, crossing the hotel carpet, Pedlar found himself going through one, two, three of these rose-arches.

Then a fourth. A scent that stopped him short. A scent ingrained in his every pore.

He looked round. Somehow he had never imagined that Katerina would come here. And somehow too he was unable to tell from her eyes whether she'd come for him, or because Press and television men expected her to.

He still couldn't tell as they embraced. Briefly. And said words that were lead in both their mouths. Lead. Are you all right? Yes, I'm all right. I was worried and so I came. You came. Yes.

Then they stopped talking and were apart. The journalists ushered them into the lift. It started smoothly upwards. The floor-indicators lit up in turn . . . 1 . . . 2 . . . 3 . . . And as easily as that Pedlar knew. It could all be over.

Because of the shadow that was between them. Monroe. The shadow of his hand, his mouth, his body on hers.

5 . . . 6 . . . 7 . . . Smoothly upwards. With Pedlar forcing himself to become calm. Cool and calm . . . Or was it cold and hard? Was it that? Exactly as she'd once said?

But then. Then in the strangest possible way Monroe came to his rescue. Just as he had on the deck of the yacht. Monroe dead, a ghost. But Monroe who was wind and sea, was instinct, animal instinct. Life.

Because all at once sweat broke out from Pedlar's body. A strange man broke out. For the first time in his life, in public, he did the thing that was crude and graceless. He raised his voice and bellowed across the narrow confines of the lift. He stood ape-like, belly forward, feet beating the mud of the lift-floor. 'Katerina!' he bellowed. 'I love you with all my heart and blasted soul!'

The journalists looked away. They were professionals, paid as much to ignore certain things as to print others. They did not see mud on lift-floors.

But Katerina did, and Pedlar knew it. He knew it too when he stood in the lights of the Press conference and looked out at the dark faces. The one face in particular, hers, as he talked first of all about the terrible Fastnet tragedy.

And then.

'About Monroe,' he said. 'I would like to say that Monroe was, just as the newspapers have reported, a very gifted designer and a remarkable sailing-man . . . But I would like to say too that there was another side to him, and that recent events have brought this out. Events in fact as recent as the explosion aboard my yacht, *Cry Havoc*. . . . Because, contrary to Press reports, this was not caused by cooking gas. It was, if the truth be known, an explosion of an entirely different nature. . . .'

There were headlines. There were policemen. There was interrogation after interrogation. And then a quiet period when other stories took over the front pages of newspapers. And it was then that two men sat together in a Plymouth hotel room. Pedlar and Wyatt.

They were both a little drunk, which meant they sat close, over a small table. And on the table was a British Airways folder.

Pedlar pointed to it. 'I'm sorry I haven't a lot of time. There's a plane to catch,' he said. 'But the thing I have to know before I leave is. . . . Have I done enough?'

'Enough?'

'To make things all right for you, square things up.'

'Yes, enough,' Wyatt said. 'More than enough.'

'No more troubles from the police then? Or from our Corsican friends?'

'Not any more,' Wyatt said. 'You see, what it needed was someone with your kind of business clout. To get the police moving in Corsica, I mean. And to get that anchor-chain pulled up off the Italian coast. . . . After that, well. . . .'

'Yes,' Pedlar said. 'Yes, and I'm glad.'

'Glad?' Wyatt asked. 'Jesus, you just don't know.' But then he leaned forward, even closer over the table. 'But there's something I don't know either. Something I just don't get.'

'What's that?'

'Why you shot your mouth off like that, in public. Why you didn't just sit tight and let the whole thing die down.'

'Yes,' Pedlar said. Then he picked the British Airways folder up from the table and showed the two tickets inside. One was in his own name, one was in his wife's. And their destination was Athens. 'We're going on holiday, just the two of us,' he said, 'for as long as the police will allow.'

'What's that supposed to mean?'

'Oh, come on now,' Pedlar said. 'You've been in Plymouth

for, what, a week now? You've talked to the crews? And you must have heard rumours about . . . about my wife going off with Monroe?'

'Yes,' Wyatt had to admit it.

'Well, I wanted her back. That more than anything.'

'But wasn't there another way of going about it?' Wyatt asked. 'I mean, a better way than shouting about Monroe to the Press? Involving yourself? Telling the whole damn world?'

'There had to be the truth,' Pedlar said. 'There had to be the whole truth.'

'Why?'

'Two reasons,' Pedlar said. 'One was that I was anyway guilty to a certain degree. I was after all Monroe's employer. I should have seen what was going on.'

'And the other?'

'The other was that I myself didn't see the truth, not all at once. Daylight had to be let into the whole business first.'

'What?' Wyatt frowned.

Pedlar leaned back in his chair. 'D'you remember a conversation we once had?' he asked. 'When I said something to the effect that, if you wanted to get to the heart of a problem, you had to go right back to its beginning?'

'Yes,' Wyatt said, 'I remember.'

'Well, in this case, the beginning wasn't that Monroe was involved with Corsicans. The beginning wasn't that I *let* him get involved because I was away so much, with business problems. Nor was it in fact those business problems, or anything to do with money.'

'Not to do with money?' Wyatt asked. 'Then what was it?'

'It was a house, an old stone farmhouse with beeches along the drive,' Pedlar said. 'It was a walled garden, and a stable-block where hounds were kennelled for the summer . . . Oh, and it was a dream too, a young boy standing with his father and looking out at the Solent, at the sails of big yachts.'

'I'm not sure if I understand,' Wyatt said.

'No, perhaps not.' Pedlar got up then, smoothed his suit down, and put the two air-tickets into his pocket. 'But, you see, there was something my wife once said to me, something important. . . . She said the English disease was fear of change.'

'Is that right?' Wyatt asked, lost.

And Pedlar saw he was lost. 'Listen,' he said, 'I'll try to tell you what I mean. . . . The really important thing about any battle is to know when to lose, when to retreat, get the hell out. . . . Even if, in this instance, it means giving up a house to the people who feel they belong there. Or even letting go of a dream.'

'A dream?' Wyatt seized on it. 'The dream of a young boy looking out at big sails? Is that what you're trying to say? You're giving up sailing?'

'No, not that. I don't think I could ever do that,' Pedlar told him. 'Let's just say that before I get back on the water, with a brand-new yacht, there are a hell of a lot of things I'm going to have to put right. On shore, I mean.'

'Yes,' Wyatt said. 'Yes, I s'pose so.'

The two men shook hands.

Which was just about the end of it, as far as Wyatt was concerned. Except for something, a small thing, that happened a day or two later. It was when he himself had an air-ticket in his pocket. When he himself had left a forwarding address with the Plymouth police . . . an address in Switzerland, by the lake of Luzern.

And when too, with an hour or two to kill, he walked around the quays at Plymouth, taking a last idle look at the yachts. . . . Because suddenly he stopped.

A craft was being towed in through the harbour entrance. A craft nearly fifty feet long, but torn and battered, with a tangle of rigging on its deck and a broken stump of a mast.

Though the lines were still there under the scarred blue paint, the fine racing lines. And the name painted in red on the stern.

Cry Havoc.